THE PLATOON LEADER TOOLBAG

ArmyToolbag.com

CPT Alexis M. Marks

BookSurge.com
5341 Dorchester Road, Suite 16
North Charleston, SC 29418

(843) 579-0000
Toll Free: 1-866-308-6235
orders@booksurge.com

PLATOON LEADER TOOLBAG

Written, compiled, and edited by Alexis M. Marks

ISBN: 1-4196-2494-6

ArmyToolbag.com

Email: armytool@armytoolbag.com

Website: www.ArmyToolbag.com

Dedication

This book is dedicated to all the Officers, Noncommissioned Officers, and Soldiers who have touched my life.

Especially MAJ John Vermeesch, LTC Janet Kirkton, and LTC Stephen Dwyer, who believed in me as a cadet. Without their help, I would have never been commissioned. My Platoon Sergeant, 1SG Franklin Blanche, who taught me to not take myself so seriously and to listen to my NCOs. CPT Jennifer Kasker who taught me to learn my profession and maintain standards in everything I do. And to fourth platoon, 401st Military Police Company, the best platoon in the Army.

Acknowledgements

Author

Alexis M. Marks
CPT, MP

Technical Editors

Bill Duesbury
COL, USA (Ret)

Brittany Meeks
CPT, MP

Rodger Clark
1SG, USA

Cover Design

Scott Saling
Primal Graphics

Many people contributed to this document by suggesting topics, reviewing the work, and proof-reading.

The following are members of Team Toolbag: COL (ret) Bill Duesbury, LTC Janet Kirkton, CPT Brittany Meeks, 1SG Rodger Clark, 2LT Jennifer McIntyre, 2LT David Rolen, and 2LT Robin Vandusen.

Thanks also to the Fort Leonard Wood JAG office, PAO office, and OIS office for reviewing this work.

Resources from various military websites contributed to this book and were considered open source. If appropriate credit was not given, please go to ArmyToolbag.com, and the issue will resolved in the second edition.

Table of Contents

The Platoon Leader Toolbag

Introduction

As a new platoon leader, you will have more questions than answers. The purpose of this book is to provide a reference where you can find the answers to those questions, or at least where to look for those answers. The idea for this book came from looking at Platoonleader.org and realizing that all new lieutenants tend to ask the same questions. Instead of writing a post and waiting for a response, this book will give you one-stop shopping for answers, examples, and the appropriate Army publications for each topic. There are also websites, important definitions, quick checks, and tips/tricks.

Platoon leaders have a ton of work to do. When I was a cadet, I studied about how to be a leader; only to find that the majority of my day was spent doing additional duties, writing training schedules, and filling out administrative paperwork. The Platoon Leader Toolbag will help make all that work go quicker, so you can go back to your main job, being a LEADER.

The intent of this book is to serve as a map for platoon leaders. This book is a good start point, but is not a substitute for professional development. Remember, "It ain't cheating to read the book." The definitions included are from FM 1-01, Operational Terms and Graphics. All references are current as of March 2006; refer to www.ArmyToolbag.com for a list of updated references. In many tasks, I have included in standards that are from regulations or a common standard. Make sure you refer to your unit's SOPs, unit policies, and commander's guidance for more specific time frames and standards.

Lanes

Part

1 Lanes

Definitions:

Chain of command: The succession of commanding officers from a superior to a subordinate through which command is exercised.

Command: The authority that a commander in the Armed Forces lawfully exercises over subordinates by virtue of rank or assignment. Command includes the authority and responsibility for effectively using available resources for planning the employment of, organizing, directing, coordinating, and controlling military forces for the accomplishment of assigned missions. It also includes responsibility for health, welfare, morale, and discipline of assigned personnel.

Command and control: The exercise of authority and direction by a properly designated commander over assigned and attached forces in the accomplishment of a mission. Commanders perform command and control functions through a command and control system.

1.1 Responsibilities

The Commissioned Officer

- Commands, establishes policy, plans, and programs the work of the Army.
- Concentrates on collective training, which will enable the unit to accomplish its mission.
- Is primarily involved with unit operations, training, and related activities.
- Concentrates on unit effectiveness and unit readiness.
- Pays particular attention to the standards of performance, training, and professional development of officers as well as NCOs.
- Creates conditions: makes the time and other resources available, so the noncommissioned officer can do the job.
- Supports and empowers the NCO.

The Noncommissioned Officer

- Conducts the daily business of the Army within established orders, directives, and policies.
- Focuses on individual training, which develops the capability to accomplish the mission.
- Primarily involved with training and leading soldiers and teams.
- Ensures each subordinate team, NCO, and Soldiers are prepared to function as an effective unit and each team member is well trained, highly motivated, ready, and functioning.
- Concentrates on standards of performance, training, and professional development of NCOs and enlisted soldiers.

- Follows orders of officers

The Warrant Officer
- Provides quality advice, counsel, and solutions to support the command.
- Executes policy and manages the Army's system.
- Commands special-purpose units and tasks-organized operational elements.
- Focuses on collective, leader, and individual training.
- Operates, maintains, administers, and manages the Army's equipment, support activities, and technical system.

FM 7-22.7 (Tables 2-5 thru 2-7)

Command vs. General Military Authority

Command authority is the authority that a commander in the armed forces lawfully exercises over subordinates by virtue of rank or assignment.	General military authority is a broad-based authority allows leaders to take corrective actions whenever a member of any armed service, anywhere, commits an act involving a breach of good order or discipline. All enlisted leaders have general military authority.

Command vs. Individual Responsibility

Command responsibility is collective or organizational accountability and includes how well units perform their mission. Leaders have responsibility for what their units do or fail to do.	Individual responsibility is accounting for your personal conduct. Members of the Army must account for their actions.

FM 7-22.7 (para 2-22 thru 2-24)

1.2 Platoon Leader Duty Description

As a platoon leader, you are in an awkward position. You are a commissioned officer responsible for the entire platoon, yet you may have less experience than your team leaders. It is your responsibility to know everything occurring in your platoon, take responsibility for your platoon's failures, give them credit for their successes, and constantly develop yourself. Your Noncommissioned Officers do not expect you to know everything, but they do expect you to learn something everyday and to continually improve. You will make mistakes; just do not make the same mistake twice.

Primary Responsibilities:

- Platoon Leadership
- Welfare of soldiers

  Know the issues of all of your Soldiers. Personally counsel the Platoon Sergeant and ensure all members of the platoon are counseled in writing. Spot check counseling packets.
- Field operations:

  Lead platoon level maneuvers (allow squad leaders to perform theirs), ensure AARs are conducted, and brief company operations on mission status
- Accountability of Platoon equipment

  Signs for all platoon equipment from commander, conducts platoon inventories, and sub-hand receipts equipment to squad/section leaders
- Maintenance (Vehicle, Commo, Weapons, NBC, SKO's, NVD's, etc)

  Battle tracks all equipment. Ensures all maintenance suspenses are met.
- Training:

  Plan platoon training and submit schedules to Company Commander for approval. Ensure training is realistic, properly prepared, and contains practical exercise for Soldiers.
- Administration of Platoon paperwork

  Personally check all paperwork that goes up to the company (Awards, NCOERs, Memorandum of Records, etc). Ensures all administrative matters meet timelines.
- Perform appointed additional duties
- Act as unit commander as needed
- Support Single Soldier Programs and the Family Readiness Group
- Protect Soldier / Family Time

1.3 Platoon Sergeant Duty Description

References:

FM 7-22.7 The Army Noncommissioned Officer Guide (Dec 02)

While "Platoon Sergeant" is a duty position, not a rank, the platoon sergeant is the primary assistant and advisor to the platoon leader, with the responsibility of training and caring for soldiers. The platoon sergeant helps the commander to train the platoon leader and in that regard has an enormous effect on how that young officer perceives NCOs for the rest of his career. The platoon sergeant takes charge of the platoon in the absence of the platoon leader. As the lowest level senior NCO involved in the company METL, platoon sergeants teach collective and individual tasks to soldiers in their squads, crews, or equivalent small units.

FM 7-22.7

Primary Responsibilities:

- Welfare of soldiers
- Platoon Leadership

  Ensures all subordinates are properly counseled in writing. Tracks all awards, chapters, evaluations, flags, and pay issues in the platoon. Counsels and serves as rater for squad leaders and senior rater for team leaders.
- Personnel Accountability

  Maintains battle roster, conducts platoon formations, maintains platoon alert roster
- Key advisor to PL

  Develops and teaches platoon leader
- Platoons physical fitness program

  Plans platoon physical fitness schedule, validates PT instructors, and supervises platoon PT. Monitors special population PT and Army Weight Control Program within the platoon.
- Field operations:

  Resources mission support, Class I, III, & V Maintenance Transportation, and Medical support
- Accountability of Platoon equipment

  Supervises squad/section leaders to ensure accountability, ensures proper procedures are maintained when loaning/borrowing equipment
- Maintenance (Vehicle, Commo, Weapons, NBC, SKO's, NVD's, etc)

  Teaches, supervises, and checks equipment maintenance, paperwork, and services. Ensures all steps are taken to identify Non-mission Capable (NMC) items and get them Fully Mission Capable (FMC)

- Training:
  Provides assessment to Platoon leader, assists in planning, resources, and validates subordinate NCO's training. Platoons senior trainer, assist, and evaluate squad training. Keeper of the duty roster (DA Form 6). Ensures Soldiers are current on 350-1 training (weapons qualification, APFT, etc)
- Discipline
  Conducts formations, inspection of soldiers, and appearance. Ensures standards in common areas and supports CSM/1SG details
- Administration of Platoon paperwork
  Supervises awards, counseling, evaluations, and promotions within platoon
- Support Single Soldier Programs and the Family Readiness Group
- Protect Soldier / Family Time

> During my years in the Army a good platoon sergeant always wanted his platoon leader to be the best in the Company and Battalion. The good officers listened to and learned from him or her the knowledge to be successful, and went on to be good commanders on up the line. No platoon sergeant wanted to be known as having a leader who wasn't knowledgeable, and that includes each level of NCOs at Company, Battalion, etc. The goal of a platoon sergeant is a platoon leader that he can be proud of- that he can brag about- and when this happens, any criticism of the platoon leader can be a source of heated discussion!
>
> **SMA Glen E. Morrell, letter 26 Aug 1997**

1.4 Platoon Lanes

Form your relationship with your platoon sergeant and squad leaders. Make time to seek their advice, but ensure they never challenge you in front of Soldiers. Always have your platoon sergeant look over anything you are turning into the company. You are a team, and you represent the platoon. A good NCO would much rather catch one of your goof-ups and laugh it over with you, than have to explain to the Operations or First Sergeant about the error. If you continually do things your own way without soliciting your NCO's advice, they may just let you, and that will lead to trouble. It is your responsibility to cultivate that relationship with your NCOs. If you get off on the wrong foot, sit down and talk it out.

One of the biggest mistakes that new Platoon Leaders make is getting out of their lane. Throughout this book, there will be quick reference tables listing suggested lanes. However, they are not written in stone. The important thing is that no one perceives that someone is either (1) stepping on someone's toes or (2) not performing their duties (shamming). You can do this through open communication with your Commander and Noncommissioned Officers.

Below is a story used by a former CSM of U.S. Army Special Operations Command during a selection of a Pre-Command Course on the subject of officer/NCO relationships.

"During the basic course for brand new lieutenants, the instructor presented them with a problem to solve. They were told that the mission was to erect a flag pole. They have one sergeant and three privates. The lieutenants were given 30 minutes to formulate a course of action, after which the instructor asked for solutions. Each lieutenant explained in detail how the job could best be accomplished. Finally he instructor gave them the right answer: "Sergeant, I want the flag pole here; I'll be back in two hours to inspect."

CSM Jimmie W. Spencer, letter 1 Sep 1997

> There are times when noncommissioned officers can accomplish a mission for the officer that seems almost impossible. We call this NCO business. It falls into many categories, but I will sum them up into four areas: shady, fishy, funny, and monkey business. Please, Lieutenant, don't get involved. If you do, sooner or later you'll get burned. For some unknown reason good, sharp, outstanding noncoms have the knack, when getting involved in this type of business- but only in order to accomplish the mission- of coming out smelling like a rose. Only when an NCO is involved for personal gain does he get burned. So it is best for the young officer to give the noncom his head when he says he can get something hopeless accomplished.
>
> **SGM Terrebonne, "NCO Meets His Junior Officer." *ARMY*, May 1967, p 66-68**

1.5 The Commander

- Legal commander, responsible for all the company does and fails to do
- Determines company policies
- Decides unit training emphasis and issues training guidance
- Issues UCMJ
- Mentors platoon leaders

1.6 The First Sergeant

- Senior noncommissioned officer in company, advisor to commander
- Primary supervisor of unit discipline, standards, and fitness
- Directly oversees family care plans, army weight control program, APFTs, Sergeants Time, and CSM details

1.7 The Operations Sergeant

- NCOIC of company operations; advises the commander
- Coordinates land, range, and ammunition for training
- Facilitates company training meeting and staff call for commander
- Publishes company training schedules
- Delegates unit missions down to platoons

Leadership

Part

2 Leadership

References:

FM 7-21.13 The Soldier's Guide (Feb 04)
FM 22-100 Army Leadership (Aug 99)

2.1 Assuming a Leadership Position

Tasks:

- Determine what your organization expects of you.
- Determine who your immediate leader is and what they expect of you.
- Determine the level of competence and the strengths and weaknesses of your soldiers.
- Identify the key people outside of your organization whose willing support you need to accomplish the mission.

Questions:

- What is the organization's mission?
- How does this mission fit in with the mission of the next higher organization?
- What are the standards the organization must meet?
- What resources are available to help the organization accomplish the mission?
- What is the current state of morale?
- Who reports directly to you?
- What are the strengths and weaknesses of your key subordinates and the unit?
- Who are the key people outside the organization who support mission accomplishment? (What are their strengths and weaknesses?)
- When and what do you talk to your soldiers about?

FM 7.22.7 (Table 2-1 and 2-2)

2.2 Officership

2.2.1 Officer Creed

I will give to the selfless performance of my duties and my mission the best that effort, thought, and dedication can provide.

To this end, I will not only seek continually to improve my knowledge and practice my profession, but also I will exercise the authority entrusted to me by the President and the Congress with fairness, justice, patience, and restraint, respecting the dignity and human rights of others and devoting myself to the welfare of those placed under my command.

In justifying and fulfilling the trust placed in me, I will conduct my private life as well as my public service so as to be free from both impropriety and the appearance of impropriety, acting with candor and integrity to earn the unquestioning trust of my fellow solders - juniors, seniors, and associates - and employing my rank and position not to serve myself but to serve my country and my unit.

By practicing physical and moral courage, I will endeavor to inspire these qualities in others by my example. In all my actions I will put loyalty to the highest moral principles and the United States of America above loyalty to organizations, persons, and my personal interest.

Suggested by the U.S. Army War College Study on Military Professionalism (1970)

2.2.2 NCO Creed

No one is more professional than I. I am a Noncommissioned Officer, a leader of soldiers. As a Noncommissioned Officer, I realize that I am a member of a time honored corps, which is known as "The Backbone of the Army". I am proud of the Corps of Noncommissioned Officers and will at all times conduct myself so as to bring credit upon the Corps, the Military Service and my country regardless of the situation in which I find myself. I will not use my grade or position to attain pleasure, profit, or personal safety.

Competence is my watchword. My two basic responsibilities will always be uppermost in my mind -- accomplishment of my mission and the welfare of my soldiers. I will strive to remain tactically and technically proficient. I am aware of my role as a Noncommissioned Officer. I will fulfill my responsibilities inherent in that role. All soldiers are entitled to outstanding leadership; I will provide that leadership. I know my soldiers and I will always place their needs above my own. I will communicate consistently with my soldiers and never leave them uninformed. I will be fair and impartial when recommending both rewards and punishment.

Officers of my unit will have maximum time to accomplish their duties; they will not have to accomplish mine. I will earn their respect and confidence as well as that of my soldiers. I will be loyal to those with whom I serve; seniors, peers, and subordinates alike. I will exercise initiative by taking appropriate action in the absence of orders. I will not compromise my integrity, nor my moral courage. I will not forget, nor will I allow my comrades to forget that we are professionals, Noncommissioned Officers, leaders!

2.2.3 Ethical Conduct

Executive Order 12371 is the federal regulation governing ethics over federal employees. The term employees refers to all Army Soldiers, NCOs, and Officers.

Executive Order 12371: Principles of Ethical Conduct for Government Officers and Employees
55 FR 42547, Oct 90

Part 1, Section 101- Principles of Ethical Conduct
To ensure that every citizen can have complete confidence in the integrity of the Federal Government, each Federal employee shall respect and adhere to the fundamental principles of ethical service as implemented in regulations promulgated under sections 201 and 301 of this order:

(a) Public service is a public trust, requiring employees to place loyalty to the Constitution, the laws, and ethical principles above private gain.
(b) Employees shall not hold financial interests that conflict with the conscientious performance of duty.
(c) Employees shall not engage in financial transactions using nonpublic Government information or allow the improper use of such information to further any private interest.
(d) An employee shall not, except pursuant to such reasonable exceptions as are provided by regulation, solicit or accept any gift or other item of monetary value from any person or entity seeking official action from doing business with, or conducting activities regulated by the employee's agency, or whose interests may be substantially affected by the performance or nonperformance of the employee's duties.
(e) Employees shall put forth honest effort in the performance of their duties.
(f) Employees shall make no unauthorized commitments or promises of any kind purporting to bind the Government.
(g) Employees shall not use public office for private gain.
(h) Employees shall act impartially and not give preferential treatment to any private organization or individuals.
(i) Employees shall protect and conserve Federal property and shall not use it for other than authorized activities.
(j) Employees shall not engage in outside employment or activities,

including seeking or negotiating for employment that conflict with official Government duties and responsibilities.

(k) Employees shall disclose waste, fraud, abuse, and corruption to appropriate authorities.

(l) Employees shall satisfy in good faith their obligations as citizens, including all just financial obligations, especially those - such as Federal, State, or local taxes - imposed by law.

(m) Employees shall adhere to all laws and regulations that provide equal opportunity for all Americans regardless of race, color, religion, sex, national origin, age or handicap.

(n) Employees shall endeavor to avoid any actions creating the appearance that they are violating the law or the ethical standards promulgated pursuant to this order.

2.2.4 Title 10, Section 3583

Requirement of exemplary conduct (Jul 05):

All commanding officers and others in authority in the Army are required:

(1) to show in themselves a good example of virtue, honor, patriotism, and subordination;

(2) to be vigilant in inspecting the conduct of all persons who are placed under their command;

(3) to guard against and suppress all dissolute and immoral practices, and to correct, according to the laws and regulations of the Army, all persons who are guilty of them; and

(4) to take all necessary and proper measures, under the laws, regulations, and customs of the Army, to promote and safeguard the morale, the physical well-being, and the general welfare of the officers and enlisted persons under their command or charge.

2.3 Counseling

References:

FM 22-100 Army Leadership (Aug 99)
FM 7-22.7 Army Noncommissioned Officers Guide (Dec 02)

Forms:

DA 4856 Developmental Counseling Form (Jun 99)

Effective Counseling:

- Purpose: Clearly define the purpose of the counseling.
- Flexibility: Fit the counseling style to the character of each soldier and to the relationship desired.
- Respect: View soldiers as unique, complex individuals, each with their own sets of values, beliefs, and attitudes.
- Communication: Establish open, two-way communication with soldiers using spoken language, nonverbal actions, gestures, and body language. Effective counselors listen more than they speak.
- Support: Encourage soldiers through actions while guiding them through their problems.
- Motivation: Get every soldier to actively participate in counseling and understand its value.

FM 7-22.7 (Figure 5-1)

COUNSELING	
P	P
Counsel your PSG (initial/quarterly)	Counsels and mentors direct subordinates
Spot check counseling packets	Responsible for the quality of all packets (PSG)
Writes local platoon-level letters of reprimand, as needed	
Read through counselings of problem Soldiers with PSG to check for specific requirements	

Leaders must demonstrate certain qualities to counsel effectively:	The Counseling Process:
- Respect for soldiers - Self and cultural awareness - Credibility - Empathy **Leaders must possess certain counseling skills:** - Active listening - Responding - Questioning **Effective leaders avoid common counseling mistakes. Leaders should avoid the influence of:** - Personal bias - Rash judgments - Stereotyping - The loss of emotional control - Inflexible methods of counseling - Improper follow-up	**1. Identify the need for counseling** **2. Prepare for counseling:** - Select a suitable place - Schedule the time - Notify the counselee well in advance - Organize information - Outline the components of the counseling session - Plan counseling strategy - Establish the right atmosphere **3. Conduct the counseling session:** - Open the session - Discuss the issue - Develop a plan of action (to include the leader's responsibilities) - Record and Close the session **4. Follow-up** - Support Plan of Action Implementation - Assess Plan of Action

Figure 5-2. Major Aspects of Counseling Process
FM 7-22.7 Army Noncommissioned Officer's Guide (Dec 02)

2.3.1 Skills

Specific skills and techniques:
- Active and interactive listening skills
- Basic attending skills
    - Minimal encouragers
    - Open/closed questions
    - Paraphrasing
    - Summarizing
    - Reflecting feelings and emotions
- Situational counseling techniques
- Feedback skills (giving/receiving)
- Career counseling techniques
- Nonverbal communications
- Supervisory/command referral techniques

Counseling Tips:
- Determine the objective of the counseling before the session begins.
- Hear the individual out.
- Treat the member as having worth and dignity.
- Show sincerity, courtesy, and personal interest in the individual.

- Give the individual the facts, whether they are pleasant or unpleasant.
- Do not brush off any problem as being too trivial.
- Do not make snap decisions.

	Advantages	Disadvantages
Non Directive	- Encourages maturity - Encourages open communication - Develops personal responsibility	- More time-consuming - Requires greatest counselor skill
Directive	- Quickest method - Good for people who need clear, concise direction - Allows counselor to actively use his experience	- Does not encourage subordinates to be part of the solution - Tends to treat symptoms, not problems - Tends to discourage subordinates from talking freely - Solution is the counselor's, not the subordinate's
Combined	- Moderately quick - Encourages maturity - Encourages open communication - Allows counselor to actively use his experience	- May take too much time for some situations

2.3.2 Required Counseling Points

For certain counselings, it is imperative that specific points are made. Those points must be included if you attempt to chapter, flag, non-select for promotion, or use UCMJ action against them. Your noncommissioned officers should conduct the counseling session as the Soldier's direct superior. However, you or your PSG should read through the DA Form 4856 before the session to make sure it is thorough.

2.3.2.1 UCMJ Statement

Any disciplinary counseling MUST include the following statement. If you eventually want to give a Soldier an Article-15 or chapter them, Staff Judge Advocate will look at their counseling packet to ensure they were advised of the potential consequences of their actions. The paragraph comes from FM 22-100, Appendix C, paragraph 1-18.

Example 1:
This counseling has been furnished to you not as a punitive measure, but as an administrative measure to stress that continued behavior of this nature may result in administrative separation proceedings being initiated to eliminate you from the U.S. Army. This counseling is required prior to initiation of involuntary separation due to (REASON; IAW AR 635-200, Chapter __*). If you are involuntarily separated, you could receive an Honorable discharge, a General (under honorable conditions) discharge, or an Other than Honorable discharge. An Honorable discharge may be awarded under any provisions. A General discharge may be awarded for separation under Chapter 5, 9, 13, and 14. An Other than Honorable discharge may be awarded for separation up to a chapter discharge, however, will disqualify you from reenlistment for some period of time and may disqualify you from transitional benefits (e.g. commissary, housing, health benefits) and the Montgomery G.I. Bill. If you receive a General discharge, you will be disqualified from reenlisting in the service for some period of time and you will be ineligible for some benefits, including the Montgomery G.I. Bill. If you receive an Other than Honorable discharge, you will be ineligible for reenlistment and for most benefits including payment for accrued leave, transportation of dependents and household goods to home, transitional benefits, and the Montgomery G.I. Bill. You may face difficulty in obtaining civilian employment, as employers have low regard for General and Under Other than Honorable discharges. Although there are agencies to which you may apply to have the character of your discharge changed, it is unlikely that such application will be successful. For further information regarding impacts of an involuntary separation contact your local Trial Defense Service Office.

Example 2:
If this behavior continues, you may be recommended for separation action under AR 635-200. If separated under chapters 13 or 14 of AR 635-200, you could receive and honorable, general, or other than honorable discharge. Honorable discharge is a separation with honor based on the quality of service, which meets the standards of acceptable conduct and performance of duty. General discharge is a separation under honorable conditions, based on a military record being satisfactory, but not sufficiently meritorious to warrant an honorable discharge. A discharge under other than honorable conditions is an administrative separation based upon a pattern of behavior or one or more acts or omissions that constitutes a significant departure from the conduct expected of the soldier. A less than honorable discharge could result in the loss of VA and military benefits (including GI Bill education documents), hardship in obtaining other

employment, or personal stigma. It is also unlikely that you will be successful in any attempt to have the character of your service changed to a more favorable characterization.

* See Chapter 3, Administrative: Chapters.

2.3.3 Common Soldier Issues

2.3.3.1 Alcohol Abuse

Key Points:

- Under the provision of Article 134 of the Uniform Code of Military Justice.
- By (STATE) state law legal drinking age is 21 years of age and .08% is considered legally intoxicated in this state. (Fact .08% is equivalent to one beer, one shot of liquor or one glass of wine.)
- It is unlawful for any soldier under the age of Twenty one to lawfully purchase, possess, provide, or consume alcoholic beverages in this Country or the state of - (STATE).
- If you are over the age of twenty-one, you will not purchase or provide alcoholic beverages to any person under the age of twenty one.
- Failure to abide by this lawful order shall be considered a violation of Article 92, of the UCMJ, and may be subject to non-judicial punishment under the provision of Article 15.

* See Figure B-1. Alcohol and/or other drug abuse process, AR 600-85. Army Substance Abuse Program (ASAP).

2.3.3.2 APFT failure

Key Point:

- Soldier's score on the APFT on (DATE).
- List passing standards for their gender and age.
- In accordance with AR 600-9 you should be flagged under AR 600-8-2 until you pass the APFT. This flag will stop all favorable actions and will only be removed upon successful completion of the APFT. This includes blocking promotion, reenlistment, and extension.
- You will be enrolled in Special Population Physical Fitness Program beginning (DATE).
- You will be barred for reenlistment.
- You will re-take the APFT in 90 days. That test will be on (DATE). Should you fail two consecutive Record APFT's you may be separated from the military.

2.3.3.3 Family Care Plan

References:

AR 600-20	Army Command Policy (Feb 06)

Forms:

DA 5304	Family Care Plan Counseling Checklist (Dec 05)
DA 5305	Family Care Plan (Dec 05)
DA 5840-R	Certificate of Acceptance as Guardian or Escort (Apr 99)
DA 5841-R	Power of Attorney (Apr 99)
DD 1172	Application for Uniformed Services ID Card (Aug 87)
DD 2558	Authorization to Start, Stop, or Change an Allotment (Nov 96)

Key Points:

- You are required to have a Family Care Plan because you are (SINGLE PARENT/DUAL MILITARY).
- You must present your completed Family Care Plan to the command 30 days from today's date.
- Failure to complete your Family Care Plan could result in a Bar to Reenlistment or separation from the military (AR 635-200, para 1-18(a))
- You must update your family care plan (1) annually, (2) after any change that makes your plan invalid, or (3) as your Chain of Command dictates.
- The chain of command has the authority to test Family Care Plan through exercises and alerts.

You are required to maintain the following forms in you Family Care Plan packet:

1. __ DA Form 5304-R (Family Care Plan Counseling) (Signed by the Commander or designated representative and Spouse's Commander or designated representative when dual military)
2. __ DA Form 5305-R (Family Care Plan) (Signed by the Commander and Spouse's Commander when dual military)
3. __ DA From 5841-R (Special Power of Attorney for Guardianship) (Copy)
4. __ DA Form 5840-R (Certificate of Acceptance for Guardianship and Escort) (Original)
5. __ DD Form 1172 (ID Card Application - one per dependent)
6. __ DD Form 2558 (Allotment Form or other proof of financial support)
7. __ Letter of Instruction to Guardian(s) and Escort (Copy)
8. __ Will (optional)

2.3.3.4 Indebtedness

Key Points:
- Your current pay with BAS/BAH is (PAY RATE).
- List which bills the Soldier is deficient in making
- Your appointment at the Unit Financial Advisor is on (DATE). You will provide a copy of your completed budget for your counseling folder.
- Failure to financial obligations could result in UCMJ

2.3.3.5 Non-select Promotion

Key Points:
- You were not selected for a promotion/waiver for the rank of (RANK) on (DATE).
- List specific reasons why Soldier was not selected.
- Outline standards the Soldier needs to meet to get promoted.
- The next date that they will considered for promotion.

2.3.3.6 Overweight (AWCP)

Key Points:
On (DATE), you were weighed in IAW AR 600-9.

1. Your authorized Screening Weight IAW AR 600-9 is: ___ lbs.
   Your current weight is ___ lbs.
   You are over your screening weight by ___ lbs.

2. Your authorized Body Fat % IAW AR 600-9 is ___ %.
   Your current BF as determined using the tape is ___ %
   You are over your allowable BF % by ___ %.

3. You will be flagged IAW AR 600-8-2 (suspends all favorable actions to include military and civilian schooling).
4. You be required to see a doctor to determine if there are any medical conditions causing this condition. Your appointment for the medical screening has been scheduled for: (DATE).
5. Your nutrition counseling appointment has been scheduled for (DATE).
6. Monthly weigh-ins will be conducted on: (DATE)
7. Special Population PT will be conducted (TIME/DAYS)

* Check AR 600-9, Figure 1. Sample Correspondence for Weight Control Program.

2.3.3.7 Pregnancy

(Pregnancy counselings are normally conducted by the Commander)

Key Points:
On (DATE), I was informed that you were pregnant. As the commander, I am required to counsel you concerning your rights and options pertaining to pregnancy. At the conclusion of this counseling session, you will be given up to 7 days in which to make your decision. You have the following options:

1. You may choose to remain in the service or separate from the service. You may request a specific separation date. However, the separation authority and your military physician will determine the separation date. The date must not be later than 30 days before the expected date of delivery, or the latest the date your military physician will authorize you to travel to your HOR or EOD destination, whichever is earlier.
2. If you **remain** on active duty, you will receive treatment in a military facility, or in a civilian facility if there is no military facility care available within 30 miles of your location. If you **separate**, you are authorized treatment only in a military facility, which has maternity care. You are not authorized care in a civilian facility at government expense.
3. You may request ordinary, advance, and excess leave in order to return home, or other appropriate place for the birth of your child or to receive other maternity care. Such leave usually terminates with onset of labor; non-chargeable convalescent leave for postpartum care is limited to the amount of time essential to meet your medical needs.
4. Military maternity uniforms will be provided to the soldier.
5. BAQ and post housing depends upon the status of quarters at your installation. See the local housing office for more information.
6. You will not normally receive PCS orders directing movement overseas during your pregnancy. However, you will be considered available for unrestricted worldwide assignment upon completion of post-partum care. If overseas, you remain assigned overseas.
7. If your performance or conduct warrants separation for **unsatisfactory** performance or misconduct, or if parenthood interferes with your duty performance, you may be separated involuntarily even though you are pregnant.
8. You must have an approved **Family Care Plan** on file stating actions to be taken in the event you are assigned to an area where dependents are not authorized or you absent from your home on

military duty. Failure to develop an approved care plan will result in a **bar to reenlistment**.

9. Discuss Agencies that could provide assistance: AER, ACS, Chaplain, Community Health Nurse, Pre-Natal Unit, Red Cross, and WIC.

Pregnancy References

1. Retention or separation	AR 635-200	para 1-16, 1-36, 5-11, and 6-3; chapter 8
	AR 600-8-24	para 2-13, 2-14, 3-11, 3-12; tbl 2-5 & 3-4; and fig 2-2, 2-3
2. Maternity care	AR 40-400	para 2-2, 2-8 and 3-9
a. Family planning services	AR 40-400	para 2-17
b. Abortions	AR 40-400	para 2-18 and 3-39
3. Leave	AR 600-8-10	para 4-27, 4-28, 5-3, 5-5, 5-6, 5-7, 5-13; tbl 4-14, 5-3, 5-4
4. Clothing and uniforms	AR 670-1 AR 700-84	chapters 4, 9, 11, and 17; para 1-6, 1-9, 1-10, 14-6 para 4-9
5. Basic Allowance Subsistence (BAS) and Basic Allowance for Housing (BAH)	AR 210-50 DOD Financial Mgmt Reg 7000	para 3-6e, 3-8e, 3-8p, 3-36b; 14-R Vol. 7A CH 26; Install Housing Office
6. Assignments	AR 614-30	para 3-3, 5-3; tbl 2-1, (13, 14) tbl 3-1 (31-33); tbl 3-2 (1d, 1e)
7. Involuntary separation for unsatisfactory performance, misconduct, or parenthood	AR 635-200	para 5-8, 11-3, and 13-2; and figure 8-1
8. Family care counseling	AR 600-8-24 AR 600-20 AR 601-280 AR 635-200	tables 2-5 and 3-4 para 5-5 para 8-4 para 8-9 and 8-10; fig 8-1
9. Pregnancy and postpartum PT	AR 40-501 DOD Directive 1308.1 FM 20-21	para 7-9 and 7-10 4.3.2
10. Additional duties	AR 40-501	para 7-9 and 7-10
11. Army Weight Control Program	AR 40-501 AR 600-9	para 7-13, para 21 and 22

Pregnant Soldiers Fact Sheet:

Can I separate from the military if I think it would be better for my child and me?

Answer: Yes. For enlisted soldiers, there are provisions commonly referred to as a "Chapter 8 separation" (AR 635-200, paragraph 8-9). You may initiate separation through your unit's Personnel Administration Center (PAC) and your chain of command at the time of your pregnancy counseling. This type of separation must be initiated prior to the delivery of your baby. According to AR 40-3, if requested at the time of your separation, maternity care in an MTF with OB/GYN capability and/or capacity will be authorized. Your care is authorized through the birth of your child, and includes a 6-week postpartum visit. Your child will be authorized one well-baby visit, the timing of which will be determined by the MTF staff. You will not be authorized care in a civilian facility at Government expense.

Do I need to buy maternity uniforms?

Answer: If you are enlisted, you will be provided two sets of maternity battle dress uniforms (BDUs) (and two sets of maternity whites if you are working in patient care or in a food service military occupational specialty. At most posts, you will need a memorandum from your commander requesting the issue of maternity uniforms and a copy of your pregnancy profile showing your due date for the central issuing facility. The maternity BDUs will be added to your clothing record and should be turned in upon your return from convalescent leave. Additional clothing may be supplied according to your local installation policy.

What about new assignments while I am pregnant?

Answer: Pregnant soldiers will not normally receive orders for overseas assignments during their pregnancies. If assigned overseas, in most situations the soldier will remain overseas. An exception to this policy exists for single pregnant soldiers stationed in some OCONUS locations (AR 614-30). Reassignments within CONUS may occur during pregnancy. The soldier will be considered available for worldwide deployment 4 months after delivery.

If I am single and living in the barracks, when will I be authorized BAH and BAS?

Answer: You will be authorized these allowances at your seventh month of pregnancy. You are required to remain in the barracks until that point, but must move out at seven months. The paperwork for BAH and BAS will be initiated through your unit PAC. Your health care provider cannot write a profile against dining facility food unless there is a clinical reason to do so, which is rare. So, do not plan on receiving BAH or BAS prior to your seventh month of pregnancy. The availability of Government quarters depends on the current housing situation at your post. Contact your installation housing office to assist you in finding non-Government housing in your area.

Can I be separated from the Army for unsatisfactory performance, misconduct, or parenthood while I am pregnant?

Answer: Yes. If your performance warrants separation for unsatisfactory performance or misconduct, you may be involuntarily separated even though you are pregnant. This is also the case if your parenthood of any other children interferes with duty performance.

Am I exempt from PT while I am pregnant?

Answer: While you are exempt from APFT until 180 days after pregnancy termination, you are not exempt from PT if you are experiencing an uncomplicated pregnancy. You should maintain the highest level of fitness possible, while ensuring the safety of your unborn child. Regular exercise (three times a week or more) is preferable to sporadic exercise. Good exercises for pregnant women are swimming, walking, riding a stationary bicycle, and low impact aerobics. You should consult your health care provider to receive approval for participation in the pregnancy PT program and to learn about appropriate exercises for yourself.

Am I exempt from duty rosters (for example, CQ, SDNCO, SDO) while I am pregnant?

Answer: No. If you are having an uncomplicated pregnancy, at the 28th week you are limited to a 40-hour workweek with a maximum 8-hour workday. You must have a 15-minute rest period every 2 hours. The duty day begins when you report for formation or duty and ends 8 hours later.

Pregnant Soldiers' Fact Sheet, A Leader's Guide to Female Soldier Readiness

2.3.3.8 Substandard Performance

Key Points:

- Close out last counseling session (Assessment Section of DA Form 4856)
- List standards the soldier is failing to achieve
- Outline past performance
- If flagged, you can be denied (except for APFT and weight) a ppointment, reappointment, reenlistment, and extension, Entry on active duty (AD) or active duty for training (ADT), reassignment, promotion or reevaluation for promotion, awards and decorations, attendance at civil or military training, unqualified resignation or discharge, retirement, advanced/excess leave, payment of enlistment bonus (EB)/selective reenlistment bonus (SRB), assumption of command, family member travel to an overseas command (when overseas), command sponsorship of family members (when overseas).*
- If you receive judicial or non-judicial punishment, you can be reduced

in rank or pay, receive extra duty and restriction. You can also receive a court-martial IAW AR 27-10, Military Justice.
- Administrative actions for not performing to standard; reduction, re-classification, separation, promotion removal board, or bar to re-enlistment
- Possible evaluations: Mental, Educational, Medical, and Personal problems
- Possible assistance: chaplain, ACS, AER, social work services, JAG, IG, and EO
- List corrective actions

* See AR 600-8-2, Suspension of Favorable Personnel Actions (Flags)

2.3.3.9 Substance Abuse

Key Points:
- Under the provision of Article 122a of the Uniform Code of Military Justice
- You may be barred from reenlistment, flagged, receive punishment under the UCMJ, and possibly processed for separation from the service pending the outcome of the investigation
- You will set up an initial meeting with a counselor at the Alcohol and Substance Abuse Program (ASAP). There you will:
  - At least 12 hours of alcohol and other drug abuse training
  - Weekly individual or group counseling sessions
  - A 2 to 4 week partial inpatient care program
  - Attendance at self-help groups such as Alcoholics Anonymous or Narcotics Anonymous
  - Rehabilitation drug testing
- Failure to abide by this lawful order shall be considered a violation of Article 92, of the UCMJ, and may be subject to non-judicial punishment under the provision of Article 15.

* See Figure B-2. Positive Drug Test Process, AR 600-85. Army Substance Abuse Program (ASAP).

2.3.4 PSG Counselings

Preparation:

- Review the NCO Counseling Checklist/Record (DA Form 2166-8-1)
- Update or review your PSG's duty description and fill out the rating chain and duty description on the working copy of the NCOER (DA Form 2166-8, Parts II and III)
- Review each of the values and responsibilities in Part IV of the NCOER and the values, attributes, skills and actions in FM 22-100. Think of how each applies to your PSG and the platoon sergeant position
- Review the actions you consider necessary for a success or excellence in each value and responsibility
- Make notes in blank spaces in Part IV of the NCOER to assist when counseling

Key Points:

- Review job description, area(s) of special emphasis, additional duties, and Army Values
- Establish platoon lanes
- Expectations in job performance and military bearing
- Personal and organizational goals – short term and long term
- Rating chain
- Platoon Status on
  - Physical fitness
  - Promotion, leaves, pay, schools
  - Training
  - Duty roster, deployments, and other readiness issues
- Other issues in the platoon

Plan of Action:

- Review Command policies and SOPs
- Review training schedule and duty roster
- Make a plan for short and long term personal and organizational goals
- Get a copy of the rating chain (if applicable)
- Update promotion packet (if applicable)
- Set time to re-look on-going platoon issues.

Leader Responsibilities:

- Complete NCOER checklist and NCOER shell
- Ensure PSG understands what your standard is for Excellence blocks
- Ensure you listen and absorb what your PSG is telling you.

Tips/Tricks:

- You and your PSG should CONSTANTLY be talking. Set one day a week that you get lunch together at the DFAC or elsewhere. Take that time away from the rest of your platoon to make sure you are both on the same sheet of music and good in your platoon lanes.
- When going over the NCOER shell, have your PSG teach you about the form and process. Let them know that you will also solicit the 1SG's help when their evaluation is due.

2.4 Leader Book

References:

FM 7-1 Battle Focus Training (Sep 03)
AR 350-17 NCODP (May 91)

It is important as a leader to know everything about EVERYTHING in your platoon. If you happen to have a photographic memory, good for you. For the rest of us, you need a Leader's Book. Make sure you make a workable book, not something fancy with lots of information you do not need. Do not put daily reports in there unless you plan on updating them daily. Below is a laundry list of things you may want in your leader's book.

Platoon Tracking

Administrative

- Alpha roster of platoon (with SSN)
- NCOER rating scheme and due dates
- Log of platoon awards
- Next of Kin Roster
- Soldier Data Sheets

Training

- Company METL
- Annual/Quarterly Training Guidance
- Long/Short Range Calendar
- Platoon Training Schedules (T-1 thru T+6)
- Battle Roster

Accountability/Maintenance

- Platoon Leader's Hand Receipt
- Sub-Hand Receipts
- Platoon NMC report
- Platoon Service's schedule

Essential Soldier Task Proficiency

- APFT Scores
- AWCP roster
- Weapons Qualification

Additional Duties

- Copies of your appointment orders

Leader Book References

Administrative
- Pass request form
- Chapter reference
- Reenlistment oath
- Pay chart
- Sample Memorandum for Record
- Privacy Act statements
- Chain of Command/NCO Support Channel
- Promotion Eligibility Table

Training
- Troop Leading Procedures
- Risk Assessment Matrix
- OPORD reference
- CTT Task List
- Common Army Reference List
- Risk Assessment
- Leader quick reference cards (GTA cards)
- Unit Packing List

Accountability/Maintenance
- Classes of Supply
- Dispatch flow
- Weapons/Equipment density List

Other
- Post Phone Numbers
- Form List
- NCO and Officer Creed
- Army Values
- Code of Conduct
- UCMJ Articles
- Alert Recall Roster
- Useful Web site list
- Daily status tracking
- Unit Lineage and Honors
- Soldier Assimilation Program Checklist

2.5 Discipline

References:

FM 27-1 Legal Guide for Commanders (Jan 92)
FM 27-14 Legal Guide for Soldiers (Apr 91)
AR 635-200 Active Duty Enlisted Administrative Separations (Jun 05)
MISC PUB 27-7 Manual for Courts-Martial (MCM) (2005)

Commander Options:

- Rehabilitative Measures
- Loss of Discretionary Benefits
- Adverse Administrative Actions
- Separations
- Non-judicial Punishments (see Chapter 3, Administrative: Legal)
- Court-Martial (see Chapter 3, Administrative: Legal)

D P	
P	P / 'S
Identify problem areas and inform NCOs	PSG/SLs approve corrective actions and make sure they match the offense
Ensures corrective actions meet unit policies	First line supervisor is physically present at corrective action
Inform Commander of serious corrective actions	

- The training, instruction, or correction given to a Soldier to correct deficiencies must be directly related to the deficiency.
- Orient the corrective action to improving the Solder's performance in their problem area.
- You may take corrective measures after normal duty hours. Such measure assume the nature of the training or instruction, not punishment.
- Corrective training should continue only until the training deficiency is overcome.
- All levels of command should take care to ensure that training and instruction are not used in an oppressive manner to evade the procedural safeguards imposing non-judicial punishment.
- Do not make notes in Soldier's official records of deficiencies satisfactorily corrected by means of training and instruction.

Figure 3-2. Corrective Training Guidelines
FM 7-21.13 The Soldier's Guide (Feb 04)

"...The discipline which makes the soldiers of a free country reliable in battle is not to be gained by harsh or tyrannical treatment. On the contrary, such treatment is far more likely to destroy than to make an army. It is possible to impart instruction and to give commands in such manner and such a tone of voice to inspire in the soldier no feeling but an intense desire to obey, while the opposite manner and tone of voice cannot fail to excite strong resentment and a desire to disobey. The one mode or the other of dealing with subordinates springs from a corresponding spirit in the breast of the commander. He who feels the respect which is due to others cannot fail to inspire in them regard for himself, while he who feels, and hence manifests, disrespect toward others, especially his subordinates, cannot fail to inspire hatred against himself..."

Major General John M. Schofield, USA, United States Military Academy, West Point, New York, 11 August 1879

Administrative

Part

3 Administrative

References:

AR 600-8-103 Battalion S1 (Sep 91)
TC 12-17 Adjutant's Call, The S1 Handbook

Tips/Tricks:

- The rules governing many administrative actions change frequently in MILPER messages. Go to S1.net and subscribe to the listserv to receive new MILPER messages to your email account.

ADM A T	
P	P
Personally edit all admin paperwork before it goes higher	Knows and enforces local admin policies and procedures
Ensures all admin paperwork is turned into PAC on time	Keeps copy of latest drafts and submitted documents for future reference
Follow-up with PAC and CO on admin actions that are delayed or have issues	Track Soldier's accomplishments in their counselings. Keeps a draft DA Form 638 and NCOER in their file

3.1 Awards

References:

AR 600-8-22 Military Awards (Feb 95)
AR 670-1 Wear and Appearance of Army Uniforms and Insignia (Feb 05)
PAM 672–6 Armed Forces Awards and Decorations (Jan 92)

Forms:

DA 638 Recommendation for Award (Nov 94)

eMILPO Reports:

AAC–C13 Loss Roster
AAC–C24 Good Conduct Medal Suspense Roster

Websites:

Army Ribbons www.armyrackbuilder.com

The objective of the DA Military Awards Program is to provide tangible recognition for acts of valor, exceptional service or achievement, special skills or qualifications, and acts of heroism not involving actual combat. **AR 600-8-2 (para 1-12)**

Quick Checks:

- Do your Soldiers have all their Good Conduct Medals (one award every 3 years of service without disciplinary action)?
- What is your unit's timetable for ETS/PCS awards?

Tips/Tricks:

- Have supervisors keep a blank DA Form 638 in each Soldier's counseling packet and writing in achievements during monthly counselings. This will make it easy to write a PCS award if they Soldier comes down on orders.
- Keep a running log of what awards are given to your Soldiers. This will help you be consistent in recommending awards.
- Ensure you have someone taking pictures at an award ceremony.
- Ensure you are planning the event when that Soldier's spouse, family, and friends can attend.

3.1.1 Approving Authority

AAM	Battalion Commander, LTC
ARCOM	Brigade Commander, COL
MSM	Division Commander, MG

> Only the approving authority can downgrade an award. If a Soldier truly deserves the award and meets the criteria for that award in AR 600-8-22 (regardless of rank), send the award forward.

3.1.2 Award List

Order of Precedence

(1) U.S. military decorations.
(2) U.S. nonmilitary decorations.
(3) Prisoner of War Medal.
(4) Good Conduct Medal.
(5) U.S. Army Reserve Components Achievement Medal.
(6) U.S. service medals and service ribbons.
(7) U.S. Merchant Marine decorations.
(8) Foreign decorations (excluding service medals and ribbons).
(9) Non-U.S. service medals and ribbons.

The order of precedence for wear within the various classes of medals and service ribbons is stated in AR 670-1, paragraph 28-6.

Decorations: Mark of heroism, meritorious service, or meritorious achievement

(1) Medal of Honor
(2) Distinguished Service Cross
(3) Distinguished Service Medal
(4) Silver Star
(5) Legion of Merit
(6) Distinguished Flying Cross
(7) Soldier's Medal
(8) Bronze Star Medal
(9) Meritorious Service Medal
(10) Air Medal
(11) Army Commendation Medal
(12) Army Achievement Medal

Good Conduct Medals: awarded for exemplary behavior, efficiency, and fidelity in active Federal military service. It is awarded on a selective basis to each soldier who distinguishes himself or herself from among his or her fellow soldiers by their exemplary conduct, efficiency, and fidelity throughout a specified period of continuous enlisted active Federal military service.

from para 4-1, AR 600-8-22

Service Medal/Ribbons: Service (campaign) medals and service ribbons denote honorable performance of military duty within specified limited dates in specified geographical areas.

from para 5-1, AR 600-8-22

Badges/Tabs:
- Combat Infantry Badge
- Combat Medical Badge
- Expert Field Medic Badge
- Parachutist Badge
- Driving Badges
- Mechanics Badges
- Marksmanship Badges

Certificates/Letters:
- Certificate of Achievement
- Certificate of Appreciation
- Accolade
- Letter of Commendation
- Letter of Appreciation

3.1.3 Good Conduct Medal

Eligibility:
- Active component enlisted soldiers
- Active guard reserve (AGR) enlisted personnel
- Serving on extended periods of active duty (for other than training) under title 10, with certain stipulations

Ineligible soldiers:
- Soldiers with an approved bar to reenlistment
- Soldiers convicted by court-martial terminates a period of qualifying service

Qualifying Period of Service:
- Each 3 years of continuous active enlisted service
- Upon ETS of less than 3 years, but more than 1 year (First award only)
- Upon termination of service of less than 1 year when final separation was by reason of physical disability or for individuals who died in the line of duty (First award only)

Disqualification:
- The commander will prepare a statement of rationale memorandum
- This memorandum will be referred to the individual concerned
- The individual will acknowledge/respond to the memorandum
- The commander will make the final decision to either (1) Award the medal or (2) Forward the disapproval memorandum to the PSB for filing and records annotation

Processing:
- PAC logs on to eMILPO. Click on REPORTS. Based on your units UIC you will print an AAA-199 roster to verify soldier information.
- Commanders will circle yes or no by each soldiers name
- S1 will be responsible for cutting the orders and maintaining an order log.

Troubleshooting

- Check eMILPO. If BASD and PEBD dates are the same, then that's a good sign
- If they are not the same, then you will need to check the soldiers enlistment contract to get the actual date in which the soldier was actually in the Army. This is the date that you will use.
- Another area that may need your attention is if the soldier was ever disqualified from receiving the GCM.

3.2 Chapters

References:

AR 635-200 Active Duty Enlisted Administrative Separations (Jun 05)

PAM 635-4 Pre-Separation Guide (Sep 97)

Chapter 3	Character of Service
Chapter 4	Separation for Expiration of Service Obligation
Chapter 5	Separation for Convenience of the Government
Chapter 6	Separation Because of Dependency or Hardship
Chapter 7	Defective Enlistment/Reenlistment and Extensions
Chapter 8	Separation of Enlisted Women - Pregnancy
Chapter 9	Alcohol or Other Drug Abuse Rehabilitation Failure
Chapter 10	Discharge in Lieu of Trial by Court-Martial
Chapter 11	Entry Level Performance and Conduct
Chapter 12	Retirement for Length in Service
Chapter 13	Separation for Unsatisfactory Performance
Chapter 14	Separation for Misconduct
Chapter 15	Discharge for Homosexual Conduct
Chapter 16	Selected Changes in Service Obligations
Chapter 18	Failure to Meet Body Fat Standards
Chapter 19	Qualitative Management Program

Table 3-2. Types of Chapter Discharges
FM 7-21.13. The Soldier's Guide (Feb 04)

3.3 Evaluations

3.3.1 Qualifcations

Qualifications

Rater:

- Immediate supervisor for at least 90 days
- Senior in grade or Date of Rank (DOR)

Intermediate Rater (OER only):

- Supervisor between the rater and senior rater for 60 days
- Senior in grade or Date of Rank to rater and rated officer

Senior Rater:

- Designated minimum of 2 rated months
- Senior to the Rater in grade or Date of Rank

Reviewer:

- Senior to the Senior Rater in grade or Date of Rank
- No minimum time period is required

Responsibilities

Rater:

- Counsel the rated NCO on paper (DA Form 4856) and record on the NCO Checklist (DA Form 2166-8-1). Specifically, review the duty description and scope.

Senior Rater:

- Review rater's comments to ensure they are IAW 623-205 or IAW 623-105. Write senior rater comments about potential, schools, and promotion. List the next three jobs. Counsels the ratee at the time of their evaluation.

Reviewer:

- Check NCOER to ensure all standards are met and evaluation is accurately supported.

3.3.2 NCOERs

References:

AR 623-205 Noncommissioned Officer Evaluation Reporting System (May 02)
PAM 623-205 The Noncommissioned Officer Evaluation Reporting System In Brief (Jan 88)

Forms:

DA 2166-8 NCO Evaluation Report (Oct 01)
DA 2166-8-1 NCO Counseling Checklist/Record (Oct 01)

eMILPO Reports:

AAC-C13 Loss Roster

NCO Evaluation Reporting System: supports the Army's personnel management programs and the career development of NCOs. It influences the NCO's career objectives, measures the quality of the NCO corps, and largely determines the senior enlisted leadership of the Army.

Noncommissioned Officer Evaluation Report (NCOER): is an important part of the OMPF. The NCOER gives recognition for the performance of duty, measures professional and personal traits, and provides a basis for counseling by the rating officials on career development. NCOERs have a significant impact on promotion, school selection, assignment, MOS classification, CSM designation, and qualitative management.

Chap 4-7, TC 12-17

NCOER Types:

Annual (02)

- Submitted 12 months after ending month of last report or effective date of promotion to sergeant
- Rater must meet 90 day minimum qualification
- Report will not be signed prior to the first day of the month following the ending month of the report

Change of Rater (03):

- Rater or Rated NCO is reassigned (over 90 days position)
- Rater will submit report upon retirement
- Report will not be signed before date change occurs (exception - report may be signed up to 10 days prior to PCS)

Complete the Record (04):

- Submitted at the rater's option on those eligible for consideration by DA centralized boards for promotion, school, and CSM Selection

Relief for Cause (05):
- Removal from position based on personal or professional conduct/performance
- Reason for relief will be stated on the report
- Rater/Senior Rater qualifications is 30 days
- Report may be signed during the closing or following month of the report

Sixty Day Rater Option (05):
- When one of the conditions described in paragraphs 3-29 through 3-31 occurs but there are fewer than 90 rated days but more than 59 rated days
- NCO must be serving overseas on a designated short tour for a period of 14 months or less
- Senior Rater must meet time in position requirements
- Senior Rater must approve submission of the report

Senior Rater Option (05):
- Senior Rater has served in that position for at least 60 rated days
- Rater meets minimum requirements to give a report
- Rated NCO has not received a report in the preceding 90 rated days
- If an evaluation would be due within 60 days after the departure of the Senior Rater, a Senior Rater Option report will be submitted

3.3.2.1 Writing

VALUES: Values tell us what we need to be, every day, in every action we take. Army values for the identity of America's Army, the solid rock upon which everything else stands. They are the glue that binds us together as members of a noble profession. They make the whole much greater than the sum of the parts. They are nonnegotiable: they apply to everyone all the time and in every situation.

COMPETENCE: The knowledge, skills, and abilities necessary to be expert in the current duty assignment and to perform adequately in other assignments within the MOS when required. Competence is both technical and tactical and includes reading, writing, speaking, and basic mathematics. It also includes sound judgment, ability to weight alternatives, form objective opinions, and make sound judgments. Closely allied with competence is the constant desire to be better, to listen and learn more, and do each task completely to the best of one's ability. Learn, grow, set standards, and achieve them, create, and innovate, take prudent risks, never settle for less than best…be committed to excellence.

PHYSICAL FITNESS AND MILITARY BEARING: Physical fitness is the physical and mental ability to accomplish the mission – combat readiness. Total fitness includes weight control, diet and nutrition, smoking cessation, control of substance abuse, stress management, and physical training. It covers strength, endurance, stamina, flexibility, speed, agility, coordination, and balance. NCOs are responsible for their own physical fitness and that of their subordinates. Military Bearing consists of posture, dress, overall appearance, and manner of physical movement. Bearing also includes an outward display of inner-feelings, fears, and overall confidence and enthusiasm. An inherent NCO responsibility is concern with the military bearing of the individual soldier, to include on-the-spot corrections.

LEADERSHIP: Influencing others to accomplish the mission. It consists of applying leadership attributes (Beliefs, Values, Ethics, Character, Knowledge, and Skills). It includes setting tough, but achievable standards and demanding that they be met; caring deeply and sincerely for subordinates and their families and welcoming the opportunity to serve them; conducting counseling; setting the example by word and act/deed; can be summarized by BE, KNOW, DO. Instill the spirit to achieve and win: Inspire and develop excellence. A soldier cared for today, leads tomorrow.

TRAINING: Preparing individuals, units, and combined arms teams for duty performance; the teaching of skills and knowledge. NCOs contribute to team training, are often responsible for unit training (Squads, Crews, Sections), but individual training is the most important, exclusive responsibility of the NCO Corps. Quality training bonds units: Leads directly to good discipline; concentrates on wartime missions; is tough and demanding without being reckless; is performance oriented; sticks to Army doctrine to standardize what is taught to fight, survive, and win as small units when wartime actions dictate. "Good training means learning from mistakes and allowing plenty of room for professional growth. Sharing knowledge and experience is the greatest legacy one can leave subordinates."

RESPONSIBILITY AND ACCOUNTABILITY: The proper care, maintenance, use, handling, and conservation of personnel, equipment, supplies, property, and funds. Maintenance of weapons, vehicles, equipment, conservation of supplies, and funds is a special NCO responsibility because of its links to the success of all missions, especially those on the battlefield. It includes inspecting soldier's equipment often, using manual or checklist; holding soldiers responsible for repairs and losses; learning how to use and maintain all the equipment soldiers use; being among the first to operate new equipment; keeping up-to-date component lists; setting aside time for inventories; and knowing the readiness status of weapons, vehicles, and other equipment. It includes knowing where each soldier is during duty hours; why he/she is going on sick call, where he/she lives, and his/her family situation; it involves reducing accidental manpower and monetary losses by providing a safe and healthful environment; it includes creating a climate which encourages young soldiers to learn and grow, and to report serious problems without fear of repercussions. Also, NCOs must accept responsibility for their own actions and for those of their subordinates.

from DA Form 2166-8-1

3.3.2.2 Example

NCO EVALUATION REPORT
For use of this form, see AR 623-205; the proponent agency is ODCSPER

SEE PRIVACY ACT STATEMENT IN AR 623-205, APPENDIX C.

PART I - ADMINISTRATIVE DATA

a. NAME *(Last, First, Middle Initial)*	b. SSN	c. RANK	d. DATE OF RANK	e. PMOSC
f. UNIT, ORG., STATION, ZIP CODE OR APO, MAJOR COMMAND			g. REASON FOR SUBMISSION	

h. PERIOD COVERED FROM (YYYY MM) THRU (YYYY MM)	i. RATED MONTHS	j. NON RATED CODES	k. NO. OF ENCL	l. RATED NCO COPY *(Check one and Date)* 1. Given to NCO 2. Forwarded to NCO *Date*	m. PSC Initials	n. CMD CODE	o. PSB CODE

PART II - AUTHENTICATION

a. NAME OF RATER *(Last, First, Middle Initial)*	SSN	SIGNATURE
RANK, PMOSC/BRANCH, ORGANIZATION, DUTY ASSIGNMENT		DATE
b. NAME OF SENIOR RATER *(Last, First, Middle Initial)*	SSN	SIGNATURE
RANK, PMOSC/BRANCH, ORGANIZATION, DUTY ASSIGNMENT		DATE
c. RATED NCO: I understand my signature does not constitute agreement or disagreement with the evaluations of the rater and senior rater. I further understand my signature verifies that the administrative data in Part I, the rating officials in Part II, the duty description to include the counseling dates in Part III, and the APFT and height/weight entries in Part IVc are correct. I have seen the report completed through Part V, except Parts IId and IIe. I am aware of the appeals process of AR 623-205.	SIGNATURE	DATE
d. NAME OF REVIEWER *(Last, First, Middle Initial)*	SSN	SIGNATURE
RANK, PMOSC/BRANCH, ORGANIZATION, DUTY ASSIGNMENT		DATE

e. ☐ CONCUR WITH RATER AND SENIOR RATER EVALUATIONS ☐ NONCONCUR WITH RATER AND/OR SENIOR RATER EVAL *(See attached comments)*

PART III - DUTY DESCRIPTION *(Rater)*

a. PRINCIPAL DUTY TITLE	b. DUTY MOSC

c. DAILY DUTIES AND SCOPE *(To include, as appropriate, people, equipment, facilities and dollars)*

d. AREAS OF SPECIAL EMPHASIS

e. APPOINTED DUTIES

f. COUNSELING DATES	INITIAL	LATER	LATER	LATER

PART IV - ARMY VALUES/ATTRIBUTES/SKILLS/ACTIONS *(Rater)*

a. **ARMY VALUES. Check either "YES" or "NO".** *Comments are mandatory for "No" entries; optional for "Yes" entries.)*		YES	NO
V A L U E S Loyalty Duty Respect Selfless-Service Honor Integrity Personal Courage	1. LOYALTY: Bears true faith and allegiance to the U. S. Constitution, the Army, the unit, and other soldiers.		
	2. DUTY: Fulfills their obligations		
	3. RESPECT/EO/EEO: Treats people as they should be treated.		
	4. SELFLESS-SERVICE: Puts the welfare of the nation, the Army, and subordinates before their own		
	5. HONOR: Lives up to all the Army values.		
	6. INTEGRITY: Does what is right - legally and morally		
	7. PERSONAL COURAGE: Faces fear, danger, or adversity (physical and moral).		
	Bullet comments		

DA FORM 2166-8, OCT 2001 REPLACES DA FORM 2166-7, SEP 87, WHICH IS OBSOLETE USAPA V1.01

Figure 3-1. Sample DA Form 2166-8 (front side)
AR 623-205. Noncommissioned Officer Evaluation Reporting System

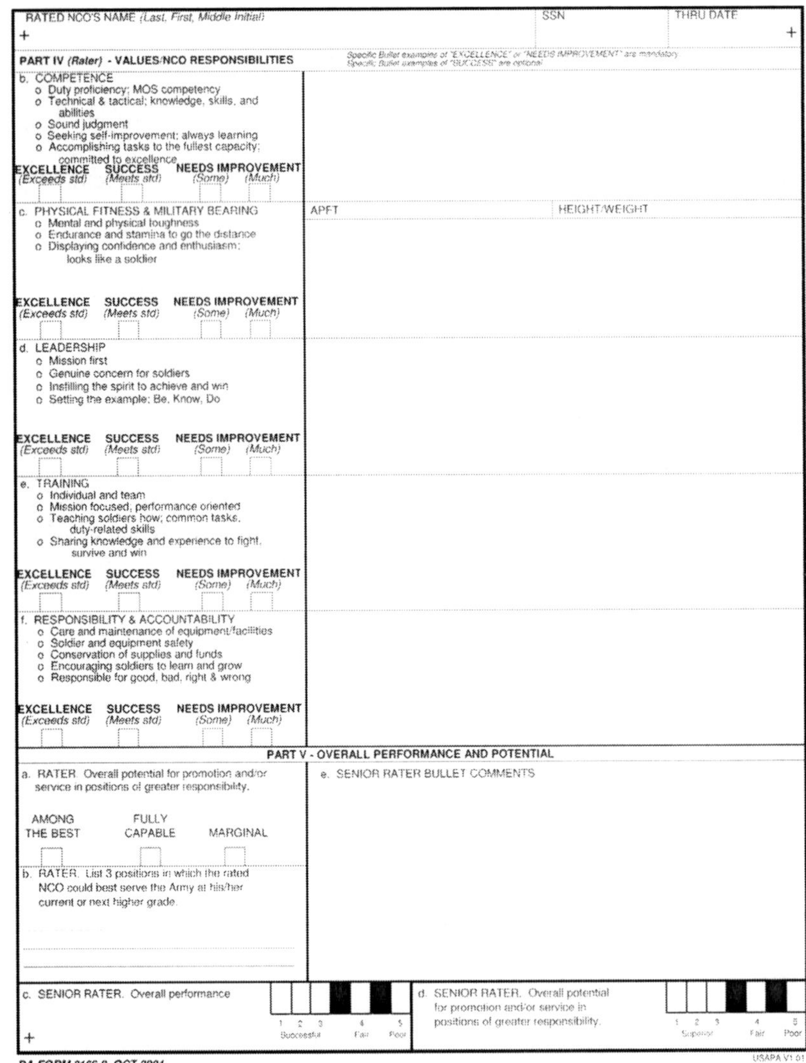

RATED NCO'S NAME *(Last, First, Middle Initial)* | SSN | THRU DATE

PART IV *(Rater)* - VALUES/NCO RESPONSIBILITIES

Specific Bullet examples of "EXCELLENCE" or "NEEDS IMPROVEMENT" are mandatory.
Specific Bullet examples of "SUCCESS" are optional.

b. COMPETENCE
- o Duty proficiency; MOS competency
- o Technical & tactical; knowledge, skills, and abilities
- o Sound judgment
- o Seeking self-improvement; always learning
- o Accomplishing tasks to the fullest capacity; committed to excellence

EXCELLENCE *(Exceeds std)* SUCCESS *(Meets std)* NEEDS IMPROVEMENT *(Some)* *(Much)*

c. PHYSICAL FITNESS & MILITARY BEARING
- o Mental and physical toughness
- o Endurance and stamina to go the distance
- o Displaying confidence and enthusiasm; looks like a soldier

APFT | HEIGHT/WEIGHT

EXCELLENCE *(Exceeds std)* SUCCESS *(Meets std)* NEEDS IMPROVEMENT *(Some)* *(Much)*

d. LEADERSHIP
- o Mission first
- o Genuine concern for soldiers
- o Instilling the spirit to achieve and win
- o Setting the example; Be, Know, Do

EXCELLENCE *(Exceeds std)* SUCCESS *(Meets std)* NEEDS IMPROVEMENT *(Some)* *(Much)*

e. TRAINING
- o Individual and team
- o Mission focused; performance oriented
- o Teaching soldiers how; common tasks, duty-related skills
- o Sharing knowledge and experience to fight, survive and win

EXCELLENCE *(Exceeds std)* SUCCESS *(Meets std)* NEEDS IMPROVEMENT *(Some)* *(Much)*

f. RESPONSIBILITY & ACCOUNTABILITY
- o Care and maintenance of equipment/facilities
- o Soldier and equipment safety
- o Conservation of supplies and funds
- o Encouraging soldiers to learn and grow
- o Responsible for good, bad, right & wrong

EXCELLENCE *(Exceeds std)* SUCCESS *(Meets std)* NEEDS IMPROVEMENT *(Some)* *(Much)*

PART V - OVERALL PERFORMANCE AND POTENTIAL

a. RATER. Overall potential for promotion and/or service in positions of greater responsibility.

AMONG THE BEST | FULLY CAPABLE | MARGINAL

b. RATER. List 3 positions in which the rated NCO could best serve the Army at his/her current or next higher grade.

e. SENIOR RATER BULLET COMMENTS

c. SENIOR RATER. Overall performance — 1 2 3 Successful, 4 Fair, 5 Poor

d. SENIOR RATER. Overall potential for promotion and/or service in positions of greater responsibility. — 1 2 3 Superior, 4 Fair, 5 Poor

DA FORM 2166-8, OCT 2001 USAPA V1.01

Figure 3-2. Sample DA Form 2166-8 (back side)
AR 623-205. Noncommissioned Officer Evaluation Reporting System

3.3.2.3 Timeline

- NCOERs are due to PSB on the last day of the rated month
- Most S1 sections require the NCOER 15 days prior.
- Most unit PAC sections require the NCOER 30 days prior.

3.3.2.4 Rating Scheme

- Rating scheme lists each Noncommissioned Officer (E-4 Corporal and above) with their rater, senior rater, and reviewer. For the each individual, it lists their name, social security number, rank, date of rank, and their duty position.
- Use the rating scheme to make sure each rater and senior rater is eligible (outranks by DOR and has been in that position long enough)
- Make sure each rater and senior rater KNOW they are rating that individual so they can counsel them and start a draft NCOER.

3.3.3 OERs

References:

AR 623-105 Officer Evaluation Reporting System (Dec 04)
PAM 623-105 The Officer Evaluation Reporting System In Brief (Oct 97)

Forms:

DA 67-9 Officer Evaluation Report (Dec 04)
DA 67-9-1 Officer Evaluation Report Support Form (Oct 97)
DA 67-9-1A Junior Officer Dev Support Form (JODSF) (Dec 04)

Officer Evaluation Reporting System (OERS): identifies officers who are best qualified for promotion and assignment to positions of higher responsibility. It also identifies officers who should be kept on active duty, those who should be retained in grade, and those who should be eliminated.

Officer Evaluation Report: The primary function of the OER (DA Form 67-9) is to provide information to HQDA for personnel management decisions. Secondary functions are to encourage officer professional development and enhance mission accomplishment. Normally, to be eligible for an OER, the rated officer must work in the same position for the same rating official a minimum of 90 calendar days.

Chap 4-2, TC 12-17

OER Types:

Annual (05)

- Mandatory on completion of one calendar year of duty following the "Thru" date of the last report

Change of Rater (03):

- Rated Officer ceases to serve under the immediate supervision of the rater
- Rater dies, relieved, declared missing, or becomes incapacitated

Change of Duty or PCS (04):

- Rated Officer has a change in principle duty, even though Rater stays the same
- Rated Officer is separated from Active Duty
- Rater declared missing or becomes a prisoner of war (rating chain time requirements do not apply)

Relief for Cause (18):

- Used when an officer is relieved based on performance of duty
- Reason for relief will be stated on the report
- Rated officer must be notified

Complete the Record (21):
- Submitted at the rater's option on those eligible for consideration by DA centralized boards for promotion (in or above the zone), school, command (Battalion or Brigade Level)

Senior Rater Option (22):
- Change in senior rater occurs
- Rated officer had not received a report in the preceding 90 calendar days
- An evaluation report is due within 60 calendar days of the change in senior rater

3.3.3.1 OER Support Forms

References:

PAM 600-3	Commissioned Officer Professional Development and Career Management (Dec 05)
DA 67-9-1	Officer Evaluation Report Support Form (Oct 97)
DA 67-9-1A	Junior Officer Dev Support Form (JODSF) (Dec 04)

The OER Support Form has two main objectives. First, viewing your rater and senior rater's forms will show you their areas of emphasis. Second, your own support form allows you to set goals and list your accomplishments during that rating period. The rater section of the OER can be somewhat subjective (ie, your rater is not required to mention certain accomplishments), so the OER support form allows you to have a record of what you have done during that period.

The Junior Officer Developmental Support Form (JODSF) is required for all LTs and WO1. This form allows you to set goals through specific categories (these match up with the box checks on your OER). This form should help you identify your strengths and weaknesses. The purpose of this form is development; not to look good. If you are weak in public speaking, you should set goals that will help you improve throughout the period (ie, Teach mandatory class to platoon or give company safety brief once a month). Your rater should give you feedback and suggest methods of improvement. Remember, no one expects you to be perfect as a LT, they just want to see you improve.

First 30 days:
- Rater and senior rater give you a copy of their support form.

- You draft a copy of your own support form, following the areas of emphasis from theirs.
- Have initial counseling with your rater and complete the draft of your support form.

During Rating Period:
- Receive quarterly and performance counseling from your rater.
- Update your accomplishments on page two of the form.

End of Rating Period:
- Complete support form
- Give support form to rater and they complete your OER
- Rater gives you OER counseling and returns support form to you.

PAM 623-105 (page 5 and 13)

3.3.4 Useful Words for Evaluations

Useful Action Words for Evaluations Reports, Awards, and Commendations

Achievements:

achieved	enforced	rated
attained	ensured	received
carried out	gained	scored
created	made	wrote
developed	mastered	
earned	provided	

Improvements:

aided	improved	reorganized
corrected	increased	repaired
enhanced	raised	strengthened
fixed	reduced	upgraded
formed	refined	updated
helped	renewed	

Leadership:

coached	headed	managed
commanded	initiated	steered
controlled	influenced	supervised
directed	inspired	tasked
guided	instilled	took
handled	led	

Training:

counseled	prepared	taught

drilled	practiced	trained
instructed	presented	tutored
mentored	shaped	planned
molded	sharpened	showed

Adjectives for OERs, NCOERs, Awards, and Commendations
Able (skilled, skillful, expert, polished)
Bold (aggressive)
Brave (dauntless, fearless)
Bright (smart, quick)
Devoted (dedicated, faithful, loyal)
Dynamic (forceful, aggressive)
Eager (earnest, intent)
Expert (skilled, skillful, adroit, polished)
Firm (resolved, steadfast, staunch)
Forceful (dynamic, aggressive)
Helpful (supportive)
Intense (acute, keen)
Matchless (unrivaled, peerless)
Outstanding
Perfect (faultless, flawless)
Precise (exact, keen)
Sharp
Skilled (skillful)
Superb (superior)

3.4 Finance

References:

AR 37-104-4	Military Pay and Allowances Policy (Jun 05)
AR 600-15	Indebtedness of Military Personnel (Mar 86)
AR 600–38	The Meal Card Management System (Mar 88)
TC 21-7	Personal Financial Readiness and Deployability Handbook (Aug 03)

Forms:

DA 2142	Pay Inquiry (Apr 82)
DA 3685	JUMPS-JSS Pay Elections (Sep 90)
DD 1351-2	Travel Voucher or Sub-voucher (Jul 04)
DD 2558	Authorization to Start, Stop, or Change an Allotment (Nov 96)
SF 1199A	Direct Deposit Sign-up Form (Jun 87)

Websites:

MyPay	https://mypay.dfas.mil/

eMILPO Reports:

AAC–P49	Cyclic JUMPS Transaction Register
AAC–P51	JUMPS Error Notice Listing

Tips/Tricks:

- Most units have a Command Financial Advisor. Send your Soldiers over there when they first arrive to your unit to do a budget. Place that budget in their counseling folder. This will help find problems your Soldiers may not want to talk to you about.
- When scheduling mandatory training on the schedule, create time for one of your NCOs to teach a class about basic finance issues; especially loans and interest rates.
- Require all junior Soldiers to consult their supervisor before making any purchase over $1000.
- Get the updated list of banned businesses from your post and place it on the bulletin board. Make sure your Soldiers to avoid those establishments that rip off Soldiers. If a business uses shady tactics on one of your Soldiers, take the time to get that business added to the post list.

3.4.1 Allowances

Allowance	Who gets it
Basic Allowance for Housing (BAH) Basic Allowance for Subsistence (BAS)	Active duty Soldiers who have not been furnished adequate government quarters for themselves or their dependents or who have been furnished inadequate quarters. BAH is intended to pay only a portion of the Soldier's housing costs. All Active duty officers and active duty Soldiers are authorized to mess separately (separate rations) or Soldiers who do not have a dining facility available.
Family Separation Allowance (FSA)	Active duty Soldiers on permanent or temporary duty for 30 consecutive days at a location where dependents may not go to at government expense and where government quarters are unavailable for the dependents. Up to $250 a month.
Clothing Maintenance Allowance Dislocation	Active duty enlisted Soldiers on the anniversary of enlistment intended to pay for replacement or military unique items required for war. Increased after the first three years. Active duty Soldiers who make a permanent change of stations intended to defray costs associated with moving that are not reimbursed through other means. Equal to two months of BAH.
Cost of Living Allowance	Active Duty Soldiers assigned and residing in specified high cost areas. Intended to compensate for a portion of non-housing costs that exceed the US average by 8% or more.
Additional Active Duty Uniform Allowance	Reserve component officers ordered to active duty or active duty for training (ADT) for 90 days or more. Payable after serving 90 consecutive days of active duty.
Per diem Allowance	Soldiers on temporary duty (TDY) when government quarters and mess are unavailable. Per diem is a tax-free daily allowance for the added expenses of buying meals and/or living in hotels while on official business.

Table 7-2. Allowances
FM 7-21.13. The Soldier's Guide (Feb 04)

3.4.2 LES

References:

LES Fact Sheet

Payments

- PAY DATE - Base pay computation date which reflects all creditable service for pay purposes (also known as PBED).
- YRS SVC - Years of service for pay.
- ETS - Expiration Term of Service. The date which a member is scheduled to complete the current term of enlistment or obligation.
- BRANCH - Branch of Service (i.e., AF or ARMY).
- ADSN/DSSN - Number used to identify the servicing finance office or disbursing activity.
- PERIOD COVERED - The pay period.
- ENTITLEMENTS - The money the member has earned by type and amount. It includes all pay and allowance earned (e.g., basic pay, basic allowance for quarters, clothing allowance, separate rations, variable housing allowance, etc.).
- EVEN $ (ENTITLEMENTS) - The unpaid money amount brought forward from the "previous" month. When the check is sent to an address, it is always paid in even dollar amounts. The remainder will be brought forward to the next month.
- DEDUCTIONS - Deductions charged against military pay entitlements, indicated by type and amount.
- EVEN $ (DEDUCTIONS) - The unpaid money amount for the "current month", which will be brought forward for the next month. When the check is sent to an address, it is always paid in even dollar amounts.
- MID-MONTH PAY - The amount of mid-month payment received for the current month when the member's pay option is twice a month.
- ALLOTMENTS - Designated amounts of a member's pay which is authorized to be paid to a designated allottee.
- AMT FWD - Dollar amount brought forward from prior period covered.
- TOT ENT - The total of all entitlements before taxes and allotments are deducted.
- TOT DED - The total of all deductions.
- TOT ALMT - The total of all allotments.
- NET AMOUNT - Net or take-home pay for the member.
- CR FWD - Amount carried forward to the net pay period.
- EOM PAY - Amount due member after subtracting amount carried forward from the net amount.

Leave

- BF BAL - Number of leave days member has at the start of the fiscal year or current enlistment (if this year).
- ERND - Leave earned this fiscal year or enlistment.
- USED - Number of leave days used this fiscal year.
- CR BAL - Current leave balance. (BF BAL + ERND - USED = CR BAL).
- ETSBAL - Number of leave days, to include current balance, which can accrue until ETS.
- LOST - Number of leave days lost the prior fiscal year.
- PAID - Number of leave days the member has cashed in after 9 Feb 76 (not more than 60 days during career).
- USE LOSE - Number of leave days that will be lost if no more leave is taken before 1 Oct.

Pay Date

- BAQ TYPE - A code which correlates to the BAQ type, i.e., with dependents, without dependents, partial or single.

- BAQ DEPN - A code for the primary dependent of the member for BAQ purposes (e.g., Spouse).
- VHA ZIP - The postal zip code for the VHA computation.
- RENT AMT - Housing cost for VHA computation.
- SHARE - Number of military sharing expenses.
- STAT - The indicator which reflects whether the member is renting (R), or a homeowner (H).
- JFTR - Joint Federal Travel Regulation code for overseas station allowance calculation (COLA, etc.).
- DEPNS - Number of dependents authorized for overseas station allowance.
- 2DJFTR - Same as JFTR. Used when member has been granted a special entitlement.
- BAS TYPE - Type of separate rations received.
- CHARITY YTD - Charitable contributions this year.
- TPC - Training Pay Category Code. The code which indicates the pay status for Guard or Reserve member.
- PACIDN - The eight digit Army Personnel Administration Center Identification Number (PACIDN) code.
- REMARKS - The remarks area will continue a line by line explanation of changes to the account throughout the month.

3.4.3 myPay

Websites:

MyPay https://mypay.dfas.mil/

Functions:

- View LES
- Start/Stop allotments
- View travel vouchers
- View Tax information
- View/Adjust Thrift Savings Plan
- View Savings Bonds issues

3.4.3.1 Getting Logon Credentials

Active Duty (AKO account):

- Go to myPay Homepage and click NEED NEW PIN
- The process will issue a new random temporary PIN to your account, which will be emailed to your pre-registered AKO email address

Active Duty (no AKO account):

- You must FAX or MAIL the following information to DFAS in order to establish a new temporary PIN:

  Name, SSN, Photocopy of Military ID, Daytime phone number, signature

DFAS-Cleveland/PMCAA
Attention myPay
1240 East 9th Street
Cleveland, Ohio 44199
FAX: 216-522-5800

- If you Fax or Mail your request, your new Temporary PIN will be set to the last five numbers of your SSN. Please wait at least two business days before attempting to use your new temporary PIN (allow additional time if you mailed your request). You will not receive any notification that your temporary PIN has been reset.

Reserves:
- Go to myPay Homepage and click NEED NEW PIN
- The process will issue a new random temporary PIN for your account, which will be mailed to your address of record currently contained in your pay system. It will arrive in 10 business days.

3.4.4 TDY Settlement

References:

AR 614-11	Temporary Duty (TDY) (Oct 79)
PAM 55-20	Uniformed Services Personnel Travel and Transportation (Nov 77)

Forms:

DD Form 1351-2 Travel Voucher or Sub-voucher (Jul 04)

TRAVEL VOUCHER OR SUBVOUCHER

Read Privacy Act Statement, Penalty Statement, and Instructions on back before completing form. Use typewriter, ink, or ball point pen. PRESS HARD. DO NOT use pencil. If more space is needed, continue in remarks.

1. PAYMENT
- Electronic Fund Transfer (EFT)
- Payment by Check

SPLIT DISBURSEMENT: The Paying Office will pay directly to the Government Travel Charge Card (GTCC) contractor the portion of your reimbursement representing travel charges for transportation, lodging, and rental car if you are a civilian employee, unless you elect a different amount. Military personnel are required to designate a payment that equals the total of their outstanding government travel card balance to the GTCC contractor.

Pay the following amount of this reimbursement directly to the Government Travel Charge Card contractor: $

2. NAME (Last, First, Middle Initial) (Print or type) | **3. GRADE** | **4. SSN**

5. TYPE OF PAYMENT (X as applicable): TDY, PCS, Dependent(s), Member/Employee, Other, DLA

6. ADDRESS. a. NUMBER AND STREET | b. CITY | c. STATE | d. ZIP CODE | e. E-MAIL ADDRESS

7. DAYTIME TELEPHONE NUMBER & AREA CODE | **8. TRAVEL ORDER/AUTHORIZATION NUMBER** | **9. PREVIOUS GOVERNMENT PAYMENTS/ ADVANCES**

10. FOR D.O. USE ONLY
a. D.O. VOUCHER NUMBER
b. SUBVOUCHER NUMBER
c. PAID BY
d. COMPUTATIONS

11. ORGANIZATION AND STATION

12. DEPENDENT(S) (X and complete as applicable): ACCOMPANIED | UNACCOMPANIED

a. NAME (Last, First, Middle Initial)	b. RELATIONSHIP	c. DATE OF BIRTH OR MARRIAGE

13. DEPENDENTS' ADDRESS ON RECEIPT OF ORDERS (Include Zip Code)

14. HAVE HOUSEHOLD GOODS BEEN SHIPPED? (X one): YES | NO (Explain in Remarks)

15. ITINERARY

a. DATE		b. PLACE (Home, Office, Base, Activity, City and State; City and Country, etc.)	c. MEANS/ MODE OF TRAVEL	d. REASON FOR STOP	e. LODGING COST	f. POC MILES
	DEP					
	ARR					
	DEP					
	ARR					
	DEP					
	ARR					
	DEP					
	ARR					
	DEP					
	ARR					
	DEP					
	ARR					
	DEP					
	ARR					

16. POC TRAVEL (X one): OWN/OPERATE | PASSENGER

17. DURATION OF TDY TRAVEL
- 12 HOURS OR LESS
- MORE THAN 12 HOURS BUT 24 HOURS OR LESS
- MORE THAN 24 HOURS

18. REIMBURSABLE EXPENSES

a. DATE	b. NATURE OF EXPENSE	c. AMOUNT	d. ALLOWED

e. SUMMARY OF PAYMENT
(1) Per Diem
(2) Actual Expense Allowance
(3) Mileage
(4) Dependent Travel
(5) DLA
(6) Reimbursable Expenses
(7) Total
(8) Less Advance
(9) Amount Owed
(10) Amount Due

19. GOVERNMENT/DEDUCTIBLE MEALS

a. DATE	b. NO. OF MEALS	a. DATE	b. NO. OF MEALS

20.a. CLAIMANT SIGNATURE | b. DATE | **c. SUPERVISOR SIGNATURE** | d. DATE

21.a. APPROVING OFFICER SIGNATURE | b. DATE

22. ACCOUNTING CLASSIFICATION

23. COLLECTION DATA

24. COMPUTED BY | **25. AUDITED BY** | **26. TRAVEL ORDER/ AUTHORIZATION POSTED BY** | **27. RECEIVED** (Payee Signature and Date or Check No.) | **28. AMOUNT PAID**

DD FORM 1351-2, JUL 2004 PREVIOUS EDITIONS ARE OBSOLETE. Exception to SF 1012 approved by GSA/IRMS 12-91.

DD Form 1351-2

Quick Checks:

- Is the Travel Voucher claim (DD Form 1351-2) an original, not a copy?
- Is the signature on the Travel Voucher an original signature?

- Does the administrative data on the Travel Voucher agree with the orders?
- Are advances and/or accrued per diem payments lists in Block 10? The traveler annotates "NONE" in block 10 if there were none.
- Is Block 16 (POC Travel) checked by the traveler if mileage is claimed? Privately Owned Conveyance (POC) mileage should be reasonable according to the mission. This includes mileage within and around TDY site, to and return from the airport, and to and return from TDY station.
- Are Reimbursable Expenses claimed authorized in travel order?
- Was rental car expense claimed? If so, was the car obtained through proper channels (ex. Carlson or SATO)?
- Are confirmation numbers of non-availability of government quarters in the remarks block of the orders? If not, and obtained after the fact, a Travel Approving Official must authorized lodging in Block 29 and sign in Block 21a.
- Is lodging claimed and support by original itemized paid receipts (regardless of amount) or a justification statement attached explaining why receipts are not available?
- Are expenses of $75.00 or more supports by a receipt or justification statement explaining why receipts are not available?
- Did the traveler list the exchange rate obtained in Block 29 when foreign currency is involved?
- Was leave taken in conjunction with the TDY? If so, was it annotated in the itinerary and in Block 29, Remarks section? Is a copy of the DA 31 attached?
- Are the required orders, receipts, statements, and justifications attached to the Travel Voucher?
- Was any deviation from the travel order in the government's best interest?
- Are there any specific items, not in the original order, that require an amended order or the authorization and signature of the Travel Approving official?
- Did the commander/reviewer sign in Block 20c and date in Block 20d.

Reviewer's Checklist to Travel Vouchers

3.4.5 TSP

Website:
TSP Homepage http://www.tsp.gov/

The TSP is a retirement benefit that is offered to employees of the U.S. Government. It is similar to "401(k)" plans available to many private sector employees. The purpose of the TSP is to give you the opportunity to participate in a long-term savings and investment plan.

Advantages:
- Before-tax contributions and tax-deferred investment earnings
- Automatic payroll deductions
- Low administrative and investment expenses
- Diversified choice of investment options, including professionally designed life-cycle funds
- Limited access to your money while you are still employed by the Federal Government
- Portable retirement account that can move with you when you retire or leave Federal service
- Variety of withdrawal options

Summary of the Thrift Savings Plan (2005)

3.5 Flags

References:

AR 600-8-2 Suspension of Favorable Personnel Actions (Flags) (Dec 04)

AR 600-9 Army Weight Control Program (Jun 87)

Forms:

DA 268 Report to Suspend Favorable Personnel Actions (Flag) (Jun 87)

Categories of Flags

Flags will be submitted when an unfavorable action or investigation (formal or informal) is started against a soldier by military or civilian authorities. Flags are classified into the two categories, transferable or non-transferable, depending upon the specific action or investigation. Transferable flags may be transferred to another unit; non-transferable flags may not be transferred to another unit. Flags transactions are completed on a DA Form 268, to initiate, delete, transfer, or remove a flag.

Transferable Flags

- Adverse Action: HQDA Directed Reassignment (Code G)
- Adverse Action: Punishment Phase (Code H)
- Army Physical Fitness Test Failure (Code J)
- Weight Control Program (Code K)

Non-Transferable Flag

- Adverse Actions (Code A)
    - Charges, restraint, or investigation
    - Court-martial
    - Absent without leave (AWOL)
    - Administrative reduction
    - Letter of admonition, censure, or reprimand not administered as non-judicial punishment
- Elimination – Field Initiated (Code B)
- Removal from Selection List – Field initiated (Code C)
- Security Violation (Code E)
- Elimination or Removal from Selection List: HQDA initiated (Code F)

Actions Prohibited by a Flag

- Appointment, reappointment, reenlistment, and extension
- Entry on active duty (AD) or active duty for training (ADT)
- Reassignment
- Promotion or reevaluation for promotion
- Awards and decorations
- Attendance at civil or military training
- Unqualified resignation or discharge
- Retirement
- Advanced or excess leave
- Payment of enlistment bonus (EB) or selective reenlistment bonus (SRB)
- Assumption of command
- Family member travel to an overseas command (when overseas)
- Command sponsorship of family members (when overseas)

APFT Flag:

- Block promotion, reenlistment, and extension only and are not initiated if the soldier has a limiting physical profile prohibiting the APFT.

Weight Control Flag:

- Flags for weight control block attendance at full-time civil or military schooling, promotion, assumption of command, and reenlistment or extension.

Awards and Decorations:

- Retirement awards and decorations for valor may be processed and presented to flagged soldiers.

3.6 Inspections

References:

AR 1-201 Army Inspection Policy (Jan 04)

Principles of Army Inspections (from AR 1-201, paragraph 2-2):

1. Purposeful
   - Related to mission accomplishment
   - Tailored to meet the commander's needs
2. Coordinated
   - Can this inspection be canceled or combined with another inspection?
   - Does this inspection duplicate or complement another inspection?
   - Do inspection reports from other agencies or other echelons of command exist that can assist in the conduct of an inspection?
3. Focused on Feedback
   - Identify root causes
   - Identify strengths and weaknesses
   - Implement corrective actions
   - Share inspection results
4. Instructive
5. Followed Up

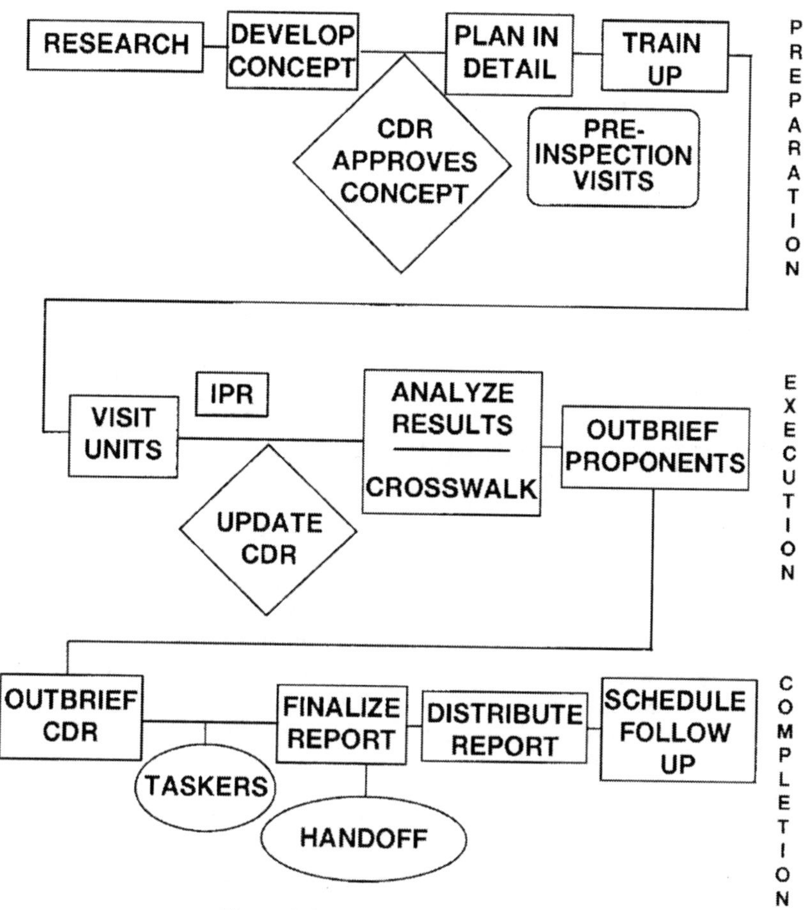

Figure 6-2. The Inspection Process
AR 20-1. Inspector General Activities and Procedure (Mar 02)

3.6.1 Internal Inspections

Types of Internal Inspections (AR 1-201, para 3-4)

- Personal observations
- Unit status report
- Strategic Readiness System
- Installation status report
- Monthly status report (TRADOC only)
- Emergency deployment readiness exercise
- Command post exercises/field training exercises
- Gunnery
- Logistics evaluations

- Joint training exercises
- Internal review audits

3.6.2 Commanders Inspection (CIP)

The CIP is a means for commanders to identify and correct deficiencies at their level. The CIP will help commanders enhance efficiencies, and assess and improve the quality of their efforts and products. The CIP must be implemented and have the direct involvement and support of the commander and personnel. Commanders will conduct a CIP at least twice a year.

CIP Checklists:

- Your higher headquarters should maintain each section's checklist. Request a copy ahead of time.

3.6.3 Inspector General Inspections

References:

AR 20-1 Inspector Activities and Procedure (Mar 02)

The Inspector General Inspection Program is designed to train personnel to perform their jobs in compliance with regulatory guidance. The inspection provides commanders an objective and independent appraisal of their performance. The inspection helps determine specific training needs, manner of performance, and the state of discipline, economy, efficiency, and morale in each functional area.

IG Checklists:

- IG inspections are usually formal and your unit will receive an MSO about 30 days prior to the inspection. You can check with your post or division Inspector General's office for a copy of the checklist.

3.6.4 Staff Inspections

Types of Staff Inspections

- Safety inspections
- Training inspections
- Command supply discipline inspections
- Automated data processing inspections
- Maintenance inspections
- Accountability inspections
- Physical security inspections of arms rooms
- Inspections of ammunition and explosives storage areas
- Resource management

from AR 1-201, para 3-4

3.7 Legal

References:

FM 27-1	Legal Guide for Commanders (Jan 92)
FM 27-14	Legal Guide for Soldiers (Apr 91)
AR 27-10	Military Justice (Nov 05)
AR 600-15	Indebtedness of Military Personnel (Mar 86)
AR 635-200	Active Duty Enlisted Administrative Separations (Jun 05)
PAM 635-4	Pre-Separation Guide (Sep 97)
MISC PUB 27-7	Manual for Courts-Martial (MCM) (2005)

eMILPO Reports:

AAC-C95 Suspension of Favorable Personnel Actions Report

3.7.1 Article 15

Article 15 Punishments:

	Summarized	Company Grade	Field Grade
Restriction	14 days	14 days	60 days
Extra Duty	14 days	14 days	45 days*
Pay Forfeiture	None	7 days	1/2 month for 2 months
Rank Reduction (E-4 & below)	None	1 grade	1 or more grades
Rank Reduction (E5 & E6)	None	None	1 grade
Rank Reduction (E-7 & up)	None	None	None

* If not extra duty is imposed, then maximum restriction is 60 days. If both restriction and extra duty are imposed, they must be served at the same time. Pay forfeiture, restriction, and extra duty may be all or partially suspended.

Table 3-1. Maximum Punishments in Article 15
FM 7-21.13. The Soldier's Guide (Feb 04)

3.7.2 Court Martial

Summary Court Martial (SCM): The SCM handles minor crimes and has simple procedures. The maximum punishment, which depends upon the rank of the accused, is limited to confinement for one month, forfeiture of two-thirds pay for one month, and reduction in grade. (See MCM, R.C.M. 1301(d) for allowable punishments.) An SCM may not try an accused against his will. If he objects, you may consider trial by a higher court-martial. The accused does not have the right to military counsel at an SCM.

Special Court-Martial (SPCM): The SPCM consists of a military judge, at least three court members (unless the accused chooses to be tried by a military judge alone), a trial counsel, and a defense counsel. The maximum sentence is confinement for six months, forfeiture of two-thirds pay per month for six months, and reduction to the lowest enlisted grade. (See MCM, R.C.M. 201(f)(2)(B).)

General Court-Martial (GCM): The GCM tries the most serious offenses. It consists of a military judge, at least five members (unless the accused elects to be tried by a military judge alone), a trial counsel, and a defense counsel; the counsel must be lawyers. Unless waived by the accused, a formal investigation must occur before a general court-martial may try the case. (See UCMJ, Article 32.) The GCM may adjudge the most severe sentences authorized by law, including dishonorable discharge. (See MCM, Part IV and Appendix 12.)

from FM 27-1, Legal Guide for Commanders

Court-Martial Punishments:

	Summary (SCM)	**Special (SPCM)**	**General (GCM)**
Restriction	60 days	- - -	- - -
Extra Duty (E4 & below)	45 days	- - -	- - -
Extra Duty (E5 & above)	- - -	- - -	- - -
Confinement (E4 & below)	30 days	6 months	Maximum for each offense
Confinement (E5 & above)	- - -		Maximum for each offense
Pay Forfeiture	2/3 of basic pay for one month	2/3 of basic pay for six months	Forfeiture of all pay and allowance
Rank Reduction (E4 & below)	Reduction to E1	Reduction to the next lower pay grade	- - -
Rank Reduction (E5 & above)	Reduction to the next lower pay grade	Reduction to the next lower pay grade	- - -

* deprivation of liberties may be combined, so long as the total punishment does not exceed the max for the most severe, i.e.: 15 days confinement, followed by 15 days restriction or extra duties

3.8 Medical Processing

References:

AR 40-501 Standards of Medical Fitness (Feb 06)
AR 600-60 Physical Performance Evaluation System (Jun 02)
AR 635-40 Evaluation for Retention/Retirement/Separation (Feb 06)
PAM 611-21 Enlisted Career Fields and MOS (Mar 99)

DA 689 Sick Call Slip (Mar 63)
DA 3349 Profile (Feb 04)

Profiles:

- See Chapter 5, Physical Fitness: Profiles

Permanent Profiles (1)

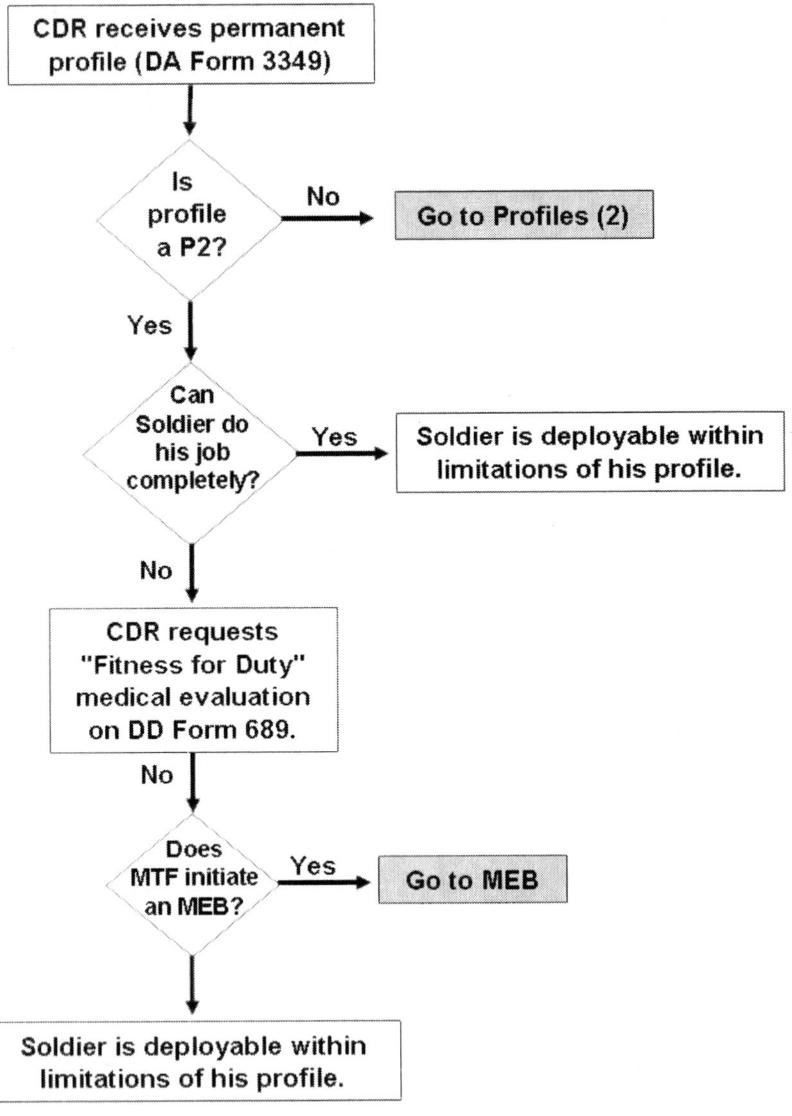

Permanent Profiles (2)

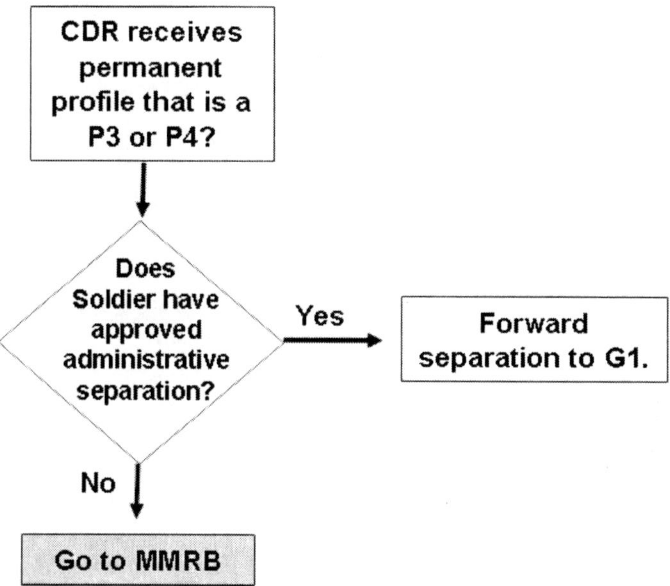

3.8.1 MMRB

MOS/Medical Retention Board (MMRB): Determine whether soldiers can perform in their PMOS or specialty code in worldwide assignments under field conditions.

MMRB Process

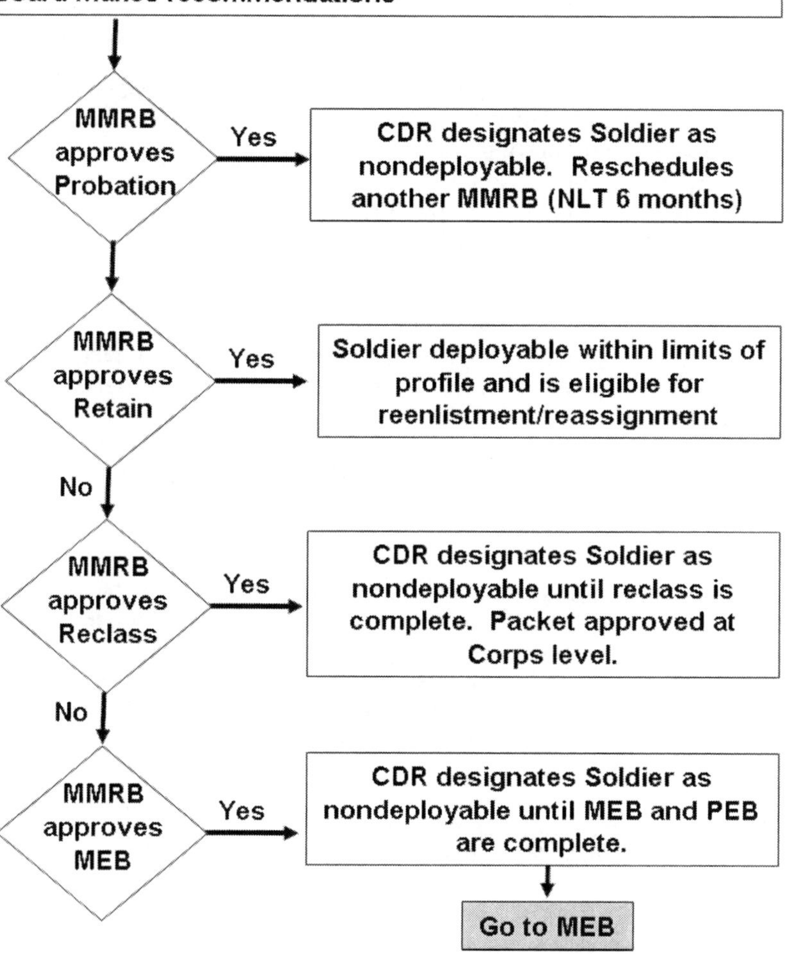
CDR notified of pending MMRB.
CDR writes evaluation on Soldier. CDR makes recommendation to board (Retain, Reclass, Probation, MEB).
CDR forwards ERB/ORB, PT card, Soldier's memo, profile, and medical record to the board. Soldier attends MMRB.
Board makes recommendations
MMRB approves Probation
Yes
CDR designates Soldier as nondeployable. Reschedules another MMRB (NLT 6 months)
MMRB approves Retain
Yes
Soldier deployable within limits of profile and is eligible for reenlistment/reassignment
No
MMRB approves Reclass
Yes
CDR designates Soldier as nondeployable until reclass is complete. Packet approved at Corps level.
No
MMRB approves MEB
Yes
CDR designates Soldier as nondeployable until MEB and PEB are complete.
Go to MEB

Considerations:
- Soldier worldwide deployable
- Basic soldier physical tasks
- Specific MOS and skill levels
- APFT

Initiation:
- Soldiers issued a permanent physical profile with a 3 or 4 in one or more of the physical profile serial (PULHES) factors are required to appear before an MMRB

Not required:
- A numerical factor of 2 in one or more of the PULHES factors
  - Commander's referral for permanent profile reevaluation
- Possessing temporary profiles
- Approved service retirements
- DA/locally imposed bars to reenlistment
- Pending administrative separation

Notification:
- Notification memorandum to unit commanders
- Commanders must write an evaluation of the soldier's physical capability and the impact on the performance of the soldier's PMOS

Options:
- Reclassification: Soldier cannot physically perform the full range of PMOS duties but possesses the physical ability to perform a current shortage or balanced MOS

- Probationary status: Condition prevents a soldier from performing PMOS in a worldwide field environment but may improve through a program of rehab and physical therapy. Period will not exceed 6 months. Commander will evaluate progress after 90 days. If progress is not noted the commander will refer the soldier to the MMRB. End of probationary period MMRB will reevaluate the soldier

- Retain: Medical condition does not preclude satisfactory performance of PMOS physical requirements in worldwide field environment.

- Physical disability system: Medical condition precludes satisfactory performance in any MOS for which the Army has a requirement in a worldwide field environment

3.8.2 MEB

Medical Evaluation Board (MEB): Documents a how a Soldier's medical status affects and/or limits their duty performance.

MEB Initiation:
- Medical Treatment Facility (MTF) Commanders (through physicians)
- General Court-martial authority Commanders
- Unit commanders (refer to medical channels for evaluation)
- Commander, PERSCOM (recommends Soldiers denied reclassification through MMRB)

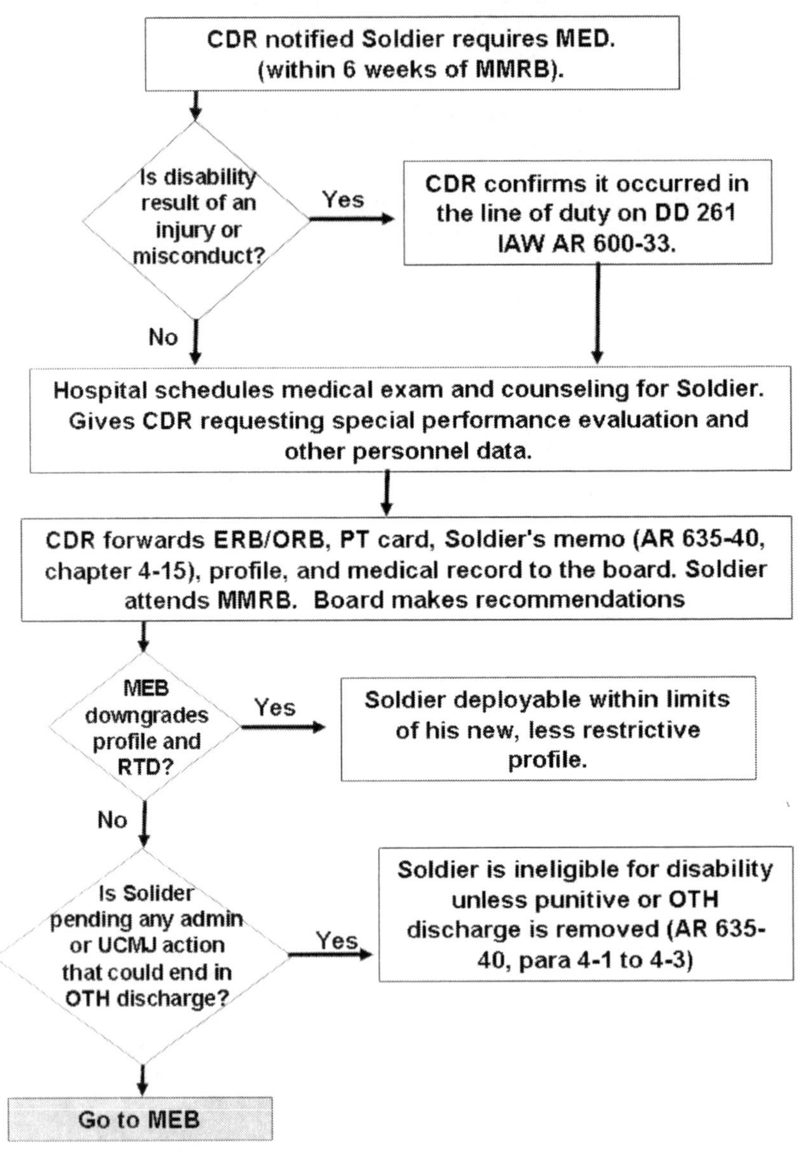
MEB Process
CDR notified Soldier requires MED. (within 6 weeks of MMRB).
Is disability result of an injury or misconduct?
Yes
CDR confirms it occurred in the line of duty on DD 261 IAW AR 600-33.
No
Hospital schedules medical exam and counseling for Soldier. Gives CDR requesting special performance evaluation and other personnel data.
CDR forwards ERB/ORB, PT card, Soldier's memo (AR 635-40, chapter 4-15), profile, and medical record to the board. Soldier attends MMRB. Board makes recommendations
MEB downgrades profile and RTD?
Yes
Soldier deployable within limits of his new, less restrictive profile.
No
Is Solider pending any admin or UCMJ action that could end in OTH discharge?
Yes
Soldier is ineligible for disability unless punitive or OTH discharge is removed (AR 635-40, para 4-1 to 4-3)
Go to MEB

3.8.3 PEB

Physical Evaluation Board (PEB): Determines whether the soldier can reasonably perform the duties of his or her primary MOS/OS and grade; and if not, determines the present severity of the soldier's physical or mental disability and rate it accordingly.

Possible Recommendations:
- Fit for Duty
- Permanent Disability Retirement
- Temporary Disability Retirement
- Separation with Severance Pay
- Separation without Disability Benefits

PEB Process

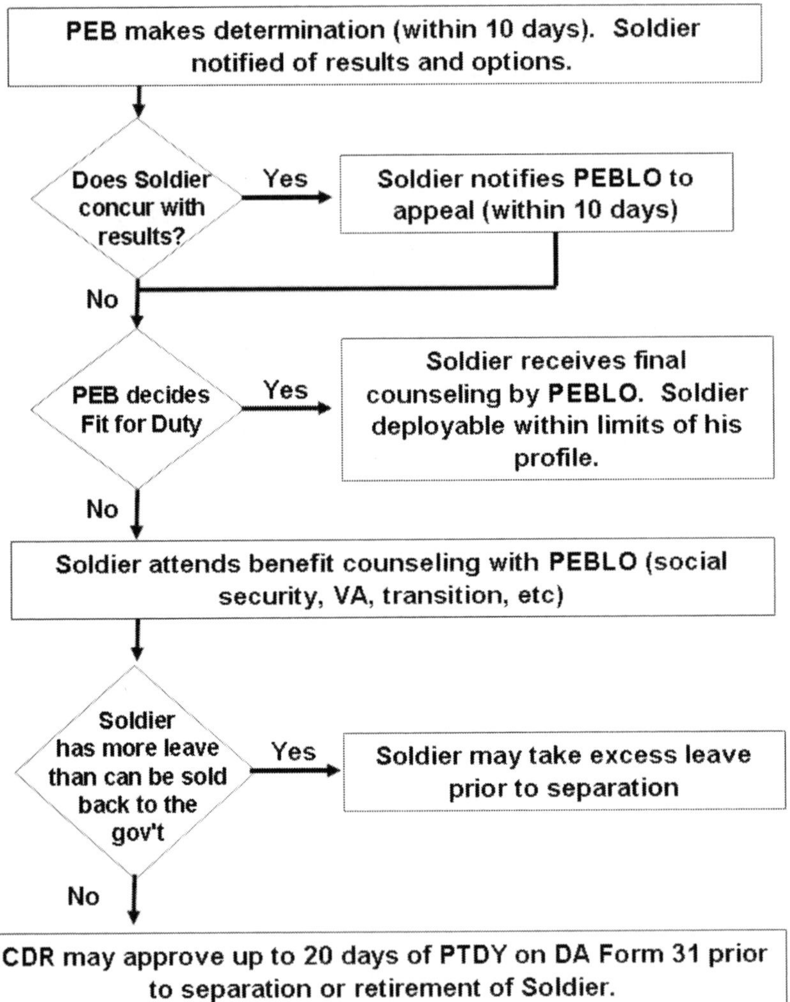

PEB makes determination (within 10 days). Soldier notified of results and options.
Does Soldier concur with results?
Yes
Soldier notifies PEBLO to appeal (within 10 days)
No
PEB decides Fit for Duty
Yes
Soldier receives final counseling by PEBLO. Soldier deployable within limits of his profile.
No
Soldier attends benefit counseling with PEBLO (social security, VA, transition, etc)
Soldier has more leave than can be sold back to the gov't
Yes
Soldier may take excess leave prior to separation
No
CDR may approve up to 20 days of PTDY on DA Form 31 prior to separation or retirement of Soldier.

3.9 Pass/Leave

References:
AR 600-8-10 Leaves and Passes (Feb 06)

Forms:
DA 31 Request and Authority for Leave (Sep 93)
DA 4179 Leave Control Log (Aug 03)

Website:
Automated Risk Assessment https://crc.army.mil/

Soldiers on active duty earn 30 days of leave a year with pay and allowances at the rate of 2 1/2 days a month.

3.9.1 Difference

Regular Pass: A short, non-chargeable, authorized absence from post or place of duty during normal off duty hours.
- The unit commander is the approval authority.
- A soldier remains in an available-for-duty-status during normal off duty hours unless absence is authorized.
- A regular pass begins and ends on post, at duty location, or at the location from where soldier normally commutes to duty. Soldier must be physically at one of these locations when departing to or returning from a regular pass.
- A regular pass will normally be from the end of normal duty hours on one day to the beginning of working hours the next duty day. The standard for calculating the period of the pass is to count calendar days, not on the number of hours to be taken.
- On weekends, a 3-day regular pass period, which includes a national holiday, begins at the end of normal duty day on Friday afternoon, and terminates at the beginning of the normal duty day on the 4th day (Tuesday).
- A regular pass period will not exceed 3 days in length, to include during public holiday weekends or public holiday periods specifically extended by the President.

Special Pass: A short, non-chargeable, authorized absence from post or place of duty

Leave: Ordinary leave is a chargeable leave granted in execution of the commander's annual leave program

Chargeable Leave

Ordinary leave	para 4-3 and 4-4
Advance leave	para 4-5 and 4-6
Emergency leave	chap 6
Environmental and morale leave (EML)	para 4-7 and 4-14
Leave awaiting orders resulting from disability separation proceedings	para 4-15 and 4-16
Leave together with Consecutive Overseas Tour	para 4-17 and 4-18
Reenlistment leave	para 4-19 and 4-20
Transition leave	para 4-21 and 4-22
Rest and recuperation (R & R) leave	para 4-23 and 4-24
Periods of leave that encompass a public holiday or weekends	para 4-25 and 4-26
Pregnancy home leave	para 4-27 and 4-28
AWOL (when excused as unavoidable)	para 4-29 and 4-30
Leave together with PCS and TDY	chap 7

3.9.2 Request Procedures

Procedures:
- Specific procedures are outlined in AR 600-8-10, Leave and Passes.
- Follow unit SOPs for routing and timeframes.

Pass/Leave Packet:
- Unit Pass/Leave Request
- POV Inspection Form
- US Safety Center (CRC) Online Risk Assessment
- Itinerary or Strip Map (with miles traveled)
- DA 31 (may be filled out later by PAC)

3.9.3 DA Form 31

REQUEST AND AUTHORITY FOR LEAVE
This form is subject to the Privacy Act of 1974. For use of this form, see AR 600-8-10.
The proponent agency is ODCSPER. *(See instructions on reverse.)*

1. CONTROL NUMBER

PART I

2. NAME *(Last, First, Middle Initial)*	3. SSN	4. RANK	5. DATE

6. LEAVE ADDRESS *(Street, City, State, ZIP Code and Phone No.)*	7. TYPE OF LEAVE ☐ ORDINARY ☐ EMERGENCY ☐ PERMISSIVE TDY ☐ OTHER	8. ORGN, STATION, AND PHONE NO.

9. NUMBER DAYS LEAVE				10. DATES	
a. ACCRUED	b. REQUESTED	c. ADVANCED	d. EXCESS	a. FROM	b. TO

11. SIGNATURE OF REQUESTOR	12. SUPERVISOR RECOMMENDATION/SIGNATURE ☐ APPROVAL ☐ DISAPPROVAL	13. SIGNATURE AND TITLE OF APPROVING AUTHORITY

14. DEPARTURE		
a. DATE	b. TIME	c. NAME/TITLE/SIGNATURE OF DEPARTURE AUTHORITY

15. EXTENSION		
a. NUMBER DAYS	b. DATE APPROVED	c. NAME/TITLE/SIGNATURE OF APPROVAL AUTHORITY

16. RETURN		
a. DATE	b. TIME	c. NAME/TITLE/SIGNATURE OF RETURN AUTHORITY

17. REMARKS

Chargeable leave is from ________ to ________

PART II - EMERGENCY LEAVE TRANSPORTATION AND TRAVEL

18. You are authorized to proceed on official travel in connection with emergency leave and upon completion of your leave and travel will return to home station *(or location)* designated by military orders. You are directed to report to the Aerial Port of Embarkation *(APOE)* for onward movement to the authorized international airport designated in your travel documents. All additional travel is chargeable to leave. Do not depart the installation without reservations or tickets for authorized space required transportation. File a no-pay travel voucher with a copy of your travel documents or boarding pass within 5 working days after your return. Submit request for leave extension to your commander. The American Red Cross can assist you in notifying your commander of your request for extension of leave.

19. INSTRUCTIONS FOR SCHEDULING RETURN TRANSPORTATION:

For return military travel reservations in CONUS call the MAC Passenger Reservation Center *(PRC)*:
Should you require other assistance call PAP:

20. DEPARTED UNIT	21. ARRIVED APOD	22. ARRIVED APOE *(return only)*	23. ARRIVED HOME UNIT

24. **PART III - DEPENDENT TRAVEL AUTHORIZATION**

25. ☐ *(Space available or required cash reimbursable)* ☐ ONE WAY ☐ ROUND TRIP
☐ *(Space required)* TRANSPORTATION AUTHORIZED FOR DEPENDENTS LISTED IN BLOCK NO. 25

DEPENDENT INFORMATION			
a. DEPENDENTS *(Last name, First, MI)*	b. RELATIONSHIP	c. DATES OF BIRTH *(Children)*	d. PASSPORT NUMBER

PART IV - AUTHENTICATION FOR TRAVEL AUTHORIZATION

26. DESIGNATION AND LOCATION OF HEADQUARTERS	27. ACCOUNTING CITATION

28. DATE ISSUED	29. TRAVEL ORDER NUMBER	30. ORDER AUTHORIZING OFFICIAL *(Title and signature)* OR AUTHENTICATION

DA FORM 31, SEP 93 EDITION OF 1 AUG 75 IS OBSOLETE **ORIGINAL 1** USAPPC V4.00

DA Form 31

3.9.4 AWOL

References:

AR 630-10 Absence Without Leave, Desertion, and Personnel in Civilian Court (Jan 06)

3.10 Promotions

References:

AR 140-158 Enlisted Personnel Classification, Promotion, and Reduction (Nov 05)
AR 600-8-19 Enlisted Promotions and Reductions (Jan 06)
AR 600-8-29 Officer Promotions (Feb 05)

Forms:

DA 3355 Promotion Point Worksheet (May 00)
DA 3355-1R Reserve Promotion Point Worksheet (Jan 98)
DA 3356 Board Member Appraisal Worksheet (May 00)
DA 3356-1R USAR Board Member Appraisal Worksheet (Sep 87)
DA 3357 Board Recommendation (May 00)
DA 3357-1R USAR Board Recommendation (Sep 87)
DA 4187 Personnel Action (Jan 00)
DA 4187-1R Personnel Action Addendum (Jan 00)

eMILPO Reports:

AAC-CO1 Enlisted Personnel Eligible for Promotion Consideration
AAC-C10 Recommended List for Promotion of Enlisted Personnel
R070 Commander's Monthly Promotion/Reduction Report

Website:

HRC Promotions https://www.hrc.army.mil/site/active/select/Promo.htm
Promotion Pt Calc http://armyawards.com/promo.shtml

Overview:

- Promotions are always sensitive
- Take a vested interest in every promotion on behalf of your commander

Tips/Tricks:

- Make sure supervisors are tracking when subordinates are in the zone for promotion consideration. Be proactive in getting waivers and promotion point worksheets on those ready for promotion. Make sure counseling packets have sufficient documentation for those in the zone that do not warrant promotion.
- When in doubt, call or visit your servicing PSB if you have any questions
- When a Soldier is in consideration for promotion, ensure supervisors are checking their training records in Operations for completeness.

3.10.1 Requirements

Automatic Non-promotion:

- AWOL, desertion, confinement
- Court-Martial, Article 15 (including period of suspended sentence)
- Flag (including overweight flag)
- MOS reclassification for inefficiency or disciplinary reasons
- Denied reenlistment
- Lack of security clearance (for MOS requiring, such as intelligence, MP)
- Board action for reduction or removal from promotion list
- Decline reenlistment or extension for assignment
- Retirement approved/accepted

If a Soldier that is non-promotable is promoted by oversight, the promotion must be voided and the Soldier returned to his/her grade.

Rank	TIS	TIG	Waiverable TIS	Waiverable TIG	Authority
PV2	6		4		Co Cdr
PFC	12	4	6	2	Co Cdr
SPC	24	6	18	3	Co Cdr
SGT	35	8	33	4	LTC
SSG	84	10	48	5	LTC

SFC-SGM announced by CDR, PERSCOM

Table 6-1. Promotion Criteria-Active Duty
FM 7-21.13. The Soldier's Guide (Feb 04)

Rank	TIS	TIG	Waiverable TIS	Waiverable TIG	Authority
PV2	6		4		Co Cdr
PFC	12	4	6	2	Co Cdr
SPC	26	4	14	3	Co Cdr
SGT	N/A	6	N/A*		LTC
SSG	N/A	8	N/A*		LTC
SFC	9 years	11	6 years*		Selection Board
MSG	13 years	12	8 years*		Selection Board
SGM	16 years	14	10 years*		Selection Board

* Cumulative Enlisted Service

Table 6-2. Promotion Criteria-Army National Guard
FM 7-21.13. The Soldier's Guide (Feb 04)

Rank	TIS	TIG	Waiverable TIS	Waiverable TIG	Authority

PV2	6				Co Cdr
PFC	12	4	6	2	Co Cdr
SPC	24	6	12	3	Co Cdr
SGT	36	12	18	8	LTC
SSG	84	15	48	8	LTC

Table 6-3. Promotion Criteria-Reserve TPU, PV2-SSG
FM 7-21.13. The Soldier's Guide (Feb 04)

3.10.2 Local Promotion

eMILPO Reports:
AAA-117/119 Unit Enlisted Advancement/Waiver Allocation Report

Local Promotions: conducted by Company Commander for PVT (E-1) through promotion to SPC (E-4)

Waivers:
20% Waiver Allocation Rule Applies (Accelerated Promotion Rule)
10% Waiver Allocation for Specialist (AR 600-8-19)

PV2 - Complete six months AFS
PFC - 12 months TIS; 4 months TIG
SPC - 26 months TIS; 6 months TIG
CPL - Lateral promotions per local SOP and DA Regulations

- Commanders may promote one Soldier per quarter without regard to the 10% restriction
- Promotion to SPC is not automatic and must be recommended
- PFC's are not eligible for Reenlistment

3.10.3 Semi-Centralized Boards

Applies to:
- Promotion to Sergeant and Staff Sergeant
- Must be recommended by unit
- Promotion authority must approve (Commander in the rank of LTC or higher)

Service Remaining Obligation:
- 3 months for Sergeant
- 12 months for Staff Sergeant
- Must extend of reenlist (if not eligible, then not promoted and removed from list)

Promotion Board

- Must meet TIS/TIG requirements for rank in which he/she will be promoted
- Must complete NCOES level School
- SGT Warrior Leader Course/SSG BNCOC (see MILPER messages for waivers)

Process
- Recommendations prepared on DA Form 3355
- When recommendation is approved, DA Form 3355 sent to local MILPO
- AR 600-200, FIG 7-1, PP 44
- Point Computation Completed by PSC

Category	Points
Military Training	100
Duty Performance	150
Awards	100
Military Education	200
Civilian Education	100
Promotion Board	150
TOTAL	800

3.10.4 Centralized Board

Applies to:
- SFC, MSG, and CSM
- Controlled by HQDA
- Individual NCOs assist themselves by reviewing and updating personnel records

Process:
- Promotion orders published by PERSCOM via Department of the Army Special Orders (DASO) at end of each month for SFC and above
- PSB verifies eligibility and issues orders the last week of month
- PSB notifies S1s for pickup
- Incur 2 year ADSO upon promotion to SFC, MSG or SGM

Board Packet:
- ERB/ORB
- Evaluations
- Awards
- DA Photo

3.10.5 2LT to 1LT

IAW AR 600-8-29
- 2 years from Active Date of Rank (ADOR)* *or* 18 months from Entered Active Duty date (whichever date is earlier is PED)
- Request S1s confirm officer Promotion Eligibility Date (PED) upon arrival to unit and cross-check with PSB
- PSB should forward 78R (Recommendation for Promotion to 1LT) to S1 at least 60-120 days prior to Promotion Eligibility Date (PED)
- S1s obtain CO CDR's recommendation and BN CDR's approval and return to PSB
- If BN CDR disapproves, there is a mandatory 6 month probationary period (MILPER Message 02-022) If after problem. period, still disapproves, final separation authority is *first O6 in chain, promotion review authority.*

Processing
- The Supervisor/Rater recommends the soldier (is/is not recommended for promotion)
- The Approving official (CDR, LTC OR ABOVE) recommends approval/disapproval of the supervisor/rater recommendation
- If approving authority recommendation leads to soldier being promoted forward 78R to serving PSB for orders
- If approving authority recommendation leads to soldier not being promoted, forward 78R to the Promotion Review Authority (PRA) as applicable
- If PRA (GCMA/COL +) directs promotion of soldier PSB will cut orders
- If PRA denies promotion soldier will be separated IAW AR 635-100 or 635-120
- The DA Form 78R will serve as the order for promotion to 1LT and CW2

3.11 Reenlistments

References:

AR 601-280 Army Retention Program (Jan 06)
AR 635-200 Active Duty Enlisted Administrative Separations (Jun 05)
AR 140-111 US Army Reserve Reenlistment Program (Feb 06)

Forms:

DA 1315 Reenlistment Data (May 98)
DA 1315-1R Status of Reenlistment Data (Dec 94)
DA 4126-R Bar to Reenlistment Certificate (Dec 94)
DA 4856 Developmental Counseling Form (Jun 99)

Website:

Army Retention http://www.stayarmy.com/

Reenlistment Oath:

"I do solemnly swear (or affirm) that I will support and defend the Constitution of the United States against all enemies, foreign and domestic; that I will bear true faith and allegiance to the same; and that I will obey the orders of the President of the United States and the orders of the officers appointed over me, according to regulations and the Uniform Code of Military Justice. So help me God."

Tips/Tricks:

- You should be honored if a Soldier or NCO asks you to reenlist them. Make sure you spent some time thinking of remarks to say about them before the oath.
- Let the Soldier/NCO choose where/when they want their ceremony. It is their day, not the chain of command's. Make sure the ceremony is at a time where their friends and family can attend.
- See if your company has a policy about letting the Soldier/NCO have a pass for reenlisting.

3.12 Separations

References:

AR 630-10	Absence Without Leave, Desertion, and Personnel in Civilian Court (Jan 06)
AR 635-200	Active Duty Enlisted Administrative Separations (Jun 05)
PAM 635-4	Pre-separation Guide (Sep 97)
	VA Benefits Handbook

Website

Veteran's Affairs http://www.va.gov/

Honorable Discharge (AR 635-200, para 3-7c)

- Standards of acceptable conduct and duty are met.
- This type of discharge depends on your behavior and performance of duty. Isolated incidents of minor misconduct may be disregarded if your overall record of service is good.

General Under Honorable Conditions (AR 635-200, para 3-7b)

- Military record is satisfactory, but not sufficiently meritorious to warrant honorable discharge.

Under Other than Honorable Conditions (AR 635-200, para 3-7c)

- This is the most severe of the administrative discharges. It may result in the loss of veteran's benefits. Such a discharge usually is given to those who have shown one or more incidents of serious misconduct.
- This discharge is used for misconduct, fraudulent entry, homosexuality, security reasons, and for the good of the service.
- Results in immediate reduction to the lowest grade IAW AR 600-200, Chpt 6, Section IV
- VA determines benefits.

Dishonorable (AR 635-200, para 3-10)

- Pursuant to sentence of General Courts-Martial
- No VA benefits

Bad Conduct (AR 635-200, para 3-11)

- Pursuant only to approved sentence of General or Special Courts-Martial
- VA determines benefits.

Entry Level Status

- This discharge applies if you are within 180 days of continuous active duty and your records do not warrant a discharge under other than honorable conditions.

3.13 Soldier Administrative Records

It is important that the unit PAC section receives and maintains an Administrative Record on each Soldier. These DA Form 201 have mostly been replaced by electronic OMPF. However, make sure the following documents are in their folder:

- Copies of orders (2)
- Enlisted Records Brief (ERB) or Officer Record Brief (ORB)
- DA 71 Oath of Office
- DA 873 Security Clearance
- DA 1315 Reenlistment Data (SSG and above)
- DA 3355 Promotions Point Worksheet
- DA 3955 Change of Address and Directory Card
- DA 2366 Montgomery GI Bill
- DA 5305-R Family Care Plan (Single Parent or Dual Military Parent)
- DD 93 Record of Emergency Data Card
- DD 1172 Application for ID Card - DEERS
- SGLV 8286 Servicemembers' Group Life Insurance

3.14 Army Writing Style

References:

AR 25-50 Preparing and Managing Correspondence (Jun 02)
PAM 600-67 Effective Writing for Army Leaders (Jun 86)

3.14.1 Memorandum Format

Types of Memorandums

- Memorandum for Record (MFR)
- Memorandum of Agreement (MOA)
- Memorandum of Understanding (MOU)

Formal memorandums. The formal memorandum is used for correspondence that is sent outside the headquarters, the command, the installation, or similarly identifiable organizational elements within the DOD; for routine correspondence to Federal Government agencies outside the DOD; for notification of personnel actions, military or civilian; and for showing appreciation or commendation to DA employees and soldiers.

Informal memorandums. The informal memorandum is used for internal correspondence within the same headquarters, same command, or similarly identifiable organizational elements. As a general rule, do not use informal memorandums when corresponding with organizations or individuals not familiar with your office symbol. Informal memorandums may be pre-printed and used as form letters.

DEPARTMENT OF THE ARMY
ORGANIZATIONAL NAME/TITLE
STANDARDIZED STREET ADDRESS
CITY, STATE, AND ZIP + 4 CODE

OFFICE SYMBOL

MEMORANDUM FOR Deputy Commandant, US Army Command General Staff College (ATZL-SWD), 1 Reynolds Avenue, Ft. Leavenworth, KS 66027-1352

SUBJECT: Using and Preparing a Memorandum

1. Paragraph 2-2 defines the use of a memorandum.

2. Single-space the text of the memorandum; double-space between paragraphs.

3. When a memorandum has more than one paragraph, number the paragraphs consecutively. When paragraphs are subdivided, designate first subdivisions by the letters of the alphabet indent them as shown below.

a. When a paragraph is subdivided, there must be at least two subparagraphs

b. If there is a subparagraph "a," there must be a "b."

(1) Designate second subdivisions by numbers in parentheses; for example (1), (2), and (3).

(2) Do not subdivide beyond the third subdivision.

(a) However, do not indent any further than the second subdivision.

(b) This is an example of the proper indentation procedure for a third subdivision.

AUTHORITY LINE:

Encl

JOHN W. SMITH
Colonel, GS
Deputy Chief of Staff for Operations

CF:
Director, Tactics Division (w/encl)

Figure 2–1. Using and preparing a memorandum
AR 25-50. Preparing and Managing Correspondence (Jun 02)

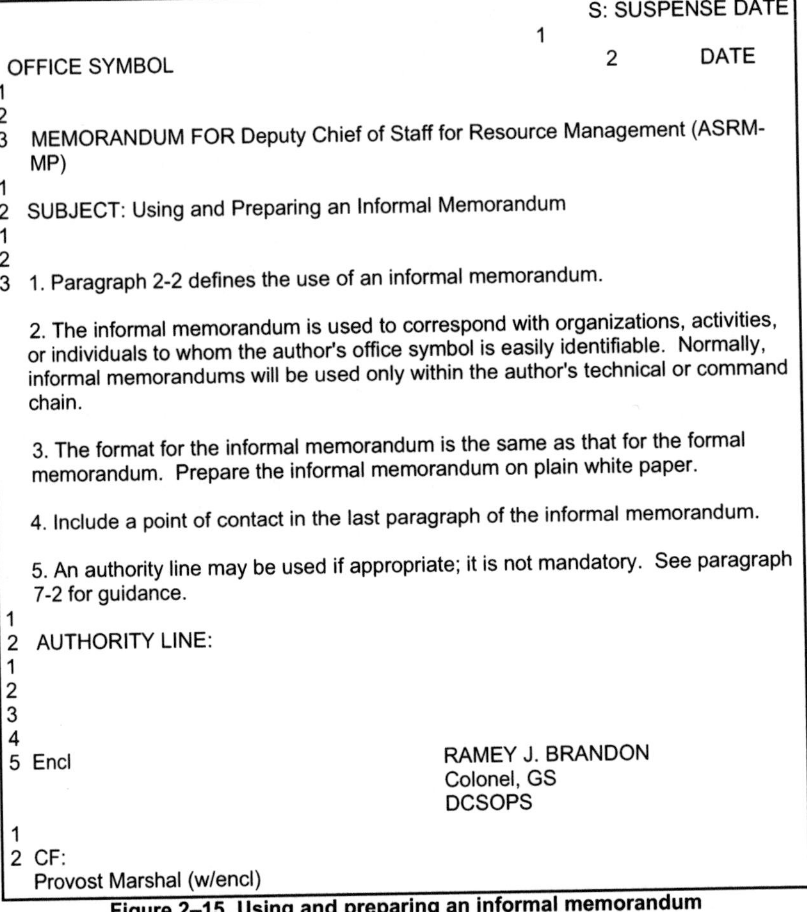

S: SUSPENSE DATE

OFFICE SYMBOL DATE

MEMORANDUM FOR Deputy Chief of Staff for Resource Management (ASRM-MP)

SUBJECT: Using and Preparing an Informal Memorandum

1. Paragraph 2-2 defines the use of an informal memorandum.

2. The informal memorandum is used to correspond with organizations, activities, or individuals to whom the author's office symbol is easily identifiable. Normally, informal memorandums will be used only within the author's technical or command chain.

3. The format for the informal memorandum is the same as that for the formal memorandum. Prepare the informal memorandum on plain white paper.

4. Include a point of contact in the last paragraph of the informal memorandum.

5. An authority line may be used if appropriate; it is not mandatory. See paragraph 7-2 for guidance.

AUTHORITY LINE:

Encl

RAMEY J. BRANDON
Colonel, GS
DCSOPS

CF:
Provost Marshal (w/encl)

Figure 2–15. Using and preparing an informal memorandum
AR 25-50. Preparing and Managing Correspondence (Jun 02)

3.14.2 Paragraph Headers

Suggested Paragraph Headers for Memorandums

1. First Paragraph: References
   - If you have none, just skip this paragraph. Do not say "None."
   - List references in the order you cite them.
   - For publications, give the type, number, date, and title. (ex. FM 21-20, Physical Fitness Training (Sep 92))
   - For correspondence, give the type, office symbol, date, and subject (ex. Memorandum for Record, AFVP-110, 10 Nov 05, Annual Training Guidance)
   - For meetings or phone calls, state the type, parties involved/

organization, date, and subject. (ex. Meeting, Brigade Staff Call, 1st Brigade, 10 Nov 05, Training Schedules)

2. Second Paragraph: Purpose.
   - Clear statement of the purpose.
   - Omit the purpose if it is clear from the title.

3. Bottom Line Up Front. Put the bottom line (your request, recommendation, summary of key points, etc) up front in a paragraph up to 75 words long.

4. Body Paragraphs.
   - See examples below

5. Last Paragraph. Point of Contact. In the last paragraph, state the point of contact (POC). List the POCs rank, name, office, and telephone number.

Examples of Paragraph Headers

PURPOSE	TYPE	HEADERS
To explain something	Information Memorandum	1. References 2. Purpose 3. Summary 4. Discussion (facts) 5. POC
To answer a question (solve a simple problem)	Reply Memorandum	1. References 2. Question (or problem) 3. Answer (or solution) 4. Discussion 5. POC
To announce a meeting	Announcement Memorandum	1. Time 2. Place 3. Purpose 4. Required Attendees 5. Agenda 6. Coordinating Instr 7. POC
To ask for something	Request Memorandum	1. References 2. Purpose 3. Request 4. Reasons 5. Coordinating Instr 6. POC
To announce a policy	Policy Memorandum	1. References 2. Purpose 3. Summary (if needed) 4. Specifics 5. POC

PURPOSE	TYPE	HEADERS
To task someone to do something	Memorandum of Instruction (MOI)	1. References 2. Purpose 3. Summary 4. Responsibilities 5. Coordinating Instructions a. Suspenses b. Sequence of Events c. Service Support d. Command and Signal 6. POC
To announce Standing Operating Procedures (SOP)	SOP Memorandum	1. References 2. Purpose 3. Summary 4. Scope 5. Definitions 6. Responsibilities 7. Procedures 8. Files
To report on progress on a project or preparations for an upcoming event	Progress Report Memorandum	1. References 2. Purpose 3. Summary 4. Actions Completed 5. Actions Yet to be Completed 6. Significant Problems 7. POC
To report on a completed action or event	After-Action Report Memorandum	1. References 2. Purpose 3. Summary 4. Review of Actions 5. Lessons Learned 6. POC
To report the results of an inspection	Inspection Report Memorandum	1. References 2. Purpose 3. Summary 4. Findings and Follow-up Actions 5. Further Actions Required 6. POC

PURPOSE	TYPE	HEADERS
To recommend a course of action on simple problem with one obvious solution	Decision Paper Memorandum	1. This is a decision paper 2. Purpose (or problem) 3. Recommendation 4. Reasons 5. Effect on Resources 6. Coordination
To report the proceedings of a meeting	Meeting Report Memorandum	1. References 2. Purpose 3. Summary 4. Attendees 5. Old Business 6. New Business 7. The Next Meeting 8. POC
To recommend a course of action on a complex issue with two or more feasible course of action	Staff Study Memorandum	1. This is a decision paper 2. Problem 3. Recommendation 4. Facts Bearing on the Problem 5. Assumptions 6. Courses of Action 7. Analysis 8. Conclusion
To reprimand a Soldier	Memorandum of Reprimand	1. Facts 2. Reprimand 3. Warning 4. Requirement for a Reply 5. Disposition of Reprimand
To present your review of a book or article	Book Review Memorandum	1. References 2. Recommendations 3. Analysis of the Author 4. Analysis of the Content 5. Analysis of the Quality 6. Lessons Learned
To present your analysis of a battle	Battle Analysis Memorandum	1. References 2. Summary 3. Strategic Setting 4. Tactical Situation 5. The Action 6. Significance of Action

3.14.3 Letter Format

DEPARTMENT OF THE ARMY
ORGANIZATIONAL NAME/TITLE
STANDARDIZED STREET ADDRESS
CITY, STATE, AND ZIP + 4 CODE

1
2 July 1, 2000

1
2 Manpower Programming Division

Mr. John Doe
123 Main Street
Nashville, Tennessee 73695-0000

1
2 Dear Mr. Doe:

Adjust margins so that the letter is framed on the page.

Type dates in civilian style and center two lines below the last line of the letterhead.

The REPLY TO ATTENTION OF line is explained in paragraph 3-7. There is no set number of lines between the REPLY TO ATTENTION OF line (when preprinted on the letterhead) and first line of the address.

Frame the letter on the page. Five lines is the general rule when the letter is two or more pages.

Do not use abbreviations in the address or signature blocks. See paragraph 3-7.

Single-space the body of a letter with double-spacing between the paragraphs.

Type the salutation on the second line, below the last line of the address. Type the first line of the text of the letter on the second line below the salutation.

Indent paragraphs as shown in this figure, figure 3-3, and figure 3-4. Do not number paragraphs, Subparagraphs may be numbered if there are more than one.

a. Use letters of the alphabet (a, b, c, d) to indicate subparagraphs.

b. Indent subparagraphs as shown in this figure.

If only one subparagraph is used, indicate that subparagraph by a hyphen as shown below.

- This is an example of how to type a subparagraph when there is only one.

When more than one page is needed, there should be a minimum of two lines of text on the second page.

Leave at least one-inch margin at the bottom of multiple-page letter.

Figure 3–1. Letter format
AR 25-50. Preparing and Managing Correspondence (Jun 02)

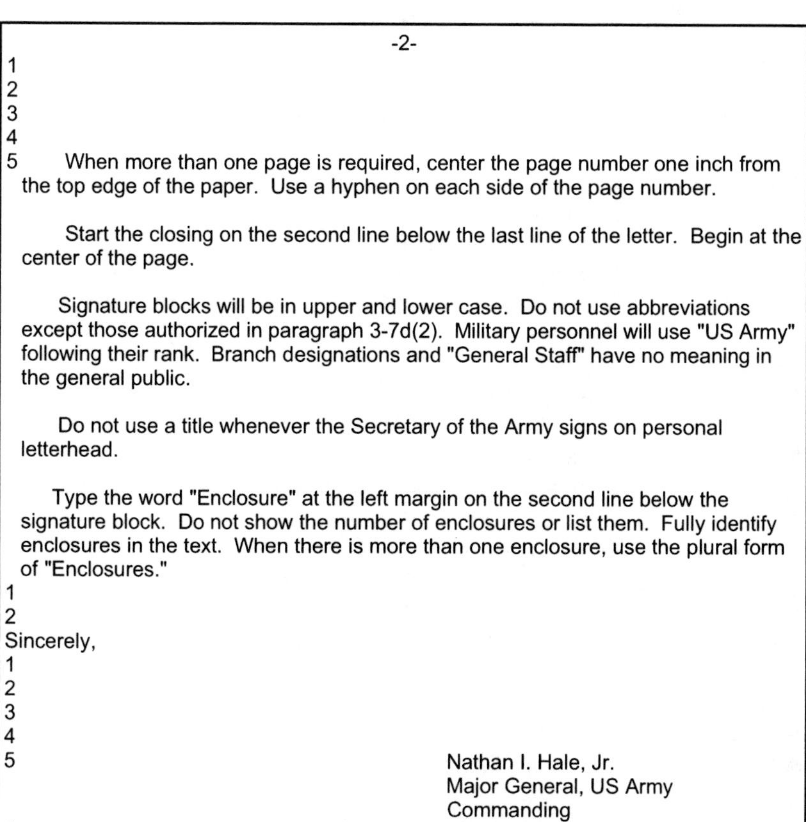

-2-

1
2
3
4
5 When more than one page is required, center the page number one inch from the top edge of the paper. Use a hyphen on each side of the page number.

Start the closing on the second line below the last line of the letter. Begin at the center of the page.

Signature blocks will be in upper and lower case. Do not use abbreviations except those authorized in paragraph 3-7d(2). Military personnel will use "US Army" following their rank. Branch designations and "General Staff" have no meaning in the general public.

Do not use a title whenever the Secretary of the Army signs on personal letterhead.

Type the word "Enclosure" at the left margin on the second line below the signature block. Do not show the number of enclosures or list them. Fully identify enclosures in the text. When there is more than one enclosure, use the plural form of "Enclosures."

1
2
Sincerely,
1
2
3
4
5 Nathan I. Hale, Jr.
Major General, US Army
Commanding

1
2 Enclosure

Figure 3–2. Continuation of a letter
AR 25-50. Preparing and Managing Correspondence (Jun 02)

3.15 eMILPO Quick Sheet

AAA-160	Report of AWOLs
AAA-162	Unit Personnel Accountability Report
AAA-165	Unit Personnel Accountability Notice
AAA-342	Human Resource Authorization Report (Alpha Roster)
AAC-CO1	Enlisted Personnel Eligible for Promotion Consideration
AAC-CO5	Unit Strength Recap
AAC-CO7	Unit Manning Report
AAC-C10	Recommended List for Promotion of Enlisted Personnel
AAC-C11	Alpha Roster
AAC-C13	Loss Roster
AAC-C15	Projected DEROS Report
AAC-C17	Educational Level Survey
AAC-C20	Personnel Actions Suspense Roster
AAC-C22	Personnel Photo Suspense Roster
AAC-C24	Good Conduct Medal Suspense Roster
AAC-C26	Personnel Medical Suspense Roster
AAC-C27	Personnel Strength Zero Balance Report
AAC-C28	Personnel Dental Suspense Roster
AAC-C32	Weight Control Program Report
AAC-C37	Personnel Qualification Roster
AAC-C40	Unit Personnel Accountability Notices
AAC-C45	Company Grade Officer/Warrant Officer Eligible for Promotion
AAC-C95	Suspension of Favorable Personnel Actions Report
AAC-PO1	Personnel Transaction Register by Unit (PTRU)
AAC-P11	Personnel Transaction Register by Originator (PTRO)
AAC-P49	Cyclic JUMPS Transaction Register
AAC-P51	JUMPS Error Notice Listing
R070	Commander's Monthly Promotion/Reduction Report

11/06/2003

Unit Personnel Accountability Report
AAA-162

Unit Name: FORT EUSTIS REPL DET **UIC: W0UV49**

ASGN/ ATCH	Name	SSN	Rank	Gain Dt	Loss Dt	Rsg Rsn	Old Duty Stn	New Duty Stn	Duty Stn Date
ASG	DOE JOHN RICKY	123-45-6789	SPC	20030930			TRA	PDY	20030930
ASG	DOE KEVIN MICHAEL	987-65-4321	PV1	20030923			TRA	PDY	20030923

Total number of ATCH personnel: 0

Total Number of Assigned Enlisted: 2
Total Number of Assigned Warrant Officers: 0
Total Number of Assigned Officers: 0

Total Number of Attached Enlisted: 0
Total Number of Assigned Warrant Officers: 0
Total Number of Assigned Officers: 0

Total number (Assigned) PRESENT FOR DUTY: 2

I certify this report reflects the personnel accountability for all soldiers assigned or attached to the unit for months indicated (Signature required only for month end report)

BRENDA D. WILLIAMS

(CDR or Auth Representative signature)

The reconciliation of the AAA-162 is an imperative tool that is used by each unit to ensure the Commander has 100% accountability of all personnel assigned to their company. This report is mandatory and required to be conducted monthly. Any discrepancies on the report need to be identified and resolved with the eMILPO section immediately. Also, copies of orders for personnel not reflected on the AAA-162 must be accompany the report (i.e. TDY, PCS, ETS, Retired, Deployed, Chapter, etc). After the report is verified and signed by the Commander, it will be provided to the eMILPO section NLT the 10th of each month.

Accountability/Maintenance

Part

4 Accountability/Maintenance

4.1 Supply Accountability

References:

FM 10-27-4 Organizational Supply for Unit Leaders (Apr 00)
AR 710-2 Supply Policy Below the National Level (Jul 05)
AR 735-5 Policies and Procedures for Property Accountability (Feb 05)
PAM 710-2-1 Using Unit Supply System (Manual Procedures) (Dec 97)

Forms:

DA 2062 Hand Receipt/Annex Number (Jan 82)
DA 3161 Request For Issue or Turn-in (Dec 00)
DA 3645a Org Clothing and Individual Equipment Record (Oct 91)
DA 3645b Org Clothing and Individual Equipment Record (Oct 91)
DA 3645-1a Additional Org Clothing and Ind Equipment Record (Dec 83)
DA 3645-1b Additional Org Clothing and Ind Equipment Record (Dec 83)
DD 362 Statement of Charges for Government Property Lost, Damaged, or Destroyed (Mar 74)
DD 1131 Cash Collection Voucher (Apr 57)

Property Accountability Definition:

Property Accountability is the obligation imposed by law, lawful order, or regulation on an officer or other person for keeping an accurate record of property, documents, or funds. It includes maintaining records of gains, losses, due-in, due-out and balances on hand or in use. The person having this obligation may or may not have actual possession of the property, documents or funds. (AR 710-2, para 1-12)

Overview:

All items should be hand-receipted down to the user level.

SUPPLY	
PL	**PSG/NCO'S**
Sign for all platoon equipment from Commander	Signs for platoon equipment not used by PL or squads/sections
Sub-hand receipts all equipment down to user level	Ensures subordinates properly account for equipment and BII
Inventories all platoon equipment and creates shortage annexes	Supervises inventory layout in -10 order
	Tracks platoon expendables and requests from supply section
	Tracks Soldier's issued equipment and initiates field loss or statement of charges when equipment is lost

4.1.1 Command Supply Discipline

Command Supply Discipline Program (CSDP) is a commander's program. It is a compilation of existing regulatory requirements put together for visibility purposes.

Purpose:
- Responsibilities of commanders and supervisory personnel to instill supply discipline in their operations.
- Guidance for evaluating supply discipline.
- Feedback through command and technical channels for improving supply policy.
- Follow-up to ensure supply discipline is maintained.

Goals:
- Establish supply discipline to ensure waste, fraud, and abuse are prevented
- Identify supply problems
- Ensure compliance with DA supply policies
- Provide responsible personnel with a single listings of all existing supply discipline requirements (inspection checklists)
- The major intent of CSDP is for the commander to direct elimination

of non-compliance with supply regulations.
- CSDP is not intended to be solely used as an inspection program. Do not wait to do things right only when you know you'll be inspected.
- Evaluations or inspections should be used to monitor performance

Definitions:
- **Supervisory personnel:** All individuals in a position of responsibility whose job involves them with supply operations within or for the U.S. Army force structure. This applies to officers, warrant officers, NCOs, and civilians.
- **Supply economy:** The conservation of material by every individual dealing with Army supplies to ensure that only the proper item in the necessary amount is used to accomplish a task. The term Stewardship of Resources is synonymous with Supply Economy.
- **Supply discipline:** The compliance with established DA regulations to effectively administer supply economy. Supply discipline applies to the use of supply funds and to all functions and levels of supply operations, (from contractor through the national and retail level, to the user).
- **Repeat finding:** A discrepancy of noncompliance noted from a previous evaluation and unresolved beyond the established suspense date.
- **Requirements listing:** A compilation of existing regulatory requirements as a single source listing, organized by level of responsibility or function.

from AR 735-5, para 11-1 to 11-3

4.1.2 Classes of Supply

Class 1: Subsistence, including free health and welfare items. (AR 30-22)

Class 2: Clothing, individual equipment, tentage, tool sets and tool kits, handtools, administrative, and housekeeping supplies and equipment (including maps). This includes items of equipment, other than major items, prescribed in authorization/allowance tables and items of supply (not including repair parts. (AR 700-84, CTA 50-900, CTA 50-970)

Class 3: POL, petroleum and solid fuels, including bulk and packaged fuels, lubricating oils and lubricants, petroleum specialty products; solid fuels, coal, and related products. (AR 11-27, AR 700-36, AR 710-2, FM 10-13, FM 10-18, FM 10-68, FM 10-69, FM 10-71, SB 710-2, TM 5-675)

Class 4: Construction materials, to include installed equipment, and all fortification/barrier materials (AR 420-17)

Class 5: Ammunition, of all types (including chemical, radiological, and special weapons), bombs, explosives, mines, fuses, detonators, pyrotechnics, missiles, rockets, propellants, and other associated items. (AR 190-59, AR 190-11, AR 190-13, AR 190-51, AR 700-19, AR 710-2, SB 700-2, SB 708-3, FM 9-38, TM 9-1300-206)

Class 6: Personal demand items (nonmilitary sales items). (AR 700-23)

Class 7: Major items: A final combination of end products which is ready for its intended use: (principal item) for example, launchers, tanks, mobile machine shops, vehicles. (AR 710-1, FM 704-28, SB 700-20, Appropriate authorization documents)

Class 8: Medical material, including medical peculiar repair parts. (AR 40-61, CTA 8-100)

Class 9: Repair parts and components, including kits, assemblies and subassemblies, reparable and non-repairable, required for maintenance support of all equipment. (AR 710-2, AR 710-1, Appropriate TMs)

Class 10: Material to support nonmilitary programs; such as, agricultural and economic development, not included in classes 1 through 9.. No additional program of instruction (POI) time is authorized. (CTA 50-909)

CLASSES OF SUPPLY		
CLASS	DESCRIPTION	SYMBOL
I	Rations	
II	Expendables	
III	POL	
IV	Barrier material	
V	Ammunition	
VI	Sundry	
VII	Major end items	
VIII	Medical	
IX	Repair parts	
X	Material to support nonmilitary programs	CA

4.1.3 Types of Property

Real Property:
Land, buildings, Utilities/Sanitary systems (things you cannot move)

Personal Property Items:
Anything except real property (anything you CAN move)

Installation Property:
Anything received from installation property book officer (IPBO). Are non-deployable items unless proper lateral transfer is conducted. (ex. lawn mowers, barracks furnitures, some electronics)

Organizational Property
Property authorized by MTOE or TDA

Organizational Clothing & Individual Equipment (OCIE)
- Items identified as deployable by CTA 50-909, Appendix B
- Basic loads
- Items in AR 840-10 (Guidons, Flags)

Classification of Property:

- **Nonexpendable:** Property that is not consumed in use and that retains its original identity during the period of use. It requires formal property book accountability. Therefore, it is managed at property book level. It is identified by ARC "N" in the AMDF (Army Master Data Files) or FEDLOG (Federal Logistics File). Example: Major end items.

- **Durable:** Property that is not consumed in use, does not require property book accountability, but because of its unique characteristics requires control when issued to the user. Identified by ARC "D" on FEDLOG. Example: Most hand tools.

- **Expendable**: Property that is consumed in use, or that looses its identity in use. It is identified with ARC of "X" in the FEDLOG. Does not require accountability, but must be controlled. Examples: Sandpaper, light bulbs, pens, paper, etc

4.1.4 Types of Responsibility

Command Responsibility: The obligation of a commander to ensure all Government property within his or her command is properly used and cared for, and that proper custody and safekeeping are provided. Command responsibility is inherent in command and cannot be delegated.

Direct Responsibility: Obligation of a person to ensure all government property for which he/she has receipted, is properly used, cared for, and that proper custody and safekeeping are provided. Direct responsibility results from assignment as an accountable officer, acceptance of property on hand receipt from an accountable officer, or receipt of formal written delegation.

Supervisory Responsibility: Supervisory responsibility is the obligation to ensure the proper use, care, and safekeeping of government property issued to or used by subordinates. Supervisors can be held liable for losses incurred by their subordinates.

Personal Responsibility: Unit personnel are responsible for all arms, hand tools, and OCIE issued to them for their use. They are responsible whether they signed for the property or not. For example, when the tool kit is issued, the mechanic assumes personal responsibility for it and all items in it. The mechanic must take proper care of the kit and secure it in the assigned storage area when it is not being used. If the mechanic forgets to secure the kit and it is lost, he is responsible for the loss.

from FM 10-27-4, page 6-2

4.1.5 Hand Receipts

A signed document acknowledging acceptance of and responsibility for items of property listed thereon that are issued for use and are to be returned.

Primary Hand Receipt: Commander's hand receipt . A hand receipt between an accountable officer and the person receiving the property and assuming direct responsibility for it. (DPAS or SPBS-R Automated)

Hand Receipt/Sub Hand Receipt: A receipt for property from a primary hand receipt holder or a sub-hand receipt holder to a person subsequently given the property for care, use, safekeeping or further issue. It does not transfer direct responsibility for the property to the sub-hand receipt holder but does transfer personal responsibility. (DA Form 2062 or ULLS-S4 Automated)
- Required for issued of non-expendable or durable items
- Signature establishes responsibility.

Component Hand Receipt: A hand receipt for a major end item with components of sets, kits and outfits (SKO), less expendable consumables. The component hand receipt is the record of responsibility for items listed on it. (DA Form 2062 or pre-printed HR on SC or TM)
- The user accepts responsibility for the end item and its components by signing the component hand receipt.
- Prepared by individual issuing property.

Temporary Hand Receipt: Used when property is issued or loaned for a period of up to 30 calendar days. (DA Form 3161)
- Inform commander of loan
- Include on temporary HR (Phone number of person receiving equipment and Date of return)

Hand Receipt Annex (Shortage Annex): It is a record validating shortages not issued to the user on a component hand receipt. Hand Receipt Annexes are prepared at the level where the Document Register is kept. (DA Form 2062)

Equipment Receipt: A DA form 3749 used to assign responsibility for property for brief recurring periods. Examples: masks, weapons
- Use to issue weapons for 24 hours or less. For over 24 hours, log issue on control sheet.
- Do not update with change of commander.

1. Keep hand receipts current.
2. Conduct inventories when required.
3. Use DA Form 3161 for issue and turn-in (Transactions between the PBO and the Hand receipt holder)
4. Post change documents :
   a. At least every six months
   b. Before change of hand receipt holder
   c. Before change of responsible officer - Inventory

4.1.5.1 DA Form 2062

References:
DA 2062 Hand Receipt/Annex Number (Jan 82)

Uses of the DA Form 2062:
- Temporary Hand Receipt (fig 5-2, PAM 710-2-1)
- Component Hand Receipt (fig 6-1, PAM 710-2-1)
- Shortage Annex
- Furniture Hand Receipt

HAND RECEIPT/ANNEX NUMBER *For use of this form, see DA PAM 710-2-1. The proponent agency is ODCSLOG.*	FROM:	TO:	HAND RECEIPT NUMBER

FOR ANNEX/CR ONLY	END ITEM STOCK NUMBER	END ITEM DESCRIPTION	PUBLICATION NUMBER	PUBLICATION DATE	QUANTITY

STOCK NUMBER *a.*	ITEM DESCRIPTION *b.*	* *c*	SEC *d.*	UI *e.*	QTY AUTH *f.*	g. QUANTITY A	B	C	D	E	F

* WHEN USED AS A:

HAND RECEIPT, enter Hand Receipt Annex Number
HAND RECEIPT FOR QUARTERS FURNITURE, enter Condition Codes
HAND RECEIPT ANNEX/COMPONENTS RECEIPT, enter Accounting Requirements Code (ARC).

PAGE ______ OF ______ PAGES

DA FORM 2062, JAN 82 EDITION OF JAN 58 IS OBSOLETE USAPPC V2.10

DA Form 2062

4.1.5.2 DA Form 3161

References:
DA 3161 Request For Issue or Turn-in (Dec 00)

Uses of the DA Form 3161:
- Issue (fig 2-2, PAM 710-2-1)
- Receipt (fig 2-17,PAM 710-2-1)

REQUEST FOR ISSUE OR TURN-IN
(DA PAM 710-2-1)

ISSUE | TURN-IN | SHEET NO. 1 | NO. SHEETS | 3. REQUEST NO. | 4. VOUCHER NO.

1. SEND TO: | 5. DATE MATERIAL REQUIRED | 6. DODAAC | 7. PRIORITY | 8. ACCOUNTING/FUNDING DATA

2. REQUEST FROM: | 9. END ITEM IDENT | 9a. NAME/MANUFACTURER | 9b. MODEL | 9c. SERIAL NO.

* CODE — ISSUE: I-Initial, R-Replacement; TURN-IN: FWT-Fair Wear And Tear, RS-Report of Survey, EX-Excess, SC-Statement of Charges | 10. PUBLICATION | 11. JOB ORDER NO.

12. ITEM NO. a	STOCK NO. b	ITEM DESCRIPTION c	UNIT OF ISSUE d	QUANTITY e	CODE* f	SUPPLY ACTION g	UNIT PRICE h	TOTAL COST i	POSTED j DATE	BY
							SHEET TOTAL		GRAND TOTAL	

13. ISSUE/TURN-IN "QUANTITY" COLM IS REQUESTED	DATE	BY	14. ISSUE QTY IN "SUPPLY ACTION" COLUMN	DATE	BY	15. REC QTY IN "SUPPLY ACTION" COLUMN	DATE	BY

DA FORM 3161, MAY 83 REPLACES EDITION OF JUN 73 WHICH WILL BE USED UNTIL EXHAUSTED. USAPPC V1.10

DA Form 3161

4.1.6 Inventories

Annual/Cyclic: Inventory 100% of property annually or on a cyclic basis, ie. (off-site units are exempted form cyclic; their method is 50% semi-annually) 10% monthly, 25% quarterly, or 50% semi-annually. Inventory Major End Items with its components. Annotate discrepancies on a memorandum to the PBO. Follow guidance from PBO's monthly memorandum.10% cyclic inventory printed 1st day of each month. Inventory is due by suspense date indicated on memorandum. Cyclic inventory can be delegated, however, indicate who conducted the inventory on the memorandum of endorsement to the PBO. Commander/PHRH is responsible for signing the original copy kept at PBO level. Attach memorandum with results.

Change of primary hand receipt holder/Change of command: Joint physical inventory between outgoing and incoming persons. 30 days allowed to complete the inventory. Use most recent Hand Receipt. Use current SC or TM for Major End Items with components. Supply personnel update sub-hand receipts as inventories are completed. Ensure quantity on hand agrees with quantity on hand receipt. Annotate shortages or overages. Offer Statement of Charges to responsible HRH for missing or damaged items. Prepare AAR's (Administrative Adjustment Reports)-DA Form 4949 for minor property book adjustments (i.e.adjust sizes, makes/models/nomenclature, NSN and obvious discrepancies of serial numbers). Prepare Financial Liability Investigation to annotate shortages when individuals refuse Statement of Charges or when accountability cannot be established. Upon completion on inventory and preparation of all adjustment documents do the following: review a new print out master hand receipt against all sub-hand receipts. Ensure all Sub-Hand Receipt Holders sign. Ensure all adjustment documents have been properly posted. Prepare signature cards (DA Form 1687) for each Supply Support Activity(SSA) along with Assumption of Command Orders. Submit DA Form 1687's (Signature Card) and copy's of Assumption of Command Orders to the PBO. Sign PBO master hand receipt immediately after the Bde Cdr's briefing. Incoming/outgoing hand receipt holder will conduct joint inventory of all property on HR.

Change of hand receipt holder: Incoming/outgoing hand receipt holder will conduct joint inventory of all property on HR. Complete within 30 days.

Sensitive items: Sensitive items are designated by the controlled inventory item code (CIIC) by Codes of 1-6, 8-9, P $, Q, R, or Y(night vision devices and navigation systems) on the Federal Logistics Catalog (FEDLOG). Responsible officer ensures weapons are inventoried by serial number monthly. NCO, WO, or Officer can conduct inventory. Unit armor's will not perform inventory. Same individual can not conduct inventory in two consecutive months. No deviations. It must be conducted monthly, without delay. Loss of sensitive item requires AR 15-6 investigation. Use DA Form 4697 (Report of Survey) only as an adjustment document/voucher to the property book. Attach 15-6 investigation results as an Exhibit to the DA Form 4697. Maintain Sensitive Item Inventory memorandum for two years in active files.

Change of property book officer: Incoming/outgoing PBO will conduct joint inventory of all property on HR. Complete within 30 days.

Weapons and ammunition: Responsible officer ensures weapons are inventoried by serial number monthly. NCO, WO, or officer can conduct inventory. Unit armorer's will not perform inventory. Same individual can not conduct inventory two months in a row. Inventory ammunition and explosives by listing it by purpose (basic load, operational load, or training) DODIC, lot number, quantity OH, and qty signed out on the inventory form. List qty shown on banded or sealed and banded containers. Inventory when custody of arms room is transferred.

Command Directed: Commanders will direct inventories be taken when there is Evidence of forced or unlawful entry, Discovery of open or unattended storage areas, Alleged misappropriation of Government property. Commanders ensure inventories are conducted after a FTX. To verify OCIE is on hand and serviceable. This is done within 15 calendar days after the exercise (30 days for USAR ad ARNG).

Tool room inventory: The tool room will be inventoried semi-annually. Inventory all tools, sets, kits, and outfits in the tool room. Record the results of the inventory, including discrepancies on a memorandum. Account for all discrepancies in accordance with AR 735-5. Inventory listings produced in automated systems will satisfy the requirement for the memorandum.

Receipt/Issue of an item (Lateral Transfer): When receiving property from an SSA. Inventory the items as follows: Make sure that the item is for your unit. Check the item to make sure it matches the description on the receipt document. Count all items. Make sure that the qty's received agrees with quantity recorded on the receipt document. Check item for completeness...use TM or SC. Verify serial numbers. Check condition of the item. If satisfied with the above procedures...sign the receipt document.

Absentee Baggage/OCIE: Handling Absentee Baggage/OCIE is critical and is the most common deficiency in supply rooms. Many Reports of Survey are initiated over Absentee Baggage (OCIE) due to improper inventories, handling, storage, and accountability. The abandoned property of a soldier absent from the unit without leave/authority (AWOL) or PCSs while on emergency leave must be inventoried without delay.

- When dropped from rolls (DFR) and PCSs while on emergency leave OCIE must be turned in to the issue point.
- If soldier resides in the unit billets, Commander must assign an Officer or WO as the witness and an NCO/E-5 or above as the designated representative to conduct the physical inventory.
- Use DA Form 3078 to annotate military clothing. Use DA Form 3645 to annotate CIF/TA-50 items.
- Items found in excess of initial issue must be annotated in the inventory against personal effects.
- Place original forms inside each container with items.
- If soldier does not return in 30 days and is DFR (dropped from rolls) all OCIE must be turned-in.
- Turn-in TA-50 items to CIF (Central Issue Facility). Initiate a Financial Liability Investigation if any items are missing. Turn-in military clothing to DOL.
- Ship personal effects to soldier's next of kin at their expense.
- If soldier is to be hospitalized for 120 hours (5 days) or more, the OCIE and personal effects must be inventoried without delay in the same manner as previously stated for AWOL personnel.
- If hospitalized over 60 days soldier OCIE will be turned in to the issue point.

Inventory	Description
Receipt and Issue of Property	When property is received from a hand receipt holder or PBO, from an SSA, from the next higher source of supply, or a lateral transfer.
Change of Primary Hand Receipt Holder	When there is a change in the officer responsible for property issued to the unit
Annual Primary Hand Receipt Holder	Within one year since the last annual inventory or within one year since the change of responsible officer, whichever is later.
Cyclic	Monthly, quarterly, or semiannually
Change of PBO	Within 30 days prior to replacement of the PBO.
Change of Custody of Arms Storage Facility	When responsibility for the custody of the keys to the arms storage facility is transferred
Command Directed	When directed by the installation commander
Sensitive Items- Other than Weapons or Ammunition	Quarterly Controlled crytographic items semiannually
Weapons and Ammunition	Monthly- weapons by serial number
Basic Loads	Monthly for Class III bulk and Class V. Semiannually for Class I, II, III Packaged and IV.
OCIE	Within 5 days of arrival or departure

Table 6-2. Types of Inventories
FM 10-27-4. Organization Supply and Services for Unit Leaders

4.1.6.1 Procedure

- Check with higher HQ for instructions and review SOP's
- Ensure change documents are posted prior to start
- Obtain publications: MTOE, property book, copies of hand receipts, etc
- DA PAM 25-30 lists current publications
- Review sub-hand receipts & reconcile against primary hand receipt
- Notify sub-hand receipt holders of inventory dates & other details
- Check item against hand receipts
- Physically count all items
- Record or verify serial numbers
- Identify & record overages and shortages
- Check property for serviceability

- Check items for completeness using TM's and SC's
- Report all differences regarding property discrepancies to the accountable officer/PBO
- Process adjustment documents:
    - Administrative adjustment report (AAR)
    - Relief from property loss: cash collection vouchers, statement of charges, and financial liability investigations
    - Update supply records
- Sign for property

4.1.7 Relief from Responsibility

References:

PAM 710-2-1 Using Unit Supply System (Manual Procedures) (Dec 97)

Forms:

DA 1659 Financial Liability Investigation of Property Loss Register (Oct 04)
DA 4949 Administrative Adjustment Report (AAR) (Jan 82)
DD 200 Financial Liability Investigation of Property Loss (Oct 99)
DD 362 Statement of Charges for Government Property Lost, Damaged, or Destroyed (Mar 74)
DD 1131 Cash Collection Voucher (Apr 57)

Liability: Financial liability is defined as "a personal, joint, or corporate statutory (monetary) obligation to reimburse the US Government for any lost, damaged, or destroyed Government property due through negligence or misconduct."

Limits of Liability: the amount equal to one month's basic pay at the time of the loss, or the actual amount of the loss to the Government, whichever is less, will be assessed. For ARNG and USAR personnel, 1 month's basic pay refers to the amount that would be received by the soldier if on active duty. For Civilian employees, financial liability for losses of Government property (including personal arms and equipment) is limited to 1/12 of their annual pay. (equal to one month's pay)

	Fault Admitted	**Fault NOT Admitted**
Fault or Neglect Present	Statement of Charges/ CCV (DD Form 362)	Financial Liability Investigation (DA Form 1659)
Fault or Neglect NOT Present	**Damaged Equipment:** Damage Statement prepared as a memorandum for record **OCIE:** Damage statement in MFR through CO within 30 days.	

Making Minor Administrative Adjustments. Property records may be adjusted when there are administrative changes or minor errors. Although they are called minor, they correct inaccuracies in the records. However, minor adjustments do not affect or correct the on hand balance on property books. These adjustments are made under the manual system by using DA Form 4949. The procedures for preparing this form are in DA Pam 710-2-1. AARs can be used on NSN changes (similar makes and models), Size corrections, Unit of issue changes, Items changing from accountable to non-accountable, and Items changing from non-accountable to accountable. (FM 10-27-4, page 6-16)

Statement of Charges/Cash Collection Voucher: When a person admits liability, they may be offered the option of reimbursing the government by using DD Form 362 or DD Form 1131. These forms may not be used for reimbursement to the government if the costs exceed one month's basic pay for that individual.

Financial liability Investigation: A means of reestablishing accountability for lost, damaged, or destroyed supplies and equipment. When there is no admission of liability for a loss or when a person admits liability for the loss but the loss is greater than one month's basic pay for that person, then a report of survey should be initiated. The Financial liability investigation is not intended as a means of punishment. The commander still retains the option of administering non-judicial punishment under Article 15 of the UCMJ or convening a court marshal. The commander will appoint a survey officer or NCO, normally of equal or higher rank than the individual who signed for the item on the hand receipt. This appointing authority commander is at or above battalion level. The investigating officer or NCO uses DA Form 4697 for recording report of survey information. DA Form 4697 along with specific guidelines and timelines are shown in AR 735-5. The timelines shown in AR 735-5 are important in seeing the matter resolved in a timely manner. (FM 10-27-4, page 6-16)

4.1.8 LOGSA

Websites:
LOGSA https://www.logsa.army.mil/
PS Magazine https://www.logsa.army.mil/psmag/psonline.cfm

Website Functions:
- AOAP
- Electronic Technical Manuals (TMs)
- FEDlog
- Parts Tracker
- PS Magazine
- Sets, Kits, Outfits, and Tools (SKOTs)
- WEBLIDB

Logon Credentials:
- Go to LOGSA webpage
- Click on System Access Request (SAR)
- Fill in the information and your supervisor's name/email
- When your supervisor approves the request, you will receive your logon.

4.1.9 Supply Book

Supply Accountability is one of the biggest pitfalls for a platoon leader. It is important to account for all of your equipment and have all necessary paperwork handy. This best way is to have a supply book for all your platoon's equipment. Encourage your squad/section leaders to have an equivalent book for their equipment. Hang on to all documents for your duration as platoon leader, plus one year.

Your hand receipts:
This includes your automated hand receipt from ULLS-S4 and any other equipment hand receipts

Sub hand receipts:
Reconcile with your master hand receipt to ensure that ALL equipment is subhand-receipted down. The only exception is property you have physical control of (ex.your computer, compass, etc.)

Adjustment Documents:
This includes all turn-in documents, AARs, statement of charges, etc. Many times you will have an adjustment done which your supply sergeant updates in the company system. However, if it is not properly reconciled with battalion, the item may reappear on your hand receipt.

Equipment Listings:
Download the technical manual for each piece of equipment you are accountable for. Print out the component listing, basic issue items, and additional authorized list for each item.

Shortage Annexes:
During inventories, create a shortage annex for each piece of equipment that is missing components or basic issue items. Ensure your commander initials and dates form. Without a shortage annex, you are accountable for every component and basic issue item that is missing from that end item.

4.2 Maintenance Process

References:

AR 385-55 Prevention of Motor Vehicle Accidents (Mar 87)
AR 750-1 Army Material Maintenance Policy (Jan 06)
FM 4-30.3 Maintenance Operations and Procedures (Jul 04)
TC 43-4 Maintenance Management (May 96)
GTA 09-10-045 Small Unit Leader's Card (Maintenance) (Oct 88)

Definitions:

Full mission-capable (FMC): Material condition of any piece of military equipment, aircraft, or training device indicating that it can perform all missions.

Not mission capable (NMC): Material condition indicating that systems and equipment are not capable of performing any of their assigned missions because of maintenance requirements.

MAINTENANCE	
PL	**PSG/NCO'S**
Knows status of all equipment in platoon and briefs CO	Knows the status of all equipment and keeps PL informed
Tracks maintenance deadlines and ensures Platoon meets them	Supervises Soldiers conducting services and installing parts
Properly hand receipts out all equipment going to direct support and depot level maintenance	Secures BII of all equipment turned in
Ensures personal equipment is properly maintained	Ensures all equipment is properly cleaned, lubricated, and calibrated
Ensures all DA 2406 and 5988-E are turned into the ULLS-G clerk and updated weekly	Supervises PMCS of all equipment, ensuring DA 2406 and 5988-Es are filled out properly using the appropriate TM

4.2.1 Command Maintenance

Areas of Emphasis:

- Vehicles
- Weapons and other sensitive items
- Radios/Communication equipment
- NBC equipment

Tasks for Command Maintenance:
- PMCS
- Dispatching
- Parts Installation
- Services (based upon service schedule)

Tips/Tricks:
- Your unit should have a schedule for the priority of work during command maintenance. Many units perform maintenance on vehicles every week, but alternate maintenance on communications, weapons, NBC, and other platoon equipment once a month.
- Command maintenance is definitely driven by your NCOs. Make sure that squad leaders and team leaders are physically present for motor stables.

COMMAND MAINTENANCE	
PL	PSG
Spot checks Command Maintenance Activities	Teach and supervise proper PMCS of all equipment
Ensures personal equipment is maintained	Knows the status of all equipment and keeps PL informed
Knows status of all equipment in platoon and briefs CO	Ensures drivers are licensed and vehicles are properly dispatched

4.2.2 5988-E

Operator:
- PMCS vehicle with TM
- Review the uncorrected faults portion of the automated Equipment Inspection / Maintenance Worksheet and ensure the faults listed reflect the current condition of the equipment.
- All operator correctable faults found will be corrected by the operator. Other faults not already on the uncorrected faults portion of the Equipment Inspection / Maintenance Worksheet, will be properly annotated on the Equipment Inspection / Maintenance worksheet. The operator and supervisor will sign the form.
- If no new faults are found the operator dates the Equipment Inspection / Maintenance Worksheet.
- After corrective action is taken on all operator level deficiencies, the operator/supervisor submits the Equipment Inspection/Maintenance worksheet to the motor office for organizational repairs, if required, or

to the dispatcher for dispatch.

NO FAULTS FOUND

Motor Pool NCO Signature

:E: 20031102 EQUIPMENT MAINTENANCE AND INSPECTION WORKSHEET DA FORM 5988-I

W91VCE 401ST MP CO.

------------------------- EQUIPMENT DATA -------------------------

ADMIN NUM: 401-6	EQUIPMENT SERIAL NUM:
JIP MODEL:	REGISTRATION NUM:
QUIP NOUN:	TYPE INSPECTION:
EQUIP NSN:	

	NUMBER	DATE	CHANGE NUMBER
BLICATION:	TM 9-2320-280-10	01/96	01
BLICATION:	TM 9-2320-280-10-1	01/96	02

SPECTORS LIC #:________ TIME: ____ SIGNATURE: ___________ TIME:____

PSG Signature

----- PARTS REQUESTED -------------------------

ULT	DOC	NUM	NIIN	NOUN	QTY DUE / REC	STATUS DATE	DATE COMP	P D R L I C
'1	3254	3117	014108794	MIRROR, H	00000 00001	BB20031017	20031101	02N
'2	3254	3117	014108794	CONTROL, D	00000 00001	BB20031017	20031101	02N
'3	3254	3117	014108794	CLAMP, LOO	00000 00001	BB20031017	20031101	02N
'4	3254	3117	014108794	SEAL, NONME	00000 00001	BB20031017	20031101	02N

------------------------- MAINTENACE FAULTS -------------------------

:M !	FAULT DATE	FAULT STATUS	FAULT DESCRIPTION	CORRECTIVE ACTION	OPER HRS	LIC#
51	20030816	-	B SERVICE COMPLETE		___	___
57	20030316	/	F/WENCH BAR BENT		___	___
'0	20030316	/	HATCH SEAL UNSERV		___	___
'1	20030816	/	L/R QUARTER PANEL		___	___
___	___	___	20031130	W	___	M1234
___	___	___	___	___	___	___
___	___	___	___	___	___	___

FAULTS FOUND

Motor Pool NCO Signature

TE: 20031102 EQUIPMENT MAINTENANCE AND INSPECTION WORKSHEET DA FORM 5988-

W91VCE 401ST MP CO.

------------------------------ EQUIPMENT DATA ------------------------------

ADMIN NUM: 401-6 EQUIPMENT SERIAL NUM:
UIP MODEL: REGISTRATION NUM:
QUIP NOUN: TYPE INSPECTION:
EQUIP NSN:

	NUMBER	DATE	CHANGE NUMBER
BLICATION:	TM 9-2320-280-10	01/96	01
BLICATION:	TM 9-2320-280-10-1	01/96	02

SPECTORS LIC # M1234 TIME: ____ SIGNATURE: __________ TIME: ____

PSG Signature

---- PARTS REQUESTED ----------------------------------

ULT	DOC	NUM	NIIN	NOUN	QTY DUE / REC	STATUS DATE	DATE COMP	PRI DLC
71	3254	3117	014108794	MIRROR, H	00000 00001	BB20031017	20031101	02N
72	3254	3117	014108794	CONTROL, D	00000 00001	BB20031017	20031101	02N
73	3254	3117	014108794	CLAMP, LOO	00000 00001	BB20031017	20031101	02N
74	3254	3117	014108794	SEAL, NONME	00000 00001	BB20031017	20031101	02N

----------------------- MAINTENACE FAULTS -----------------------

EM M	FAULT DATE	FAULT STATUS	FAULT DESCRIPTION	CORRECTIVE ACTION	OPER HRS	LIC#
61	20030816	-	B SERVICE COMPLETE			
67	20030816	/	F/WENCH BAR BENT			
70	20030816	/	HATCH SEAL UNSERV			
71	20030816	/	L/R QUARTER PANEL			
	Date	/	Problem			

4.2.3 Dispatching

Dispatch Clerk:

- Check for all required forms and manuals are present and up to date.
- Check automated Operators ID Card to verify that the operator is licensed on the requested equipment
- Check Dispatch Request for operator and supervisor signature
- Ensure a mechanic performed a proper QAQC and signed the

5988-E.
- Check 5988-E to ensure it is signed by licensed driver and supervisor, dated, all faults are notated, and the current mileage is annotated.

4.2.4 Licensing

References:

FM 21-305	Manual for the Wheeled Vehicle Driver (Aug 93)
AR 58-1	Management, Acquisition, and Use of Motor Vehicles (Aug 04)
AR 385-55	Prevention of Motor Vehicle Accidents (Aug 87)
AR 600-55	The Army Driver and Operator Standardization Program (Dec 93)
TC 21-305-100	The Military Commercial Driver's License Driver's Manual (Aug 96)
TC 21-305	Wheeled Vehicle Accident Avoidance (Apr 03)
TC 21-305-1	Heavy Expanded Mobility Tactical Truck (HEMTT) (Oct 95)
TC 21-305-2	Night Vision Goggle Driving Operations (Sep 98)
TC 21-305-3	M939 Series 5-ton Tactical Cargo Truck (Aug 97)
TC 21-305-4	High Mobility Multi-purpose Wheeled Vehicle (May 91)
TC 21-305-5	Equipment Transporters (C-HET, MET, and LET) (Dec 91)
TC 21-305-6	Tractor and Semi-trailer (M915, M931, AND M932) (Dec 91)
TC 21-305-7	Light Vehicles (Sep 92)
TC 21-305-8	Medium Vehicles (Sep 92)
TC 21-305-9	Heavy Equipment Transporter System (Jun 97)
TC 21-305-10	Palletized Load System (Sep 94)
TC 21-305-11	Family of Medium Tactical Vehicles Operator (May 99)
TC 21-306	Tracked Combat Vehicle Driver Training (Feb 02)

Forms:

DA 348-1R	Equipment Operator's Qualification Record (Feb 86)
DA 5984-E	Equipment Operator License (Electronic)

Requirements for Military Driver's License:
- Commander's Interview
- Driver's Training (conducted by a Master Driver)
- Road Test
- Civilian Driver's License

Operators Must Be Competent At:
- PMCS all vehicles licensed on
- Correctly fill out DA Form 5988-E
- Operate vehicle on and off-road
- Operate vehicle at night
- Operate vehicle in black-out drive
- Perform recovery of vehicle

Physical Fitness

Part

5 Physical Fitness

References:

FM 21-20 Physical Fitness Training (Sep 92)
AR 600-9 Army Weight Control Program (Jun 87)

Websites:

Army Physical Fitness School https://www.infantry.army.mil/usapfs/

Definition (from FM 21-20):

Physical fitness is the ability to function effectively in physical work, training, and other activities and still have enough energy left over to handle any emergencies which may arise.

PHYSICAL FITNESS	
PL	**PSG/NCO'S**
Supervise platoon PT	Run PT sessions
Recommend areas of emphasis for PT schedule	Create platoon PT schedule and risk assessments

5.1 Fitness Information

Components of Fitness:

- **Cardio-respiratory (CR) endurance:** the efficiency with which the body delivers oxygen and nutrients needed for muscular activity and transports waste products from the cells.
- **Muscular strength:** the greatest amount of force a muscle or muscle group can exert in a single effort.
- **Muscular endurance:** the ability of a muscle or muscle group to perform repeated movements with a sub-maximal force for extended periods of times.
- **Flexibility:** the ability to move the joints (for example, elbow, knee) or any group of joints through an entire, normal range of motion.
- **Body composition:** the amount of body fat a soldier has in comparison

from FM 21-20, pg 1-3

Principles of Fitness (PROVRBS):

- **Progression:** The intensity (how hard) and/or duration (how long) of exercise must gradually increase to improve the level of fitness.
- **Regularity:** To achieve a training effect, a person must exercise often. One should strive to exercise each of the first four fitness components at least three times a week. Infrequent exercise can do more harm than good. Regularity is also important in resting, sleeping, and following a good diet.
- **Overload:** The work load of each exercise session must exceed the normal demands placed on the body in order to bring about a training effect.
- **Variety:** Providing a variety of activities reduces boredom and increases motivation and progress.
- **Recovery:** A hard day of training for a given component of fitness should be followed by an easier training day or rest day for that component and/or muscle group(s) to help permit recovery. Another way to allow recovery is to alternate the muscle groups exercised every other day, especially when training for strength and/or muscle endurance.
- **Balance:** To be effective, a program should include activities that address all the fitness components, since overemphasizing any one of them may hurt the others.
- **Specificity:** Training must be geared toward specific goals. For example, soldiers become better runners if their training emphasizes running. Although swimming is great exercise, it does not improve a 2-mile-run time as much as a running program does.

from FM 21-20, pg 1-4

Factors of Fitness:

- **Frequency**: Army Regulation 350-15 specifies that vigorous physical fitness training will be conducted 3 to 5 times per week. For optimal results, commanders must strive to conduct 5 days of physical training per week. Ideally, at least three exercise sessions for CR fitness, muscle endurance, muscle strength, and flexibility should be performed each week to improve fitness levels. Thus, for example, to obtain maximum gains in muscular strength, soldiers should have at least three strength-training sessions per week. Three physical activity periods a week, however, with only one session each of cardio-respiratory, strength, and flexibility training will not improve any of these three components.
- **Intensity**: Exercise for CR development must be strenuous enough to elevate the heart rate to between 60 and 90 percent of the heart rate reserve (HRR). Those with low fitness levels should start exercising at a lower training heart rate (THR) of about 60 percent of HRR. For muscular strength and endurance, intensity refers to the

percentage of the maximum resistance that is used for a given exercise. When determining intensity in a strength-training program. For strength development, the weight used should be a 3-7 correctly performed repetitions. On the other hand, the person who wants to concentrate on muscular endurance should use a 12 or more correctly performed reps.

- **Time**: At least 20 to 30 continuous minutes of intense exercise must be used in order to improve cardio-respiratory endurance. For muscular endurance and strength, exercise time equates to the number of repetitions done.
- **Type**: The basic rule is that to improve performance, one must practice the particular exercise, activity, or skill he wants to improve.

from FM 21-20, pg 1-5 thru 1-7

FITT FACTORS				
Cardio-respiratory Endurance	**Muscular Strength**	**Muscular Endurance**	**Muscular Strength and Muscular Endurance**	**Flexibility**
F requency 3-5 times/ wk	3 times/wk	3-5 times/wk	3 times/wk	Stretch before and after each exercise session
Intensity 60-90% HRR	3-7 RM	12+ RM	8-12 RM	Tension and slight discomfort, NOT PAIN
Time 20 min or more	Time req to do 3-7 repetitions	Time req to do 12 repetitions	Time required to do 8-12 repetitions	Warmup: 10-15 sec Dev: 30-60 sec
Type Running Swimming CC Skiing Rowing Cycling Jump Rope Walking Hiking Stairs	Free Weights Resistance Machines Partner-resisted Exercises Body-Weight Exercises (Pushups, situps, Pullups, Dips)			Stretching: Static Passive P.N.F.

* HRR: Heart Rate Reserve
* RM: Repetition Maximum

Figure . FITT Factors
FM 21-20. Physical Fitness

5.2 Types of Exercise

5.2.1 Cardiovascular

Conditioning Drill 1

1. The Bend and Reach
2. The Rear Lunge
3. The High Jumper
4. The Rower
5. The Squat Bender
6. The Windmill
7. The Forward Lunge
8. The Prone Row
9. The Bent-leg Body Twist
10. The Push-up

Conditioning Drill 2

1. The Push-up
2. The Sit-up
3. The Pull-up

Pocket Physical Fitness Guide, US Infantry School.

Activity Selection Guide									
Activity	**MS**	**ME**	**CR**	**Flex**	**Body Comp**	**Speed/ Agility**	**Coord**	**Team work**	**Soldier Skills**
Aerobics		X	X	X	X		X		
Bicycling		X	X		X				
Circuits		X	X	X	X	X	X	X	X
Competitive Sports						X	X	X	X
Calisthenics		X		X		X	X		
Cross Country Ski	X	X	X	X	X		X		
Grass/Guerilla Drills	X	X	X		X		X		
Obstacle Courses	X	X	X		X	X	X	X	X
Partner Resisted Exercise	X	X					X	X	
Relays		X	X		X	X	X	X	
Rifle Drills	X	X					X		X
Road Marching	X	X	X		X				X
Running		X	X		X				
Stretching				X					
Weight Training	X	X				X	X		

* Muscular Strength (MS), Muscular Endurance (ME), Cardio-Respiratory (CR)

Page 2-11. Activity Selection Guide.
FM 21-20. Physical Fitness Training

5.2.2 Muscular Strength/Endurance

Exercise Chart for Muscular Strength and Endurance:

Partner-Resisted Exercises								
Exercises	**Lower Legs**	**Upper Legs**	**Waist**	**Chest**	**Upper Arms**	**Lower Arms**	**Shoulder**	**Back**
Split Squat		X						
Single Leg Squat		X						
Leg Extension		X						
Leg Curl		X						
Heel Raise	X							
Toe Raise	X							
Push-Up				X	X			
Seated Row					X			X
Overhead Press					X		X	
Pull-Down					X			X
Shrug							X	
Triceps Extension							X	
Biceps Curl					X			
Abdominal Twist			X					
Abdominal Curl			X					
Abdominal Crunch								

Exercise with Equipment (Barbell/Dumbbell)								
Exercises	**Lower Legs**	**Upper Legs**	**Waist**	**Chest**	**Upper Arms**	**Lower Arms**	**Shoulder**	**Back**
Squat		X						
Heel Raise	X							
Bench Press				X	X			
Bent-over Row					X			
Overhead Press					X		X	
Shrug							X	
Triceps Extension					X			
Biceps Curl					X			
Wrist Curl						X		
Bent-leg Dead Lift		X					X	X

Exercise with an Exercise Machine								
Exercises	Lower Legs	Upper Legs	Waist	Chest	Upper Arms	Lower Arms	Shoulder	Back
Leg Press		X						
Leg Extension		X						
Leg Curl		X						
Toe Raise	X							
Bench Press	X			X	X			
Seated Row					X			X
Lat Pull-Down					X			X
Shrug							X	
Parallel Bar Dip				X	X			
Chin-Up					X			X
Triceps Extension					X			
Biceps Curl					X			
Back Extension								X
Sit-Up			X					
Incline Sit-Up			X					
Abdominal Twist			X					
Abdominal Crunch			X					

Page 3-5. Exercise Chart for Muscular Strength and Endurance. FM 21-20. Physical Fitness Training.

5.2.3 Flexibility

Rotations: Neck, Arms/Shoulders, Hips, Knee Ankle

Stretches: Neck/Shoulder, Abdominal, Chest, Upper-back, Overhead Arm Pull, Thigh, Hamstring (Standing/Seated), Groin (Standing/ Seated/Seated Straddle), Calf (Normal/Toe Pull), Hip/Back

Calisthenics: Side Straddle Hop, Mule Kick, Ski Jump, Flutter Kick, Bend and Reach, High Jumper, Squat Bender, Lunger, Knee Bender, Swimmer, Supine Bicycle, Engine, Cross-country skier, Push-up, Sit-up, Chin-up, and Dips.

5.3 Unit Fitness Plan

Usually the Master Fitness Trainer or First Sergeant completes the Unit Fitness Plan. If your unit does not have one, or you want to create a platoon fitness plan, here is the format below. Make sure that you rely on your Noncommissioned Officers for their assessment of the unit's fitness and their suggestions for the plan.

Physical Fitness Evaluation: Usually consists of APFT scores and other evaluations

Mission: A physical fitness mission for your specific unit

Fitness Objectives: Specific objectives for your unit. This should not only reflect APFT goals, but goals for your Soldiers performance in any strenuous tasks.

Unit Assessment: Current assessment of your Soldiers identifying strengths and weaknesses.

Training Requirements: Schedule of unit training requirements (future EXEVALs, NTC rotations)

Fitness Tasks: Physically strenuous tasks your Soldiers need to perform (such as litter carry, MK-19 carry)

Schedules: Past and future PT schedules

Special Population PT: APFT Failures, Overweight Soldiers, Pregnant Soldiers, and Profiles

Battle Focused PT: Plan for conducting tactical based PT (tasks such as road march, water jug carry, HMMWV push)

5.4 PT Evaluation Sheet

Physical Fitness Training Session Performance Evaluation Checklist		
Risk Assessment	GO	NO GO
Conducted risk assessment		
Formation Commands	GO	NO GO
Brought group to attention and formed group into ranks		
Extend to the left, MARCH		
Arms downward, MOVE		
Left, FACE		
Extend to the left, MARCH		
Arms downward, MOVE		
Right, FACE		
From front to rear, COUNT OFF		
Even numbers to the left, UNCOVER		
Warm Up	GO	NO GO
Slow jog in place or walk for 1-3 minutes		
Slow joint rotation exercises		
Slow static stretching		
Calisthenics exercises		
Warm up for 5-7 minutes		
Conditioning	GO	NO GO
Brought group to attention before beginning each exercise		
Calisthenics exercises		
Provided sufficient training intensity		
Session included CR, muscular endurance, and/or strength training		
Cool Down	GO	NO GO
Conducted cool down		
Repeated the stretches done in the warm-up		
Held stretches 30 seconds or more		
Conducted cool down for 5-7 minutes		
Close Session	GO	NO GO
Brought group to attention		
Assemble to the Right, MARCH		
OVERALL EVALUATION:	GO	NO GO

5.5 APFT

References:

FM 21-20 Physical Fitness Training (Sep 92)

DA 705 Army Physical Fitness Test Scorecard (Jun 98)
DA 705c Situp Standards
DA 705d Pushup Standards
DA 705e Run Standards (1)
DA 705f Run Standards (2)

APFT Script:

A copy of FM 21-20 and TWO stop watches are required for the administration of an APFT. If they are not present, a Soldier can appeal a failure. The script for the APFT is found on pages 14-11 through 14-18 of FM 21-20.

Tips/Tricks:

- Do not forget your Soldiers that take the alternate events. Make your platoon do the 2.5 mile walk, bike test, or swim test one day for PT to appreciate the difficulties of those events.

APFT	
PL	**PSG/NCO'S**
As a leader, it is important to do well on your APFT. It is highly recommended to take your test at the same time as your Soldiers so they see you	Prepare risk assessment and setup APFT course
	Read APFT script
Let your NCOs run the PT test, but be visible. Cheer on your Soldiers, especially the ones that you know will struggle	Grade APFT events
	Pace Soldiers on run event
	Conduct weigh-in and tape
Supervise weigh-in and tape as necessary	Complete APFT cards and turn in to Operations

APFT Incentives:
Incentives are usually dictated by company policy. Check your company's policy letter for incentives. If you company does not have any, ask your commander if it is possible to establish some.

Possible Incentives:
- Passes
- Unit coin
- Certificate of Achievement (gives promotion points)
- Recognition (300-club plaque, APFB plaque)
- Army Physical Fitness Badge (APFB)
- PT less often (be careful of taking all of your studs away from PT and be wary of letting leaders miss PT unless their whole team/squad achieves that standard)

5.6 AWCP

References:

AR 40-25 Nutrition Standards and Education (Jun 01)
AR 600-9 The Army Weight Control Program (Jul 87)
AR 600-9-I1 Interim Change: The Army Weight Control Program (Mar 94)

DA 5500-R Body Fat Content Worksheet (Male) (Dec 85)
DA 5501-R Body Fat Content Worksheet (Female) (Dec 85)
DA 5511-R Personal Weight Loss Progress (Feb 86)

Overweight: A soldier is considered overweight when his or her percent body fat exceeds the standard specified in AR 600-9, paragraph 20*c* of this regulation.

Satisfactory progress: Progressing toward a point to meet the body fat standards described in AR 600-9, paragraph 19*c*. Weight loss of 3 –8 pounds per month is required for satisfactory progress.

Screening and Weight Control Actions: See Figure 2. Flow process guide for screening and weight control actions, AR 600-9. Army Weight Control Program.

Age Group: 17-20 **Male (% body fat):** 20% **Female (% body fat)**: 30%
Age Group: 21-27 **Male (% body fat):** 22% **Female (% body fat)**: 32%
Age Group: 28-39 **Male (% body fat):** 24% **Female (% body fat)**: 34%
Age Group: 40 & older **Male (% body fat):** 26% **Female (% body fat)**: 36%

Table 2. Maximum Allowable percent body fat standards. AR 600-9, Interim Change 1. Army Weight Control Program.

5.7 Injuries

Many common injuries are caused by overuse, that is, exercising too much and too often and with too rapid an increase in the workload. Most overuse injuries can be treated with rest, ice, compression and elevation (RICE).

Extrinsic Risk Factors for Injuries
- Training errors
- Type of training
- Environmental conditions
- Equipment
- Technique

Intrinsic Risk Factors for Injuries
- Flexibility
- Physical fitness
- Inadequate rehabilitation

Acute injuries. Acute traumatic injuries result when ligaments, bones or muscle-tendon units are subjected to an abrupt force, such as twisting an ankle on a trail or breaking a bone in contact with an obstacle, i.e., an opponent's jaw. The two most common traumatic injuries are sprains and strains.

- **Sprains:** Injuries to ligaments are termed sprains. Ligaments are connective tissues that connect bones or cartilage; they provide support and strength to joints. Sprains are classified into three categories: first, second, and third degree.
    - **First-degree sprains**. First-degree sprains occur when the fibers within the ligament are stretched. There is mild pain and swelling but no joint instability.
    - **Second-degree sprains**. Second-degree sprains are more severe, with partial tearing of the ligament and possibly the joint capsule. There is severe pain and swelling and considerable loss of strength. A second-degree sprain inadequately treated may result in further injury or complete tearing of the ligament.
    - **Third-degree sprains**. Third-degree sprains result from a complete tear of the ligament. There is severe pain at the time of injury and obvious joint instability. Third degree sprains usually require reconstructive surgery and should be promptly evaluated by an orthopedic surgeon (bone doctor).

- **Strains**. Strains are commonly referred to as “muscle pulls” and generally result from stretching or tearing muscle tissue. Strains are classified as first-, second- or third-degree strains by the severity of muscle damage and the resulting loss of function.

- **First-degree strains**. First-degree strains produce mild signs and symptoms with minimal local pain. There is often a sensation of muscle tightness with activity.
- **Second-degree strains**. Second-degree strains are more severe, with partial tearing of the injured muscle. There is substantial pain, considerable loss of function, and discoloration from bruising.
- **Third-degree strains**. Third-degree strains cause marked muscle disruption and possible avulsion of the muscle-tendon unit. These injuries usually require surgical intervention and should also be promptly evaluated by a bone doctor.
- **Muscle strain restoration**. Most strains of the lower extremity are mild to moderate in severity but may require up to three weeks for recovery. More severe muscle strains may require several months to heal. Muscle strains often recur, particularly if there has been inadequate rehabilitation. Both flexibility and strength of the injured part should be restored to near full capacity before returning to activity.

- **Fractures and dislocations**. Fractures (broken bones) and dislocations (separation of joints) are more serious but less frequent injuries. Individuals with these injuries should be immobilized and transported immediately to an appropriate medical facility for evaluation and treatment.

- **Blisters**. Blisters result from friction between the skin and equipment. The blister top should remain intact and be covered with sterile dressing to promote faster healing and reduce the risk of infection. If the blister is painful and must be punctured, this should be done in sterile conditions. The area should remain clean and covered.

Chronic injuries. Overuse injuries result from small, repetitive, overload forces on the musculoskeletal system. Although some degree of trauma is likely with any training program, these small repetitive forces may eventually result in a noticeable injury. Common overuse injuries include tendinitis, strains, sprains, and stress fractures.

- **Tendinitis**. Tendinitis, or painful inflammation of a tendon, results from the repetitive stress of forceful muscle contractions. Tendon overload occurs more frequently with eccentric (lengthening) muscle contractions, such as running downhill or lowering weight, than with concentric contractions (shortening).

- **Sprains and strains**. Many sprains and strains are acute injuries. When they result from or are aggravated by overuse, they are then classified as chronic injuries. Whatever the cause, the symptoms are the same as for acute injuries but are generally milder. Treatment is the same as for acute injuries.
- **Stress fractures**. Most stress fractures from overuse occur to the lower extremities, especially in the tibia of the leg and metatarsals of the feet. They occur in response to repetitive overloading forces to bones during activities such as running, walking or marching. Any individual with aching bone pain from exercise which does not abate in a few days or worsens should be evaluated by appropriate medical personnel.
- **Shin splints**. "Shin splints" (i.e., shin soreness) is a vague term for overuse injuries involving the lower leg. This injury may involve inflammation or stresses to the muscle-tendon units attached to the tibia or the bone itself. Rapid changes in intensity, frequency or duration of activities such as running, walking, marching, or biking can result in these conditions.
- **Lower back injuries**. Low back pain is a common symptom of injury either associated with or exacerbated by exercise. Low back pain resulting from a musculoskeletal injury may indicate damage to the vertebrae, discs, or the back and abdominal muscles. If neurologic symptoms develop, i.e., pain radiating into the buttocks or down one or both legs, numbness or tingling in the legs, or weakness, a physician should be consulted. Chronic back pain of unknown origin and severe pain are additional reasons to consult a physician.

Type	Location	Signs/Symptoms	Treatment
Bursitis	Bony prominence Bursae	Pain, swelling, warmth, limitation of motion.	RICE* Anti-inflammatory**
Tendinitis	Tendon	Pain, swelling, limitation of motion.	RICE* Anti-inflammatory**
Patellar-femoral syndrome	Knee cap, patellar tendon, cartilage, ligament	Pain, grating, instability.	RICE* Anti-inflammatory**
Sprain	Ligament	Same as acute but milder.	RICE* Anti-inflammatory**
Strain	Muscle, muscle-tendon unit	Same as acute but milder.	RICE* Anti-inflammatory**
Stress fracture	Bone	Persistent pain, X-ray/Bone scan.	RICE* Anti-inflammatory**
Low back injury	Vertebrae, disk, ligament, muscles of back	Pain, limitation of motion, neurological symptoms.	RICE* Anti-inflammatory**
Shin splints	Bone, tendon, fascia of lower leg	Pain, swelling.	RICE* Anti-inflammatory**
Metatarsalgia	Bone, joint, nerves of foot	Pain, swelling.	RICE* Anti-inflammatory**

* RICE = Active Rest, Ice, Compression, Elevation.
** Anti-inflammatory
*** Reconstructive surgery may be required.

Figure 1. Summary of Common Physical Training Induced Chronic (Overuse) Injuries

Jones BH, Reynolds KL, Rock PB, Moore MP, "Exercise-Related Musculoskeletal Injuries: Risks, Prevention, and Care", Resource Manual for Guidelines for Exercise Testing and Prescription, American College of Sports Medicine, 2nd ed., Lea & Febiger, Philadelphia, PA, 1993:378-393.

5.7.1 Heat/Cold Injuries

Signs and Symptoms of Heat Injuries

If you experience any of the below symptoms of heat cramps, heat exhaustion, or heatstroke, immediately stop your physical activity.

- **Heat Cramps:** Muscular Twitching, Cramping, Muscular Spasms in Arms, Legs or Abdomen
- **Heat Exhaustion (Requires Medical Attention):** Excessive Thirst, Fatigue, Lack of Coordination, Increased Sweating, Cool/Wet Skin, Dizziness and/or Confusion
- **Heatstroke (Dial 911):** No Sweating, Hot/Dry Skin, Rapid Pulse, Rapid Breathing, Coma, Seizure, Dizziness and/or Confusion, Loss of Consciousness

Signs and Symptoms of Cold Weather Injuries

During exercise in the cold, your body usually produces enough heat to maintain its normal temperature. As you get fatigued, however, you slow down and your body produces less heat. Hypothermia develops when the body cannot produce heat as fast as it is losing it.

- **Hypothermia:** Shivering, Loss of Judgment, Slurred Speech, Drowsiness, Muscle Weakness,
- **Frostbite:** A white or grayish-yellow skin area, Skin that feels unusually firm or waxy, Numbness in body parts exposed to the cold such as the nose, ears, feet, hands, and skin

Hydration

Water is the preferred hydration fluid before during and after physical training activities.

- Drink 13 to 20 ounces of cool water at least 30 minutes before beginning exercise (approximately 2 glasses of water).
- After the activity, drink to satisfy thirst, then drink a little more.
- After exercise, avoid alcoholic beverages and soft drinks because they are not suitable for proper hydration and recovery. Sports drinks may be consumed, but are not required and contain a considerable number of additional calories.

from Pocket Physical Fitness Guide, US Infantry School

5.8 Profiles

References:

AR 40-501 Standards of Medical Fitness (Feb 06)

DA 689 Sick Call Slip (Mar 63)
DA 3349 Profile (Feb 04)

Overview:

- Profiles are written on a DA From 3349.
- The severity of the profile depends on the PULHES scale (Physical capacity, Upper extremities, Lower extremities, Hearing-ears, Vision-eyes, Psychiatric). The letter determines the type of capacity that is limited and the number (1-4) determines to what degree function is limited. See Table 7-1. Physical Profile Functional Capacity Guide, AR 40-501.

Temporary profiles:

- Given if the condition is considered temporary, the correction or treatment of the condition is medically advisable, and correction usually will result in a higher physical capacity.
- Soldiers on active duty and RC soldiers not on active duty with a temporary profile will be medically evaluated at least once every 3 months
- Profiling officer must review previous profiles before making a decision to extend a temporary profile
- Any extension of a temporary profile must be recorded on DA Form 3349, and must contain the following statement: **"This temporary profile is an extension of a temporary profile first issued on (date)."**
- Should specify an expiration date. If no date is specified, the profile will automatically expire at the end of 30 days from issuance of the profile.
- In no case will soldiers carry a temporary profile that has been extended for more than 12 months. If a profile is needed beyond the 12 months the temporary profile should be changed to a permanent profile.

Permanent profiles

- Considered permanent unless a modifier of "T" (temporary) is added
- May be amended at any time if clinically indicated
- Soldier's commander may also request a review of a permanent profile
- If a P3 or P4, Soldier will receive a MEB.

from para 7-4, AR 40-501

Medical Boards:
- See Chapter 3, Administrative: Medical

Tips/Tricks:
- Have supervisors check profiles to ensure they list they are an extension if the Soldier has had a previous profile for the same injury/illness. If the doctor fails to annotate it, take the Soldier back to the TMC and speak to one of the NCO supervisors at the front.
- Have supervisors keep a running log of Soldier's profiles. This will help you recommend if a Soldier should have a Medical Evaluation Board (MEB).

5.9 Target Heart Rate Worksheet

Heart rate is one of the most effective ways to see how hard a Soldier is exerting himself.

Percent Maximum Heart Rate Method: With this method, the Target Heart Rate is figured using the estimated maximal heart rate. When using the MHR method, one must compensate for its built-in weakness. A person using this method may exercise at an intensity which is not high enough to cause a training effect. To compensate for this, a person who is in poor shape should exercise at 70 percent of his MHR; if he is in relatively good shape, at 80 percent MHR; and, if he is in excellent shape, at 90 percent MHR.

Max Heart Rate	(220 – age)	
Target (Lower)	(MRR x 0.70)	
Target (Mid)	(MRR x 0.80)	
Target (Upper)	(MRR x 0.80)	

HRR Method: A more accurate way to calculate Target Heart Rate is the percent Heart Rate Reserve method.

Resting Heart Rate	(# beats per minute)	
Max Heart Rate	(220 – age)	
Heart Rate Reserve	(Max. HR - Rest HR)	
Target (Lower)	(HRR x 0.60)	
Target (Upper)	(HRR x 0.80)	

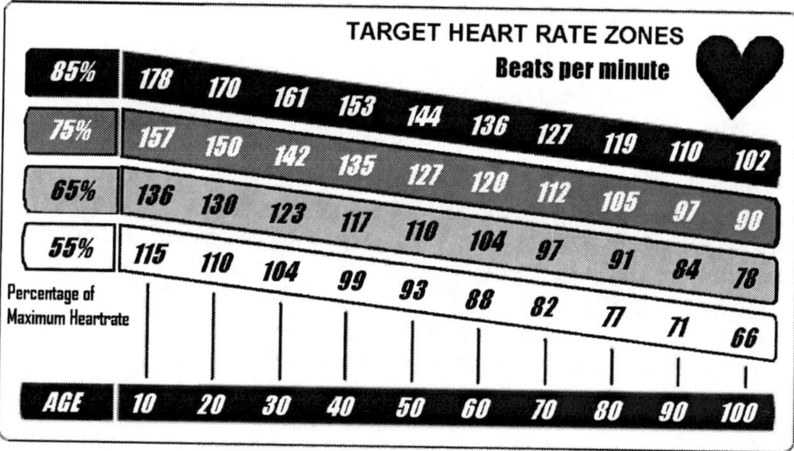

TARGET HEART RATE ZONES

Beats per minute

Percentage of Maximum Heartrate										
85%	178	170	161	153	144	136	127	119	110	102
75%	157	150	142	135	127	120	112	105	97	90
65%	136	130	123	117	110	104	97	91	84	78
55%	115	110	104	99	93	88	82	77	71	66
AGE	10	20	30	40	50	60	70	80	90	100

Tips/Tricks:

- See if your company can get a few heart rate monitors. These are a great tool for Soldiers to see how hard they are actually running. They are also great for special population PT because they left supervisors know how hard to push Soldiers.

5.10 Choosing Shoes

Proper footwear may play a role in injury prevention. Choosing a running shoe that is suitable for your particular type of foot can help you avoid some common running related injuries. It can also make running more enjoyable and help you get more mileage out of your shoes.

- Ask the salesperson to match your specific foot type to a specific shoe type. **High arched feet should go into cushioned shoes; normal arches into stability shoes; and low or no arches into motion control shoes.**
- Always tie and untie shoes when putting them on and taking them off.
- Expect shoes to be comfortable when you try them on. If they are not, then do not buy them.
- How a shoe looks is not as important as proper fit or comfort.
- Replace running shoes when they begin to show visible wear or after 500 miles of use, whichever occurs first.
- The best shoe for you may not be the most expensive. Always try on both shoes and walk around the store to ensure they fit before purchasing.
- If possible, shop for shoes at the end of the day instead of in the morning. Your feet swell from being in shoes and moving around all day.

from Pocket Physical Fitness Guide, US Infantry School.

Foot Type Test:

- Get your foot wet and step on a dry surface (like a paper towel)
- Normal foot has a flare but shows the forefoot and the heel connected by a wide band
- Flat feet (low arch) leave an imprint of the whole sole with very little arch remaining
- High-arched foot's imprint shows a flare with a very small band connecting the heel and forefoot.
- Also see, Figure E-1. How to Select the Right Shoe, FM 21-20. Physical Fitness Training.

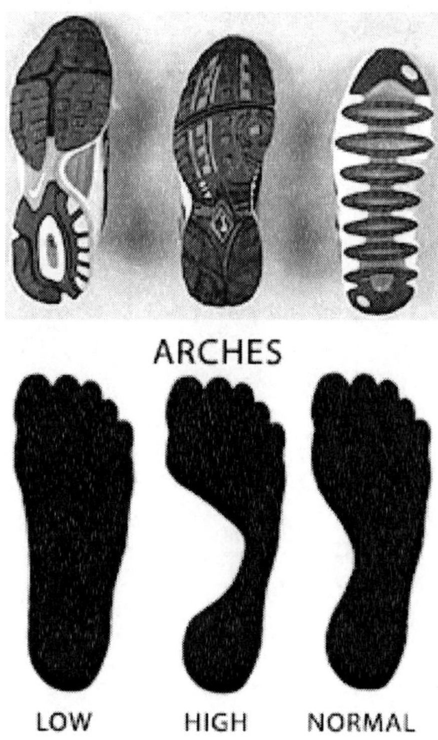
ARCHES
LOW
HIGH
NORMAL

Warrior Tasks

Part

6 Warrior Tasks

This section outlines warrior tasks that you should be proficient in as a platoon leader. They are not outlined due to operational security, but the appropriate references are listed in each sub-section. Seek out your Noncommissioned Officers to help you learn. They want to see a positive attitude and a willingness to learn, not a Platoon Leader that thinks he/she knows it all.

6.1 ABCS Systems

References:

ABCS-LRG 6.2	Army Battle Command System Leader's Reference (Feb 02)
TB 11-7010-326-10-1	FBCB2/BFT Operator's Pocket Guide
	FBCB2 Digital Operator's Guide (DOG)
	FBCB2 On-line Software User's Manual (SUM)
	FKSM 71-1 Digital Supplement- Platoon and Company Digital Operations
	FKSM 17-97-10 (EXFOR) The Brigade and Reconnaissance Troop
TB 11-5895-1500-10-2	MCS Software User's Guide

FBCB2/Blue Force Tracker Tasks:

- Find current location
- Send text message to higher
- Send MEDEVAC report
- Perform digital stand-to
- Conduct PCC of system
  - Clear Logs and Queues
  - Create messages and Folders
  - Establish message and address groups
  - Establish transmission settings
  - Pre-set filter settings
  - Pre-set Platform settings
  - Pre-set Medevac frequencies and call signs
  - Perform communication equipment checks
  - FBCB 2 system checks

MCS-Light:

- Find current location
- Send text message to higher
- Send MEDEVAC report
- Create an overlay

6.2 Call For Fire

References:

FM 6-20 Fire Support in the AirLand Battle (May 88)
FM 6-20-10 Tactics, Techniques, and Procedures for the Targeting Process (May 96)
FM 6-30 Tactics, Techniques and Procedures for Observed Fire (Jul 91)
JP 3-09.3 Joint Tactics, Techniques, and Procedures for Close Air Support (Dec 95)
GTA 07-01-032 Observed Fire Reference Card (Jun 87)

Call for Fire Tasks:

- Call for Field Artillery Fire (Grid)
- Call for Field Artillery Fire (Polar)
- Adjust/Shift Fire
- Call for Close Air Support
- Call for Naval Gun Fire

Effects of Fire:

Destruction: Destruction puts a target out of action permanently.
Neutralization: Neutralization knocks a target out of action temporarily. Most missions are neutralization fire.
Suppression. Suppression of a target limits the ability of the enemy Personnel in the target area to perform their jobs. The effect of suppressive fires usually lasts only as long as the fires are continued.

Definitions:

Add: In artillery, mortars, and naval fire support, a correction used by an observer/spotter to indicate that an increase in range along the spotting line is desired.
Adjust Fire: An order or request to initiate an adjustment on a designated target.
Close air support (CAS): Air action by fixed- and rotary-wing aircraft against hostile targets that are in close proximity to friendly forces and which require detailed integration of each air mission with the fire and movement of those forces.
Danger close: In close air support, artillery, mortar, and naval gunfire support fires, it is the term included in the method of engagement segment of a call for fire which indicates that friendly forces are within close proximity of the target. The close proximity distance is determined by the weapon and munition fired.

Description of target: In artillery, mortar, and naval fire support, an element in the call for fire in which the observer or spotter describes the installation, personnel, equipment, or activity to be taken under fire.

Destroy: A tactical mission task that physically renders an enemy force combat-ineffective until it is reconstituted. To damage a combat system so badly that it cannot perform any function or be restored to a usable condition without being entirely rebuilt. (30% casualties or material damage)

Neutralize: To render enemy personnel or material incapable of interfering with a particular operation. (10% casualties or material damage (12-24 hours)

No-fire area (NFA): Land area, designated by the appropriate commander, into which fires or their effects are prohibited.

Shift fire: The command to move the cone of fire in a direction away from a friendly maneuvering force so that enemy forces continue to be struck by the beaten zone at the same time the friendly unit moves.

Suppress: A tactical mission task that results in temporary degradation of the performance of a force or weapons system below the level needed to accomplish the mission (Limits enemy's performance)

6.3 Civil Disturbance

References:

FM 3-07	Stability Operations and Support Operations **(Feb 03)**
FM 3-19.15	Civil Disturbance Operations (Apr 05)
GTA 19-08-004	Non-lethal Munitions (Oct 01)
GTA 21-02-007	Civil Disturbance Instructions (Dec 70)
CALL 00-7	Preventing Civil Disturbance Tactics, Techniques, and Procedures

Civil Disturbance Tasks:

- Form platoon into riot formation (line, echelon, and diamond and circle)
- Understand the use of force
- Employ non-lethal munitions
- Employ riot control shields and batons
- Utilize an extraction team
- Employ obstacles effectively to control crowds

Definitions:

Civil disturbances: Riots, acts of violence, insurrections, unlawful obstructions or assemblages, or other disorders prejudicial to public law and order. The term “civil disturbances” includes all domestic conditions requiring or likely to require the use of Federal Armed Forces pursuant to the provisions of Chapter 15 of Title 10, United States Code.

6.4 Communications

References:

FM 6-02.72	Tactical Radios Multi-Service Communications Procedures for Tactical Radios in a Joint Environment (Jun 02)
FM 11-32	Combat Net Radio Operations (Oct 90)
FM 11-43	Signal Leader's Guide (Jun 95)
FM 24-18	Tactical Single-Channel Radio Communications Techniques (Sep 87)
FM 24-19	Radio Operator's Handbook (May 91)
TC 24-21	Tactical Multi-channel Radio Communications Techniques (Oct 88)
CALL 03-15	Radio Telephone Operators (RTO) Handbook
CALL 05-18	Radiotelephone Operator (RTO) Handbook Vol II
TM 11-5820-890-30P-3	Radio Set AN/PRC-119F, 87F, 88F, 89F, 90F, 91F, and 92F
TM 11-5985-357-13	Antenna Group, OE-254/GRC

Communication Tasks
- Communicating via Tactical Radio (SITREP, SPOTREP, Call for Fire, and MEDEVAC)
- Use visual signaling techniques

Radio Tasks:
- Loading a Radio with a Secure Fill
- Setting/Switching Channels
- Adjust Radio Time
- Understand limitations of radio systems (effective ranges, etc)
- Understand communication batteries

Tips/Tricks:
- Ensure you have redundant communications (example, ICOM radios, handheld walkie-talkies, etc)
- Ensure you have alternate means (establish hand/arm signals, convoy procedures, if communications go down)
- Have a quick card for each vehicle listing your organic unit

frequencies/callsigns and MEDEVAC frequencies.
- Have a strip map of adjacent AOs you operate in with callsigns/frequencies. Ensure those frequencies are programmed into specific channels before SP. Have SLs do communication checks with units as you enter their AO.

6.5 Convoy Operations

References:

FM 4-01.011	Unit Movement Operations (Oct 02)
FM 4-01.30	Movement Control (Sep 03)
FM 55-30	Army Motor Transport Units and Operations (Sep 91)
GTA 55-03-030	HMMWV Uparmored Emergency Procedures Performance Measures (May 05)
GTA 55-03-031	Water Egress HMMWV Uparmored Performance Measures (Jul 05)
GTA 90-01-004	Logistics Convoy Operations Smart Card (Sep 04)
CJTF-7 Smart Card 2	Convoy Operations
CJTF-7 Smart Card 3	Convoy Operations
CALL 04-27	Convoy Leader Training Handbook v2.0
CALL 04-24	Special Operations Command (USSOCOM) Combat Convoy Handbook
CALL 03-31	Route Clearance Handbook
CALL 03-6	Tactical Convoy Operations
CALL 04-27	Convoy Leader's Handbook ver 5 (Nov 04)
TSP 55-Z-0001	Convoy Survivability (Aug 04)

Convoy Tasks:
- Conduct a Convoy Brief
- Choose a primary and alternate route
- Dismount a vehicle
- Secure at a halt
- React to contact (small arms, IED, RPG, indirect fire)
- React to ambush (blocked)
- React to ambush (unblocked)
- React to indirect fire
- React to chemical attack
- Break contact
- Evacuate injured personnel from vehicle
- Recover a disabled vehicle

Definitions:

Alternate supply route (ASR): A route or routes designated within an area of operations to provide for the movement of traffic when main supply routes become disabled or congested.

Convoy: A group of vehicles organized for the purpose of control and orderly movement with or without escort protection that moves over the same route at the same time under one commander.

Herringbone: An arrangement of vehicles at left and right angles to the line of march used to establish security during an unscheduled halt.

Main supply route (MSR): The route or routes designated within an operational area upon which the bulk of traffic flows in support of military operations.

March column: A group of two to five serials using the same route for a single movement, organized under a single commander for planning, regulating, and controlling.

March serial: A subdivision of a march column consisting of a group of two to five march units using the same route for a single movement, organized under a single commander for planning, regulating, and controlling.

March unit: The smallest subdivision of a march column; a group of normally no more than 25 vehicles using the same route for a single movement organized under a single commander for planning, regulating, and controlling.

Reserved route: In road traffic, a specific route allocated exclusively to an authority or formation.

6.6 Cordon Search

References:

FM 3-07 Stability Operations and Support Operations (Feb 03)

CALL 04-16 Cordon and Search Handbook (Jul 04)

Cordon Search Tasks:
- Perform an inner cordon of an objective
- Perform an outer cordon of an objective
- Conduct a search of a building
- Employ as a cordon/search reserve force
- Properly account for and secure evidence/property
- Evacuate EPWs

Tips/Tricks:
- Ensure you plan and rehearse for what you will do after the search is complete and your departure from the objective.

6.7 Defense

References:

FM 3-0 Army Operations (Jun 01)
FM 3-90 Tactics (Jul 01)
FM 7-8 Infantry Rifle Platoon and Squad (Apr 92)
GTA 07-04-006 Building the Company Team for Defense (May 94)
GTA 05-08-001 Survivability Positions (Aug 93)
GTA 07-04-006 Building the Company Team for Defense (May 94)
GTA 07-06-001 Fighting Position Construction (Jan 94)

Defense Tasks:
- Use OCOKA to analyze the terrain
- Conduct a quartering party
- Establish a platoon perimeter
- Establish Fighting Positions (Individual/Vehicle)
- Create a platoon sector sketch

Definitions:

Active Defense: The employment of limited offensive action and counterattacks to deny a contested area or position to the enemy.

Alternate position – A defensive position that the commander assigns to a unit or weapon for occupation when the primary position becomes untenable or unsuitable for carrying out the assigned task.

Area defense: A type of defensive operation that concentrates on denying enemy forces access to designated terrain for a specific time rather than destroying the enemy outright.

Base defense: The local military measures, both normal and emergency, required to nullify or reduce the effectiveness of enemy attacks on, or sabotage of, a base, to ensure that the maximum capacity of its facilities is available to US forces.

Battle position: A defensive location oriented on a likely enemy avenue of approach.

Concealment: The protection from observation or surveillance.

Cover: Protection from the effects of fires.

Dead space: An area within the maximum range of a weapon, radar, or observer, which cannot be covered by fire or observation from a particular position because of

intervening obstacles, the nature of the ground, the characteristics of the trajectory, or the limitations of the pointing capabilities of the weapon.

Defensive operations: Operations that defeat an enemy attack, buy time, economize forces, or develop conditions favorable for offensive operations. Defensive operations alone normally cannot achieve a decision. Their purpose is to create conditions for a counteroffensive that allows Army forces to regain the initiative.

Delay: A form of retrograde in which a force under pressure trades space for time by slowing the enemy's momentum and inflicting maximum damage on the enemy without, in principle, becoming decisively engaged.

Field of fire: The area which a weapon or a group of weapons may cover effectively with fire from a given position.

Forward operations base (FOB): In special operations, a base usually located in friendly territory or afloat that is established to extend command and control or communications or to provide support for training and tactical operations. Facilities may be established for temporary or longer duration operations and may include an airfield or an unimproved airstrip, an anchorage, or a pier. A forward operations base may be the location of special operations component headquarters or a smaller unit that is controlled and/or supported by a main operations base.

Grazing fire: Fire approximately parallel to the ground where the center of the cone of fire does not rise above one meter from the ground.

Harassing fire: Fire designated to disturb the rest of the enemy troops, to curtail movement, and, by threat of losses, to lower morale.

Primary position: The position that covers the enemy's most likely avenue of approach into the area of operations.

Sector of fire: That area assigned to a unit, crew-served weapon, or an individual weapon within which it will engage targets as they appear in accordance with established engagement priorities.

Successive positions:

Supplementary position: A defensive position located within a unit's assigned area of operation that provides the best sectors of fire and defensive terrain along an avenue of approach that is not the primary avenue along where the enemy is expected to attack.

6.8 Deployment Operations

References:

FM 4-01.011 Unit Movement Operations (Oct 02)
AR 220-1 Unit Status Reporting (Mar 06)
GTA 55-07-003 Air Deployment Planning Guide (Feb 96)

DD 1750 Packing List (Sep 70)

Deployment Tasks:

- Track deployability of platoon
- Inventory platoon equipment on DD Form 1750
- Load vehicles on a rail car
- Load vehicles on a aircraft

Definitions:

Relief in place (RIP): An operation in which, by direction of higher authority, all or part of a unit is replaced in an area by the incoming unit. The responsibilities of the replaced elements for the mission and the assigned zone of operations are transferred to the incoming unit. The incoming unit continues the operation as ordered.

Time-phased force and deployment data (TPFDD): The Joint Operation Planning and Execution System database portion of an operation plan; it contains time-phased force data, non-unit-related cargo and personnel data, and movement data for the operation plan, including the following: a. In-place units; b. Units to be deployed to support the operation plan with a priority indicating the desired sequence for their arrival at the port of debarkation; c. Routing of forces to be deployed; d. Movement data associated with deploying forces; e. Estimates of non-unit related cargo and personnel movements to be conducted concurrently with the deployment of forces; and f. Estimate of transportation requirements that must be fulfilled by common-user lift resources as well as those requirements that can be fulfilled by assigned or attached transportation resources.

6.9 Detainees

References:

FM 3.19-1 Internment and Resettlement Operations (Mar 01)
FM 3-19.40 Military Police Internment/Resettlement Operations (Aug 01)
FM 27-10 The Law of Land Warfare (Jul 56)
FM 34-52 Intelligence Interrogation (Sep 92)
FM 3-25.150 Combatives (Jan 02)
FMI 3-63.6 Command and Control of Detainee Operations (Sep 05)
AR 195-5 Evidence Procedures (Nov 05)
AR 190-8 Enemy Prisoners of War, Retained Personnel, Civilian Internees, and Other Detainees (Oct 97)
JP 3-63 Joint Doctrine for Detainee Operations (Mar 05)
GTA 19-08-004 Non-lethal Munitions (Oct 01)

CALL Tactical Questioning: Soldier's Handbook

Training Support Packages:

191-D-0001 Point of Capture
191-D-0002 Detainee Collecting Point or Detainee Holding Area
191-E-0001 Internment/Resettlement Facility

Forms:

DA 2823 Sworn Statement (Dec 98)
DA 4137 Evidence/Property Custody Document (Jul 76)
DA 5976 Enemy Prisoner of War Capture Tag (Jan 91)

Enemy Prisoner of War Tasks:

- Apply Levels of Force
- Conduct a personnel search
- Employ non-lethal munitions
- Properly account for and secure evidence/property
- Complete a DA Form 2823, Sworn Statement
- Complete a DA 5976 EPW Tag
- Transport a detainee

Definitions:

Detainee: An individual who is captured by or placed in the custody of a duly constituted governmental organization for a period of time.

Dislocated civilian: A generic term that describes a civilian who has been forced to move by war, revolution, or natural or man-made disaster from his or her home to some other location. Dislocated citizens include displaced persons, refugees, evacuees, stateless persons, and war victims. Legal and political considerations define the subcategories of a dislocated civilian.

Displaced person: An internally displaced person is a civilian involuntarily outside his area or region within his country.

Enemy prisoner of war (EPW): An individual or group of individuals detained by friendly forces in any operational environment who meet the criteria as listed in Article 4 of the Geneva Convention Relative to the Handling of Prisoners of War.

Internment and resettlement (I/R): A military police mission that involves enemy prisoners of war/civilian internee handling, US military prisoner handling, and populace and resource control. Internment and resettlement operations address military police and criminal investigation division (CID) roles in control of populations (enemy prisoners of war/civilian internees, US military prisoners, and dislocated civilians). This function involves those measures necessary to provide shelter, sustain, guard, protect, and account for populations.

Noncombatant: An individual, in an area of combat operations, who is not armed and is not participating in any activity in support of any of the factions or forces involved in combat. An individual, such as chaplain or medical personnel, whose duties do not involve combat.

Prisoner of war (POW): A detained person as defined in Articles 4 and 5 of the Geneva Convention Relative to the Treatment of Prisoners of War of August 12, 1949. In particular, one who, while engaged in combat under orders of his or her government, is captured by the armed forces of the enemy. As such, he or she is entitled to the combatant's privilege of immunity from the municipal law of the capturing state for warlike acts which do not amount to breaches of the law of armed conflict. For example, a prisoner of war may be, but is not limited to, any person belonging to one of the following categories who has fallen into the power of the enemy: a member of the armed forces, organized militia, or volunteer corps; a person who accompanies the armed forces without actually being a member thereof; a member of a merchant marine or civilian aircraft crew not qualifying for more favorable treatment; or individuals who, on the approach of the enemy, spontaneously take up arms to resist the invading forces.

Refugee: A person who, by reason of real or imagined danger, has left their home country or country of their nationality and is unwilling or unable to return.

Tips/Tricks:
- Each squad should have an make-shift EPW kit with flexi-cuffs, ziplock bags, permanent markers, index cards, field dressings (for first aid and as blindfolds), and appropriate paperwork.

6.10 First Aid

References:

FM 4-25.11	First Aid (Dec 02)
PAM 40-13	Training in First Aid and Emergency Medical Treatment (Aug 85)
TC 8-800	Semi-Annual Combat Medic Skills Test (Jun 02)
GTA 08-01-004	MEDEVAC Request Form (Aug 02)

First Aid Tasks:
- Evaluate a casualty
- Perform first aid for open wound (abdominal, chest, & head)
- Perform first aid for bleeding of extremity
- Select temporary fighting position
- Call Nine Line MEDEVAC via Tactical Radio
- Send Nine Line MEDEVAC using FBCB2/Blue Force Tracker
- Use the Combat Application Tourniquet (CATS) system

Definitions:

Aid station: The first medical treatment facility that can provide advanced trauma management to a battlefield casualty. It provides first level of triage evaluation of casualties and conducts routine sick call.

Medical Treatment Facility (MTF):

Triage: The evaluation and classification of wounded for purposes of treatment and evacuation. It consists of the immediate sorting of patients according to type and seriousness of injury, and likelihood of survival, and the establishment of priority for treatment and evacuation to assure medical care of the greatest benefit to the largest number.

Levels of care:
- **Level I:** Immediate lifesaving measures, emergency medical treatment, advanced trauma management (ATM), and evacuation from supported unit to supporting medical treatment facility (MTF). Medics, CLS, and Aid Station.
- **Level II:** Capabilities duplicate Level I and operational dental care, laboratory, x-ray, patient holding capabilities, mental health and forward surgical team (FST)

- **Level III:** Combat support hospital (CSH)
- **Level IV:** Landstuhl
- **Level V** (CONUS Support Base)**:** Walter Reed, Brooks Army Medical Center, Bethesda Naval Hospital

Tips/Tricks:
- Each squad or section should have a body bag/blanket in the event of a KIA. It is a leader's responsibility to recover the body and cover it so Soldiers can focus on their mission instead of seeing a dead comrade.
- Ensure each squad has a CLS bag and it is stocked. Also, work to get CATS tourniquets and Quik Clot for your unit.

6.11 Force Protection

References:

FM 5-34	Engineer Field Data (Jul 05)
FM 5-103	Survivability (Jun 85)
AR 525-13	Anti-Terrorism (Jan 02)
TC 19-210	Access Control Handbook (Oct 04)
JP 3-26	Homeland Security (Aug 05)
JP 3-07.2	Joint Tactics, Techniques, and Procedures for Antiterrorism (Mar 98)
GTA 19-04-003	Individual Protective Measures (Nov 01)
GTA 90-01-003	Vehicle Search Techniques Smart Card (Aug 04)
CJTF-7 Smart Card 5	Vehicle Search Techniques
CJTF-7 Smart Card 4	The IED and VBIED
CALL 05-24	Forward Operating Base Newsletter (Sep 05)
CJCS 5260	A Self-Help Guide to Anti-Terrorism (Oct 02)
CJCS 5260	Commander's Handbook for Antiterrorism Readiness (Jan 97)
DoD O-2000.12-H	DOD Anti-Terrorism Handbook (Feb 04)
MIL-HDBK-1013/12	Evaluation and Selection Analysis of Security Glazing for Protection against Ballistic, Bomb, and Forced Entry Tactics (Mar 97)
MIL-HDBK-1013/14	Selection and Application of Vehicle Barriers (Feb 97)
TRADOC DCSINT 1	A Military Guide to Terrorism in the Twenty-First Century (Aug 05)
UFC 4-012-01	Security Engineering: Entry Control Facilities / Access Control Points (Jan 00)
UFC 4-010-01	DOD Minimum Anti-Terrorism Standards for

Buildings (Oct 03)

Websites:
AT Training http://at-awareness.org/

Force Protection Tasks:
- Perform a vulnerability assessment for your unit
- Conduct an Entry/Access Control Point (ECP/ACP)
- Conduct Random Anti-Terrorism Measures
- Conduct a vehicle search

Definitions:
Checkpoint: A place where military police check vehicular or pedestrian traffic in order to enforce circulation control measures and other laws, orders, and regulations.
Antiterrorism (AT): Defensive measures used to reduce the vulnerability of individuals and property to terrorist acts, to include limited response and containment by local military forces.
Force protection (FP): Actions taken to prevent or mitigate hostile actions against Department of Defense personnel (to include family members), resources, facilities, and critical information. These actions conserve the force's fighting potential so it can be applied at a decisive time and place and incorporates the coordinated and synchronized offensive and defensive measures to enable the effective employment of the joint force while degrading opportunities for the enemy. Force protection does not include actions to defeat the enemy or protect against accidents, weather, or disease.
Terrorism: The calculated use of unlawful violence or threat of unlawful violence to inculcate fear; intended to coerce or to intimidate governments or societies in the pursuit of goals that are generally political, religious, or ideological.

6.12 Host Nation Training

References:
FM 3.19-1 Military Police Operations (Mar 01)
FM 3.19-13 Military Police Investigations (Jan 05)
FM 19-10 Law Enforcement (Sep 87)
AR 570-9 Host Nation Support (Mar 06)
TC 19-138 Civilian Law Enforcement and Security Officer Training (Aug 01)

Host Nation Training Tasks:
- Develop METL tasks for Host Nation unit
- Train applicable skill level 1-4 tasks to Host Nation

- Develop cohesion within Host Nation unit
- Learn basic phrases in Host Nation language
- Conduct lane training for Host Nation unit
- Evaluate Host Nation unit

6.13 Improvised Explosive Devices

References:

FMI 3-34.119	Improvised Explosive Device Defeat (Sep 05)
TC 9-21-01	Soldier's Improvised Explosive Device (IED) Awareness Guide Iraq & Afghanistan Theaters of Operation (May 04)
TC 20-32-5	Commander's Reference Guide: Land Mine and Explosive Hazards (Iraq) (Feb 03)
GTA 90-01-001	Improvised Explosive Device (IED) and Vehicular Borne Improvised Explosive Device (VBIED) Smart Card (May 04)
CJTF-7 Smart Card	Improvised Explosive Device (IED)
CALL 05-023	Counter IED TTP Handbook
CALL	IED Safe Standoff Distance Cheat Sheet

IED Tasks:
- Visually identify a possible Improvised Explosive Device (IED)
- React to a Possible IED (dismounted and mounted)
- Cordon an IED for Explosive Ordnance Disposal (EOD)

6.14 Intelligence

References:

FM 34-3 Intelligence Analysis (Mar 90)
FM 34-52 Intelligence Interrogation (Sep 92)
FM 34-130 Intelligence Preparation of the Battlefield (Jul 94)
FMI 2-91.4 Intelligence Support to Operations in the Urban Environment (Jun 05)
ST 2-22.7 Tactical Human Intelligence and Counterintelligence Operations (Apr 02)
ST 2-50.4 Combat Commander's Handbook on Intelligence (Sep 01)
ST 2-91.1 Intelligence Support to Stability Operations and Support Operations (Nov 04)

CALL COE Smartcard
CALL Tactical Questioning

Intelligence Tasks:

- SALUTE report
- Understand and brief subordinates on INSUM report
- Intelligence Preparation of the Battlefield
    - Analyze Terrain using OCOKA
    - Analyze Weather using the five aspects of weather
    - Analyze enemy end state and courses of action
- Conduct tactical questioning of a witness/suspect

Definitions:

Analysis: The process by which collected information is evaluated and integrated with existing information to produce intelligence that describes the current, and predicts the future, impact of the threat and/or environment on operations.

High-value target (HVT): A target the enemy commander requires for the successful completion of the mission. The loss of high-value targets would be expected to seriously degrade important enemy functions throughout the friendly commander's area of interest.

Human intelligence (HUMINT): A category of intelligence derived from information collected and provided by human sources. Covers a wide range of activities encompassing reconnaissance patrols, aircrew reports and debriefs, debriefing of refugees, interrogations of prisoners of war, and the conduct of counterintelligence force protection source operations.

Intelligence: The product resulting from the collection, processing, integration, analysis, evaluation, and interpretation of available information concerning foreign countries or information and knowledge about an adversary obtained through observation, investigation, analysis, or understanding.

Intelligence preparation of the battlefield (IPB): The systematic, continuous process of analyzing the threat and environment in a specific geographic area. Intelligence preparation of the battlefield (IPB) is designed to support the staff estimate and military decisionmaking process. Most intelligence requirements are generated as a result of the IPB process and its interrelation with the decisionmaking process.

Intelligence, surveillance, and reconnaissance (ISR): An enabling operation that integrates and synchronizes all battlefield operating systems to collect and produce relevant information to facilitate the commander's decisionmaking.

Interrogation: Systematic effort to procure information by direct questioning of a person under the control of the questioner. (Army) The systematic effort to procure information to answer specific collection requirements by direct and indirect questioning techniques of a person who is in the custody of the forces conducting the questioning.

Templates:

Doctrinal template: Model based on known or postulated adversary doctrine. Doctrinal templates illustrate the disposition and activity of adversary forces and assets conducting a particular operation unconstrained by the effects of the battlespace. They represent the application of adversary doctrine under ideal conditions. Ideally, doctrinal templates depict the threat's normal organization for combat, frontages, depths, boundaries and other control measures, assets available from other commands, objective depths, engagement areas, battle positions, and so forth. Doctrinal templates are usually scaled to allow ready use with geospatial products.

Event template: Guide for collection planning. The event template depicts the named area of interest where activity, or its lack of activity, will indicate which course of action the adversary has adopted. (Army) A model against which enemy activity can be recorded and compared. It represents a sequential projection of events that relate to space and time on the battlefield and indicate the enemy's ability to adopt a particular course of action. The event template is a guide for collection and reconnaissance and surveillance planning.

Situation template: Depiction of assumed adversary dispositions, based on adversary doctrine and the effects of the battlespace if the adversary should adopt a particular course of action. In effect, the situation templates are the doctrinal templates depicting a particular operation modified to account for the effects of the battlespace environment and the adversary's current situation (training and experience levels, logistic status, losses, dispositions). Normally, the situation template depicts adversary units two levels of command below the friendly force, as well as the expected locations of high-value targets. Situation templates use time-phase lines to indicate movement of forces and the expected flow of the operation. Usually the situation template depicts a critical point in the course of action. Situation templates are one part of an adversary course of action model. Models may contain more than one situation template.

6.15 Land Navigation

References:

FM 3-25.26 Map Reading and Land Navigation (Jan 05)

TB 11-5825-291-10 Satellite Signal Navigation Sets, AN/PSN-11
TB 11-5825-291-10-2 Soldier's Guide for Precision Lightweight GPS Receiver (PLGR)
TB 11-5825-291-10-3 The PLGR Made Simple

Land Navigations Tasks:

- Navigate Dismounted using Lensatic Compass and Map
- Navigate using Terrain Association
- Determine location on ground (terrain association, map, & GPS)
- Move over, through, or around obstacles (except minefields)
- Find location using AN/PSN-11 PLGR
- Set waypoint using AN/PSN-11 PLGR
- Find location using a commercial GPS unit
- Set waypoint using a commercial GPS unit

Definitions:

Way point: A designated point or series of points loaded and stored in a global positioning system or other electronic navigational aid system to facilitate movement.

6.16 MOUT

References:

FM 3-06 Urban Operations (Jun 03)
FM 3-06.1 Multi-service Aviation Urban Operations (Jul 05)
FM 3-06.11 Combined Arms Operations in Urban Terrain (Feb 02)
TC 90-1 Training for Urban Operations (Apr 02)

CALL 03-4 Small Unit Leader's Guide to Urban Operations
CALL 99-16 Urban Combat Operations

MOUT Tasks:

- Perform movements techniques during an urban operation
- Engage targets during an urban operation
- Enter/clear a building during an urban operation

Tips/Tricks:

- Understand the different types of structures (brick, dry wall, etc) and what your fires will do to them.

6.17 MOOTW

References:

FM 100-23-1 HA Multi-Service Procedures for Humanitarian Assistance Operations (Oct 94)
JP 3-07.3 Joint Tactics, Techniques, and Procedures for Peace Operations (Feb 99)

CALL 06-01 Staff Officer's Catastrophic Disaster Relief Handbook
CALL 93-6 Disaster Assistance
CALL 94-4 Operations Other Than War (OOTW) Handbook

MOOTW Tasks:
- Escort humanitarian supplies
- Provide security to a logistics distribution point
- Apply Levels of Force

Definitions:

Military operations other than war (MOOTW): Operations that encompass the use of military capabilities across the range of military operations short of war. These military actions can be applied to complement any combination of other instruments of national power and occur before, during, and after the war.

6.18 NBC

References:

FM 3-3 Chemical and Biological Contamination Avoidance (Sep 94)
FM 3-5 Decontamination Operations (Jan 02)
FM 3-7 NBC Field Handbook (Sep 94)
TC 3-10 Commander's Tactical NBC Handbook (Sep 94)
GTA 03-05-015 Chemical Protection and Decon (Dec 95)
GTA 03-06-008 NBC Warning and Reporting System (Aug 96)

DA 1971-10-R NBC 4 Radiation Dose Rate Measurements or Chemical/Biological Areas of Contamination (Oct 92)
DA 1971-7-R NBC 1 Observer's Initial or Follow-Up Report (Oct 92)

NBC Tasks:
- Conduct unmasking procedures
- Understand NBC alarms and how to employ them
- Cross a contaminated area
- Conduct MOPP Gear Exchange
- Conduct individual decontamination
- Send NBC 1 report
- Send NBC 4 Report

Definitions:

Biological agent: A microorganism that causes disease in personnel, plants, or animals or causes the deterioration of materiel.

Chemical Agent: Any toxic chemical intended for use in military operations. A chemical substance which is intended for use in military operations to kill, seriously injure, or incapacitate personnel through its physiological effects. The term excludes riot control agents, herbicides, and substances generating smoke and flames.

MOPP/ Equip	MOPP READY	MASK ONLY	MOPP ZERO	MOPP 1	MOPP 2	MOPP 3	MOPP 4
Mask	Carried	Worn	Carried	Carried	Carried	Worn[1]	Worn
Over-garment	Ready[3]	Note	Avail[4]	Worn[1]	Worn[1]	Worn[1]	Worn
Vinyl Overboot	Ready[3]	Note	Avail[4]	Avail[4]	Worn	Worn	Worn
Gloves	Ready[3]	Note	Avail[4]	Avail[4]	Avail[4]	Avail[4]	Worn
Helmet, Pro cover	Ready[3]	Note	Avail[4]	Avail[4]	Worn	Worn	Worn
Chem Pro Under Garment (CPU)[2]	Ready[3]	Note	Avail[4]	Worn[1]	Worn[1]	Worn[1]	Worn[1]

1 In hot weather, coat or hood can be left open for ventilation
2 The CPU is worn under the BDU (primarily applies to SOF) or CVC coveralls
3 Must be available to the Soldier within two hours. Second set available in six hours
4 Must be within arm's reach of Soldier.

Table 1-1. Seven Levels of MOPP
FM 1-02. Operational Terms and Graphics

6.19 Offensive Operations

References:

FM 1-02 Operational Terms and Graphics (Sep 04) formerly FM 101-5-1
FM 3-0 Operations (Jun 01)
FM 7-8 Infantry Rifle Platoon and Squad (Apr 92)
GTA 07-06-001 Fighting Position Construction (Jan 94)

Offensive Tasks:

- Conduct a hasty attack
- Conduct a deliberate attack
- Conduct an ambush
- Conduct actions on the objective
- Shift fires through audio and visual means

Definitions:

Actions on Contact: A series of combat actions, often conducted simultaneously, taken upon contact with the enemy to develop the situation.

Ambush: A form of attack by fire or other destructive means from concealed positions on a moving or temporarily halted enemy.

Assault: To make a short, violent, but well-ordered attack against a local objective, such as a gun emplacement, a fort, or a machine gun nest.

Assault position: A covered and concealed position short of the objective, from which final preparations are made to assault the objective.

Assembly area: An area in which a command is assembled preparatory to further action.

Attack: An offensive operation that destroys or defeats enemy forces, seizes and secures terrain, or both.

Attack position: The last position occupied by the assault echelon before crossing the line of departure.

Base of fire: Direct fire placed on an enemy force or position to reduce or eliminate the enemy's capability to interfere by fire and/or movement with friendly maneuver element(s). It may be provided by a single weapon or a grouping of weapons systems.

Counterattack: Attack by part or all of a defending force against an enemy attacking force, for such specific purposes as regaining ground lost, or cutting off or destroying enemy advance units, and with the general objective of denying to the enemy the attainment of the enemy's purpose in attacking. In sustained defensive operations, it is undertaken to restore the battle position and is directed at limited objectives.

Covering fire: Fire used to protect troops when they are within range of enemy small arms.

Deliberate attack: A type of offensive action characterized by preplanned coordinated employment of firepower and maneuver to close with and destroy or capture the enemy.

Demonstration: A form of attack designed to deceive the enemy as to the location or time of the decisive operation by a display of force. Forces conducting a demonstration do not seek contact with the enemy. In stability operations and support operations, an operation by military forces in sight of an actual or potential adversary to show military capabilities.

Envelopment: A form of maneuver in which an attacking force seeks to avoid the principal enemy defenses by seizing objectives to the enemy rear to destroy the enemy in his current positions. At the tactical level, envelopments focus on seizing terrain, destroying specific enemy forces, and interdicting enemy withdrawal routes.

Exploitation: An offensive operation that usually follows a successful attack and is designed to disorganize the enemy in depth.

Feint: A form of attack used to deceive the enemy as to the location or time of the actual decisive operation. Forces conducting a feint seek direct fire contact with the enemy but avoid decisive engagement.

Frontal attack: A form of maneuver in which the attacking force seeks to destroy a weaker enemy force or fix a larger enemy force in place over a broad front.

Hasty attack: In land operations, an attack in which preparation time is traded for speed in order to exploit an opportunity.

Infiltration: A form of maneuver in which an attacking force conducts undetected movement through or into an area occupied by enemy forces to occupy a position of advantage in the enemy rear while exposing only small elements to enemy defensive fires. .

Maneuver: Place the enemy in a disadvantageous position through the flexible application of combat power.

Meeting engagement: A combat action that occurs when a moving force, incompletely deployed for battle, engages an enemy at an unexpected time and place.

Named area of interest: Geographical area where information that will satisfy a specific information requirement can be collected. Named areas of interest are usually selected to capture indications of adversary courses of action, but also may be related to conditions of the battlespace.

Offensive operations: Operations which aim at destroying or defeating an enemy. Their purpose is to impose US will on the enemy and achieve decisive victory.

Penetration: A form of maneuver in which an attacking force seeks to rupture enemy defenses on a narrow front to disrupt the defensive system.

Pursuit: An offensive operation designed to catch or cut off a hostile force attempting to escape, with the aim of destroying it.

Raid: An operation, usually small scale, involving a swift penetration of hostile territory to secure information, confuse the enemy, or to destroy installations. It ends with a planned withdrawal upon completion of the assigned mission.

Spoiling attack: Tactical maneuver employed to seriously impair a hostile attack while the enemy is in the process of forming or assembling for an attack. A form of attack that preempts or seriously impairs an enemy attack while the enemy is in the process of planning or preparing to attack.

Support by fire: Tactical mission task in which a maneuver force moves to a position where it can engage the enemy by direct fire in support of another maneuvering force.

Turning movement: A form of maneuver in which the attacking force seeks to avoid the enemy's principal defensive positions by seizing objectives to the enemy rear and causing the enemy to move out of his current positions or divert major forces to meet the threat.

6.20 Rear Detachment

References:

CALL 04-28	Rear Detachment Operations (Oct 04)

Website:

Army Rear-D	http://reardcommander.army.mil
MyArmyToo	http://www.myarmylifetoo.com
Army FRG	http://www.armyfrg.org/
OneSource	http://www.armyonesource.com/

Rear-Detachment Tasks:

- Inventory and sign for Rear Detachment property
- In-process new Soldiers
- Supervise an FRG meeting
- Initiate chapter paperwork
- Counsel and supervise Family Care Plans
- Supervise financial issues and assist in AER loan paperwork
- Refer family members to appropriate agencies for assistance
- Update unit roster and distribute to FRG members

6.21 SASO/SOSO

References:

FM 3-07	Stability Operations and Support Operations (Feb 03)
FM 3-07.31	Conducting Peace Operations (Oct 03)
FMI 3-07.22	Counterinsurgency Operations (Oct 04)
TC 7-98-1	Stability and Support Operations (Jun 97)
CALL 02-8	Operation Enduring Freedom Tactics, Techniques and Procedures
CALL 03-20	Army & USMC TTP - Stability Operations & Support Operations (SOSO)
CALL 03-35	Operation Enduring Freedom Handbook II
CALL 04-7	Interpreter Operations Handbook
CALL 05-6	Operation Enduring Freedom III
CALL 05-11	Ranger Tactics, Techniques, and Procedures
CALL 05-17	Company-Level Stability Operations and Support Operations
CALL 05-26	Company-Level Stability Operations and Support Operations, Vol II
CALL 05-27	Company-Level Stability Operations and Support Operations, Vol III
CALL 05-28	Level Stability Operations and Support Operations, Vol IV
CALL 05-37	Company-Level Stability Operations and Support Operations, Vol V

SASO/SOSO Tasks:
- Conduct a snap/flash checkpoint
- Conduct a traffic control point (TCP)
- Conduct critical site security
- Conduct a VIP escort
- Perform a joint patrol with Host Nation assets (mounted/dismounted)
- Effectively use an interpreter

Definitions:

Checkpoint: A place where military police check vehicular or pedestrian traffic in order to enforce circulation control measures and other laws, orders, and regulations.

Demonstration: An operation by military forces in sight of an actual or potential adversary to show military capabilities.

Peace enforcement: Application of military force, or the threat of its use, normally pursuant to international authorization, to compel compliance with resolutions or sanctions designed to maintain or restore peace and order.

Peacekeeping: Military operations undertaken with the consent of all major parties to a dispute, designed to monitor and facilitate implementation of an agreement (ceasefire, truce, or other such agreement) and support diplomatic efforts to reach a long-term political settlement.
Peacemaking: The process of diplomacy, mediation, negotiation, or other forms of peaceful settlements that arranges an end to a dispute and resolves issues that led to it.
Stability operations: Operations that promote and protect US national interests by influencing the threat, political, and information dimensions of the operational environment through a combination of peacetime developmental, cooperative activities and coercive actions in response to crisis.

Interpreter Tips/Tricks:
- Show respect for Host Nation interpreters. Ensure Soldiers understand what these individuals risk by assisting US Forces.
- Ensure you explain your intent to your interpreter. There is a distinct difference between saying "Please put your arms out to be searched" and "Get your hands up before I shoot." Ensure your interpreter's understand what you want the locals to do.
- Ensure you protect your interpreters through your actions and giving them equipment. If you have the same interpreter on a long term basis, incorporate them into your battle drills so they understand their role when your unit is attacked.

6.22 Tactics and Doctrine

References:

FM 1-02	Operational Terms and Graphics (Sep 04) formerly FM 101-5-1
FM 3-0	Operations (Jun 01)
FM 5-0	Army Planning and Orders Production (Jan 05)
FM 3-90	Tactics (Jul 01)

Tactics and Doctrine Tasks:
- Analyze terrain using OCOKA
- Understand the different tactical tasks
- Direct subordinates using task and purpose
- Issue a WARNO (verbal and written)
- Issue a FRAGO (verbal and written)
- Issue an OPORD (verbal and written)
- Create a graphical overlay (map and electronic)
- Write a decision paper and conduct decision brief

Definitions:

Doctrine: Fundamental principles by which the military forces or elements thereof guide their actions in support of national objectives. It is authoritative but requires judgment in application.

Tactics: The employment of units in combat. It includes the ordered arrangement and maneuver of units in relation to each other, the terrain, and the enemy in order to translate potential combat power into victorious battles and engagements.

6.22.1 Levels of War

Strategic level of war: The level of war at which a nation, often as a member of a group of nations, determines national or multinational (alliance or coalition) strategic security objectives and guidance, and develops and uses national resources to accomplish these objectives. Activities at this level establish national and multinational military objectives; sequence initiatives; define limits and assess risks for the use of military and other instruments of national power; develop global plans or theater war plans to achieve these objectives; and provide military forces and other capabilities in accordance with strategic plans.

Operational level of war: The level of war at which campaigns and major operations are planned, conducted, and sustained to accomplish strategic objectives within theaters or operational areas. Activities at this level link tactics and strategy by establishing operational objectives needed to accomplish the strategic objectives, sequencing events to achieve the operational objectives, initiating actions, and applying resources to bring about and sustain these events. These activities imply a broader dimension of time or space than do tactics; they ensure the logistic and administrative support of tactical forces, and provide the means by which tactical successes are exploited to achieve strategic objectives.

Tactical level of war: The level of war at which battles and engagements are planned and executed to accomplish military objectives assigned to tactical units or task forces. Activities at this level focus on the ordered arrangement and maneuver of combat elements in relation to each other and to the enemy to achieve combat objectives.

6.22.2 Military Operations

Types of Military Operations:
Offense
Defense
Stability
Support

Characteristics of the Offense
Surprise
Concentration
Tempo
Audacity

Types of Offensive Operations
Movement to Contact
Attack
Exploitation
Pursuit

Forms of Maneuver
Envelopment
Turning Movement
Frontal Attack
Penetration
Infiltration

Forms of the Attack
Ambush
Spoiling Attack
Counterattack
Raid
Feint
Demonstration

Characteristics of the Defense
Preparation
Security
Disruption
Mass
Flexibility

Types of Defensive Operations

Mobile Defense
Area Defense
Retrograde

Types of Stability Operations
Peace Operations
Foreign Internal Defense
Security Assistance
Humanitarian & Civic Assistance
Support to Insurgencies
Support to Command Operations
Combating Terrorism
Noncombatant Evacuation Operations
Arms Control
Show of Force

Types of Support Operations
Domestic Support Operations
Foreign Humanitarian Assistance

Forms of Support Operations
Relief Operations
Support to Incidents Involving WMD
Support to Civilian Law Enforcement
Community Assistance

from Figure 2-1. FM 3-90

6.22.3 Enabling Operations

Types of Enabling Operations:
Information Operations
Combat Service Support

Types of Tactical Enabling Operations:
Troop Movement
- Administrative Movement
- Approach March
- Road March

Combined Arms Breach Operations
River Crossing Operatoins
Relief in Place
Passage of Lines
Tactical Information Operations

Reconnaissance Operation
- Zone
- Area
- Route
- Reconnaissance in Force

Security Operations
- Screen
- Guard
- Cover
- Area (includes route and convoy
- Local

from Figure 2-1. FM 3-90

6.22.4 Tactical Terms

Mission statement: A short paragraph or sentence describing the task and purpose that clearly indicates the action to be taken and the reason thereof. It usually contains the elements of who, what, when, and where, and the reason thereof, but seldom specifies how.

Task: A clearly defined, measurable activity accomplished by individuals and organizations. Tasks are specific activities which contribute to the accomplishment of encompassing missions or other requirements. A task should be definable, attainable, and decisive.

Purpose: The desired or intended result of the tactical operations stated in terms relating to the enemy or to the desired situation

Tactical Tasks (FM 3-90)		
Enemy	**Terrain**	**Friendly**
Assault	Clear	Breach
Attack by Fire	Control	Bypass
Block	Occupy	Combat Search & Rescue
Canalize	Retain	Consolidation and Reorganization
Contain	Secure	Disengage
Counterrecon	Seize	Exfiltrate
Defeat		Follow and Assume
Destroy		Follow and Support
Disengagement		Linkup
Disrupt		Reconstitution
Exfiltrate		
Fix		
Interdict		
Isolate		
Neutralize		
Reduce		
Suppress		
Support by Fire		
Turn		

Purposes
Allow
Cause
Create
Deceive
Divert
Draw
Enable
Envelop
Facilitate
Influence
Support
Open
Prevent
Surprise

Missions:

Block: A tactical mission task that denies the enemy access to an area or prevents his advance in a direction or along an avenue of approach.

Canalize: A tactical mission task in which the commander restricts enemy movement to a narrow zone by exploiting terrain coupled with the use of obstacles, fires, or friendly maneuver.

Clear: A tactical mission task that requires the commander to remove all enemy forces and eliminate organized resistance in an assigned area.

Contain: To stop, hold, or surround the forces of the enemy or to cause the enemy to center activity on a given front and to prevent the withdrawal of any part of the enemy's force for use elsewhere.

Control: A tactical mission task that requires the commander to maintain physical influence over a specified area to prevent its use by an enemy.

Defeat: A tactical mission task that occurs when an enemy force has temporarily or permanently lost the physical means or the will to fight. The defeated force's commander is unwilling or unable to pursue his adopted course of action, thereby yielding to the friendly commander' s will, and can no longer interfere to a significant degree with the actions of friendly forces. Defeat can result from the use of force or the threat of its use.

Deny: To hinder or prevent the enemy from using terrain, space, personnel, supplies, or facilities.

Destroy: A tactical mission task that physically renders an enemy force combat-ineffective until it is reconstituted. To damage a combat system so badly that it cannot perform any function or be restored to a usable condition without being entirely rebuilt.

Disrupt: A tactical mission task in which a commander integrates direct and indirect fires, terrain, and obstacles to upset an enemy's formation or tempo, interrupt his timetable, or cause his forces to commit prematurely or attack in piecemeal fashion.

Fix: A tactical mission task where a commander prevents the enemy from moving any part of his force from a specific location for a specific period of time.

Interdict: A tactical mission task where the commander prevents, disrupts, or delays the enemy's use of an area or route.

Isolate: A tactical mission task that requires a unit to seal off - both physically and psychologically - an enemy from his sources of support, deny an enemy freedom of movement, and prevent an enemy unit from having contact with other enemy forces.

Neutralize: To render enemy personnel or material incapable of interfering with a particular operation.

Reduce: A tactical mission task that involves the destruction of an encircled or bypassed enemy force.

Secure: A tactical mission task that involves preventing a unit, facility, or geographical location from being damaged or destroyed as a result of enemy action.

Seize: A tactical mission task that involves taking possession of a designated area using overwhelming force.

Suppress: A tactical mission task that results in temporary degradation of the performance of a force or weapons system below the level needed to accomplish the mission.

Turn: A tactical mission task that involves forcing an enemy force from one avenue of approach or movement corridor to another. A tactical obstacle effect that integrates fire planning and obstacle effort to drive an enemy formation from one avenue of approach to an adjacent avenue of approach or into an engagement area.

Other Definitions:

Centers of gravity (COG): Those characteristics, capabilities, or sources of power from which a military force derives its freedom of action, physical strength, or will to fight.

Combat effectiveness – The ability of a unit to perform its mission. Factors such as ammunition, personnel, status of fuel, and weapon systems are assessed and rated.

Combat power: The total means of destructive and/or disruptive force which a military unit/formation can apply against the opponent at a given time.

Combined arms: The synchronized or simultaneous application of several arms - such as infantry, armor, field artillery, engineers, air defense, and aviation - to achieve an effect on the enemy that is greater than if each arm were used against the enemy in sequence.

Commander's critical information requirements (CCIR): A comprehensive list of information requirements identified by the commander as being critical in facilitating timely information management and the decisionmaking process that affect successful mission accomplishment. The two key subcomponents are critical friendly force information and priority intelligence requirements. Elements of information required by commanders that directly affect decisionmaking and dictate the successful execution of military operations.

Commander's intent: A clear, concise statement of what the force must do and the conditions the force must meet to succeed with respect to the enemy, terrain, and desired end state.

Common operational picture (COP): An operational picture tailored to the user's requirements, based on common data and information shared by more than one command.

Concept of operations (CONOP): How commanders see the actions of subordinate units fitting together to accomplish the mission. As a minimum, the description includes the scheme of maneuver and concept of fires. The concept of operations expands the commander' s selected course of action and expresses how each element of the force will cooperate to accomplish the mission.

Decisive point: A geographic place, specific key event, critical system or function that allows commanders to gain a marked advantage over an enemy and greatly influence the outcome of an attack.

Decisive engagement: In land and naval warfare, an engagement in which a unit is considered fully committed and cannot maneuver or extricate itself. In the absence of outside assistance, the action must be fought to a conclusion and either won or lost with the forces at hand.

Economy of force: One of the nine principles of war: Allocate minimum essential combat power to secondary efforts.

Exploitation: Taking full advantage of success in military operations, following up initial gains,and making permanent the temporary effects already achieved. An offensive operation that usually follows a successful attack and is designed to disorganize the enemy in depth.

Forward edge of the battle area (FEBA): The foremost limits of a series of areas in which ground combat units are deployed, excluding the areas in which the covering or screening forces are operating, designated to coordinate fire support, the positioning of forces, or the maneuver of units.

Forward line of own troops (FLOT): A line which indicates the most forward positions of friendly forces in any kind of military operation at a specific time. The forward line of own troops (FLOT) normally identifies the forward location of covering and screening forces. The FLOT may be at, beyond, or short of the forward edge of the battle area. An enemy FLOT indicates the forward-most position of hostile forces.

Main effort: The activity, unit, or area that commanders determine constitutes the most important task at that time.

Objective (OBJ): The clearly defined, decisive, and attainable goals towards which every military operation should be directed.

Phase: A specific part of an operation that is different from those that precede or follow. A change in phase usually involves a change of task.

Scheme of maneuver: Description of how arrayed forces will accomplish the commander's intent. It is the central expression of the commander's concept for operations and governs the design of supporting plans or annexes.

Screen: A task to maintain surveillance; provide early warning to the main body; or impede, destroy, and harass enemy reconnaissance within its capability without becoming decisively engaged. A form of security operation that primarily provides early warning to the protected force.

6.22.5 Graphic Control Measures

Area of operations (AO): An operational area defined by the joint force commander for land and naval forces. Areas of operations do not typically encompass the entire operational area of the joint force commander, but should be large enough for component commanders to accomplish their missions and protect their forces.

Avenue of approach (AA): An air or ground route of an attacking force of a given size leading to its objective or to key terrain in its path.

Axis of advance: An axis of advance designates the general area through which the bulk of a unit's combat power must move.

Engagement area (EA): An area where the commander intends to contain and destroy an enemy force with the massed effects of all available weapons and supporting systems.

Final protective fire (FPF): An immediately available prearranged barrier of fire designed to impede enemy movement across defensive lines or areas.

Final protective line (FPL): A line of fire selected where an enemy assault is to be checked by interlocking fire from all available weapons and obstacles.

Limit of advance (LOA): A phase line used to control forward progress of the attack. The attacking unit does not advance any of its elements or assets beyond the limit of advance, but the attacking unit can push its security forces to that limit.

Line of departure (LD): A phase line crossed at a prescribed time by troops initiating an offensive operation.

Phase line (PL): A line utilized for control and coordination of military operations, usually an easily identified feature in the operational area.

Rally point: An easily identifiable point on the ground at which units can reassemble and reorganize if they become dispersed.

Release point (RP): A location on a route where marching elements are released from centralized control.

Start point (SP): Well defined point on a route at which a movement of vehicles begins to be under the control of the commander of this movement. It is at this point that the column is formed by the successive passing, at an appointed time, of each of the elements composing the column. In addition to the principal start point of a column there may be secondary start points for its different elements. A location on the route where the marching element falls under the control of a designated march commander.

6.22.6 Leader's Reference

METT-C
Mission
Enemy
Terrain and Weather
Troops Available
Time Available
Civilian Considerations

OCOKA
Observation and Fields of Fire
Cover and Concealment
Obstacles
Key Terrain
Avenues of Approach

Five Point Contingency Plan (GOTWA)
Going, where the PL/SL is going
Others, who is going with him
Time, how long they will be gone
What, what happens if they do not return
Actions, actions on enemy contact

Principles of War
Mass
Objective
Simplicity
Economy of Force
Security
Maneuver
Offensive
Unity of Command
Surprise

Tenets of Army Operations
Agility
Initiative
Depth
Synchronization
Versatility

Elements of Combat Power
Maneuver
Firepower
Leadership
Information

Battlefield Operating Systems
Intelligence
Maneuver
Fire Support
Air Defense
Mobility/Counter mobility/Survivability
Combat Service Support
Command and Control

6.22.7 Command and Support Relationships

Command Relationships:
- **Organic:** TO&E or TDA.
- **Assigned:** Placed in an organization on a permanent basis for its primary function. Controlled and administered by unit to which assigned.
- **Attached:** Placed in an organization on a temporary basis. Controlled by and logistically supported by unit attached to. UCMJ/Administrative normally retained by unit of assignment.
- **Operational Control (OPCON):** Unit provided to another commander to accomplish specific missions or tasks. Administrative and logistical support from assigned unit. OPCON does not include UCMJ, administrative or logistic responsibility

Support Relationships:
- **General Support (GS):** The action given to a supported force as a whole rather than to a particular subdivision thereof.
- **Mutual Support:** The action that units render each other against an enemy because of their assigned tasks, their position relative to each other and to the enemy, and their inherent capabilities.
- **Direct Support (DS):** A mission requiring a force to support another specific force and authorizing it to answer directly the supported force 's request for assistance.
- **Close Support:** The action of the supporting force against targets or objectives that are sufficiently near the supported force as to require detailed integration or coordination of the supporting action with fire, movement, or other actions of the supported force.

2-30-2-34, FM 3-0, Army Operations

6.22.8 MDMP

References:

FM 5-0 Army Planning and Orders Production (Oct 04)

Military Decision Making Process (MDMP)		
Input	**Steps**	**Output**
- Mission received from higher - HQs or deduced by commander and staff	**Step 1: Receipt of Mission**	- Cdr's Initial Guidance - WARNO
- Higher HQs order/plan - Higher HQs IPB - Staff Estimates	**Step 2: Mission Analysis**	- Restated mission - Initial Cdr's intent and planning guidance - Initial CCIR - Updated staff estimates - Initial IPB products - Initial ISR Plan - Preliminary movement
- Restated mission - Initial Cdr's intent, planning guidance, and CCIR - Updated staff estimates - Initial IPB products	**Step 3: COA Development**	- Updated staff estimates and products - COA statements and sketches - Refined Cdr's intent and planning guidance
- Refined Cdr's intent and planning guidance - Enemy COAs - COA statements and sketches	**Step 4: COA Analysis (War Game)**	- War-Game results - Decision support templates - Task organization - Mission to subordinate units - Recommended CCIR
- War-Game results - Criteria for comparison	**Step 5: COA Comparison**	- Decision Matrix
- Decision Matrix	**Step 6: COA Approval**	- Approved COA - Refined Cdr's intent - Refined CCIR - High pay-off target list
- Approved COA - Refined Cdr's intent and guidance - Refined CCIR	**Step 7: Orders Production**	- OPLAN/OPORD

Figure 3-1. The Military Decision Making Process
FM 5-0. Army Planning and Orders Production

6.22.9 Products

6.22.9.1 Orders

References:

FM 1-02	Operational Terms and Graphics (Sep 04) formerly FM 101-5-1
FM 3-0	Operations (Jun 01)
FM 5-0	Army Planning and Orders Production (Jan 05)

6.22.9.1.1 WARNO

Warning order (WARNO): Preliminary notice of an order/action to follow.

[Classification]
(Change from verbal orders, if any) (Optional)
[Heading data is the same as for OPLAN/OPORD]

WARNING ORDER [number]
References: Refer to higher headquarters OPLAN/OPORD, and identify map sheets for operation (Optional).
Time Zone Used Throughout the Order: (Optional)
Task Organization: (Optional) (See paragraph 1c.)

1. SITUATION.

a. Enemy forces. Include significant changes in enemy composition, dispositions, and COAs. Information not available can be included in subsequent WARNOs.

b. Friendly forces. (Optional) Address only if essential to the WARNO.

(1) Higher commander's mission.

(2) Higher commander's intent.

c. Environment. (Optional) Address only if essential to the WARNO.

(1). Terrain.

(2). Weather.

(3). Civil considerations.

Attachments and detachments. Initial task organization. Address only major unit changes.

2. MISSION. Issuing headquarters' mission. This may be the higher headquarters' restated mission or commander's decisions during the MDMP.

3. EXECUTION.

Intent:

a. Concept of operations. This may be "to be determined" for the initial WARNO.

b. Tasks to maneuver units. Any information on tasks to units for execution, movement to initiate, reconnaissance to initiate, or security to emplace.

c. Tasks to other combat and combat support units. See paragraph 3b.

d. Coordinating instructions. Include any information available at the time of the issuance of the WARNO. It may include the following:

- CCIR.
- Risk guidance.
- Time line.
- Deception guidance.
- Orders group meeting information.
- Specific priorities, in order of completion.
- Earliest movement time and degree of notice.
- Guidance on orders and rehearsals.

4. SERVICE SUPPORT. (Optional) Include any known logistics preparations.

a. Special equipment. Identify requirements and coordinate transfer to using units.

b. Transportation. Identify requirements, and coordinate for pre-position of assets.

5. COMMAND AND SIGNAL. (Optional)

a. Command. State the chain of command if different from unit SOP.

b. Signal. Identify the current SOI. Pre-position signal assets to support operation.

ACKNOWLEDGE:
[Authentication data is the same as for OPLAN/OPORD]
ANNEXES:
DISTRIBUTION:

[Classification]

Figure G-7. Warning Order Format
FM 5-0. Army Planning and Orders Production (Jan 05)

6.22.9.1.2 OPLAN/OPORD Outline

Operation order (OPORD): A directive issued by a commander to subordinate commanders for the purpose of effecting the coordinated execution of an operation. Also called the five paragraph field order, it contains as a minimum a description of the task organization, situation, mission, execution, administrative and logistics support, and command and signal for the specified operation.

Operation plan (OPLAN): An operation plan for the conduct of joint operations that can be used as a basis for development of an operation order (OPORD). An OPLAN identifies the forces and supplies required to execute the CINC's Strategic Concept and a movement schedule of these resources to the theater of operations. The forces and supplies are identified in TPFDD files. OPLANs will include all phases of the tasked operation. The plan is prepared with the appropriate annexes, appendixes, and TPFDD files as described in the Joint Operation Planning and Execution System manuals containing planning policies, procedures, and formats.

[Classification]
[Change from verbal orders, if any]

Copy ## of ## copies
Issuing headquarters
Place of issue
Date-time group of signature
Message reference number

OPERATION PLAN/ORDER [number] [code name]
References
Time Zone Used Throughout the OPLAN/OPORD:
Task Organization
1. SITUATION.
  a. Enemy forces.
  b. Friendly forces.
  c. Environment
    (1). Terrain.
    (2). Weather.
    (3). Civil Considerations.
  d. Attachments and detachments.
  e. Assumptions.
2. MISSION.
3. EXECUTION.
  Intent:
  a. Concept of operations.
    (1) Maneuver.
    (2) Fires.
    (3) Intelligence, Surveillance, and Reconnaissance.
    (4) Intelligence.
    (5) Engineer.
    (6) Air and Missile Defense.
    (7) Information Operations.
    (8). Nuclear, Biological, Chemical.
    (9). Military Police.
    (10) Civil-Military Operations.
  b. Tasks to maneuver units.
  c. Tasks to other combat and combat support units.
  d. Coordinating instructions.
    (1) Time or condition when the plan/order becomes effective.
    (2) CCIR (PIR, FFIR).
    (3) Risk reduction control measures.
    (4) Rules of engagement.
    (5) Environmental considerations.
    (6) Force protection.
    (7) As required.
4. SERVICE SUPPORT (Support Concept).

[Classification]

[Classification]

OPLAN/OPORD [number] [code name]—[issuing headquarters]

b. Materiel and services.

c. Health service support.

d. Personnel.

e. As required.

5. COMMAND AND SIGNAL.

a. Command.

b. Signal.

ACKNOWLEDGE:
[Commander's last name]
[Commander's rank]
OFFICIAL:
[Authenticator's Name]
[Authenticator's Position]
ANNEXES:
DISTRIBUTION:

[Classification]

Figure G-2. OPLAN/OPORD Outline Format
FM 5-0. Army Planning and Orders Production (Jan 05)

6.22.9.1.3 Annexes

Annex A (Task Organization)
Annex B (Intelligence)
  Appendix 1 (Intelligence Estimate)
  Appendix 2 (Intelligence Synchronization Plan)
  Appendix 3 (Counterintelligence)
  Appendix 4 (Weather)
  Appendix 5 (IPB Products)
Annex C (Operation Overlay)
Annex D (Fire Support)
  Appendix 1 (Air Support)
  Appendix 2 (Field Artillery Support)
  Appendix 3 (Naval Gunfire Support)
Annex E (Rules of Engagement)
  Appendix 1 (ROE Card)
Annex F (Engineer)
  Appendix 1 (Obstacle Overlay)
  Appendix 2 (Environmental Considerations)
  Appendix 3 (Terrain)
  Appendix 4 (Mobility/Countermobility/ Survivability Execution Matrix and Timeline)
  Appendix 5 (Explosive Ordnance Disposal)
Annex G (Air and Missile Defense)
Annex H (Command, Control, Communication, and Computer Operations)
Annex I (Service Support)
  Appendix 1 (Service Support Matrix)
  Appendix 2 (Service Support Overlay)
  Appendix 3 (Traffic Circulation and Control)
  Tab A (Traffic Circulation Overlay)
  Tab B (Road Movement Table)
  Tab C (Highway Regulation
  Appendix 4 (Personnel)
  Appendix 5 (Legal)
  Appendix 6 (Religious Support)
  Appendix 7 (Foreign and Host-Nation Support)
  Appendix 8 (Contracting Support)
  Appendix 9 (Reports)
Annex J (Nuclear, Biological, and Chemical Operations)
Annex K (Provost Marshal)
Annex L (Intelligence, Surveillance, and Reconnaissance Operations)
  Appendix 1 (ISR Tasking Plan/ Matrix.)
  Appendix 2 (ISR Overlay)
Annex M (Rear Area and Base Security)
Annex N (Space)
Annex O (Army Airspace Command and Control)
Annex P (Information Operations)
  Appendix 1 (OPSEC)
  Appendix 2 (PSYOP)
  Appendix 3 (Military Deception)
  Appendix 4 (Electronic Warfare)
  Appendix 5 (IO Execution Matrix)
Annex Q (Civil-Military Operations)
Annex R (Public Affairs)

Figure G-3. Sequence of Annexes and Appendixes to OPLANs/OPORDS FM 5-0. Army Planning and Orders Production (Jan 05)

6.22.9.1.4 Movement Order

[Classification]
(Change from verbal orders, if any)
[Heading data is the same as for OPLAN/OPORD]

MOVEMENT ORDER [number]
References:
Time Zone Used Throughout the Order:
Task Organization:

1. SITUATION.
   a. Enemy forces.
   b. Friendly forces.
   c. Attachments and detachments.
2. MISSION.
3. EXECUTION.
   a. Concept of movement.
   b. Tasks to subordinate units.
   c. Detailed timings.
   d. Coordinating instructions.
   (1) Order of March.
   (2) Routes.
   (3) Density.
   (4) Speed. (Include catch-up speed.)
   (5) Method of movement.
   (6) Defense on move.
   (7) Start, release, or other critical points.
   (8) Convoy control.
   (9) Harbor areas.
   (10) Instructions for halts.
   (11) Lighting.
   (12) Air support.
4. SERVICE SUPPORT.
   a. Traffic control (performed by MPs).
   b. Recovery.
   c. Medical.
   d. Petroleum, oils, and lubricants.
   e. Water.
5. COMMAND AND SIGNAL.
   a. Command.
      (1) Location of commander and chain of command.
      (2) Locations of key individuals or particular vehicles.
   b. Signal.

ACKNOWLEDGE:
[Authentication data is the same as for OPLAN/OPORD]
ANNEXES:
DISTRIBUTION:

[Classification]

Figure G-6. Movement Order Format
FM 5-0. Army Planning and Orders Production (Jan 05)

6.22.9.1.5 FRAGO

Fragmentary order (FRAGO): An abbreviated form of an operation order (verbal, written, or digital) usually issued on a day-to-day basis that eliminates the need for restating information contained in a basic operation order. It may be issued in sections. It is issued after an operation order to change or modify that order or to execute a branch or sequel to that order.

[Classification]
(Change from verbal orders, if any)

Copy ## of ## copies
Issuing headquarters
Place of issue
Date-time group of signature
Message reference number

FRAGMENTARY ORDER [number]
References: Refer to the order being modified.
Time Zone Used Throughout the Order:
1. SITUATION. Include any changes to the existing order or state, "No change"; for example, "No change to OPORD 02-XX."
2. MISSION. List the new mission or state, "No change."
3. EXECUTION. Include any changes or state, "No change."
Intent:
a. Concept of operations.
b. Tasks to subordinate units.
c. Coordinating instructions. Include statement, "Current overlay remains in effect "or "See change 1 to annex C, Operations Overlay." Mark changes to control measures on the overlay or issue a new overlay.
4. SERVICE SUPPORT. Include any changes to existing order or state, "No change."
5. COMMAND AND SIGNAL. Include any changes to existing order or state, "No change."
ACKNOWLEDGE:
[Commander's last name]
[Commander's rank]
OFFICIAL:
[Authenticator's Name]
[Authenticator's Position]
ANNEXES:
DISTRIBUTION:

[Classification]

Figure G-8. Fragmentary Order Format
FM 5-0. Army Planning and Orders Production (Jan 05)

6.22.9.2 Staff Study

Office Symbol (Marks Number) Date

MEMORANDUM FOR

SUBJECT:

1. PROBLEM.
2. RECOMMENDATION.
3. BACKGROUND.
4. FACTS.
5. ASSUMPTIONS.
6. COURSES OF ACTION.
7. CRITERIA.
a. Screening Criteria.
b. Evaluation Criteria.
c. Weighing of Criteria
8. ANALYSIS
a. COAs Screened Out.
b. COA 1
(1) Advantages
(2) Disadvantages
c. COA 2 (Use the same sub-subparagraphs as COA1)
9. COMPARISON.
10. CONCLUSION
11. COORDINATION
XO, UNIT CONCUR/NONCONCUR _______ CMT____________ DATE: ________
CDR, UNIT CONCUR/NONCONCUR _______ CMT____________ DATE: ________
12. APPROVAL/DISAPPROVAL
a. That the (state the approving authority and recommended solution).
APPROVED __________ DISAPPROVED ____________ SEE ME ___________
b. That the (Approving authority) sign the implementing directive(s) (TAB A).
APPROVED __________ DISAPPROVED ____________ SEE ME ___________
13. POINT OF CONTACT

[#] Encl **[SIGNATURE BLOCK]**
1. Implementing Document
2. Tasking Document
3. Coordination List
4. Nonconcurrences
5. Other supporting documents, list as separate annexes

Figure A-1. Format for Staff Study
FM 5-0. Army Planning and Orders Production (Jan 05)

6.22.9.3 Decision Paper

Office Symbol (Marks Number) Date
MEMORANDUM FOR
SUBJECT:
1. For **DECISION.**
2. PURPOSE.
3. RECOMMENDATION.
4. BACKGROUND AND DISCUSSION.
5. IMPACTS.
6. COORDINATION.
XO, UNIT CONCUR/NONCONCUR _______ CMT____________ DATE: ________
CDR, UNIT CONCUR/NONCONCUR _______ CMT____________ DATE: ________
7. APPROVAL/ DISAPPROVAL.
a. That the (state the approving authority and recommended solution).
APPROVED____________DISAPPROVED____________SEE ME____________
b. That the (approving authority) sign the implementing directive(s) (TAB A).
APPROVED____________DISAPPROVED____________SEE ME____________
8. POINT OF CONTACT.
[#] Encl **[SIGNATURE BLOCK]**
1. Implementing document (TAB A)
2. Tasking document (TAB B)
3. Coordination list (TAB C)
4. Nonconcurrences (TAB D)
5. Other supporting documents, listed as separate enclosures (TABS E through Z)

Figure A-2. Format for a Decision Paper.
Figure A-1. Format for Staff Study

6.22.9.4 Meetings/Briefings

References:
TC 25-30 A Leader's Guide to Company Training Meetings (Apr 94)

1. Analyze Situation and Prepare a Briefing Outline. **a. Audience.** • Number? • Composition? Single service/joint? Civilians? Foreign nationals? • Who are the ranking members? • What are their official positions? • Where are they assigned? • How well do they know the subject? • Are they generalists or specialists? • What are their interests? • What are their personal pref? • What is the anticipated reaction? **b. Purpose and Type.** • Information briefing (to inform)? • Decision briefing? • Mission briefing? • Staff briefing? **c. Subject of Briefing.** • What is the specific subject? • What is the desired coverage? • How much time will be allocated? **d. Physical Facilities/Support Needed** • Where is the briefing presented? • What arrangements are required? • What are the visual aid facilities? • What are the deficiencies? • What actions are needed to overcome deficiencies? **e. Prepare Schedule.** • Finish analysis of the situation. • Prepare preliminary outline. • Determine requirements • Edit or redraft. • Schedule rehearsals, facilities, and critiques. • Arrange for final review	**2. Construct Briefing.** **a. Collect Material.** • Research. • Become familiar with the subject. • Collect authoritative opinions/facts. **b. Prepare First Draft.** • State problem (if necessary). • Isolate key points (facts). • Identify courses of action. • Analyze and compare COAs (State advantages/disadvantages.) • Conclusions & recommendations. • Prepare draft outline. • Include visual aids. • Fill in appropriate material. • Review with appropriate authority. **c. Revise First Draft and Edit.** • Ensure facts are important and necessary. • Include all necessary facts and answers to anticipated questions. • Polish material. **d. Plan Use of Visual Aids.** • Check for simplicity and readability. • Develop method for use. **e. Practice.** • Rehearse (with visual aids). • Polish. • Isolate key points. • Memorize outline. • Develop transitions. • Use definitive words. **3. Deliver Briefing.** **4. Follow-up.** **a.** Ensure understanding. **b.** Record decision. **c.** Inform proper authorities.

Figure B-3. Briefing Checklist
FM 5-0. Army Planning and Orders Production (Jan 05)

6.22.9.4.1 Information Brief

1. Introduction

a. Greeting. Address the audience. Identify yourself and your organization.

b. Type and Classification of Briefing. For example, "This is an information briefing. It is classified SECRET."

c. Purpose and Scope. Describe complex subjects from general to specific.

d. Outline or Procedure. Briefly summarize the key points and general approach. Explain any special procedures (such as, demonstrations, displays, or tours). For example, "During my briefing, I'll discuss the six phases of our plan. I'll refer to maps of our area of operations. Then my assistant will bring out a sand table to show you the expected flow of battle." The key points may be placed on a chart that remains visible throughout the briefing.

2. Main Body

a. Arrange the main ideas in a logical sequence.
b. Use visual aids to emphasize main ideas.
c. Plan effective transitions from one main point to the next.
d. Be prepared to answer questions at any time.

3. Closing

a. Ask for questions.
b. Briefly recap main ideas and make a concluding statement.
c. Announce the next speaker.

Figure B-1. Information Brief Format
FM 5-0. Army Planning and Orders Production (Jan 05)

6.22.9.4.2 Training Meeting

Training meetings:

- Are non-negotiable at battalion and company level.
- Focus on:
  - Battalion level: training management issues for the next 6 to 8 weeks.
  - Company, battery, troop level: specifics of executing scheduled training to standard.
  - Platoon and squad level:
    - Identify essential platoon/squad/crew collective, leader, and individual soldier task(s) training requirements.
    - Input those identified platoon/squad/crew, leader, and individual soldier training requirements.
    - Brief and review published training schedules with the platoon/squad/crew.
- Are conducted by commanders; CSMs and 1SGs assist commanders.
  - Post unit training schedules.
  - Are routinely scheduled on the same week day and same time.
  - Follow a published agenda and do not exceed allotted time.
  - Are conducted weekly for AC and monthly for RC at battalion and company level.
- CSMs and 1SGs ensure that individual soldier training supports collective unit training.
- Are a vehicle for leader development.
- Are a forum to:
  - Ensure that training is METL-related.
  - Solicit evaluation feedback.
  - Solicit training requirement input from platoon leaders and platoon sergeants.
  - Assess current status of training proficiency.
  - Identify key soldier changes and resource requirements.
  - Review commander's current training guidance, short-range plan, and projected resources.
  - Provide guidance on pre-execution checks.
  - Ensure that risk management is integrated into pre-execution checks.
  - Monitor pre-execution checks.
  - Resolve problems identified during pre-execution checks updates.
  - Identify and coordinate multi-echelon training opportunities.
  - Share training tactics, techniques, and procedures (TTP).
  - Allocate resources and approve ongoing near-term training.
- Result in a coordinated and locked-in training schedule

Figure 4-48. Training Meetings
FM 7-1. Battle Focused Training

6.22.9.4.3 Decision Brief

1. Introduction
- **a. Greeting**. Address the decision maker. Identify yourself and your organization.
- **b. Type and Classification of Briefing**. For example, "This is a decision briefing. It is UNCLASSIFIED."
- **c. Problem Statement.**
- **d. Recommendation.**

2. Body
- **a. Facts**. An objective presentation of both positive and negative facts bearing upon the problem.
- **b. Assumptions**. Necessary assumptions made to bridge any gaps in factual data.
- **c. Solutions**. A discussion of the various options that can solve the problem.
- **d. Analysis**. The criteria by which you will evaluate how to solve the problem (screening and evaluation). A discussion of each course of actions relative advantages and disadvantages.
- **e. Comparison**. Show how the courses of action rate against the evaluation criteria.
- **f. Conclusion**. Describe why the selected solution is best.

3. Closing
- **a.** Questions?
- **b.** Restatement of the recommendation.
- **c.** Request a decision.

Figure B-2. Decision Brief Format
FM 5-0. Army Planning and Orders Production (Jan 05)

6.22.10 Training Process

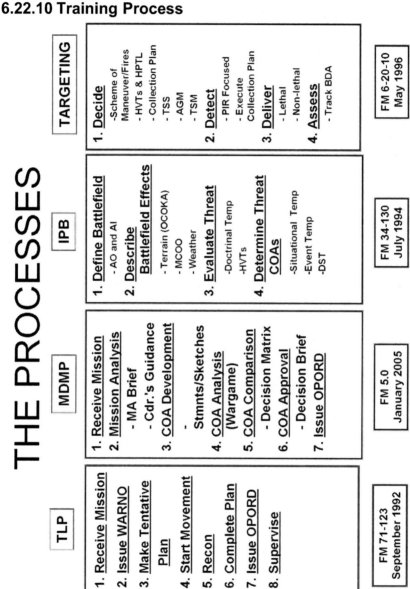

THE PROCESSES

TLP

1. Receive Mission
2. Issue WARNO
3. Make Tentative Plan
4. Start Movement
5. Recon
6. Complete Plan
7. Issue OPORD
8. Supervise

FM 71-123
September 1992

MDMP

1. Receive Mission
2. Mission Analysis
   - MA Brief
   - Cdr.'s Guidance
3. COA Development
   - Stmnts/Sketches
4. COA Analysis (Wargame)
5. COA Comparison
   - Decision Matrix
6. COA Approval
   - Decision Brief
7. Issue OPORD

FM 5.0
January 2005

IPB

1. Define Battlefield
   - AO and AI
2. Describe Battlefield Effects
   - Terrain (OCOKA)
   - MCOO
   - Weather
3. Evaluate Threat
   - Doctrinal Temp
   - HVTs
4. Determine Threat COAs
   - Situational Temp
   - Event Temp
   - DST

FM 34-130
July 1994

TARGETING

1. Decide
   - Scheme of Maneuver/Fires
   - HVTs & HPTL
   - Collection Plan
   - TSS
   - AGM
   - TSM
2. Detect
   - PIR Focused
   - Execute Collection Plan
3. Deliver
   - Lethal
   - Non-lethal
4. Assess
   - Track BDA

FM 6-20-10
May 1996

6.23 Weapon Systems

References:

FM 3-22.9	Rifle Marksmanship M16A1, M16A2/3, M16A4 and M4 Carbine (Apr 05)
FM 3-22.27	MK 19, 40-mm Grenade Machine Gun, Mod 3 (Nov 03)
FM 3-22.31	40-MM Grenade Launcher, M203 (Feb 03)
FM 3-22.65	Browning Machine Gun, Caliber .50 HB, M2 (Mar 05)
FM 3-22.68	Crew-served Machine Guns, M249, 5.56mm Machine Gun; M60, 7.62mm Machine Gun; M240B, 7.62mm Machine Gun (Jan 03)
FM 3-23.35	Combat Training with Pistols, M9 and M11 (Sep 05)
FM 23-10	Sniper Training (Aug 94)
TM 9-1005-317-10	Semiautomatic, 9mm, M9
TM 9-1005-319-10	Carbine, 5.56mm, M4A1
TM 9-1005-201-10	Machine Gun, 5.56mm, M249
TM 9-1005-213-10	Machine Guns, Caliber .50, M2
TM 9-1005-313-10	Machine Gun, 7.62mm, M240B

Weapons Tasks

- Know effective ranges and how to employ all weapons systems in your unit
- Engage targets, correct malfunctions, and PMCS:
    - M4/M16A2 Rifle
    - M203 grenade launcher
    - M9 Pistol
    - M249 machine gun
    - M240B machine gun
    - M2 50cal machine gun
    - MK-19 machine gun
- Engage targets with weapon using a night vision sight (AN/PVS-4, AN/PAS-13, AN/TVS-5)
- Engage targets using an aiming light (AN/PEQ-2A, AN/PAQ-4)
- Employ mines and hand grenades

Training/Operations

Part

7 Training/Operations

References:

AR 350-1	Army Training and Education (Jan 06)
FM 1-02	Operational Terms and Graphics (Sep 04) formerly FM 101-5-1
FM 3-0	Operations (Jun 01)
FM 5-0	Army Planning and Orders Production (Jan 05)
FM 7-0	Training the Force (Oct 02)
FM 7-1	Battle Focused Training (Sep 03)
FM 25-4	How To Conduct Training Exercises (Sep 84)
FM 25-5	Training for Mobilization and War (Jan 85)
FM 100-14	Risk Management (Apr 98)
FM 101-5-2	US Army Report and Message Formats (Jun 99)

Quick Checks:
- What is your platoon's status on collective tasks (Trained, needs Practice, or Untrained)?
- Read the evaluation of your platoon's performance on the last formal evaluation and talk to your NCOs about the strengths and weaknesses of your platoon.

Tips/Tricks:
- It is not cheating to read the book. Get a copy of the Mission Training Plan for your unit and print it to fit in your cargo pocket. In the MTP, it lists all the subtasks under each collective task.

TRAINING	
PL	**PSG/NCO'S**
Looks up specific tasks and forms platoon training schedule. Turns into Company Operations.	Gives PL assessment of Platoon training. Recommends future training. Gives PL estimated time needed to train each task.
Uses PSG's recommendations for instructors for training	Ensures all instructors validate their training before execution.
Briefs CO/Operations Sergeant at Training Meetings	Resources training.
Supervises training. Conducts AAR with leaders after training.	Executes training.

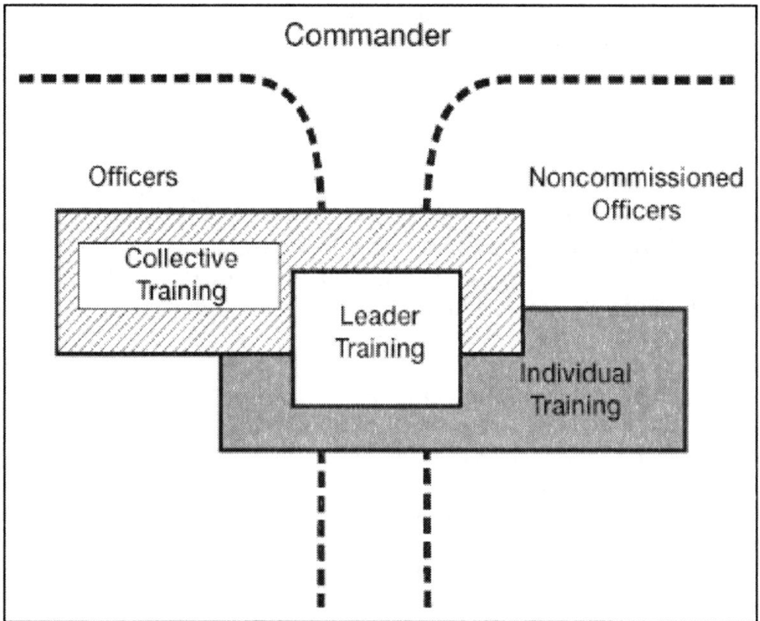

Figure 2-5. Overlapping Training Responsibilities
FM 7-0. Training the Force (Oct 02)

7.1 Responsibilities

Commander's Responsibility:

- Wartime readiness of all elements in the formation
- Using appropriate doctrine and mission training plans (MTPs), develops the unit's METL and creates unit training plan. Develop, publish, and enforce individual, collective, and unit performance standards. Publish their training philosophy, annual/quarterly training guidance.
- Primary trainer of the organization, responsible for ensuring that training is with the unit's mission essential task list (METL), are actively engaged in the training process, and adhere to the 10 principles of training
- Responsible for resourcing, ensuring stability and predictability, protecting training from interference, and executing and assessing training.
- Ensure MTP standards are met during all training. Retrain until the tasks are performed to standard. Train to standard, not to time.
- Commanders conduct unit training to prepare soldiers and leaders for unit missions by:
  - Be present at training to maximum extent possible.

- Base training on mission requirements.
- Train to applicable Army standards.
- Assess current levels of proficiency.
- Provide the required resources.
- Develop and execute training plans that result in proficient individuals, leaders, and units.

- Commanders delegate authority to NCOs in the support channel as the primary trainers of individuals, crews, and small teams. Commanders hold NCOs responsible for conducting standards-based, performance-oriented, battle-focused training and provide feedback on individual, crew, and team proficiency.

NCO Responsibility:

- Responsible for the individual training of soldiers, crews, and small teams.
- Continuation of the soldierization process of new soldiers when they arrive in the unit.
- NCO Support Channel (leadership chain) parallels and complements the chain of command.
- Responsible for conducting standards-based, performance-oriented, battle-focused training by:
  - Identify specific individual, crew, and small team tasks that support the unit's collective mission essential tasks.
  - Plan, prepare, rehearse, and execute training.
  - Evaluate training and conduct AARs to provide feedback to the commander on individual, crew, and small team proficiency.
- Senior NCOs coach junior NCOs to master a wide range of individual tasks.

Unit Responsibility:

- Collective training that is derived directly from METL and MTPs
- Leader development that is embedded in the collective training tasks and in discrete individual leader focused training
- Individual training that establishes, improves, and sustains individual soldier proficiency in tasks directly related to the unit METL.

1-30 to 1-34, FM 7-0. Training the Force (Oct 02)

7.2 Types of Training

How the Army Trains:

- Develop trust soldier-to-soldier, leader to led, unit-to-unit in the Army and grow the war-fighting confidence of the force.
- Train for decisive war-fighting.
- Train soldiers now, and grow leaders for the next conflict.
- Ensure that our soldiers are physically and mentally prepared to dominate the next battlefield—no soldier goes into harm's way untrained.
- Our soldiers must be comfortable and confident in the elements—fieldcraft, fieldcraft, fieldcraft.

1-1, FM 7-0. Training the Force (Oct 02)

Collective training:

- Derived directly from METL and MTPs

Leader development:

- Embedded in the collective training tasks and in discrete individual leader focused training

Individual training:

- Establishes, improves, and sustains individual soldier proficiency in tasks directly related to the unit METL.

1-34, FM 7-0. Training the Force (Oct 02)

Essential task: A task that must be executed to accomplish the mission.

Implied task: A task that must be performed to accomplish the mission, but is not stated in the higher headquarters order.

Specified task: A task specifically assigned to a unit by its higher headquarters.

10 Principles of Training

1. Commanders are responsible for training.
2. NCOs train individuals, crews, and small teams.
3. Train as a combined arms and joint team.
4. Train for combat proficiency.
   - Realistic conditions.
   - Performance-oriented.
5. Train to standard using appropriate doctrine.
6. Train to adapt.
7. Train to maintain and sustain.
8. Train using multi-echelon techniques.
9. Train to sustain proficiency.
10. Train and develop leaders.

Figure 2-1. Principles of Training
FM 7-0. Training the Force (Oct 02)

7.3 METL

METL:

A mission essential task is a collective task in which an organization has to be proficient to accomplish an appropriate portion of its wartime operational mission.

Para 3-1. FM 7-1. Battle Focused Training

Fundamental Concepts Used in METL Development:

- METL is derived from the organization's war plans and related tasks in external guidance.
- METL must apply to the entire organization. METL does not include tasks assigned solely to subordinate organizations.
- METL must support and complement the METL of higher headquarters. METL for CS and CSS units must also support and complement the supported unit METL.
- Resource availability does not affect METL development. METL is an unconstrained statement of tasks required to accomplish wartime missions.
- METL is not prioritized. However, all tasks may not require equal training time.
- Commanders use BOS to apply combat power.

Figure 3-3. FM 7-1. Battle Focused Training

METL Crosswalk:

Your unit should have a METL Crosswalk. This starts with the unit's METL tasks, then breaks them down by collective, leader, and individual tasks. It should list the task name, number, and reference for each one.

METL Task: Protect the Force

Collective Task	Leader Task	Individual Task
- Establish a company defensive position (STP 21-1-SMCT: 071-326-5703)	- Supervise Construction of a Fighting Position (STP 19-95B24-SM: 071-326-5704)	- Construct Individual Fighting Positions (STP 21-1-SMCT: 071-326-5703)
	- Control Use of Night Vision Devices (STP 19-95C24-SM : 071-710-0004)	- Operate Night Vision Goggles AN/PVS-7 (STP 19-95B1-SM: 071-710-0008)

Example from METL Crosswalk

7.4 Training Cycles

Green Cycle

- Training focus primarily on collective tasks with individual and leader tasks integrated during multi-echelon training.
- Maximum soldier attendance at prime time, mission essential training.
- Coincides with availability of major resources and key training facilities or devices.
- Administrative and support requirements that keep personnel from participating in training eliminated to the maximum extent possible.
- Leaves and passes limited to the minimum essential.

Amber Cycle

- Small unit, crew, leader and individual soldier training emphasized.
- Provides time for soldier attendance at education and training courses.
- Some sub-organizations may be able to schedule collective training.
- Scheduling of periodic maintenance services.
- Selected personnel diverted to support requirements when all available personnel in organizations in red period are completely committed to support requirements.

Red Cycle

- Maximize self development.
- Diverts the minimum essential number of personnel to perform administrative and support requirements.
- Sub-organizations take advantage of all training opportunities to conduct individual, leader, and crew training.
- Support missions/details accomplished with unit integrity to exercise the chain of command and provide individual training opportunities for first line supervisors, as time permits. Unit taskings can be used to reduce the number of permanent special duty personnel within installations and communities.
- Leaves and passes maximized. When appropriate, block leave may be scheduled.
- Routine medical, dental, and administrative appointments coordinated and scheduled with installation support facilities.

Figure 4-6. Green-Amber-Red Time Management System
FM 7-0. Training the Force (Oct 02)

7.5 Timeframes

Weeks T-8 to T-6

- Assess training and identify specific collective, leader, and individual soldier tasks that require additional training.
- Platoon leaders and sergeants, squad leaders and team leaders provide input on tasks that require additional training.
- Approve draft training schedules
- Request Class I, III, IV, and V supplies, TADSS, training areas, ranges, and other requirements.
- Provide pre-execution checks guidance
- Begin pre-execution checks.

Week T-5

- Company commander finalizes and signs training schedules.
- Battalion commander approves and signs training schedules.
- NCOs provide commander with individual soldier training objectives.
- Confirm support requests; lock in resources.
- Identify trainer, evaluator, OC, and OPFOR rehearsal requirements.
- Resolve scheduling conflicts.

Week T-4

- Post training schedules in the company area.
- Identify and brief trainers, evaluators, OCs, and OPFOR on responsibilities.
- Conduct initial trainer, evaluator, OC, and OPFOR backbriefs.

Week T-3

- Begin rehearsals for trainers, evaluators, OCs, and OPFOR.
- Continue to resolve scheduling conflicts.
- Recon training areas, ranges, firing points, Ops, and simulation facilities.
- Conduct IPR for trainers, evaluators, OCs, and OPFOR.

Week T-2

- Continue trainer, evaluator, OC, and OPFOR rehearsals and preparation.
- Conduct final IPR.

Week T-1

- Draw and test engagement simulation equipment and other training aids.
- Complete pre-execution checks. This includes trainer, evaluator, OC, and OPFOR rehearsals, and training site preparation (replicate training exercise conditions).
- Brief soldiers on details of training.

T Week

- Conduct pre-combat checks.
- Conduct training.
- Conduct AARs.

- Conduct retraining as necessary.

Week T+1

- Conduct recovery. This includes those actions to complete accountability actions for organizational and individual equipment and all after-operations PMCS.
- Conduct final AAR for the training event.
- Solicit training evaluation feedback.
- Solicit training requirement input from platoon leaders and platoon sergeants.
- Assess current status of training proficiency.

Figure 4-52, FM 7-1. Battle Focused Training

7.6 Training Records

Individual Training Records (ITR): must be maintained by the unit for all Soldiers. It is important to ensure these are updated. Most Soldiers packets will be reviewed for promotion boards and NCOES schools (PLDC, BNCOC). Training records include:

- Enlisted Records Brief (ERB) or Officer Record Brief (ORB)
- Weapons Qualification
- Physical Fitness Test Scorecards (DA Form 705)
- Physical Profiles (DA Form 3349)
- Driver's Record (DA Form 3626)
- Driver's License (DA Form 348)
- Technical skills (Aviations, MPOC)
- CTT Test Sheet
- AT Level 1 Training Certificate

7.7 8 Step Training Model

The 8-Step Training Model:
- Plan the Training
- Train and Certify Leaders
- Reconnoiter the Site
- Issue the Plan
- Rehearse
- Execute
- After Action Review
- Retrain

One Third, Two Thirds Rule:
One third of the time is yours for planning, two-thirds of the time belongs to your NCOs to execute the training.

7.7.1 Planning

References:
TC 25-1 Training Land (Mar 04)
TC 25-8 Training Ranges (Apr 04)

Preparation for Training
- Select tasks
- Plan the training
- Back-brief higher commander on major training events
- Train the trainers
- Recon the site
- Conduct risk management/assessment
- Issue the training plan
- Rehearse
- Conduct pre-execution checks

7.7.1.1 Training Schedules

The first step of preparation for training is to select the tasks. You should sit down with your NCOs and get their recommendations for future training. Look up the information (task name, task number, and reference) and come up with a tentative schedule. Have your NCOs recommend how long it takes to train each task and your platoon sergeant will help assign instructors.

Training schedules should:

- Specify when training starts and where it takes place.
- Allocate adequate time for scheduled training and retraining as required to correct anticipated deficiencies.
- Specify individual, leader, and collective tasks to be trained.
- Provide concurrent training topics that will efficiently use available training time.
- Specify who conducts the training and who evaluates the training.
- Provide administrative information concerning uniform, weapons, equipment, references, and safety precautions.

Figure 4-53. Training Schedule Content
FM 7-1. Battle Focused Training

Tips/Tricks

- Have an excel spreadsheet with all the CTT and MOS-specific tasks you train on (Task number, Task Name, Skill Level, and Reference). This will make it easier to "shop" for tasks when planning and provide all the information you need to make your schedule.

7.7.1.1.1 Formats

Websites:

SATs Homepage http://www.sats.army.mil/
DTMS Homepage https://dtms.army.mil/

Standard Army Training System (SATS)
SATS is the legacy software used by Army units to create their unit training schedules. It has officially been replaced by CATS, but many units still use it.

Combined Arms Training Strategy (CATS)
CATS is the new web-based training software that fills the same purpose as SATS. It has the same functionality to SATS, but allows higher echelons to view your training status. Has many tools like METL creator, QTB format, etc.

Digital Training Management System (DTMS)
DTMS is the higher echelon version of CATS. DTMS also accesses post master schedules (with installation schools, holidays, etc) and has a bulletin board for questions.

Other Formats
Although most companies will use an automated system, they will probably give you a standardized format in Microsoft Word or Excel for you to fill in and give to the Training NCO.

7.7.1.2 Resourcing

Resourcing training is part of your NCO's lane. Once you give them the training task and your initial guidance, you should not have to get involved. Only get involved if you have had problems in the past.

Definitions:

Basic load: The quantity of supplies required to be on hand within, and which can be moved by, a unit or formation. It is expressed according to the wartime organization of the unit or formation and maintained at the prescribed levels.

Combat load: The minimum mission-essential equipment, as determined by the commander responsible for carrying out the mission, required for soldiers to fight and survive immediate combat operations.

7.7.1.2.1 Training Aids

References:

PAM 350-9 Index and Description of Army Training Devices (Sep 02)

In order to make training realistic, it is important to have training aids available. Make sure all training has practical exercise. Do not fall into the Powerpoint trap; slides are not a substitution for hands on practice. Make sure that you have adequate quantities of training aids (do not have 2 MK-19s on hand when 30 Soldiers need to learn assembly/disassembly). Below is a list of training aids available at most installation TASC.

Training Aids:
- IV Arms
- Resuscitation Annies
- Moulage Kits
- MARK-1 Kits / Diazepam Injectors
- Rifle Rest
- Target Paddle
- Riddle Device
- M16 Sighting Device
- LMTS
- MACS

Weapon Aids:
- Mine Kits (U.S. Mines) TIED Kit
- AT4 Trainers and Subcaliber
- Plastic M16s

- Training Claymores
- Training IEDs/Munitions

Other Training Aids:
- Coffins and Flags
- Mapboards (Limited Quantities)
- Small Noise Simulator
- Static Displays
- Artillery Simulator
- Vehicle ID Kit
- Warlock Trainer
- Grenade ID Kit

7.7.1.2.2 OPFOR

References:

FM 7-100	Opposing Force Doctrinal Framework and Strategy (May 03)
FM 7-100.1	Opposing Force Operations (Dec 04)
FM 100-60	Armor and Mechanized-Based Opposing Force (Jul 97)
FM 100-63	Infantry-Based Opposing Forces (Apr 96)

Opposing Forces (OPFOR) are also essential to making training realistic. Ensure your OPFOR understands their role and the Tactics, Techniques, and Procedures of the enemy forces their resembling. Designate a section leader of the OPFOR and brief them on their mission and the overall effect they need to generate. If you unit is operating at a crawl pace, ensure OPFOR does not attack with sophisticated attacks. On the other end of the spectrum, ensure that when operating at a run phase, OPFOR uses sound tactics and challenges the Blue Force.

Opposing Forces (OPFOR) Aids:
- Shirts
- Weapons (In Limited Quantities)
- Pyrotechnics (Artillery Simulators, IED Simulators)
- Unexploded Ordnance (UXO)

7.7.1.3 Risk Assessment

References:

FM 3.100-4 Environmental Considerations in Military Opns (Jun 00)
FM 3-100.12 Risk Management (Feb 01)
GTA 21-08-001 Risk Management Information Card (Jun 00)

Forms:

DA 7566 Composite Risk Management Worksheet (Apr 05)

Websites:

US Army Safety Center http://crc.army.mil/

Definitions:

Risk assessment: The identification and assessment of hazards (first two steps of risk management process).

Risk management (RM): The process of identifying, assessing, and controlling risk arising from operational factors, and making informed decisions that balance risk cost with mission benefits.

Risk **E:** Extremely High **H:** High **M:** Moderate **L:** Low		HAZARD PROBABILITY				
		Frequent	**Likely**	**Occasional**	**Seldom**	**Unlikely**
SEVERITY	**Catastrophic**	**E**	**E**	**H**	**H**	**M**
	Critical	**E**	**H**	**H**	**M**	**L**
	Marginal	**H**	**M**	**M**	**L**	**L**
	Negligible	**M**	**L**	**L**	**L**	**L**

HAZARD PROBABILITY (The likelihood that an event will occur).

- **Frequent** -- The event occurs often in a soldier's career or is continuously experienced by all soldiers exposed.
- **Likely** – There is a good possibility that an event will occur several times in a soldier's career and is experienced a lot by the soldiers exposed.
- **Occasional** -- The event occurs once in a while such as, once in the

career of a soldier, or sporadically to all soldiers exposed.

- **Seldom** – There is a remote possibility that an event will occur in the career of a soldier. For a fleet or inventory, it would be unlikely but can be expected and would occur seldom to all soldiers exposed.
- **Unlikely** -- The possibility that an event would occur to in the career of a soldier is so rare that you can assume that it will not occur. It would most likely not occur within the fleet or inventory and very rarely occurs to all soldiers exposed.

SEVERITY (The expected consequence of an event in terms of degree of injury, property damage or other mission-impairing factors).
- **Catastrophic --** results in death or permanent total disability, a systems loss, or major property damage.
- **Critical** – results in severe injury. That is, permanent partial disability or temporary total disability in excess of three months for personnel, and major systems damage or significant property damage.
- **Marginal --** results in minor injury or lost workday accident for personnel. Minor systems or property damage.
- **Negligible --** first aid or less required. Minor systems impairment.

RISK LEVELS
- **E** (Extremely High) – Loss of ability to accomplish mission.
- **H** (High) – Significant degradation of mission capabilities in terms of required mission standard.
- **M** (Moderate) – Degradation of mission capabilities in terms of required mission standards.
- **L** (Low) – Little or no impact on accomplishment of mission.

7.7.2 Training Validation

When the training schedule is approved, the instructors should be locked in (at T+6). It is important that all instructors validate their training with the platoon sergeant at least two weeks out. This accomplishes the following:

- Ensures the instructor is well versed in the training subject
- Validates that the allotted time in the training schedule is adequate
- Ensures all resources are laid on
- Ensures training includes adequate practical exercise (hands-on training) for the Soldiers

7.7.3 Reconnaissance

Purpose:
- Determine suitability of site
- Ensure area meets training needs IAW doctrine, regulations, safety, etc
- Use as an opportunity for leaders to backbrief training plan
- Certify leaders (TEWT)
- Helps for producing graphics and terrain products, if necessary.

7.7.4 Issue the Plan

References:

FM 5-0 Army Planning and Orders Production (Jan 05)

When issuing the plan, remember that an 80% solution on time is better than a late 100% solution. The formats for WARNOs and OPORDs are in FM 5-0, as well in Chapter 7, Warrior Tasks, Tactics and Doctrine. Ensure the mission is clear and that you give a working timeline in your plan.

7.7.5 Rehearsals

References:
CALL 03-34 Mission Rehearsal Exercise

Rehearsal: An event in which one or more members of a unit practice, recite, recount, repeat, or drill a set of tasks or procedures to prepare for a formal performance. Used to ensure team members understand what they and other members of the team must accomplish to perform a task successfully.

Purpose:
- Serve as leader certification and training
- Help maximize training

Types:
- Radio Rehearsal
- Map Rehearsal
- Sketch Map Rehearsal
- Leader Rehearsal
- Rock Drill/ Sand Tables
- Reduced Forces Rehearsal
- Full Dress Rehearsal

7.7.6 Execution

Preparation for Training:	Conduct of Training:	Recovery from Training:
- Select Tasks - Plan the Training - Train the Trainers - Recon the Site - Conduct Risk Assessment - Issue Training Plan - Rehearse - Conduct Pre-Execution Checks	- Conduct Pre-Combat Checks - Supervise, Evaluate Hazard Controls - Implement Hazard Controls - Execute Training - Conduct After Action Reviews - Retrain at First Opportunity	- Conduct After Operations Maintenance Checks & Services - Equipment Accountability - Turn in Support Items - Close out training sites - Conduct After Action Reviews - Individual Soldier Recovery - Conduct Final Inspections - Conduct Risk Management Assessment and Review

Figure 5-1. Training Execution
FM 7-1. Battle Focused Training

7.7.6.1 Pre-execution Checklist

Sample Pre-Execution Checks
- Have previous lessons learned been integrated? - Have leaders identified and eliminated training distractors? - Have simulations, simulators, and other TADSS been included? - Have T&EOs and training outlines been acquired or prepared? - Have lane books been prepared? - Have TSPs been prepared? - Have SOPs been updated? - Have leaders been trained and their proficiency verified on leader and collective tasks? - Have OCs been identified, equipped, and trained? - Has the OPFOR been identified, equipped, and trained? - Have the OCs and OPFOR been verified on their task proficiency? - Have Soldiers been trained and verified on prerequisite individual (Soldier and leader) tasks, collective tasks, and battle drills prior to execution? - Have pre-LTX rehearsals been conducted? - Has rehearsal time been programmed during each LTX? - Are slice elements of other units integrated into planning and execution of training? - Have sufficient AARs been scheduled? - Is adequate time programmed for AARs? - Has a risk assessment been completed? - Has safety considerations been incorporated? - Have leaders been briefed on environmental protection rules and considerations? - Has a reconnaissance been conducted? - Are range or maneuver area books on hand? - Are leaders certified to conduct range operations? - Have convoy clearances been submitted and approved? - Has transportation been arranged? - Are organizational equipment and special tools oh hand? - Have TADSS been identified, requested, and acquired? - Can trainers operate all equipment, to include TADSS and targetry? - Have all equipment been tested, to include communications equipment? - Has Class I (rations) been requested and arranged? - Has Class III (POL) been requested and allocated? - Has Class IV (construction and barrier materials) been requested and picked up? - Has Class V (repair parts) been requested and pick-up times coordinated? - Are latrine facilities adequate? Have portable toilets been pre-positioned? - Are sufficient expendable supplies on hand? If not, have they been requested and arranged? - Has a back-brief to the chain of command been coordinated?

7.7.6.2 Constraints

References:
FM 3-07 Stability Operations and Support Operations (Feb 03)

When you are performing operations on a deployment, you are going to have certain constraints in which to operate in. Some examples are rules of engagement, Geneva Conventions, media policies, and general orders. It is important to incorporate these into all training. Being in a war zone is not the time to introduce new concepts to your Soldiers. During training, ensure you brief these constraints as part of the mission brief. As an Observer/Controller (OC) for training, make sure these constraints are followed.

Constraint: A restriction placed on the command by a higher command. A constraint dictates an action or inaction, thus restricting the freedom of action a subordinate commander has for planning.
Rules of engagement (ROE): Directives issued by competent military authority that delineate the circumstances and limitations under which United States forces will initiate and/or continue combat engagement with other forces encountered.

7.7.7 After Action Review

References:
TC 25-20 A Leader's Guide to After-Action Reviews (Sep 93)
GTA 25-06-023 After Action Review Techniques (Jan 97)

Tips/Tricks:
- Review what was supposed to happen (training plan).
- Establish what happened (to include OPFOR point of view).
- Determine what was right or wrong with what happened.
- Determine how the task should be done differently next time.

THE AFTER ACTION REVIEW SEQUENCE

1. State the training objectives.
2. Have the OPFOR leader restate his mission and present his plan.
3. Have the unit leader restate his mission and present his plan.
4. Review actions before first detection or contact.
5. Review first detection or contact.
6. Review report of first detection or contract.
7. Review reaction to detection or contract.
8. Review FRAGO if used.
9. Review events during engagement.
10. Review subsequent events.
11. Review extent to which unit met training objectives. [Trained/Practice Required/Untrained performance]
12. Have participants summarize the major learning points. [Basis for training objectives in next exercise]
13. Describe clear and concise training objectives for the next exercise. [Objectives must be measurable or observable.]

AFTER ACTION REVIEW TECHNIQUES

1. Use leading questions to guide the participants. [An example of a leading question is "Do you think that was a proper way to establish security?]
2. Cut off inappropriate discussion, particularly excuses and doctrinal debates.
3. Keep the review short and simple.
4. Allow all participants to contribute, not just the unit leaders.
5. Don't allow the participants to point fingers, attack or humiliate each other.
6. Let the participants identify their own mistakes, the controller does not critique.
7. Guide the participating leaders to identify the major learning points and let them decide if they met the training objective standard.
8. End the review with a concise summary of lessons learned and training objectives met and not met. **DO NOT CRITIQUE.** State the remedial training needs and the training objectives for the next exercise.

GTA 25-06-023, After Action Review (Aug 97)

Formal AAR	Informal AAR
- Conducted (or facilitated) by external OCs	- Conducted by internal chain of command
- More time to prepare	- Less time to prepare
- More time to conduct	- Less time to conduct
- Complex training aids	- Simple training aids
- Scheduled before-hand	- Scheduled or held when needed
- Conducted where best supported	- Conducted at the training site
- Conducted to gain maximum training benefit	- Conducted when resources are limited
- Normally for company-level and above	- Normally for Soldier, crew, squad, and platoon-level training
	- Support higher-level formal AAR
	- Held prior to higher-level formal AAR

7.7.8 Retrain

After you have identified training shortcomings in your After Action Review, develop a plan to correct the deficiencies. As platoon leader, your main mission is to allocate time for your NCOs to retrain Soldiers. Decide which tasks to add to the training schedule. Also emphasis which tasks are priority for hip pocket or other informal types of training. Set specific goals for when you will re-evaluate the training.

7.8 Crawl-Walk-Run

In crawl-walk-run training, the task and the standard remain the same, but the conditions may vary. Commanders change the conditions by increasing

- The difficulty of the conditions under which the task is being performed.
- The tempo of the task being trained.
- The number of tasks being trained.
- The number of personnel involved in the training.

from para 5-11, FM 7-1. Battle Focused Training

Crawl	Walk	Run
Soldiers: - Train each task step - Train task steps in sequence - Training complete task until done correctly	Soldiers: - Train to training objective standard - Train with more realism - Learn transfer skills that link other tasks. - Work as crews or small units	Soldiers: - Train collectively to achieve and sustain proficiency - Train under conditions that simulate actual combat - Develop effective team relationships
Leaders/Trainer: - Talk through and demonstrate each task - Supervise step-by-step practice - Coach frequently - Control the environment	Leaders/Trainer: - Walk through task using more realism - Increase complexity - Demonstrate authorized field expedients - Participate as leader of crew or small units - Observe, coach, and review	Leaders/Trainer: - Add realism and complexity - Combine tasks - Review Soldier and collective performance - Practice leader tasks - Work with Soldiers as a team - Coach and teach subordinate leaders

Figure 5-2. Crawl-Walk-Run Training
FM 7-1. Battle Focused Training

7.9 Garrison Training (Crawl)

In order to have success with training, it is important to train individual tasks in garrison. These tasks will be conducted mostly during Red cycle and some of Amber cycle.

7.9.1 350-1 Training

References:

AR 350-1 Army Training and Leader Development (Jan 06)
AR 600-20 Army Command Policy (Feb 06)
AR 690-12 Equal Opportunity Policy (Mar 88)
PAM 350-20 Unit Equal Opportunity Training Guide (Jun 94)

Forms:
DA 5287 Training Record Transmittal Jacket

Mandatory training is regulated by AR 350-1, Army Training and Leader Development (Jan 06), and the post equivalent (each post will have its own version. example: Fort Hood is FH 350-1).

SUBJECT	REFERENCE	FREQ
Weapons Qualification	AR 350-1: 4-14	T
Physical Fitness Combatives	AR 350-1: 4-12, 4-13	T
NBC	AR 350-1:4-15	T
PR Code of Conduct SERE	AR 350-1 4-17 AR 350-30	P
Law of War Detainee Ops	AR 350-1: 4-18	P
SAEDA	AR 381-12	P
Preventive Medicine	AR 40-5	P
Public Affairs	AR 360-81	P
AT/FP	AR 350-1: 4-19	I/P
Army Family Team Building	AR 608-99	I/P
Ethics	HQDA Letter	I/P
Cmd Climate EO Homosexual Fraternization	AR 600-20	I
Army Safety Program	AR 385-10 AR 385-63	I
Prevention of Motor Vehicular Accidents	AR 385-55	I
Military Justice	AR 27-10	I
Substance Abuse and Risk Reduction	AR 600-85	I
Employment and Reemployment Rights	DODI 1205.12	I for RC

T: Training during unit training
P: Predeployment: Train before deploying on operational mission
I: Inprocessing: Train when individual is assigned to unit

Table G-1. Common Military Training Requirements in Units
AR 350-1. Army Training and Leader Development (Jan 06)

Attendance
It is important that you and your platoon sergeant/squad leaders attend this training. If Soldiers see that their entire chain of command is using the time to type counselings, then they will assume the training is not important. Even though you are busy, make sure you are there for most of it and ensure that there is leadership from the platoon present at all times.

Additionally, mandatory training is a challenge for MOS's that do shift work (MPs, cooks, etc). Make sure that you schedule the training before or after shift and that you have multiple days scheduled. Having a Soldier come in during their rest schedule or on a day off is a result of poor planning and leadership.

Tracking/Paperwork
It is important to have a method of tracking who attended training. This becomes a big issue during commander's and inspector general inspections. Have a sign in roster for all training and schedule make up days for those that miss training.

7.9.2 Common Core Tasks

Soldier Training Plans:
21-1-SMCT Soldier's Manual of Common Tasks, SL 1 (Oct 05)
21-24-SMCT Soldier's Manual of Common Tasks, SL 2-4 (Aug 03)

Leader Duties:
- Select CTT tasks from current FY list (download from Reimer Digital Library)
- Evaluate tasks through collective field training or individual stations
- Assure proper equipment is available for training and evaluation

Evaluations:
All AA and AGR Soldiers in skill levels 1 through 4 will take a CTT annually. Other unit personnel may take the CTT at the discretion of the unit commander. All RC Soldiers in skill levels 1 through 4 will take the CTT every 2 years, or more frequently if desired by the unit commander.

from para 4-6b, AR 350-1

Tips/Tricks:
- Once your Commander has determined which of the current FY common core tasks the unit will test on, make a handbook with the tasks, conditions, standards, as well as the performance steps for all

those tasks. Take the book to the print plant and have copies made for all team leaders and above that will fit in a cargo pocket. This will facilitate hip pocket and other opportunity training on CTT.
- One Soldiers complete refresher training on Common Core Tasks, ensure they are able to perform them under more realistic conditions. For example, it a Soldier is applying a pressure dressing, the role player should not be laying still or goofing off. Have the role player writhe around and scream as if they were actually wounded.

7.9.3 Sergeant's Time

Commanders must institute sergeant's time training (STT) as a regular part of the unit's training program. Sergeant's time training recognizes that certain tasks are best trained by NCOs in a small group environment. The topics selected for STT must fit into the unit's overall training program and training plans. The topics will be based on the small unit leader's assessment of training areas that need special attention. The small unit leader recommends the training to be conducted at unit training meetings. When approved by the commander, it is properly resourced.

para 4-8, AR 350-1

Platoon Leader's Role:
- Plan tasks on training schedule
- Ensure PSG is validating instructors ahead of time
- Brief Commander on training
- Check on training (ensure you are in the same uniform as Soldiers)
- Conduct leader AAR with squad leaders and platoon sergeant

7.10 Unit Training Exercises (Walk)

References:

FM 21-18	Foot Marches (Jun 90)
FM 21-31	Topographic Symbols (Jun 61)
FM 21-60	Visual Signals (Sep 87)
FM 21-75	Combat Skills of the Soldier (Mar 84)
FM 25-4	How to Conduct Training Exercises (Sep 84)
TC 63-1	Combat Service Support LFX (Dec 04)
TC 7-9	Infantry Live-Fire Training (Sep 93)

Types of Training Events

- Joint Training Exercise (JTX)
- Situational Training Exercise (STX)
- Command Field Exercise (CFX)
- Command Post Exercise (CPX)
- Logistic Exercise (LOGEX)
- Live Fire Exercise (LFX)
- Map Exercise (MAPEX)
- CTC Rotations (CTC)
- Combined Training Exercise (CTX)
- Tactical Exercise Without Troops (TEWT)
- Deployment Exercise (DEPEX)
- Combined Arms Live Fire Exercise (CALFEX)
- Field Training Exercise (FTX)
- Fire Coordination Exercise (FCX)
- BCTP/BCBST and other Simulations

Figure 4-8. Types of Training Events
FM 7-0. Training the Force (Oct 02)

OBJ	MAPEX	TEWT	CPX	CFX	FCX	LFX	FTX
Use of Terrain		X		X		X	X
Maneuver				X	X	X	X
Staff Procedures	X		X	X			X
Weapons Employm		X		X	X	X	X
Fire Support/Coord			X	X	X	X	X
Combat Support				X		X	X
NBC Operations			X	X			X
Systems Integr	X		X	X	X		X
Survivability			X	X			X
Contingency Op	X		X				
Commo			X	X			X
Intelligence			X	X			X
Direct/Indirect Fire Control/Dist				X	X	X	X
Air Defense	X		X	X			X
Airspace Mgmt			X	X	X		X
Engineer Sys	X	X	X	X			X

Table 2. Exercise Effectiveness
FM 25-4. How to Conduct Training Exercises

Field exercise: An exercise conducted in the field under simulated war conditions in which troops and armament of one side are actually present, while those of the other side may be imaginary or in outline.

Live fire exercises (LFXs) closely replicate battlefield conditions and provide significant advantages. LFXs-

- Develop confidence and esprit-de-corps.
- Provide soldiers with a realistic experience of the danger, confusion, and speed of combat operations.
- Require demonstrated proficiency at lower echelons before LFXs are conducted at higher echelons.

Situational training exercises (STXs) are mission-related, limited exercises designed to train one collective task, or a group of related tasks and drills, through practice. STXs teach the doctrinally-preferred method for carrying out a task. STXs usually include drills, leader tasks, and individual soldier tasks. STX training is structured to expose leaders and soldiers to unexpected situations, favorable and unfavorable.

Phases of Exercises:

- Pre-Exercise: Planning and preparation. Ends with the STARTEX.
- Execution: Unit participates in exercise. Ends with ENDEX.
- Post-Exercise: Unit conducts After Action Review and completes reports.

7.10.1 Troop Leading Procedures

References:

FM 1-02	Operational Terms and Graphics (Sep 04) formerly FM 101-5-1
FM 3-0	Operations (Jun 01)
FM 5-0	Army Planning and Orders Production (Jan 05)
FM 71-123	Combined Arms Heavy Forces (Sep 92)

The Troop Leading Procedures

Receive the mission. Once you receive your mission, analyze to determine what exactly has to be done and what other factors will affect your ability to do it.
Issue warning order. As soon as you understand the mission, let subordinates know so they can begin planning.
Make a tentative plan. After analyzing the mission, develop some different ways (course of action -COA) to get it done. Then compare these COAs to determine which one is best.
Initiate movement. Begin Soldier's and equipment movement to where they will be needed or where they will rehearse the operations.
Conduct reconnaissance. Survey, as much as possible, the ground on which you will operate. At a minimum, conduct a map reconnaissance.
Complete the plan. Based on the reconnaissance and any changed in the situation complete the plan of action.
Issue the order. Fully brief Soldiers on what has to get done, the Commander's intent, and how you are going to accomplish the task.
Supervise and assess. Supervise preparation for the mission through rehearsals and inspections.

Figure 1-3. The Troop Leading Procedures
FM 7-21.13 The Soldier's Guide (Feb 04)

Definitions:

Backbrief: A briefing by subordinates to the commander to review how subordinates intend to accomplish their mission.

Confirmation brief: A briefing subordinate leaders give to the higher commander immediately after the operation order is given. It is their understanding of his intent, their specific tasks, and the relationship between their mission and the other units in the operation.

7.10.2 Precombat Inspections/Checks

Sample Precombat Checks (PCC)
- Security maintained (e.g. ground, NBC) - Weapons, vehicles, and equipment issued and camouflaged. - MILES mounted, operational, and zeroed. - Other required TADSS on hand and operational. - Personnel camouflaged - OPORD briefed. Leaders and Soldiers know the mission, commander's intent, and what is expected of them. - Individual and small element task rehearsal conducted (e.g. synchronization drills) - Safety checks and briefings completed - Safety equipment on hand. - Medical support present and prepared - Environmental concerns and controls identified. - Leaders' equipment inspected (compass, strip maps, binoculars, etc) - Soldiers and equipment inspected (weapons, LBE, ID tag, Driver licenses, and meal card) - Soldier packing lists checked and enforced. - Compasses, maps, and strip maps present (with graphics posted) - Communications checks completed (higher, lower, adjacent, and range control) - Class 1 (rations) drawn and issued. - Class III (POL) drawn and vehicles topped off - Class IV (construction and barrier materials) on hand - Class V (ammunition) drawn, issued, prepared, and accounted for - Class IX (repair parts) on hand - Reference materials available (TMs, TACSOP) - Motor pool gate opened and transportation present on time. - Precombat (before operations) and combat (during operations) preventive maintenance checks and services (PMCS) completed on vehicles, weapons, communication, and NBC equipment - Vehicle load plans checked and confirmed, cargo secured - Convoy route and plan briefed - Quartering party briefed and dispatched - Slice (CA, CS, and CSS) elements integrated) - OPFOR Soldiers deployed and read to execute their OPORD.

7.10.3 Battle Drills

Battle drills are the backbone of any operation. Official Army drills are outlined in the ARTEP -DRILL series listed below:

3-207-10-DRILL	NBC Recon
3-327-10-DRILL	CBRN
3-457-10-DRILL	Smoke/Decon.
5-DRILL	Engineer
7-7J-DRILL	Bradley Fighting Vehicle

7-8-DRILL	Infantry Rifle
7-90-DRILL	Infantry Mortar
7-91-DRILL	Anti-Armor (TOW)
19-100-10-DRILL	Military Police
19-100-SRT-DRILL	Special Reaction Team (SRT)
34-357-10-DRILL	Ground Surveillance Systems (GSS)
34-387-10-DRILL	Shadow 200 TUAV
34-388-10-DRILL	AN/MLQ-40(V)3 Prophet System
34-396-10-DRILL	AN/TSQ-179 Common Ground System (CGS)
34-396-11-DRILL	Trojan Spirit II (AN/TSQ-190(V)1/2/3) (AN/TSQ-226(V) 1/2/3)
34-398-12-DRILL	AN/TLQ-17A(V)3 Trafficjam Countermeasure Set
44-117-11-DRILL	Stinger Team
44-117-21-DRILL	Avenger Team
44-176-15-DRILL	FAAD C4I Subsystem
44-177-14-DRILL	Bradley Stinger Fighting Veh/Linebacker
44-635-11 DRILL	Patriot Crew: Electric Power Plant and Antenna
44-635-12-DRILL	Patriot Crew: Info Coordination Center (ICC)
44-635-13-DRILL	Patriot Crew: Engagement Control
44-635-15-DRILL	Patriot Crew: PAC-2/PAC-3 Launching Station

Definitions:

Battle Drill: Standardized actions made in response to common battlefield occurrences. They are designed for rapid reaction situations. (FM 7-10). Collective action rapidly executed without applying a deliberate decision-making process

Crew drill: Collective action that the crew of a weapon or piece of equipment must perform to use the equipment; a trained response to a particular situation.

Tips/Tricks:

- Sit with your peers and NCOs and develop your own unit battle drill book. Use any small missions that are performed by a crew, team, or squad and always performed in the same manner. Examples might be setting up communications, recovery of vehicles, etc. Print copies of your "playbook" and have junior leaders use it for hip-pocket training.

7.10.4 Lane Training

References:

TC 25-10 A Leader's Guide to Lane Training (Aug 96)

Other References:

PB 19-97-2 Lane Training Explained (COL Treuting)

Lane training exercise (LTX): It is an exercise used to train company-size and smaller units on one or more collective tasks (and prerequisite soldier and leader individual tasks and battle drills) supporting a unit's METL; however, it usually focuses on one primary task. An LTX consists of assembly area (AA), rehearsal, lane execution, after-action review (AAR), and retraining activities which culminate the lane training process. An LTX is an STX conducted using lane training principles and techniques.

Training Execution Model: Steps One-Eight from COL Treuting's "Lane Training Explained"

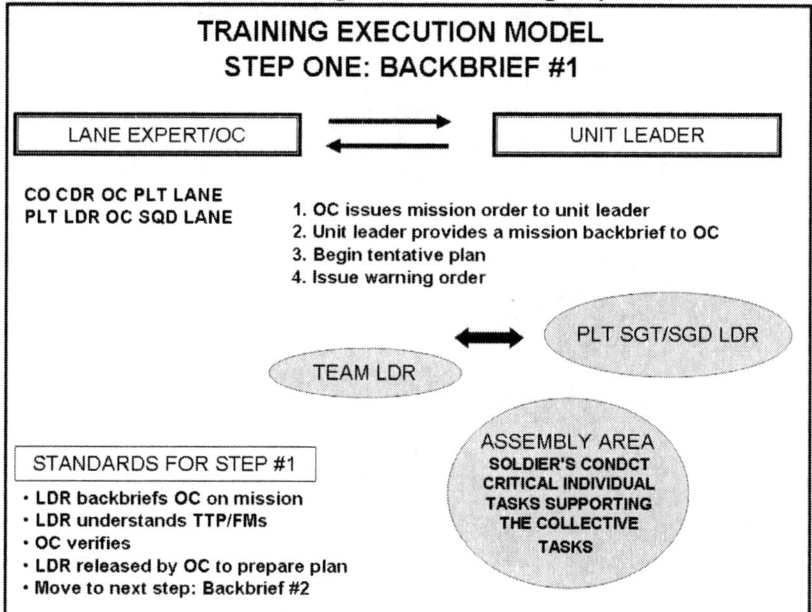

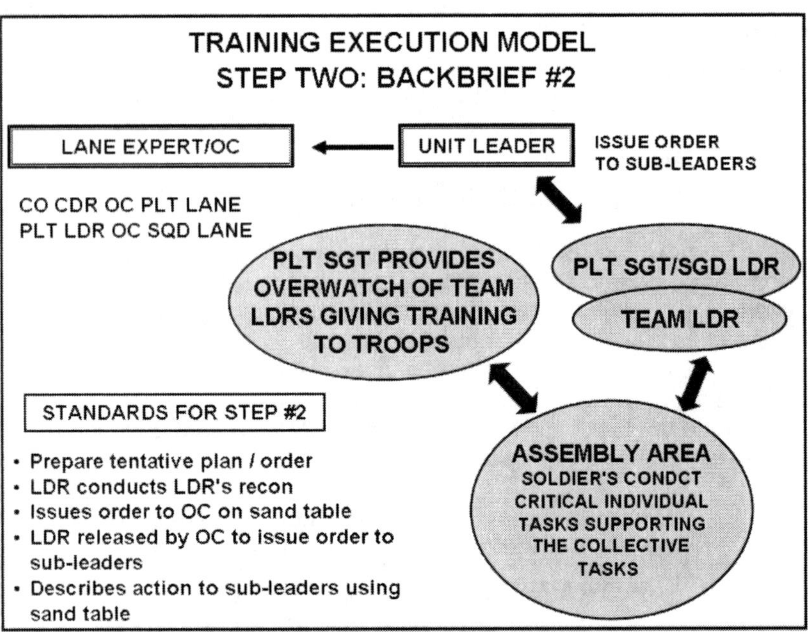
TRAINING EXECUTION MODEL
STEP TWO: BACKBRIEF #2
LANE EXPERT/OC
UNIT LEADER
ISSUE ORDER TO SUB-LEADERS
CO CDR OC PLT LANE
PLT LDR OC SQD LANE
PLT SGT PROVIDES OVERWATCH OF TEAM LDRS GIVING TRAINING TO TROOPS
PLT SGT/SGD LDR
TEAM LDR
STANDARDS FOR STEP #2
• Prepare tentative plan / order
• LDR conducts LDR's recon
• Issues order to OC on sand table
• LDR released by OC to issue order to sub-leaders
• Describes action to sub-leaders using sand table
ASSEMBLY AREA
SOLDIER'S CONDCT CRITICAL INDIVIDUAL TASKS SUPPORTING THE COLLECTIVE TASKS

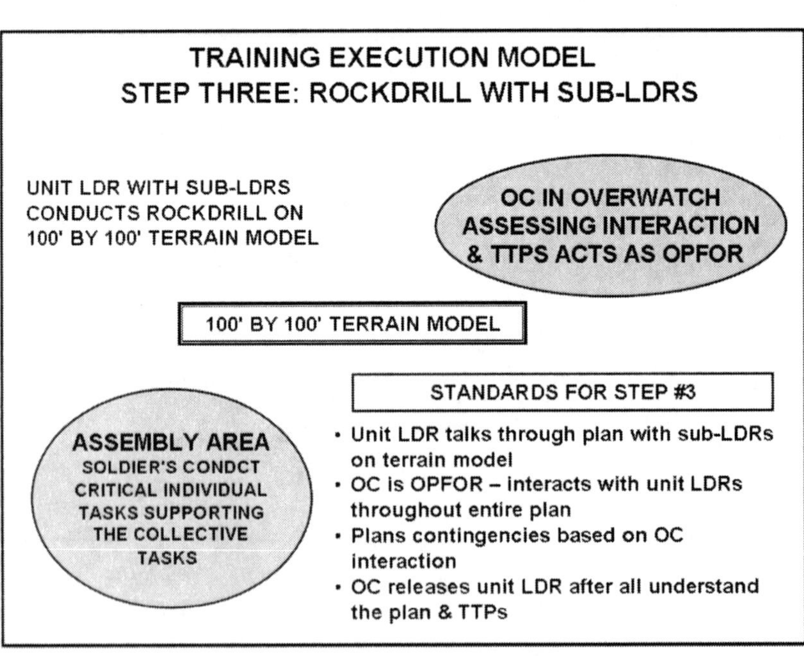
TRAINING EXECUTION MODEL
STEP THREE: ROCKDRILL WITH SUB-LDRS
UNIT LDR WITH SUB-LDRS CONDUCTS ROCKDRILL ON 100' BY 100' TERRAIN MODEL
OC IN OVERWATCH ASSESSING INTERACTION & TTPS ACTS AS OPFOR
100' BY 100' TERRAIN MODEL
STANDARDS FOR STEP #3
ASSEMBLY AREA
SOLDIER'S CONDCT CRITICAL INDIVIDUAL TASKS SUPPORTING THE COLLECTIVE TASKS
• Unit LDR talks through plan with sub-LDRs on terrain model
• OC is OPFOR – interacts with unit LDRs throughout entire plan
• Plans contingencies based on OC interaction
• OC releases unit LDR after all understand the plan & TTPs

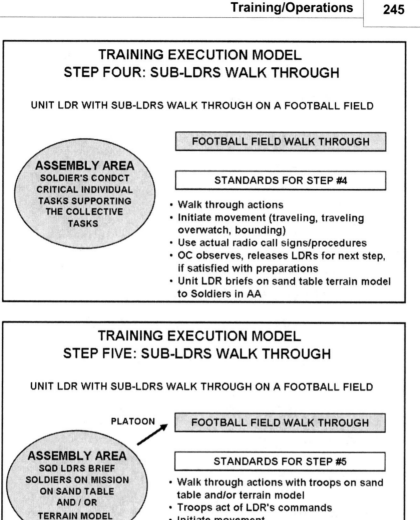

TRAINING EXECUTION MODEL
STEP FOUR: SUB-LDRS WALK THROUGH

UNIT LDR WITH SUB-LDRS WALK THROUGH ON A FOOTBALL FIELD

ASSEMBLY AREA
SOLDIER'S CONDCT CRITICAL INDIVIDUAL TASKS SUPPORTING THE COLLECTIVE TASKS

FOOTBALL FIELD WALK THROUGH

STANDARDS FOR STEP #4

- Walk through actions
- Initiate movement (traveling, traveling overwatch, bounding)
- Use actual radio call signs/procedures
- OC observes, releases LDRs for next step, if satisfied with preparations
- Unit LDR briefs on sand table terrain model to Soldiers in AA

TRAINING EXECUTION MODEL
STEP FIVE: SUB-LDRS WALK THROUGH

UNIT LDR WITH SUB-LDRS WALK THROUGH ON A FOOTBALL FIELD

ASSEMBLY AREA
SQD LDRS BRIEF SOLDIERS ON MISSION ON SAND TABLE AND / OR TERRAIN MODEL

PLATOON → FOOTBALL FIELD WALK THROUGH

STANDARDS FOR STEP #5

- Walk through actions with troops on sand table and/or terrain model
- Troops act of LDR's commands
- Initiate movement
- Use actual radio call signs/procedures
- OC observes, releases unit for next step if satisfied that unit understands LDRs plan and TTPs

TRAINING EXECUTION MODEL STEP SIX: RUN IN ACTUAL LANE	**TRAINING EXECUTION MODEL STEP SEVEN: EXECUTION**
UNIT CONDUCTS DRY RUN OF MISSION FOLLOWING LDR'S PLAN ON THE ACTUAL LANE	UNIT EXECUTES THE MISSION
STANDARDS FOR STEP #6	STANDARDS FOR STEP #7
ACTUAL LANE DRY RUN THROUGH • Conducts mission to MTP standards • Identify weak sub-tasks • Retrain weakness • Do the lane again • OC releases unit to execute at war speed if satisfied with performance	ACTUAL LANE • Conducts mission to MTP standards • Full use of OPFOR/miles • Force on force free play • OC controls OPFOR • OC calls ENDEX

TRAINING EXECUTION MODEL
STEP EIGHT: AFTER ACTION REVIEW

UNIT CONDUCTS AAR OF TRAINING EVENT

STANDARDS FOR STEP #8

- OC facilitates AAR
- State training objectives (task, conditions, standards)
- Bottom-up discussion
- Have Soldiers identify mistakes
- Have Leaders identify mistakes
- Conduct on training lane or objective
- OC assess task IAW MTP (T,P,U)
- Assessment "T": Go to next training objective
- Assessment "P" or "U": Do it again.

Lane Book Contents:
- Cover Sheet
- Table of contents
- Introduction
- List of collective tasks trained

- List of collective tasks for OPFOR
- List of individual tasks
- General and specific situations
- Orders
- Lane diagram
- Lane or LTX timeline/schedule
- Unit task summary sheet
- T&EOs for training
- T&EOs for OPFOR
- Individual task descriptions
- Safety and environmental guidance
- Risk assessment model and worksheet
- Rules of engagement

3-24. Lane Book Contents, TC 25-10

7.10.5 Reports

References:

FM 101-5-2	US Army Report and Message Formats (Jun 99)
AR 310-50	Authorized Abbreviations, Brevity Codes, and Acronyms (Nov 85)
AR 385-40	Accident Reporting and Records (Nov 94)

Most units now use internal reports instead of the Army standard. Refer to your unit TACSOP for those reports and the frequency by which you need to send them.

REPORT	TITLE	MSG	PG
Accident Report/Serious Incident	SIR	A001	II-1
Battle Damage Assessment	BDAREP	B005	II-38
Closure	CLOSEREP	C030	II-72
Commander's Situation	SITREP	C035	II-73
Decontamination Request	DECONREQ	D010	II-81
Detained Civilian Personnel	DETAINCIVREP	D020	II-83
EN/Friendly/Unit Minefield/Obstacle	MINOBREP	E025	II-96
Enemy/Prisoner of War	EPOW	E030	II-98
Explosive Ordnance Disposal Sup	EODSPT	E040	II-101
Fragmentary Order	FRAGO	F050	II-122
Intelligence	INTREP	I001	II-130
Intelligence Summary	INTSUM	I002	II-131
Logistics Situation	LOGSITREP	L005	II-135
Lost Sensitive Item	LOSTITEM	L010	II-138
Maintenance Support Request	MAINTSPTREQ	M005	II-140
Media Contact	MEDIACOTREP	M025	II-146

Medical Evacuation Request	MEDEVAC	M030	II-147
NBC Situation	NBCSITREP	N000	II-164
NBC 1 ROTA	NBC1	N001	II-166
NBC 4	NBC4	N004	II-173
Operation Order	ORDER	O001	II-179
Patrol	PATROLREP	P001	II-186
Personnel Status	PERSTAT	P005	II-187
Request for Information	RFI	R050	II-270
Response to Request for Info	RRI	R055	II-211
Route	ROUTEREP	R065	II-215
Sensitive Item	SENITREP	S035	II-229
Slant	SLANTREP	S045	II-231
Spot	SPOTREP	S060	II-234
Warning Order	WARNORD	W005	II-269

Commonly Used Reports
FM 101-5-2. Army Report and Message Formats (Jun 99)

7.10.6 Battle Tracking

References:

FM 1-02 Operational Terms and Graphics (Sep 04)
formerly FM 101-5-1
FM 3-0 Operations (Jun 01)
FM 5-0 Army Planning and Orders Production (Jan 05)
AR 220-15 Journals and Journal Files (Dec 83)
AR 220-45 Duty Rosters (Nov 75)

Forms:

DA 1594 Daily Status Journal (Nov 62)

- Your battle tracking should be thorough enough for your commander to enter your TOC and understand the entire situation without saying a word.
- Maintain personnel, fuel, equipment, ammunition, and sensitive items status at all times
- Conduct future planning based upon your battle tracking
- Maintain a DA 1594, Daily Status Journal, with all pertinent data.

7.11 External Evaluations (Run)

7.11.1 EXEVAL

An External Evaluation (EXEVAL) evaluates all mission essential task list (METL) tasks using the appropriate Army training and evaluation program (ARTEP) or mission training plan (MTP). An EXEVAL gives the commander an unbiased opinion of unit readiness. Finally, the evaluation should not be used as a performance measure of the commander's ability, but rather a detailed examination of the unit itself.

The EXEVAL evaluates not only your platoon's execution, but the leadership's ability to plan and prepare for those missions. The observer/controllers (O/Cs) are usually battalion staff officers brought in as impartial evaluators.

Tips/Tricks:

- Get a copy of the Mission Training Plan for your unit and print it to fit in your cargo pocket. In the MTP, it lists all the subtasks under each collective task. The MTP also lists tasks by specific duty description ("the Platoon leader will.....the Squad Leader will...)
- Seek out your commander and the senior platoon leaders for advice on how your higher headquarters runs lanes.
- Get a copy of the formal AAR from your evaluation. Use that as a suggestion for future training.

7.11.2 Training Centers

References:

AR 350-50 Combat Training Center Program (Jan 03)

Websites:

NTC Homepage http://www.irwin.army.mil/
JRTC Homepage http://www.jrtc-polk.army.mil/
JMRC Homepage http://www.jmrc.hqjmtc.army.mil/

Purposes:

- Focus on a wartime mission essential task list (METL) and combat operations.
- Stress realistic, sustained, multi-echelon, and fully integrated training for combat, combat support, and combat service support units.
- Focus on performance-oriented training in a realistic tactical environment measured against established tasks, conditions, and standards.
- Support achieving and sustaining leader development and

warfighting readiness using a combination of live, virtual, and constructive simulations and simulators.
- Validate training proficiency through live-fire exercises tailored to the operational environment, optimally from platoon to brigade level, based on CTC warfighting focus and capability.
- Include instrumented urban operations training experience during the rotation.
- Incorporate reception, staging, onward movement, and integration (RSOI) operations, regeneration, and deployment training.

from para 1-5, AR 350-50

National Training Center (NTC), Fort Irwin, CA:
The NTC provides realistic joint and combined arms training focused on developing soldiers, leaders, and units of America's Army for success on the 21st-century battlefield. The NTC trains up to a task-organized brigade and selected division maneuver assets to conduct and rehearse combined arms operations across the spectrum of conflict from high intensity combat to stability operations. It also provides DTLOMS feedback to improve the Army.

Joint Readiness Training Center (JRTC), Fort Polk, LA:
JRTC provides realistic joint and combined arms training focused on developing soldiers, leaders, and units of our nation's joint contingency forces for success on future battlefields. JRTC trains up to a task organized brigade, selected division maneuver assets, special operations forces, and selected multi-echeloned combat support and combat service support to conduct and rehearse combined arms operations across the spectrum of conflict from mid-intensity to stability and support operations. Training occurs under tough, realistic, combat like conditions across a wide range of likely tactical operations and mission rehearsal exercises capable of full integration into higher level exercises and scenarios. It also provides DTLOMS feedback to improve the Army.

Joint Multi-National Readiness Center (JMRC)*, Hohenfels, Germany:
The JMRC is in a forward deployed environment at Hohenfels, Germany, provides realistic joint and combined arms training focused on developing soldiers, leaders, and units for success on current and future battlefields. JMRC trains up to a task organized brigade combat team and selected division maneuver assets across the entire spectrum of conflict from high-intensity combat to stability and support operations. It also provides DTLOMS feedback to improve the Army.
* formerly known as the Combined Maneuver Training Center (CMTC)

from para 1-5, AR 350-50

7.12 Range Operations

References:

FM 3-23.35	Combat Training with Pistols, M9 and M11 (Sep 05)
FM 3-22.9	Rifle Marksmanship M16A1, M16A2/3, M16A4 and M4 Carbine (Apr 05, Chg 3)
FM 3-22.27	MK 19, 40-mm Grenade Machine Gun, Mod 3 (Nov 03)
FM 3-22.31	40-MM Grenade Launcher, M203 (Feb 03)
FM 3-22.34	TOW Weapon System (Jan 03)
FM 3-22.37	Javelin Medium Anti-Armor Weapon System (Jan 03)
FM 3-22.65	Browning Machine Gun, Caliber .50 HB, M2 (Mar 05)
FM 3-22.68	Crew-served Machine Guns, M249, 5.56mm Machine Gun; M60, 7.62mm Machine Gun; M240B, 7.62mm Machine Gun (Jan 03)
FM 3-23.30	Grenades and Pyrotechnic Signals (Jun 05)
FM 3-23.35	Combat Training with Pistols, M9 and M11 (Sep 05)
FM 23-10	Sniper Training (Aug 94)
AR 5-13	Training Ammunition Management (Mar 05)
AR 385-63	Range Safety (May 03)
PAM 350-38	Standards in Weapons Training FY03/FY04
GTA 07-01-30	Range Operations Checklist (Jun 87)

Forms:

DA 85-R	M249/M60/M240B Machine Gun Scorecard (Oct 02)
DA 88-R	Combat Pistol Qualification Scorecard(Sep 05)
DA 581	Request For Issue/Turn-in of Ammunition (Jul 99)
DA 581-1	Request For Issue/Turn-in of Ammunition Continuation (Jul 99)

Definitions:

Ammunition supply point (ASP): An area designated to receive, store, reconfigure, and issue Class V material.

Cease fire: A command given to any unit or individual firing any weapon to stop engaging the target.

RANGES	
PL	**PSG/NCO'S**
Coordinates land, range, and ammunition with Company Operations	Recommends the best way to conduct that type of range to the PL.
Writes OPORD, risk assessment, and range brief for range. Briefs CO or Bn Cdr on range.	Writes Service Support section and coordinates all resources. Implements risk assessment.
Serves as OIC of the range. Signs for range with RSO.	Serves as NCOIC of the range and supervises tower, safeties, RTO, ammo point, and concurrent training.
Ensures all reports and range scorecards are turned into Company Operations	Supervises the safety, discipline, and accountability on the range.

7.12.1 OPORDs

If you are the OIC for a range, you will normally have to write an OPORD and briefing at least 6 weeks out. Follow the normal five paragraph OPORD format, but focus your attention on the Tasks to Subordinates and Timeline (Annex AA). Your NCOs should be able to run a range in their sleep, but whether or not you delegate all tasks and properly backwards plan can make a big difference.

7.12.2 Briefings

As a Range OIC, you will usually brief your Battalion Commander about 6 weeks prior to the range. Ensure you are well prepared because your brief reflects on your unit and on your Noncommissioned Officers. Ensure you brief through your OPORD in the five paragraph format.

Areas of Emphasis:
- Timeframes
- Duty assignments (especially hazmat handlers for ammo)
- Risk Assessment and controls
- Pre-Marksmanship Instruction (PMI)
- Concurrent Training Plan and Instructors
- Medical Support
- Transportation Plan
- Communications Plan

Tips/Tricks:

- Ensure you have a hard copy of the OPORD and briefing slides. Put the slides in a three ring binder in document protectors so you can brief from it if needed.
- Bring your NCOIC (usually your PSG) with you to the briefing. A good NCO will be able to help you if you do not know an answer.
- Have a visual aid of the range to brief off of. A terrain model or range sketch (enlarged at TASC) are useful.
- Recon the range prior to conducting planning for the range. This will help you get a visual for how you will occupy site.

7.12.3 Range Checklist

Appendix E-4, FM 3-22.9, Rifle Marksmanship (Apr 05)

Section I. MISSION ANALYSIS	
1. Who will be firing on the range? Number of personnel Units	
2. What weapons and course will be used? Weapons: Course:	
3. Where will the training be conducted? **Range:**	
4. When is the range scheduled for operations? **Date:** **Opens:** **Closes:**	

Section II. DOUBLE CHECK	
1. Has sufficient ammunition been requested for the number of personnel?	
2. Are the range facilities adequate for the type of training to be conducted?	
3. Has enough time been scheduled to complete the training?	
4. Have conflicts that surfaced been resolved?	

Section III. BECOME AN EXPERT	
1. Review TMs and FMs on the weapons to be fired.	
2. Talk with the armorer and other personnel experienced with the weapons to be fired.	
3. Review AR 385-63.	
4. Visit range control and read installation range instructions.	
5. Reconnoiter the range (preferably while it is in use).	
6. Check ARTEPs to see if training tasks can be integrated into the range training plan.	

Section IV. DETERMINE REQUIREMENTS	
A. PERSONNEL:	
1. OIC	
2. Range Safety officer	
3. Assistant safety officer	
4. NCOIC	
5. Ammunition NCO	
6. Ammunition personnel (determined by type of range)	
7. Target detail and target operators	
8. Tower operator	
9. Concurrent training instructors	
10. Assistant instructors	
11. RATELO	
12. Guards (range requirements)	
13. Medic(s)	
14. Air guard	
15. Armorer	
16. Truck driver (range personnel and equipment)	
17. Mechanic for vehicles	
18. Have you overstaffed your range?	

Section IV. DETERMINE REQUIREMENTS	
B. EQUIPMENT:	
1. Range packet and clearance form	
2. Safety fan and diagram if applicable	
3. Other safety equipment (aiming circle, compass)	
4. Appropriate publications pertaining to the training that will be conducted	
5. Lesson plans, status reports, and reporting folder	
6. Range flag and light (night firing).	
7. Radios	
8. Field telephone and wire	
9. 292 antenna, if necessary	
10. PA set with backup bullhorn(s)	
11. Concurrent training markers	
12. Training aids for concurrent training stations	
13. Sandbags	
14. Tentage (briefing tent, warm-up tent)	
15. Space heaters, if needed	
16. Colored helmets for control personnel	
17. Safety paddles and vehicle flag sets or lights	
18. Ambulance or designated vehicle	
19. Earplugs	
20. Water for drinking and cleaning	
21. Scorecards	
22. Master score sheet	
23. Armorers tools and cleaning equipment for weapons	
24. Brooms, shovels, and other cleaning supplies and equipment	
25. Tables and chairs, if needed	
26. Target accessories	
27. Fire extinguishers	
28. Tarp, stakes, and rope to cover the ammunition	
29. Toilet paper	
30. Spare weapons and repair parts as needed	
31. Tow bar and slave cables for vehicles	
32. Fuel and oil for vehicles and target mechanisms	

Section V. DETERMINE AVAILABLE RESOURCES	
1. Fill personnel spaces	
2. Keep unit integrity.	
3. Utilize NCOs.	
4. Coordinate with supporting organizations: Ammunition Transportation Training aids Medics Weapons Other equipment	

Section VI. FOOLPROOFING	
1. Write an overall lesson plan for the range.	
2. Organize a plan for firing: Determine range organization. Outline courses of fire to be used. Have fire commands typed for use on the range. Set rotation of stations.	
3. Rehearse concurrent training instructors and assistants.	
4. Rehearse concurrent training instructors and assistants.	
5. Brief and rehearse reporting NCO on range operation and all his duties	
6. Collect and concentrate equipment for use on the range in one location	
7. Obtain training aids	
8. Pick up targets from range warehouse, if required.	
9. Report to range control for safety briefing (if required) and sign for any special items.	
10. Publish LOI/OPORD: Uniform of range and firing personnel (helmets and earplugs). Mode of transportation, departure times and places. Methods of messing to be used. Any special requirements being placed on units.	

Section VII. OCCUPYING THE RANGE AND CONDUCTING TRAINING	
A. OCCUPY THE RANGE:	
1. Request permission to occupy the range	
2. Establish good communications	
3. Have designated areas prepared: Parking Ammunition point/Armorer Medical station/ Helipad Water point/Mess Concurrent training	
4. Inspect range for operational condition.	
5. Raise flag when occupying or firing according to the local SOP	
6. Check ammunition to ensure it is correct type and quantity	
7. Ensure range personnel are in proper uniform and equipment in position	
8. Receive firing units.	
9. Conduct safety checks on weapons.	
10. Check for clean, fully operational weapons	
11. Conduct safety briefing (to include administrative personnel on range).	
12. Organize personnel into firing orders (keep unit integrity if possible).	
13.Request permission to commence firing from range control	

Section VII. OCCUPYING THE RANGE AND CONDUCTING TRAINING	
B. CONDUCT OF FIRING:	
1. Are communications to range control satisfactory?	
2. Commands from tower clear and concise?	
3. Range areas policed?	
4. Ammunition accountability maintained?	
5. Master score sheet updated?	
6. Personnel accountability maintained?	
7. Vehicles parked in appropriate areas?	
8. Air guard on duty and alert?	
9. Personnel in proper uniform?	
10. Earplugs in use?	
11. Troops responding properly to commands?	
12. Corrections for those with poor techniques or who fail to hit the target?	
13. Conservation of ammunition enforced?	
14. Weapons cleared before they are taken from the firing line?	
15. Personnel checked for brass or ammo before they leave the range?	
16. Anyone standing around not involved in training or support?	

Section VIII. CLOSING OF RANGE	
1. Close down range according to the local SOP.	
2. Remove all equipment and ammunition from range.	
3. Police range.	
4. Re-paste and resurface targets as required by range instructions	
5. Perform other maintenance tasks as required by local SOP.	
6. Request a range inspector from range control when ready to be cleared.	
7. Submit after-action report to headquarters.	
8. Report any noted safety hazards to proper authorities.	

Section IX. KNOWN DISTANCE RANGE	
A. PERSONNEL:	
1. NCOIC of pit detail.	
2. Assistant safety officer for pit area.	
B. EQUIPMENT:	
1. Sound set for pit area.	
2. Positive communication from the firing line to the pit area.	
3. Pasters	
4. Glue and brushes for resurfacing targets.	
5. Lubricant for target frames.	
6. Proper targets mounted in target frames.	
7. Briefing on how to operate a KD range.	
8. Procedure for marking targets.	
9. Procedure for pit safety.	

7.12.4 Range Control

Range Control controls all training areas on the installation. Most members of Range Control are civilians that are retired military and have been working on that installation for many years. They are subject matter experts on those training areas and the regulations and SOPs governing them. One of the biggest pitfalls for a LT running their first range is that they will attempt to argue with Range Control. If you have an issue, seek out your NCOs since they have more experience with ranges. Get a copy of the Range Control SOP for your post and actually READ it. When you sign for the range, you are certifying that you read that document, allow with PAM 385-63, Range Safety. Those regulations can get your range shut down if you do not follow them.

You need to go to range control to get certified to be an OIC. This usually consists of a class or watching a video. Your higher headquarters must submit a memorandum through range control listing their officers and NCOs for range operations. Ensure your name is on the memorandum, or you will be unable to sign for a range.

7.12.5 Range Duties

Officer in Charge (OIC): The officer, warrant officer, or noncommissioned officer responsible for personnel conducting firing or operations within the training complex. (usually an E6 and above)

Range Safety Officer (RSO): The range safety officer (RSO) is responsible for the safe operation of the range to include conducting a safety orientation before each scheduled live-fire exercise. He ensures that a brass and ammunition check is made before the unit leaves the range. He ensures that all personnel comply with the safety regulations and procedures prescribed for the conduct of a live-fire exercise. He ensures that a dry-fire exercise is conducted and the weapon is rodded before a firer leaves the firing line. He ensures that all left-handed firers use left-handed firing devices. This officer should not be assigned any other duties. (usually an E6 and above)

NCOIC: The NCOIC assists the OIC and safety officer, as required; for example, by supervising enlisted personnel who are supporting the live-fire exercise.

Ammunition Detail: This detail is composed of one or more ammunition handlers whose responsibilities are to break down, issue, receive, account for, and safeguard live ammunition. The detail also collects expended ammunition casings and other residue.

Unit Armorer. The unit armorer repairs the rifles to include replacing parts, as required.

Assistant Instructor. One assistant instructor (AI) is assigned for each one to ten firing points. Each assistant ensures that all firers observe safety regulations and procedures, and he assists firers having problems.

Medical Personnel. They provide medical support as required by regulations governing live-fire exercises.

Control Tower Operators. They raise and lower the targets, time the exposures, sound the audible signal, and give the fire commands. If possible, two men should be chosen to perform these functions.

Maintenance Detail. This detail should be composed of two segments: one to conduct small-arms repair and one to perform minor maintenance on the target-holding mechanisms.

See para 1-6, PAM 385-63 for specific duties

7.12.6 PMI

References:
GTA 07-01-043 Basic Rifle Marksmanship (May 00)

Pre-Marksmanship Instruction is essential to conducting a successful range. However, it occurs BEFORE the range. It is a supervisor's responsibility to conduct PMI with their subordinates prior to the day of the range. At the range, you should have a PMI station set up for BOLOs or for Soldiers that have already completed the concurrent training.

Types of PMI:
- Dime and Washer drills
- Weaponeer
- Engagement Skills Trainer

BOLOs:
- Ensure that Soldiers that do not qualify receive corrective training before returning to the firing line
- Pair of the Soldier with a coach, preferably one of their supervisors
- Have an armorer check their weapon to make sure their is not a problem, such as a bent sight post

7.12.7 Concurrent Training

Concurrent training is specific training conducted at the range to minimize time that Soldiers are sitting waiting for their firing order. As OIC, you should select the tasks in advance, as well as the instructors. Your NCOIC should resource the training and have instructors validate the classes. This is a great opportunity to knock out CTT tasks and train on battle and crew drills. Although the tasks can be anything within your METL, it is highly suggested to tie it into the range. For example, if you are conducting a M2, 50 cal range, concurrent tasks could be assembly/disassembly of the M2, crew drills with the M2, and sighting of night visions devices.

Additional Duties

Part

8 Additional Duties

Additional duties can take the majority of a platoon leader's time if they are not proactive and organized.

Continuity Books: When assuming an additional duty, you should get a continuity book. However, many times you will get very little from your predecessor. Use that first week of learning your job to assemble a new book. General continuity book contents are listed below. Add the specific lists under each duty.
- Table of Contents
- Appointment Orders
- Policy Letters (if applicable)
- Copies of listed References
- Common Tasks
- Recent Inspection and Evaluation Results
- Lessons Learned/TTPs
- Summary of Ongoing Actions

from Building a Useful Continuity Book
by CPT Leonel Nascimento (CALL)

Standard Operating Procedures: Many times an unit SOP is out of date. At a minimum, make sure the current SOP has your commander's signature block and lists the current references (many Field Manuals, Army Regulations, and DA Pamphlets are newer than 2000). Go through your SOP and make necessary suggestions. If some procedures do not make sense, then update them; it is YOUR responsible as that officer. Below are generic SOP contents. Add the specific contents under each duty. SOPs should be in memorandum for record format. Take SOPs to your Post Publication office and have copies run for each platoon and section.
- Applicability (who does the SOP apply to)
- References (Department of Army, plus Post regulations)
- Duties/Responsibilities
- Mission Statement

Additional Duty Tips/Tricks:
- Actually read the regulations and pamphlets for your duty.
- Sit down with your duty's NCO and ask them about common mistakes, what systems/SOPs are in place, and decide your lanes.
- Make contact with your higher point of contact (whether it is at battalion or a civilian agency). Put their name, phone number, and email address in your continuity book and in your cell phone.

8.1 AER/CFC Officer

References:

AR 930-4	Army Emergency Relief (Aug 94)
5 CFR Part 950	Federal Personnel for Contributions to Private Voluntary Organizations
DODD 5035.1	Combined Federal Campaign (CFC) Fund-Raising (May 99)

Forms:

DA 4908	Army Emergency Relief Fund Campaign (Jan 01)
DD 0139	Pay Adjustment Authorization (May 53)

Websites:

AER	http://www.aerhq.org/
CFC Homepage	http://www.opm.gov/cfc/

Timeframes:

AER Season	1 March through 15 May
CFC Season	1 September through 15 December

Responsibilities:

- Fully brief Commander on the AER campaign
- Designate platoon representatives to collect donations
- Request the Commander/1SG reinforce the importance of the campaign
- Keep Commander informed of the results throughout the campaign period.
  - Track the number of Soldiers contacted
  - Track the number of Soldiers who contributed
  - Track overall unit contribution

AER Guidance:

- Base campaign on voluntary contributions. Assure that each soldier is given the opportunity through on-the-job solicitations, and other fund-raising events, to contribute voluntarily under policies and procedures in this regulation. Practices that involve compulsion, coercion, or reprisal to soldiers because of the size of their contributions or their failure to contribute must be avoided.
- Dollar goals may be set at the installation level.
- Individual goals, quotas, or prescribed amounts for individual contributions are not permitted nor will lists of non-contributors be compiled for any reason.
- Each individual will have the option of disclosing or keeping his or her contribution confidential.

- No awards or rewards initiated within the Army will be made to individual solicitors for achievements in a fund drive. Comments on efficiency reports, plaques, passes, training holidays, relief from guard duty or details, and all other incentives or rewards to those who contribute to fund drives, likewise are not permitted.
- Awards from higher HQ to their subordinate units or their commanders for goal accomplishment or percent of participation, will not be used.
- Recognition, such as letters of commendation, for exceptional performance in organization or administration of a campaign, is appropriate.

from para 5-3, AR 930-4

CFC Guidance:

- Activities contrary to the non-coercive intent of Federal fundraising policy are not permitted in campaigns. They include, but are not limited to:
- Supervisory inquiries about whether an employee chose to participate or not to participate or the amount of an employee's donation. Supervisors may be given nothing more than summary information about the major units that they supervise.
- Setting of 100 percent participation goals.
- Establishing personal dollar goals and quotas.
- Developing and using lists of non-contributors.
- Providing and using contributor lists for purposes other than the routine collection and forwarding of contributions and allotments.
- Using as a factor in a supervisor's performance appraisal the results of the solicitation in the supervisor's unit or organization.
- Employee solicitations shall be conducted during duty hours using methods that permit true voluntary giving and shall reserve to the individual the option of disclosing any gift or keeping it confidential. Campaign kick-offs, victory events, awards, and other non-solicitation events to build support for the CFC are encouraged.
- Special CFC fundraising events, such as, raffles, lotteries, auctions, bake sales, carnivals, athletic events, or other activities not specifically provided for in these regulations are permitted during the 6-week campaign period if approved by the appropriate agency head or government official, consistent with agency ethics regulations.

- In all approved special fundraising events the donor must have the option of designating to a specific participating organization or federation or be advised that the donation will be counted as an undesignated contribution and distributed according to these regulations.

from 5 CFR Part 950, §950.108 and §950.602

Tips/Tricks:
- Go to the AER and CFC office to get free publicity items (posters, handouts, etc)
- Make sure you keep accurate tracking of all contributions and have someone else re-count the money/checks, verifying the total on a Memorandum for Record.
- Turn all forms, cash, and checks in DAILY to AER or CFC office.

8.2 Budget Officer

References:

AR 37-47	Representation Funds of the Secretary of the Army (Mar 04)
AR 710-2	Supply Policy Below the National Level (Jul 05)
FAR	Federal Acquisition Regulation
DFARS	DOD Federal Acquisition Regulation Supplement
DOD 5500.7-R	Joint Ethics Regulation
DFAS 37-1	Finance & Accounting Policy Implementation

Fiscal Year: The fiscal year runs from October through September.
- First Quarter October to December
- Second Quarter January to March
- Third Quarter April to June
- Fourth Quarter July to September

Responsibilities:
- Be familiar with the unit's quarterly and annual budget

Budget Book:
- Annual and Quarterly Budget
- Recon Report
- CO's memorandums authorizing IMPAC purchases
- Spending Spreadsheets

Quick Checks:

- Are transactions recorded from the past 12 months?
- Are there signed memorandums (or other paperwork) signed by the commander authorizing all local purchases?
- Do you have a running record of the amount remaining in the quarter?

Tips/Tricks:

- Make a one page SOP for inputting new transactions to the budget and give to the Supply Sergeant and PLL clerk. (Example: Receipts or reports of money spent will be turned into the Budget Officer within 48 hours. The first Tuesday of every month we will conduct a full reconcile)
- Have your Commander and all platoons and sections submitted their "dream list" of supply requests. Put them in a spreadsheet with the Item, Quantity, NSN (or other identifying number), Price per item, and Total Price. Give the list to your Commander to prioritize requests. This spreadsheet will make it easy to drop requests as soon as your unit gets more money.

BUDGET	
OIC	**SUPPLY NCO**
Work with the S4 for unit budget constraints	Keep running log of all purchases (IMPAC, GSA, Class II)
Conduct monthly reconcile	Compile monthly reconcile
Compile Unit Funds Request (UFR) for Commander	Look up specific details for Unit Funds Request

8.3 Casualty Operations

References:

FM 8-55	Planning for Health Service Support (Sep 94)
AR 600-8-1	Army Casualty Operations/Assistance/Insurance (Oct 94)
AR 638-2	Care and Disposition of Remains and Personal Effects (Dec 00)
PAM 608-4	Guide for Survivors of Deceased Army Members (Feb 89)
PAM 638-2	Care and Disposition of Remains and Personal Effects (Dec 00)

Other References:
Casualty Assistance Officer Guide (Jul 05)

Forms:

DA 1155	Witness Statement of Individual (Jun 66)
DA 1156	Casualty Feeder Report (Jun 66)
DA 2204-R	Casualty Assistance Report (May 86)
DA 2386	Agreement for Interment (Jun 82)
DA 4475-R	Info from the NOK of a Deceased Service Member (Dec 75)
DA 7302	Disposition of Remains Statement (Dec 00)
DD 1300	Report of Casualty (Mar 04)
DD 1375	Request for Payment of Funeral and/or Interment Expenses (Oct 03)
DD 2656-7	Verification of Survivor Annuity (Jun 05)

Websites:

Casualty Assistance	http://www.armycasualty.army.mil
VA Benefits	http://www.vba.va.gov/

Casualty Operations Book:
- Unit Next of Kin (NOK) roster
- Duty Roster (DA 6) of Casualty Officers (CAO and CNO)
- Phone roster of qualified Casualty Assistance and Notification Officers
- Copy of Casualty Assistance Officer Guide (Jul 05)

Definitions:

Casualty: Any person who is lost to the organization by having been declared dead, duty status-whereabouts unknown, missing, ill, or injured. (Army) Any person who is lost to his organization by reason of having been declared dead, wounded, injured, diseased, interned, captured, retained, missing in action, beleaguered, besieged, or detained.

Casualty Assistance Officer (CAO)
The CAO must be a CPT (O-3) and above or MSG (E-8) and above. The CAO is assigned to the family to help with arranging the funeral, receiving benefits, and other issues.

Casualty Notification Officer (CNO):
Should be an officer, and whenever possible, should be equal to or higher than the rank of the casualty. The CNO informs the next of kin of the death of their loved one using the speech below.

"The Secretary of the Army has asked me to express his deep regret that your (RELATIONSHIP, NAME) (DIED/WAS KILLED IN ACTION) in (COUNTRY/STATE) on (DATE).
(CIRCUMSTANCES)
The Secretary extends his deepest sympathy to you and your family in your tragic loss."

Summary Court Martial Officer:
Usually a lieutenant. This officer takes care of all legal business left by the casualty, as well as clearing the casualty from post.

Escort Officer:
Must be equal or high than the rank of the casualty. Accounts for the body of the deceased and escorts the body to the place of burial.

Quick Checks:
- Does your PAC have completed SGLI (DD 93) on each Soldier? Are the forms signed?

Tips/Tricks:
- Have each Soldier fill out an index card with their next of kin's Name, Date of birth, and Social security number. In the event of the Soldier's death, the Casualty Notification Officer can take that index card to fill out the notification form. This allows them to not have to ask those questions during the next of kin's grief.

8.4 Environmental Coordinator

References:

FM 3-100.4	Environmental Considers in Military Opns (Jun 00)
AR 11-27	Army Energy Program (Feb 97)
TC 3-34.489	The Soldier and the Environment (May 01)

Graphical Training Aids:

GTA 05-08-002 Environmental-related Risk Assessment (Oct 99)
GTA 05-08-004 Soldier's Environmental Card (Jan 02)
GTA 05-08-005 Environmental Unit Leader's Field Guide, Assessment, and Quality Checklist (Jan 99)
GTA 05-08-013 Training and Environment Field Card (Jul 05)
GTA 05-08-014 Unit Pre-Deployment and Load Plan (Jan 03)
GTA 05-08-015 Unit Deployment/Sustainment Checklist (Jan 03)
GTA 05-08-016 Environment: How to Clear a Base Camp (Jan 03)
GTA 05-08-017 Tactical Risk/Spill Reaction Procedures (Jan 03)

Responsibilities:
- Complete post Environmental Coordinator school
- Ensure mandatory training is conducted
- Ensure your unit is in compliance with environmental policies
- Conduct monthly inspection of company area
- Conduct quarterly hazmat inventory

Sub-Sections:
- Energy Conservation
- Recycling
- Spill Prevention

Environmental Book
- Post Environmental Inspection Checklist
- Past Formal Inspection results
- Unit Monthly Inspections
- Annual HAZMAT Inventory
- Spill Prevention Plan
- Motor Pool Map (with safety and waste disposal sites)

Quick Checks:
- Check training records to see if required training is being conducted (should be on training schedules and have sign in rosters).
- Check motor pool for spill kits, disposal of POL, and eye wash station.
- Does unit have blue recycling bins? Are they used? Check the dumpster and see how many recyclables are being thrown in the normal trash.

Tips/Tricks:
- Ask Post Environmental to give you a courtesy inspection. Keep their contact information handy. Also, ask them for a copy of their inspection checklist.

- If Soldiers are repeatedly not using recycling bins (despite training and warnings), ask the 1SG for a detail to sift through the trash dumpster to remove recyclables.

ENVIRONMENTAL	
OIC	**MOTOR POOL NCO**
Coordinates with Training NCO to have environmental training on the unit training schedule. Ensures training is conducted	Primary instructor for environmental training. Trains the trainer for the unit
Checks all paperwork and assembles the Unit Environmental Book	Conducts annual HAZMAT inventory
Conducts random inspections of safety points, POL disposal, recycling, and common areas	Conducts monthly inspections of safety points, POL disposal, recycling, and common areas

8.5 Equal Opportunity Advisor

References:

AR 600-20	Army Command Policy (Feb 06)
AR 690-12	Equal Opportunity Policy (Mar 88)
FM 22-51	Leader's Manual for Combat Stress Control (Sep 94)
PAM 350-20	Unit Equal Opportunity Training Guide (Jun 94)
PAM 600-15	Extremist Activities (Jun 00)
PAM 600-24	Suicide Prevention (Sep 88)
PAM 600-69	Unit Climate Profile Handbook (Oct 86)
PAM 600-70	Prevention of Suicide/Self-Destructive Behavior (Nov 85)
PAM 600-85	Army Substance Abuse Program (Mar 06)
TC 26-6	Commander's Equal Opportunity Handbook

Forms:

DA 7279-R	Equal Opportunity Complaint Form (Apr 99)
DA 7279-1R	Equal Opportunity Complaint Resolution (Apr 99)

Responsibilities:
- Primary trainer for all EO training
- Ensures a record of training is maintained
- Ensures EO training occurs QUARTERLY (Prevention of Sexual Harassment)
- Completes quarterly report
- Point of Contact for all EO complaints
- Advises the commander on command climate as it relates to EO

EO Book:
- Quarterly Narrative and Statistics Report (QNSR)
- Last Command Climate Survey Results
- EO Representative Roster (up through installation level)
- Schedule of EO Training

Timeframes:

Victim to Report	60 days from incident
Unit to Notify GCM	72 hours from Soldier report
Unit to Investigate	14 days (may be granted 14 day extension)

Quick Checks:
- Check past training schedules and see if the required Equal Opportunity training has been conducted. Also, check to see if sign-in rosters are still on hand from that training.
- Ask Soldiers if they know who their Equal Opportunity

Representatives are.

Tips/Tricks:

- Involve platoon leadership in all training. Ensure Soldiers know that their chain of command is their PRIMARY route of filing complaints; the EO rep the secondary.
- Ensure you have an EO bulletin board in a highly visible place in the unit. Include pictures and contact information for unit and higher representatives. Also post the flow chart on informal and formal complaints.

EQUAL OPPORTUNITY	
CO COMMANDER	**EO REP**
Ensures all training is conducted	Coordinates with Training NCO to schedule mandatory training
Provides command emphasis for unit Equal Opportunity program	Primary instructor for EO training
Conducts Command Climate Survey in unit	Advises the CO on potential EO problem areas in the company

8.6 Financial Liability Officer

(formerly the Report of Survey)

References:

FM 10-27-4	Org Supply and Services for Leaders (Apr 00)
AR 735-5	Policies and Procedures for Property Accountability (Feb 05)
PAM 735-5	Survey Officer's Handbook (Mar 97)

Forms:

DA 1659	Financial Liability Investigation of Property Loss Register (Oct 04)
DA 2823	Sworn Statement (Dec 98)
DA 7531	Checklist and Tracking Document for Financial Liability Investigations (Aug 04)
DD 200	Financial Liability Investigation of Property Loss (Oct 99)

Overview:

Financial liability investigation is a means of reestablishing accountability for lost, damaged, or destroyed supplies and equipment. When there is no admission of liability for a loss, or when a person admits liability for the loss but the loss is greater than one month's basic pay for that person, then a financial liability investigation should be initiated. The financial liability investigation is not intended as a means of punishment. The commander still retains the option of administering non-judicial punishment under Article 15 of the UCMJ or convening a court martial. The commander will appoint a survey officer or NCO, normally of equal or higher rank than the individual who signed for the item on the hand receipt. This appointing authority commander is at or above battalion level. The investigating officer or NCO uses DD Form 200 for recording financial liability investigation information. DA Form 1659 along with specific guidelines and timelines are shown in AR 735-5. The timelines shown in AR 735-5 are important in seeing the matter resolved in a timely manner. (FM 10-27-4, page 6-16)

Responsibilities:

- Determine the proximate cause for loss/damage to equipment using DA Pam 735-5.
- Complete the DD Form 200 with your findings (also may have to explain on a memorandum for record)
- Brief the Approving Authority (usually Battalion Commander) or Executive Officer on your findings

Appointing an Investigating Officer:
A commander at any level can appoint an officer or a board of officers to make an informal investigation. The appointment may be oral or written. It should specify the purpose and scope of the investigation, the nature of the findings, and the recommendation(s) needed.

Time Hacks:
- You have 30 days to complete the investigation. (Must do a memorandum for record if late in which your cite the reason)

With An Appointing Authority:
- Processing steps: Figure 13-10, AR 735-5
- Processing time: Figure 13-1, AR 735-5.

Without An Appointing Authority:
- Processing steps: Figure 13-9, AR 735-5
- Processing time: Figure 13-2, AR 735-5.

Financial Liability Book
- Appointment orders
- Letter of Lateness (if needed)
- DD Form 200
- DA Form 7531
- Sworn statements from all involved personnel (DA Form 2823)
- All paperwork exhibits (hand receipts, etc)
- Memorandum for Record with Facts, Findings, and Recommendations (if required by higher)
- Copy of DA PAM 735-5

Quick Checks:
- Ensure you are on appointment orders for the investigation. Check the date of the orders because that determines your due date, not the date when you received the packet.
- Check enclosures to make sure you have all applicable hand receipts and statements of persons involved.

Tips/Tricks:
- Get sworn statements (DA Form 2823) from all persons involved. Have them write their statement, then ask questions on the form.
- Write your findings in a Memorandum for Record outlining the Facts, Findings (with citations from PAM 735-5), and your Recommendation. This gives you a record of your investigation and logic in your findings.
- If you find someone liable, sit down with them and explain your findings to them face to face. Do not let them find out when their

Supply NCO gives them the paperwork.

FINANCIAL LIABILITY	
APPOINTED LT	**SUPPLY NCO**
Interviews all involved personnel	Initiates paperwork through S4 when discrepancy is found
Uses DA PAM 735-5 to determine liability	Makes copies of all related documents and provides them as exhibits
Complete all necessary paperwork	

8.7 Fire Marshal

References:

AR 385-10 Army Safety Program (Feb 00)
AR 420-90 Fire and Emergency Services (Sep 97)

Forms:

DA 5381-R Building- Fire Risk Management Survey (Dec 96)
DA 5382-R Hazard/Deficiency Survey Record (Sep 92)

Responsibilities:

- Ensure fire extinguishers are in place and current
- Make/post fire escape plan
- Ensure smoke detectors/fire alarms are functional

Fire Marshal Book

- Fire Exit Plan
- Fire Point of Contacts
- Inspection records
- Extinguisher inspection due dates
- Chart explaining different types of fire extinguishers

Quick Checks:

- Check to make sure you have adequate fire extinguishers in your company area (including barracks, motor pool, etc). The fire department will determine the type, size, and location of extinguishers per NFPA Standard 10.
- Check inspection dates on fire extinguishers to make sure all are

current.
- Make sure the fire escape plan is posted in each office.

Tips/Tricks:
- Ask for a courtesy inspection of your unit.

8.8 Food Service

References:

FM 10-23	Field Feeding and Class 1 Opns (Apr 96)
FM 10-23-2	Food Preparation and Class 1 Opns Mgmt (Sep 93)
AR 30-22	The Army Food Program (May 05)
PAM 30-22	Operating Procedures for the Food Program (Aug 02)
GTA 10-01-003	Kitchen Equipment, Emersion Heater (Dec 75)
GTA 10-01-007	Kitchen Equipment, Layout, Sanitation (Dec 75)
GTA 10-01-011A	Insulated Food Container User Maint (Apr 94)
GTA 10-01-011B	Insulated Food Container Guide (Apr 94)

Forms:
DA 5914-R Ration Control Sheet (Jun 90)

Website:

DFAC Manager	http://www.dfacmanager.com/
Logistical Network	https://lognet.bcks.army.mil/

Food Service Book
- Copy of Food service section's schedule
- Inspections/awards your section received
- MKT layout chart (from TM)

Tips/Tricks:
- Schedule a meeting with your Food Service NCO's supervisor at the DFAC. Bring a NCOER shell with you. Ask that supervisor for mentorship so you can give your NCO an accurate and fair evaluation.

8.9 Family Readiness Group Officer

References:
PAM 608-47 Army Family Action Plan (ACAP) Program (Dec 04)

Other References:
Spouse's Handbook

Website:
FRG Website http://frg.army.mil

Virtual FRG http://www.armyfrg.org/
Virtual ACS Site http://www.myarmylifetoo.com/
One Source http://www.militaryonesource.com/

Family Readiness Book:
- Family Roster
- Schedule of Meetings/events
- List of Post agencies

Quick Checks:
- Have lunch with the head of the family readiness group and have them update you on the current status of the group, problems, and ongoing projects.

Tips/Tricks:
- Make sure your BOSS (Better Opportunities for Single Soldiers) representative is tied in with the Family Readiness Group. Many times their will be an unit event for families, and there is nothing for the single Soldiers to do. Make sure your events are balanced.
- Most posts have a program at the hospital where families can take a class, and then pick up over the counter medications for free. Try to have a medical representative teach that class at an FRG meeting. This is an incentive for families to attend and a valuable resource.

8.10 Funds Officer

References:

AR 37-47 Representation Funds of the Army (Mar 04)
AR 215-1 Non-appropriated Fund Instrumentalities and MWR Activities (Sep 05)
AR 600-29 Fundraising within the Department of the Army

Funds Book:
- Company Budget
- Receipts for all purchases
- Memorandum of Records for all incoming money (with two signatures)

8.10.1 Cup & Flower

Cup and Flower Book
- Company Budget
- Receipts for all purchases
- Memorandum of Records for all incoming money (with two signatures)

Tips/Tricks:
- Sit down with CO/1SG and ask them what they want to fund. Make a budget.
- Most posts have a Arts & Crafts center. Have each platoon send one Soldier to the framing class there. By having Soldiers frame gifts, you only pay for materials which saves about 50% of the cost.

8.10.2 Fundraising

Fundraising Ideas:
- Car Wash
- Civilian clothes day ($5 to wear civilian clothes to work. Make sure you get higher's permission first)
- Soda and Snack sales
- Unit auction (sell Parking spots, pie in the face, boot shinings, etc)

Tips/Tricks:
- Fundraising is a touchy task. Call JAG before implementing an program.
- If you are going to sell sodas and snacks, look at buying in bulk to save money. Many value stores, such as SAMs Club, offer cards for military units that allow multiple authorized purchasers.

8.10.3 Unit Funds Officer

The unit funds officer is responsible for the management of the unit's additional funds (outside of operational budget) meant for MWR, improvement of soldier quality of life, and unit cohesion. The unit funds officer is the head member of the unit's "Unit Fund Council" that collectively decides what the unit should use the money for. The Unit Fund officer must maintain inspectable expenditure balance sheets, receipts, and abide by local regulations governing what the unit may use the funds for. Each unit gets a small amount of money deposited into an account each month (based upon number of assigned Soldiers)

Tips/Tricks:
- Ensure your unit has an account set up for unit funds.
- Ensure you update your unit's information as it changes.
- Talk to the Comptroller or other representative that runs the unit funds program at your installation.
- The unit funds budget is just like regular budget, going from FY to FY. Make sure you spend it before by 1 Sept.

8.11 Honor Book

References:
AR 672-11 Jeremiah P. Holland Award (Mar 93)

Responsibilities:
- Produce a Honor Book monthly which includes pictures and descriptions of your units accomplishments.

Honor Book (by month or quarter)
- Awards (Individual and Unit)
- Civilian Education
- Disciplinary Actions
- Military Education
- NCOES
- Physical Fitness averages
- Promotions
- Reenlistments
- Training assessments
- Weapons Qualification

Quick Checks:
- Make sure they is someone taking pictures at every promotion, reenlistment, company function, etc
- Make sure PAC/Training knows what statistics you need from them

(number of awards, APFT average) and give them a suspense of when you need them.

Tips/Tricks:

- Give PAC and Training a form they can fill in their numbers on (example: APFT Average for March: __) and list the suspense on the top. Have them handwrite in the numbers to minimize their time.
- Ask the battalion rep to view the winning book from last month. Ask them what they are specifically looking for in a book.
- On a monthly status, review current honor book status and discuss what is required from platoons and sections.

8.12 Investigations Officer

Appointing an Investigating Officer:
A commander at any level can appoint an officer or a board of officers to make an informal investigation. The appointment may be oral or written. It should specify the purpose and scope of the investigation, the nature of the findings, and the recommendation(s) needed.

8.12.1 15-6 Investigating Officer

References:

AR 15-6	Procedures for Investigating Officers and Boards of Officers (May 88)
AR 195-2	Criminal Investigations Activities (Oct 85)

Forms:

DA 1574	Report of Proceedings by Investigating Officer (Mar 83)
DA 2823	Sworn Statement (Dec 98)
DA 3881	Rights Warning Procedure/Waiver Certificate (Nov 89)

Requirements:
- Investigating officers must be an commissioned officer, warrant officer, or DA Civilian (>GS13)

AR 15-6 Investigation Book
- DA Form 1574
- Appointment Order
- Initial information collected
- Rights warnings statements
- Chronology
- Exhibits (with an index)

Function of investigations and boards:
The primary function of any investigation or board of officers is to ascertain facts and to report them to the appointing authority. It is the duty of the investigating officer or board to ascertain and consider the evidence on all sides of each issue, thoroughly and impartially, and to make findings and recommendations that are warranted by the facts and that comply with the instructions of the appointing authority.
from para 1-5, AR 15-16.

8.12.2 Line of Duty Officer

References:

AR 600-8-4	Line of Duty Procedures, and Investigations (Apr 04)
AR 385-40	Accident Reporting and Records (Nov 94)

Forms:

DA 285	Abbreviated Ground Accident Report (Jul 94)
DA 2173	Medical Examination and Duty Status (Oct 72)
DA 2823	Sworn Statement (Dec 98)
DD 261	Line of Duty (Oct 95)

Line of Duty Determination:
Line of duty determinations are essential for protecting the interest of both the individual concerned and the U.S. Government where service is interrupted by injury, disease, or death. Soldiers who are on active duty (AD) for a period of more than 30 days will not lose their entitlement to medical and dental care, even if the injury or disease is found to have been incurred not in LD and/or because of the soldier's intentional misconduct or willful negligence, Section 1074, Title 10, United States Code (10 USC 1074). A person who becomes a casualty because of his or her intentional misconduct or willful negligence can never be said to be injured, diseased, or deceased in LD. Such a person stands to lose substantial benefits as a consequence of his or her actions; therefore, it is critical that the decision to categorize injury, disease, or death as not in LD only be made after following the deliberate, ordered procedures described in this regulation.

from para 2-1, AR 600-8-4

Rules to Determine Line of Duty:

Rule 1: Injury, disease, or death directly caused by the individual's misconduct or willful negligence is not in line of duty.

Rule 2: Mere violation of military regulation, orders, or instructions, or of civil or criminal laws, if there is no further sign of misconduct, is no more than simple negligence.

Rule 3: Injury, disease, or death that results in incapacitation because of the abuse of alcohol and other drugs is not in line of duty.

Rule 4: Injury, disease, or death that results in incapacitation because of the abuse of intoxicating liquor is not in line of duty.

Rule 5: Injury or death incurred while knowingly resisting a lawful arrest, or while attempting to escape from a guard or other lawful custody, is incurred not in line of duty.

Rule 6: Injury or death incurred while tampering with, attempting to ignite, or otherwise handling an explosive, firearm, or highly flammable liquid in disregard of its dangerous qualities is incurred not in line of duty.

Rule 7: Injury or death caused by wrongful aggression or voluntarily taking part in a fight or similar conflict in which one is equally at fault in starting or continuing the conflict, when one could have withdrawn or fled, is not in line of duty.

Rule 8: Injury or death caused by a soldier driving a vehicle when in an unfit condition of which the soldier was, or should have been aware, is not in line of duty.

Rule 9: Injury or death because of erratic or reckless conduct, without regard for personal safety or the safety of others, is not in the line of duty.

Rule 10: A wound or other injury deliberately self-inflicted by a soldier who is mentally sound is not in line of duty.

Rule 11: Misconduct or willful negligence of another person is attributed to the soldier if the soldier has control over and is responsible for the other person's conduct, or if the misconduct or neglect shows enough planned action to establish a joint venture.

Rule 12: The line of duty and misconduct status of a soldier injured or incurring disease or death while taking part in outside activities, such as business ventures, hobbies, contests, or professional or amateur athletic activities, is determined under the same rules as other situations.

from Appendix B, AR 600-8-4

8.12.3 Congressional Inquiry

References:

AR 1-20 Legislative Liaison (Jan 04)
AR 340-21 Privacy Act Program (Jul 85)

Forms:

DA 2823 Sworn Statement

Process:

- Address all allegations raised in the inquiry. If there are issues that the command cannot answer, provide the reason. If the response raises related issues, you should answer them as well; providing all the facts and findings in our initial response will prevent subsequent inquiries to obtain omitted facts.
- Write drafts in clear, concise and courteous language. Keep in mind the official response will be from a civilian (the Secretary of the Army) to a civilian (the Member of Congress). Avoid the use of Army jargon, acronyms, abbreviations and military time identification whenever possible; however, abbreviations or acronyms **may be used** in the text after the full term has been spelled out and identified. Ensure that responses address the allegations and provide all the facts.
- Give special attention to inquiries of a compassionate or time sensitive nature, such as deaths, injury or sickness (especially suicide threats), or other grave circumstances relating to service personnel or members of their families.

- Do not list or refer to enclosures. If a finding is based on a supplementary document, then clearly state the facts regarding the document. Be sure to include copies of the supplemental documents with your response.

Elements of a Good Response:
- Self-contained
- Describes Army policy
- Stresses rationale used
- Describes the case facts
- Describes the results, impact, and alternative(s)
- Courteous tone

A/Chief, Congressional Inquiry Division

Time Hacks:
- Special Interest (White House, Secretary of the Army or Secretary of Defense): 1-3 days
- Hardcopy/written inquiries: 3-5 days
- Telephonic inquiries: 2 days
- Fear-for-life: 1-4 hours
- Suicide threat: 1 hour

Tips/Tricks:
- Ensure the chain of command thoroughly reviews your findings before they are forwarded.

8.13 Key Control Custodian

References:

AR 190-11 Physical Security of Arms, Ammunition, and Explosives (Feb 98)

Forms:

DA 5513-R Key Control Registry and Inventory (Aug 93)
DA 2062 Hand Receipt/Annex Number (Jan 82)

Procedures:

- Inventory keys and locks twice a year
- Make sure keys to the box are counted and that missing keys are accounted for when there is a change of duty officer/NCO. Record this as part of the duty log.
- Make sure that only authorized persons have access to the key box and to the keys inside. Keep the list of authorized persons near the box, but away from public view.
- Store keys to arms rooms, weapons racks, and containers away from other keys. Do not allow these keys to be left unattended.
- Do not leave keys unattended or in an unsecured area.
- Do not take keys for secure area, arms rooms, rack, or containers outside the unit's operating area.
- Change locks at once whenever keys are lost, misplaced, or stolen.
- Make sure key control registers and inventory logs are kept up to date.
- Change combinations to locks on secured areas twice a year.

from Table 6-1, FM 10-27-4

Key Control Book:

- All 5513-R inventories
- Physical Security checklist (for key control)
- Your monthly inspections (on MFR)
- Sub-hand receipts for all keys to platoon/section custodians

Quick Checks:

- Make sure all key boxes are locked and not left open. Ensure key box key is not left in a desk drawer or other unsecure location.
- Make sure all keys are signed out by the key custodian on a DA Form 5133-R.
- Ensure all key custodians have current appointment orders signed by you.
- Ensure each lock has two keys (one in the key box and one retained on a master ring by the key control officer)
- Ensure each key inspection is notated on a Memorandum for Record

and retained in the Key Control Continuity Book.

Tips/Tricks:

- Have supply order extra locks (5500 series) so you can replace locks as needed. Before deployments, order as many locks as you can, so you have a reserve during the deployment.

8.14 Maintenance Officer

References:

AR 750-1 Army Material Maintenance Policy (Jan 06)
FM 4-30.3 Maintenance Operations and Procedures (Jul 04)
TC 43-4 Maintenance Management (May 96)

Forms:

DA 2062 Hand Receipt/Annex Number (Jan 82)
DA 2404 Equipment Inspection and Maintenance Worksheet (Apr 79)
DA 5988-E Equipment Inspection and Maintenance Worksheet

Websites:

Logistical Network https://lognet.bcks.army.mil/
Electronic TMs https://www.logsa.army.mil/
MotorPool.org http://www.themotorpool.org/
Ordnance University https://ommu.army.mil/

Training:

- Maintenance Officer Course (local post)
- Maintenance Leader Course (Correspondence: 171 Q12)

Quick References:

- Logistics Cheat Sheet
- ULLS-G Commander's Guide
- Maintenance Leader Book
- Julian Date Calendar

Responsibilities:

- Brief Commander on status of all Non-mission capable (NMC) equipment
- Review monthly TMDE print-out. Ensure all calibration items are submitted on time.
- Review monthly Services report. Check to see if any equipment requires services in the next 90 days. Vehicles are due services by date OR mileage, whichever comes first.

Sub-Sections:

- AOAP
- Arms Room
- Calibrations
- Communications
- Motor Pool
- NBC

- Tool Room

ULLS-G Reports:
- Commander's Exception Report
- Parts Received/Not Installed
- Commander's Financial Transaction
- Dispatch Report
- Services
- PLL Zero Balance
- Licensed Driver Roster

Definitions:
Prescribed load: The quantity of combat essential supplies and repair parts (other than ammunition) authorized by major commanders to be on hand in units and which is carried by individuals or on unit vehicles. The prescribed load is continuously reconstituted as used.

General Maintenance Book:
- Weekly ULLS-G Reports
- Levels of Maintenance Smartcard
- Logistics Cheat Sheet
- Julian Date Calendar
- Point of Contacts for Post Direct Support and Depot

Role of Battalion Maintenance Officer: The BMO usually works directly for the battalion XO. He is the subject matter expert on all maintenance matters. It is extremely important to have a good relationship with the BMO. Seek out his guidance and mentorship to learn more about maintenance, as well as a go-to person when you cannot resolve maintenance matters at the company level.

8.14.1 Arms Room Officer

References:

FM 4-30.13 Ammunition Handbook: Tactics, Techniques, and Procedures for Munitions Handlers (Mar 01)
AR 190-11 Physical Security of Arms, Ammunition, and Explosives (Feb 98)
AR 190-51 Physical Security of Arms, Ammunition and Explosives (Sep 93)
AR 710-2 Supply Policy Below the National Level (Jul 05)

Forms:

DA 2062 Hand Receipt/Annex Number (Jan 82)
DA 2404 Equipment Inspection and Maintenance Worksheet (Apr 79)
DA 5988-E Equipment Inspection and Maintenance Worksheet (Electronic)
SF 701 Activity Security Checklist (Aug 85)
SF 702 Security Container Checksheet (Aug 85)
* Property Issue and Turn-in Log/Register
* Property Inventory by Serial Number

* Form number differs by installation. Check installation publications for form number.

Arms Room Inspection Book:

- Physical Security Numbers
- Last Inspections
- Access Rosters (accompanied/unaccompanied)
- Appointment Orders
- Local Records Check
- Armorer Certificate of Training
- Construction Statement
- Unit Physical Security SOP (example provided)
- SF 701s / 702s
- Copy of Master Authorization List (MAL)
- DEH Memo for Fabricated Arms Racks
- Property Hand receipts/Transfer Documents
- Commander's Authorization of Other Than AA&E
- Inventory Instructions
- Inventories
- Key Control (Armorer)
- Privately Owned Weapon Storage/Registration
- SARPs
- Required References
- Division Check Lists
- Sample Memos

Arms Room Tracking Book:
- Unit Master Authorization List
- NMC/deadline list
- Gauging/Service Schedule
- Parts Received Not Installed Report
- Unit Alpha and Battle Roster
- Sensitive Item schedule/roster
- Arms Room Hand Receipt
- Hand receipts of weapons at Direct Support/Depot

Quick Checks:
- Opening/Closing Inventories: Every time armorers end/begin a shift, an inventory should be conducted on a DA Form 2062. The hand receipt should list the types of weapons and the count (serial numbers not required).
- Weapons Signed out: Every weapon that is not physically in the arms room should have either a weapons card or DA Form 2062. Make sure the 550 sign out roster matches what weapons are not in.

Tips/Tricks:
- Make sure all platoons have their MALs and weapons cards updated prior to a large weapons draw. Make sure the Property Issue and Turn-in Log/Register is pre-printed with all information (Soldier's name, SSN, Weapon, Serial, Rack, etc). Sort the 550 by Soldier name so each Soldier can sign for their sensitive items without flipping pages.
- Have pre-printed DA Form 2062's for Soldier's without weapons cards (Fill in NSN, LIN, and Nomenclature, and FROM box). Make sure only one sensitive item is signed out on each form.
- If possible, re-number your rack numbers to go in order by serial number. This will make inventories and accountability much easier; however, you will have to re-do all weapons cards and MALs. Do not do if you anticipate getting new weapons any time soon.
- Post the component and basic issue item lists for each end item on the wall. Make sure that you could for those items with the end item (rifle straps, NVG mounts, etc)
- Ensure the Soldiers assigned to the arms room have not had that duty for more than a year if that is not their MOS.
- Designate a "platoon armorer" for each platoon. Initiate local files checks on these Soldiers and add them to the access roster. This will give you more help in the arms room on days when the entire unit is drawing weapons.

A S ROOM	
OIC	**ARMS ROOM NCO**
Spot checks physical security, accountability, maintenance, and administrative paperwork	Signs for all Arms Room equipment and ensures proper opening/closing inventories occur. Responsible for all armorers and the DA 6 Duty Roster
Pre-inspects all Commander's/outside agency inventories of Arms Room. Oversees all monthly inspections	Facilitates all inventories of the Arms Room
Briefs CO on NMC, Parts Received not Installed, and Services due	Conducts -20 maintenance on Arms Room equipment. Ensures platoons conduct proper PMCS on their equipment
Ensures platoons update weapons cards information, MALs, and all other paperwork	Completes paperwork and turns-in equipment to Direct Support and Depot as needed
Briefs Arms Room maintenance at Bn maintenance meeting	Subject Matter Expert (SME) for all Arms Room training in the unit. Coordinates with Training NCO and CO to implement training
Ensures Arms Room section of CO TACSOP and Maintenance SOP are updated and implemented to lowest level	Works with Arms Room Officer to update SOPs

8.14.2 Commo Officer

References:

AR 25-2	Information Assurance (Nov 03)
FM 11-43	Signal Leader's Guide (Jun 95)
FM 24-18	Tactical Single-Channel Radio Communications Techniques (Sep 87)
FM 24-19	Radio Operator's Handbook (May 91)

Forms:

DA 2062	Hand Receipt/Annex Number (Jan 82)
DA 2404	Equipment Inspection and Maintenance Worksheet (Apr 79)
DA 5988-E	Equipment Inspection and Maintenance Worksheet

Commo Book:
- NMC/deadline list
- Service Schedule
- Calibrations
- Parts Received Not Installed Report
- Commo Hand Receipt
- Hand receipts of equipment at Direct Support/Depot
- List of Commo Tasks (in unit METL)

Quick Checks:
- Make sure every user account on the network has a signed user's agreement on hand and a valid computer user's test.
- Make sure you have adequate batteries on hand or on order for each piece of equipment.
- Ensure you have a training fill available for training
- Ensure all sensitive communication is properly secured in a safe.
- Check with PSG's to make sure that all NMC commo equipment is showing on the NMC report (means the 5988-E or DA Form 2404 has been turned in and inputted into the ULLS-G box). Make sure any needed parts are on order, parts received are installed, and any items with faults above unit level are turned in.

Tips/Tricks:
- Attempt to turn in old communications equipment that your unit no longer uses.
- Have unit test long range communications once a month during command maintenance. Have commo section set up OE-254 and have vehicles go out a few clicks and do communication checks (radio and ABCS systems). This will help identify problems with radios, power amps, antennaes, etc before field exercises.

COMMO	
OIC	**COMMO NCO**
Pre-inspects all inventories of communications equipment	Signs for all communication equipment and ensures it is properly sub hand receipted and filed properly
Briefs CO on NMC, Parts Received not Installed, and Services due	Conducts -20 maintenance on Commo equipment. Ensures platoons conduct proper PMCS on their communication equipment
Ensures platoons give Commo Section what they need (paperwork, Soldiers, etc)	Completes paperwork and turns-in equipment to Direct Support and Depot as needed
Briefs Commo maintenance at Bn maintenance meeting	Subject Matter Expert (SME) for all communications training in the unit. Coordinates with Training NCO and CO to implement Commo Training
Ensures Commo section of CO TACSOP and Maintenance SOP are updated and implemented to lowest level	Works with Commo Officer to update SOPs

8.14.3 Motor Pool Officer

References:

AR 600-55	The Army Driver and Operator Standardization Program (Dec 93)
FM 21-305	Manual for the Wheeled Vehicle Driver (Aug 93)

Forms:

DA 2062	Hand Receipt/Annex Number (Jan 82)
DA 2404	Equipment Inspection and Maintenance Worksheet (Apr 79)
DA 5988-E	Equipment Inspection and Maintenance Worksheet

Responsibilities:

- Attend command maintenance and make sure all vehicles are PMCSed and dispatched
- Ensure all parts received are installed
- Ensure vehicles receive services on time.
- Check AOAP and make sure your unit is current.
- Review monthly TMDE print-out. Ensure all calibration items are submitted on time.

Motor Pool Book

- NMC/deadline list
- Service Schedule
- Calibrations
- Parts Received Not Installed Report
- Motor Pool Hand Receipt
- Hand receipts of vehicles at Direct Support/Depot
- List of Vehicle Tasks (in unit METL)
- Dispatch Flow
- Tool Room Sign-out log

Quick Checks:

- Spot check vehicle log books. Ensure all PMCS checks are annotated on current 5988-E (a new 5988-E should be printed on Command Maintenance with new notations). Ensure vehicle is properly dispatched to a licensed driver.
- Check service schedule. Remember that vehicles are due services based upon time or mileage, whichever is soonest.

MOTOR POOL	
OIC	**MOTOR POOL NCO**
Briefs CO on NMC, dispatches, Parts Received not Installed, and Services due	Performs QAQC, services, conducts -20 maintenance and parts installation.
Ensures platoons give Motor Pool what they need (paperwork, Soldiers, etc)	Responsible for cleanliness and safety of the motor pool
Pre-inspects all inventories of Motor Pool equipment	Supervises mechanics and PLL clerk
Briefs company maintenance at Bn maintenance meeting	

8.14.4 NBC Officer

References:

FM 3-5	Decontamination Operations (Jan 02)
FM 3-7	NBC Field Handbook (Sep 94)
TC 3-10	Commander's Tactical NBC Handbook (Sep 94)

Forms:

DA 2062	Hand Receipt/Annex Number (Jan 82)
DA 2404	Equipment Inspection and Maintenance Worksheet (Apr 79)
DA 5988-E	Equipment Inspection and Maintenance Worksheet

NBC Book:
- NMC/deadline list
- Service Schedule
- Calibrations
- Parts Received Not Installed Report
- NBC Hand Receipt
- Hand receipts of equipment at Direct Support/Depot
- List of NBC Tasks (in unit METL)

Quick Checks:
- Make sure all Soldiers are assigned a protective mask and that is has a current PATS test.
- Make sure there are batteries on hand or on order for NBC equipment.
- Make sure all NBC equipment has current calibrations.

N C	
OIC	**N C NCO**
Pre-inspects all inventories of NBC equipment	Signs for all NBC equipment and ensures it is properly sub hand receipted and filed properly
Briefs CO on NMC, Parts Received not Installed, and Services due	Conducts -20 maintenance on NBC equipment. Ensures platoons conduct proper PMCS on their NBC equipment
Ensures platoons give NBC section what they need (paperwork, Soldiers, etc)	Completes paperwork and turns-in equipment to Direct Support and Depot as needed
Briefs NBC maintenance at Bn maintenance meeting	Subject Matter Expert (SME) for all NBC training in the unit. Coordinates with Training NCO and CO to implement NBC Training
Ensures NBC section of CO TACSOP and Maintenance SOP are updated and implemented to lowest level	Works with NBC Officer to update SOPs

8.15 Postal Operations

References:

FM 12-6 Personnel Doctrine (Sep 94)
AR 600-8-3 Postal Operations (Dec 89)

Unit Mail Clerks:

- Receive mail and sort it by location to the lowest remaining unit levels.
- Deliver mail to addressees.
- Collect 100 percent of retrograde mail from unit soldiers and forward it to the postal services platoon via the MDPs.
- Forward retrograde mail to the postal services platoon/mail delivery point separated by outgoing and intra-theater (local) military mail.
- Ensure that all mail is safeguarded and handled IAW DOD postal regulations (without exception).
- Coordinate with the S1 to maintain an accountability roster by location of unit soldiers to ensure efficient mail redirect for soldiers who become casualties or change location.
- Appropriately label and redirect casualty mail to the postal services platoon for forwarding.
- Deliver accountable mail to soldiers and civilians IAW DOD postal regulations.
- Immediately report any postal problems to the commander and/or unit S1.

Quick Checks:

- Are your unit's mail clerks on appointment orders? Do they have their Mail Handler's card?
- Are the mail room hours posted? Check during those times to make sure it is opened.

Tips/Tricks:

- Do not put problem Soldiers in the mail room as an extra duty. Ensure you are choosing responsible Soldiers for this duty that have the hours to do the job properly.
- Ensure the mail room hours are workable for Soldiers on shift duty to pick up their packages.
- Make sure Soldiers fill out a change of address card through the mail room when they inprocess.

8.16 Safety Officer

References:

AR 190-40 Serious Incident Report (Feb 06)
AR 385-10 Army Safety Program (Feb 00)
AR 385-40 Accident Reporting and Records (Nov 94)
FM 100-14 Risk Management (Apr 98)
PAM 385-1 Small Unit Safety Officer/NCO Guide

Forms:

DA 285-AB-R US Army Abbreviated Ground Accident Report (AGAR) (Jul 94)

Websites:

US Army Safety Center http://crc.army.mil/
POV Risk Assessment https://crcapps.army.mil/ASMIS2

Tools:

POV Toolbox
Safety Posters
Motorcycle Safety Packet

Responsibilities:

- Ensure leader's give safety briefs before weekends/briefs
- Ensure leaders conduct POV Inspections
- Complete (or help leader's complete) the necessary paperwork when accidents occur

Safety Book:

- Past incident reports
- Serious Incident Report format
- Motorcycle riders
- Past safety inspections
- Sign-in sheets from safety briefs

Quick Checks:

- Check operations records and see if they maintain sign in rosters from safety briefs.
- Identify the motorcycle operators in your unit and ensure they have signed the Motorcycle Safety Packet and have received proper licensing.
- Ensure POV Inspection sheets and risk assessments are maintained till after the Soldier signs in from pass/leave.

Sample Incident Report:

<table>
<tr><td>Reporting Unit:</td><td></td><td>DTG:</td><td>140001JAN06</td><td>Report Type:</td><td>Initial</td></tr>
<tr><td>Subject:</td><td colspan="5">Alcohol Related: Yes_X___ No_____</td></tr>
<tr><td colspan="2">Person Filing Report:</td><td colspan="4">2LT Smith</td></tr>
<tr><td colspan="2">Persons Involved:</td><td colspan="4">Subject:
(Rank, Name, SSN, Duty Position)
Victim:
(Rank, Name, SSN, Duty Position)
Witness:
(Rank, Name, SSN, Duty Position)</td></tr>
<tr><td colspan="2">Summary of Incident:</td><td colspan="4"></td></tr>
<tr><td colspan="2">Where Incident Took Place:</td><td colspan="4">Location with as much information as available</td></tr>
<tr><td colspan="2">DTG (of incident):</td><td colspan="4">140001JAN06</td></tr>
<tr><td colspan="2">Commander's Assessment: (Why the Incident Occurred)</td><td colspan="4"></td></tr>
<tr><td colspan="2">Actions Taken:</td><td colspan="4"></td></tr>
</table>

Accidents:

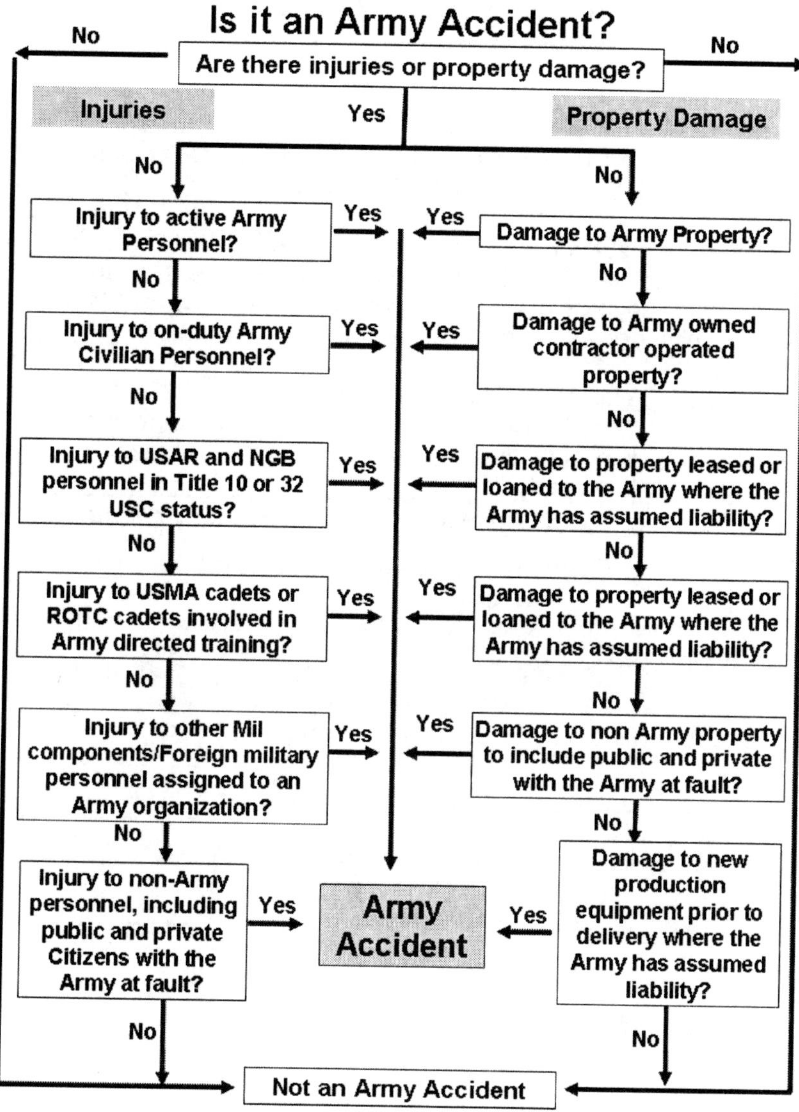

Is it an Army Accident?
No
Are there injuries or property damage?
No
Injuries
Yes
Property Damage
No
No
Injury to active Army Personnel?
Yes
Yes
Damage to Army Property?
No
No
Injury to on-duty Army Civilian Personnel?
Yes
Yes
Damage to Army owned contractor operated property?
No
No
Injury to USAR and NGB personnel in Title 10 or 32 USC status?
Yes
Yes
Damage to property leased or loaned to the Army where the Army has assumed liability?
No
No
Injury to USMA cadets or ROTC cadets involved in Army directed training?
Yes
Yes
Damage to property leased or loaned to the Army where the Army has assumed liability?
No
No
Injury to other Mil components/Foreign military personnel assigned to an Army organization?
Yes
Yes
Damage to non Army property to include public and private with the Army at fault?
No
No
Injury to non-Army personnel, including public and private Citizens with the Army at fault?
Yes
Army Accident
Yes
Damage to new production equipment prior to delivery where the Army has assumed liability?
No
No
Not an Army Accident

Class A. The resulting total cost of reportable damage is $1,000,000 or more; an Army Aircraft or missile is destroyed, missing, or abandon; or an injury and/or occupational illness results in a fatality or permanent total disability.

Class B. The resulting total cost or reportable property damage is $200,000 or more but less than $1,000,000, an injury and/or occupational illness results in permanent partial disability, or three or more personnel are inpatient hospitalized.

Class C. The resulting total cost of property damage is $20,000 or more but less than $200,000 or a nonfatal injury, illness, or disability that causes any loss of time from work beyond the day or shift on which it occurred or disability at any time (lost-time case).

Class D. The resulting total cost of property damage is $2,000 or more but less than $20,000. Note. Nonfatal injuries/illnesses (restricted work activity, light duty, or profile) will only be recorded in conjunction with recordable property damage accidents

Ground Accident Notification and Reporting Requirements & Suspenses					
	Peacetime			Combat	
	Phone Notification	AGAR	DA Form 285	Phone Notification	AGAR only
On-Duty					
A	Immediately	N/A	IAI/CAI 90days	Immediately	NLT 30 days
B	Immediately	N/A	IAI/CAI 90days	Immediately	NLT 30 days
C	N/A	Within 30 days	N/A	N/A	NLT 30 days
D	N/A	Within 30 days	N/A	N/A	NLT 30 days
Off-Duty					
A	Immediately	Within 30 days	N/A	Immediately	NLT 30 days
B	Immediately	Within 30 days	N/A	Immediately	NLT 30 days
C	N/A	Within 30 days	N/A	N/A	NLT 30 days
D	N/A	Within 30 days	N/A	N/A	NLT 30 days

Table E-2. Ground Accident Notification
AR 385-40. Accident Reporting and Records.

8.17 Security Officer

References:

AR 380-67 Army Personnel Security Program (Sep 88)
AR 604-5 Department of the Army Personnel Security Program (Feb 84)
AR 604-10 Military Personnel Security (Sep 69)

Forms:

DA 5247-R Request for Security Determination (Sep 83)
DA 5248-R Report of Unfavorable Information for Security Determination (Sep 83)

eMILPO Reports:
AAC-C37 Personnel Qualification Roster

Definitions:
Need to know: A criterion used in security procedures that requires the custodians of classified information to establish, prior to disclosure, that the intended recipient must have access to the information to perform his or her official duties.

8.17.1 Crime Prevention

Quick Checks:
- The PMO should have a Crime Prevention section. Stop by and they should be able to give you materials for the bulletin board, etc.

8.17.2 Force Protection Officer

References:
AR 525-13 Anti-Terrorism (Jan 02)

Other References:
FBI Bomb Threat Card

Force Protection Book:
- Exercises and Plans
- Current Threats
- FPCON and Homeland Security levels

Force Protection Condition (FPCON): A Chairman of the Joint Chiefs of Staff-approved program standardizing the Military Services' identification of and recommended responses to terrorist threats against US personnel and facilities. This program facilitates inter-Service coordination and support for antiterrorism activities.

FPCON ALPHA: This condition applies when there is a general threat of possible terrorist activity against personnel and facilities, the nature and extent of which are unpredictable, and circumstances do not justify full implementation of FPCON BRAVO measures. However, it may be necessary to implement certain measures from higher FPCONs resulting from intelligence received or as a deterrent. The measures in this FPCON must be capable of being maintained indefinitely.

FPCON BRAVO: This condition applies when an increased and more predictable threat of terrorist activity exists. The measures in this FPCON must be capable of being maintained for weeks without causing undue hardship, affecting operational capability, and aggravating relations with local authorities.

FPCON CHARLIE: This condition applies when an incident occurs or intelligence is received indicating some form of terrorist action against personnel and facilities is imminent. Implementation of measures in this FPCON for more than a short period probably will create hardship and affect the peacetime activities of the unit and its personnel.

FPCON DELTA: This condition applies in the immediate area where a terrorist attack has occurred or when intelligence has been received that terrorist action against a specific location or person is likely. Normally, this FPCON is declared as a localized condition.

Tips/Tricks:
- Ensure all Soldiers take the Anti-Terrorism Level I training online when your unit does Soldier Readiness Preparation (SRP). File their certificates in their SRP packets.
- When in the field or deployed, walk your unit's AO and do a vulnerability assessment. Encourage your unit to alter unit schedules and activities to not be so predictable.

8.17.3 Information Assurance Security (IASO)

References:
AR 25-2 Information Assurance (Nov 03)

Training:
IASO Training http://ia.gordon.army.mil/iaso/

IASO Book:
- IASO training certificate
- User agreements and user tests
- Anti-virus and Windows Update lists

Quick Checks:
- Ensure you have a list of all authorized users on the post domain. Maintain the user agreement and user test for each user.

Tip/Tricks:
- Have the commander designate that all government computers have the default background. Do not allow Soldiers to personalize them.
- Install software to make all anti-virus and Windows Updates automatic.

- Set the Commander and 1SG as Power Users on their systems so they can install basic software and programs themselves.
- Create a quick sheet with the TCP/IP and proxy settings for each computer.
- Create a list of useful post websites and post in the company.
- Go to DOIM and build a relationship with them. Have their Help Desk number on speed dial.

8.17.4 OPSEC Officer

References:

FM 3-13	Information Operations (Nov 02)
AR 530-1	Operations Security (Sep 05)

Websites:

Army OPSEC https://opsec.1stiocmd.army.mil/

Definitions:

Operations security: A process of identifying essential elements of friendly information and subsequently analyzing friendly actions attendant to military operations and other activities to: identify those actions that can be observed by adversary intelligence systems, determine indicators hostile intelligence systems might obtain that could be interpreted or pieced together to derive critical information in time to be useful to adversaries, and select and execute measures that eliminate or reduce to an acceptable level the vulnerabilities of friendly actions to adversary exploitation.

OPSEC Book:

- Current OPSEC messages
- List of unit Soldiers with military blogs
- Levels security classifications

Tips/Tricks:

- Find out which Soldiers in your company have Blogs about the military (especially during deployment). Make sure they register with the Army and check them personally to make sure they say in good OPSEC practice.
- Make sure unit publications have proper classifications on them (such as For Official Use Only).

8.17.5 Physical Security Officer

References:

FM 3-19.30	Physical Security (Jan 01)
AR 190-11	Physical Security of Arms, Ammunition, and Explosives (Feb 98)

AR 190-13 The Army Physical Security Program (Sep 93)
AR 190-16 Physical Security (May 91)
AR 380-67 Army Personnel Security Program (Sep 88)
PAM 190-51 Risk Analysis for Army Property (Sep 93)

Forms:
DA Form 7278-R Risk Level Worksheet (Aug 93)
* High Value Forms
* Form number differs by installation. Check installation publications for form number.

Definitions:
Physical security: That part of security concerned with physical measures designed to safeguard personnel; to prevent unauthorized access to equipment, installations, material, and documents; and to safeguard them against espionage, sabotage, damage, and theft.

Responsibilities:
- Conduct quarterly inspections of the arms room.
- Conduct periodic walk-thru's of the motor pool to check security of the vehicles and communication systems
- Conduct Risk Analysis for everything your unit owns (company area, motor pool, etc) on DA Form 7278-R. This needs to be completed every three years.

Physical Security Book
- High value forms
- Inspection checklists
- Past Inspections

Quick Checks:
- Check to see if Soldiers fill out high value forms (Personal Property Records) on their property.
- Check the date on the last Risk Analysis for your unit.

Item No	Name of Item	Qty	Brand Name, Model, or Style	Serial No	Date Acq	Value	Signature

Example Fields of High Value Form

8.18 Supply Officer

References:

AR 710-2	Supply Policy Below the National Level (Jul 05)
AR 735-5	Policies and Procedures for Property Accountability (Feb 05)
AR 735-11-2	Reporting of Supply Discrepancies (Aug 01)
FM 10-27-4	Organizational Supply for Unit Leaders (Apr 00)
CTA 50-900	Clothing and Individual Equipment (Aug 90)
CTA 50-909	Field and Garrison Furnishings and Equip (Jun 89)
CTA 50-970	Expendable/Durable Items (Sep 90)
PAM 710-1-1	Using Unit Supply System (Manual) (Dec 97)
PAM 735-5	Survey Officer's Guide (Mar 97)
PAM 738-751	Users Manual for TAMMS-A (Mar 91)
ULLS-S4	Commander's Guide for Unit Level Logistics - Supply

Forms:

DA 1659	Financial Liability Investigation of Property Loss Register (Oct 04)
DA 1687	Notice of Delegation of Authority (Jan 82)
DA 2062	Hand Receipt/Annex Number (Jan 82)
DA 3161	Request For Issue or Turn-in (Dec 00)
DA 3294	Ration Request/Issue/Turn-in Slip (Jul 02)
DA 3645a	Org Clothing/Indiv Equip Record (Oct 91)
DA 3645b	Org Clothing/Indiv Equip Record (Oct 91)
DA 3645-1a	Additional Org Clothing/Indiv Equip Record (Dec 83)
DA 3645-1b	Additional Org Clothing/Indiv Equip Record (Dec 83)
DA 3749	Equipment Receipt (Jan 82)
DA 4949	Administrative Adjustment Report (Jan 82)
DA 5914-R	Ration Control Sheet (Jun 90)
DA 7531	Checklist for Financial Liability Investigations (Aug 04)
DD 200	Financial Liability Investigation of Property Loss (Oct 99)
DD 362	Statement of Charges for Government Property Lost, Damaged, or Destroyed (Mar 74)
DD 1131	Cash Collection Voucher (Apr 57)

Websites:

Logistical Network	https://lognet.bcks.army.mil/
Electronic TMs	https://www.logsa.army.mil/

Training:
Supply Officer Course (local Post)
Unit Supply Specialist Course (Correspondence: 101 M40-M42)

Responsibilities:
- Manage cyclic and sensitive item inventories. Make sure they are conducted on time and the commander is provided with the proper paperwork.

Supply Book:
- Commander's Master Hand Receipt
- Sub Hand Receipts
- Lateral Transfers
- Turn-in paperwork, Statement of Charges
- Equipment Listings (Components, Basic Issue Items, and Additional Authorized for each type of equipment of in your unit)

Quick Checks:
- Is there a highly visible chart listing all primary hand receipt holders, date of last inventory, last hand receipt update, and projected departure date of holder?
- Does the Supply NCO have a listing of all missing equipment/components not on valid requisition due to funding constraints? Does it reference relief documents?
- Is there a file on hand containing copies of mandatory commander's 10% inventories?
- Is there an excessive amount of unserviceable property awaiting turn-in on hand?
- Is the Supply Clerks ULLS-S4 certified?
- Does your unit's ULLS-S4 box match print outs from the PBO?
- Get a reconnaissance report of supplies ordered and make sure you have a valid status (BA,BB) on everything.

SUPPLY	
OIC	**SUPPLY NCO**
Coordinate inventories, transfers, etc on the commander's schedule	Safeguards supplies and property stored in unit supply room and storage areas
Responsible for the CO's book of components, BII, and AAL for all property book items	Prepares and maintains supply and property book records
Briefs Commander on shortages, transfers, inventories, and discrepancies	Requests, receives, and issues supplies. Prepares adjustment documents for lost, damaged, or destroyed property
Checks recon report to make sure all requests have a current status	Coordinates delivery of supplies from field trains forward
	Coordinates issue and turn in of unit property between company and personnel

Role of the Property Book Officer: The PBO usually works directly for the battalion XO. He is the subject matter expert on all supply matters. It is extremely important to have a good relationship with the PBO. Seek out his guidance and mentorship to learn more about supply, as well as a go-to person when you cannot resolve supply matters at the company level. Ensure that you get the updated ULLS-S4 hand receipt for your commander and that you are tracking on when inventories are due to the PBO.

8.18.1 Transactions

Lateral Transfer: A lateral transfer is an exchange of non-expendable excess property from one organization to another organization where a shortage exists.

- Prepared on DA Form 3161, IAW DA PAM 710-2-1, figure 3-3, Prepared in enough copies. Transfer equipment in 10/20 standard condition (Fully Mission Capable-FMC).
- Must be approved by losing PBO's assign document number from Document Register.
- Losing and gaining PBO's assign document number from Document

Register.
- You do not have to accept items if not in serviceable condition

DA 3161
- Ensure you have all TM -10/-20 on hand and
- Have a component hand receipt if any components are missing
- Have a shortage annex for any basic issue items (BII) that are missing

Turn-ins:
- Major End items that are excess or unserviceable must be turned-in within 10 days. A technical inspection (TI) is required prior to the turn-in. Prepare Maintenance request DA Form 2407, take item to appropriate SSA for inspection.
- Immediately after inspection schedule an appointment with the SSA.
- Prepare DA Form 2765-1 with correct information from the HR.
- Obtain a document number from the PBO 3 days prior to the turn-in day. Bring DA Form 2765-1 to PBO along with DA Form 2407 to obtain a document number.
- Items that are serviceable and authorized by TDA or MTOE will not be turned-in regardless if item is used or not. Unit must prepare a DA Form 4610-R if PHRH wants to delete item form TDA or MTOE.

Adjustments:
DA Form 4949-AAR is used to make minor property book adjustments. It is not used to replace one item for another. The only exception is if the maintenance form or manufacturer's exchange document indicates that the items were exchanged and both serial numbers are shown on the document. Attach document to the AAR. Use and AAR to adjust sizes, makes, models, NSN, LIN, ARC, or to adjust a serial number when it is obvious a number has been transposed or mistyped.

Document Numbers:
The PBO will give you the UIC for types of equipment: Durable, Expendable, Nonexpendable, Class IX. The next four digits is the Julian Date. The last four is the actual number.

8.19 Tax Officer

Forms:

IRS 1040 EZ
IRS 1040

Websites:

IRS Homepage http://www.irs.gov/

Responsibilities:

- Check with Platoon Sergeants to ensure all Soldiers receive their W-2s (usually January).
- Be an alarm clock to remind Soldiers to file their taxes (or at least an extension) before April 15.

Tips/Tricks:

- After a safety brief, attempt to persuade Soldiers not to go to Check-cashing places for their refunds.

8.20 Unit Movement Officer

References:

Fort Eustis 97-1	Unit Movement Deployment Handbook
FM 3-35.4	Deployment Fort to Port (Jun 02)
FM 4-01.011	Unit Movement Operations (Oct 02)
FM 4-01.30	Movement Control (Sep 03)
FM 4-01.45	Multi-service Tactics, Techniques, and Procedures for Convoy Operations (Mar 05)
FM 55-1	Transportation Operations (Oct 95)
FM 55-15	Transportation Reference Data (Oct 97)
FM 100-17	Mobilization, Deployment, Redeployment, Demobilization (Oct 92)
AR 59-3	Movement of Cargo by Scheduled Military Air Transportation (Apr 01)
AR 59-9	Special Assignment Airlift Mission Regulations (Mar 85)
TB 55-46-1	Characteristics for Transportability of Military Vehicles and Other Equipment
TB 43-0244	Unit Level Procedures for Handling Service Supplies, Hazardous Materials, and Waste (Aug 92)

Forms:

DD 836	Shippers Declaration of Dangerous Goods (Apr 05)
DD 1249	SAAM/JCS Airlift Request (Jul 81)
DD 1384	Transportation Control and Movement Document (Oct 00)
DD 1387	Military Shipping Label (Jul 99)
DD 1750	Packing List (Sep 70)
DD 2133	Joint Airlift Inspection Record (Oct 98)
DD 2781	Container/Vehicle Packing Certificate (Jun 05)

Websites:

Deployment Homepage http://www.deploy.eustis.army.mil/

Sub-Sections:

- Rail Load Planner
- Air Load Planner
- 463-L Pallets

Responsibilities:

- Update unit Deployment Equipment List (DEL) at DOL
- Identify unit rail load and air load teams and ensure those Soldiers attend training.

- Ensure DD Form 1750 is filled out when packing out
- Ensure all vehicles/containers are property blocked/braced
- Ensure all Military Shipping Labels (MSLs) and RF tags are properly affixed to equipment

Definitions:

Advance Party: A team that coordinates the convoy's arrival at the destination. It may move with the main body initially but must arrive at the destination sufficiently ahead of the main body.

Aerial port of debarkation (APOD): An airfield for sustained air movement at which personnel and materiel are discharged from aircraft. Aerial ports of debarkation normally serve as ports of embarkation for return passengers and retrograde cargo shipments.

Aerial port of embarkation (APOE): An airfield for sustained air movement at which personnel and materiel board or are loaded aboard aircraft to initiate aerial movement. Aerial ports of embarkation may serve as ports of debarkation for return passengers and retrograde cargo shipments.

Marshalling area: A location in the vicinity of a reception terminal or pre-positioned equipment storage site where arriving unit personnel, equipment, materiel, and accompanying supplies are reassembled, returned to the control of the unit commander, and prepared for onward movement.

Port of debarkation (POD): The geographic point at which cargo or personnel are discharged. This may be a seaport or aerial port of debarkation; for unit requirements, it may or may not coincide with the destination.

Port of embarkation (POE): The geographic point in a routing scheme from which cargo and personnel depart. This may be a seaport or aerial port from which personnel and equipment flow to a port of debarkation; for unit and non-unit requirements, it may or may not coincide with the origin.

Sea port of debarkation (SPOD): A marine terminal for sustained port operations at which personnel and materiel are discharged from ships. Sea ports of debarkation normally act as ports of embarkation on return passenger and retrograde cargo shipments.

Sea port of embarkation (SPOE): A marine terminal for sustained port operations at which personnel board and materiel is loaded aboard ships. Sea ports of embarkation normally act as ports of debarkation on return passenger and retrograde cargo shipments.

Unit Movement Book:
- Unit Deployment Equipment List
- Packing Lists (DD Form 1750) for all containers
- Hazmat Paperwork (DD Form 843)
- Serial Number lists of sensitive items

Quick Checks:
- Check unit movement book for most recent DEL
- Check Alert procedures and movement SOPs
- Check containers for seaworthiness

Tips/Tricks:
- Ensure you have new locks for all containers. Ensure all hand receipt holders are physically present when the container is opened.

8.21 UPL

References:

AR 600-85 Army Substance Abuse Program (ASAP) (Mar 06)
DA 8003 ASAP Referral Form

Other References:

Commander's Guide and Unit Prevention Leader (UPL) Collection Handbook, ACSAP (Nov 01)

Responsibilities:

- Complete the ASAP UPL certification program
- Conduct unannounced unit urine collection
- Coordinate required drug and alcohol classes (350-1 training)
- Ensure commander's selection for testing is purely random and unpredictable
- Maintain unit ASAP bulletin board with current drug trends, marketing, and prevention materials
- Train and supervise unit observers

Objectives:

- Deterrence
- Early identification of users
- Enable commanders to assess the security, military fitness, good order, and discipline in their units
- Monitor rehabilitation
- Determine the presence of illegal drugs
- Research

Conditions for Directing Bio-Testing

- Unit inspections
- Search and seizures/probably cause
- Command directed/ reasonable suspicion
- Rehabilitation
- Voluntary

Tips/Tricks:

- Make sure all unit urinalysis tests are random.

8.22 USR Officer

References:

AR 220-1 Unit Status Reporting (Mar 06)
AR 220-20 Army Status of Resources and Training System (ASORTS) - Basic Identity Data Elements (BIDE) (Mar 04)
AR 680-29 Military Personnel, Organization, and Type of Transaction Codes (Mar 96)

Websites:

ASORTS Software http://www.pc-asorts.com/

eMILPO Reports:

AAA 162	Unit Personnel Accountability Report	AAC C15	Projected DEROS Report
AAC C01	Enlisted Personnel Eligible for Promotion Consideration	AAC C27	Personnel Strength Zero Balance Report
AAC C05	Unit Strength Recap	AAC–C37	Personnel Qualification Roster
AAC C10	Recommended List for Promotion of Enlisted Personnel	AAC–C40	Unit Personnel Accountability Notices
AAC C11	Alpha Roster	AAC–C47	Roster of Senior Enlisted Personnel
AAC C13	Loss Roster	AAC-C49	Roster of Officers

Websites:

PC-ASORTS Software http://www.pc-asorts.com

Monthly Requirements:

- ASORTS output (MTF file)
- USR Powerpoint brief
- BN/BDE Spreadsheet

Continuity/Tracking Book:

- Unit Log (List personnel, equipment, training status by month)
- Higher echelon's USR Memorandum of Instruction
- MTF Output (monthly)
- Powerpoint Slides (monthly, 6 to a page)
- Higher echelon spreadsheet
- Non-deployable list

Tips/Tricks:

- Learn ASORTS. To read a MTF, find the file on your computer, Right-Click, and OPEN WITH Notepad.
- Although there are many spreadsheets and other tools out there, when you first get USR, make your own Excel spreadsheet using the formulas in Chapter 4 of AR 220-1. It will help you understand where the values come from.
- Do not PROCRASTINATE! The key to USR is to have good tracking throughout the month, not pulling all-nighters two days before.
- Give your commander a suspense for turning in their comments (GENTEXT, etc). The comments are one of the most important parts and you need to give them time to think through them. Give them a printout of their comments from the previous turn-in and have them return them the day prior to you.

8.23 Voting Officer

References:

AR 608-20 Army Voting Assistance Program (Oct 04)

Website:

Federal Voting Assistance http://www.fvap.gov

Responsibilities:

- Assist Soldiers to register to vote
- Assist Soldiers in obtaining absentee ballots
- Remind unit of upcoming elections and the suspense

Tips/Tricks:

- In July or August (3-4 months prior to election), set up a bulletin board about voting. Create a flyer with the links for each state's voting registration website. Include the suspense for registering and requesting absentee ballots.
- Remind Soldiers about registering to vote/requesting absentee ballots at an end of day formation.

Branch References

Part

9 Branch References

References:

PAM 600-2 The Armed Forces Officer (Feb 88)

Combat Arms	Combat Support	Combat Service Support
11- Infantry	21- Engineer	27- Paralegal
13- Field Artillery	25- Signal Operations	38- Civil Affairs (RC)
14- Air Defense Artillery	31- Military Police	42- Adjutant General
15- Aviation	35- Military Intelligence	44- Financial Management
18- Special Forces	37- Psychological Ops	46- Public Affairs
19- Armor	74- Chemical	55- Ammunition
21- Engineer	88- Transportation	56- Religious Support
		60 thru 62- Medical
		63- Dental
		64- Veterinary
		66- Nurse
		67- Medical Service
		89- Ammunition
		91- Ordnance
		92- Quartermaster

9.1 Combat Arms

Combat arms : Units and soldiers who close with the enemy and destroy enemy forces or provide firepower and destructive capabilities on the battlefield.

- **AIR DEFENSE ARTILLERY**
  - Short Range
  - Theater Air Defense
  - Theater Ballistic Missile Defense
- **ARMOR**
  - Armor
  - Armored Cavalry
  - Light Cavalry
- **AVIATION**
  - Attack
  - Assault
  - Air Cavalry
- **ENGINEERS**
  - Mobility
  - Counter-mobility
  - Survivability
- **INFANTRY**
  - Light
  - Mechanized
  - Motorized
  - Air Assault
  - Airborne
- **FIELD ARTILLERY**
  - Target Acquisition
  - Cannon Artillery
  - MLRS/ATACMS
- **SPECIAL OP FORCES**
  - Ranger
  - Special Forces
  - Special Ops Aviation

Figure A-1. Combat Arms Capabilities
FM 3-90. Tactics (Jul 01)

9.1.1 Air Defense

References:

FM 3-01.4	Joint Suppression of Enemy Air Defense (May 05)
FM 3-01.7	Air Defense Artillery Brigade Operations (Oct 00)
FM 3-01.11	Air Defense Artillery Reference Handbook (Oct 00)
FM 3-01.15	Integrated Air Defense System (IADS) (Oct 04)
FM 3-01.16	Theater Missile Defense Intel Prep of Battlespace (Mar 02)
FM 3-01.20	Joint Air Operations Center and Army and Missile Defense Cmd Coordination (JAOC/AAMDC) (Mar 04)
FM 3-01.48	Air/Missile Defense Sentinel Platoon Operations (Dec 03)
FM 3-01.51	Joint Theater Missile Target Development (Nov 03)
FM 3-01.80	Visual Aircraft Recognition (Jan 06)
FM 3-01.85	Patriot Battalion and Battery Operations (May 02)
FM 3-01.86	Air Defense Artillery Patriot Brigade Gunnery (Sep 04)
FM 3-01.87	Patriot Tactics, Techniques, and Procedures (Sep 00)
FM 3-01.94	Air and Missile Defense Command Operations (Apr 05)
FM 44-8	Combined Arms for Air Defense (Jun 99)
FM 44-18	Air Defense Employment: Stinger (May 85)
FM 44-18-1	Stinger Team Operations (Dec 84)
FM 44-43	Bradley Stinger Fighting Vehicle PLT/Squad Opns (Oct 95)
FM 44-44	Avenger Platoon, Section, and Squad Operations (Oct 95)
FM 44-100	US Army Air and Missile Defense Operations (Jun 00)
PAM 600-3-14	Air Defense Artillery (Aug 87)

Websites:

Air Defense Branch	https://www.hrc.army.mil/site/active/opada/adanews.htm
ADA Knowledge Ctr	https://www.us.army.mil/suite/collaboration/comm_V.do?ci=3968&load=true

ARTEP:

44-117-11-DRILL	Drills for the Stinger Team (Feb 99)
44-117-21-DRILL	Drills for the Avenger Team (Jan 01)
44-176-15-DRILL	Drills for the FAAS C41 Subsystems (Aug 01)
44-177-14-DRILL	Drills for Bradley Stinger Vehicle/Linebacker (Jun 03)
44-635-11-DRILL	Patriot Drills for Power Plant/Antenna Mast (Jun 03)
44-635-12-DRILL	Patriot Drills for Infor Coordination Central with EPU, Comm Relay Group, and TCS (Oct 03)
44-635-13-DRILL	Patriot Drills for Engagement Control Station (Jul 03)
44-635-14-DRILL	Patriot Drills for PAC-2/3 Missile Reload (Oct 03)
44-635-15-DRILL	Patriot Drills for PAC-2/3 Forklift Missile Reload (Oct 03)
44-115-MTP	ADA Battalion (Light, ABN, and AA)
44-117-11-MTP	Stinger Platoon
44-117-22-MTP	Avenger Platoon
44-117-30-MTP	ADA Battery, Gun or Stinger
44-175-MTP	ADA Battalion Heavy Division (Nov 03)
44-176-15-MTP	Sentinel Platoon
44-177-15-MTP	Bradley Stinger Fighting Vehicle/Linebacker Platoon
44-177-30-MTP	ADA Battery, Bradley, Stinger Fighting Vehicle
44-177-35-MTP	ADA Battery (Light, ABN, AA, Heavy Div/Corps) (Aug 02)

44-413-34-MTP	SHORAD Battery
44-637-30-MTP	ADA Battery, Patriot

Soldier Training Plans (STP):

9-27T14-SM-TG	MOS 27T, Avenger System Repairer, SL 1-4 (Sep 01)
9-27X14-SM-TG	MOS 27X, Patriot System Repairer, SL 1-4 (Nov 01))
9-35R13-SM-TG	MOS 35R, Avionic Systems Repairer, SL 1-3 (Jun 04)
9-35T14-SM-TG	MOS 35T, Avenger System Repairer, SL 1-4 (Mar 05)
44-14E14-SM-TG	MOS 14E, Patriot Fire Control, SL 1-4 (Jul 04)
44-14J14-SM-TG	MOS 14J, C4I TOC Maintainer, SL 1-4 (Nov 02)
44-14S14-SM-TG	MOS 14S, Avenger Crew Member, SL 1-4 (Sep 04)
44-14T14-SM-TG	MOS 14T, Patriot Launching Station, SL 1-4 (Mar 02)

9.1.2 Armor

References:

FM 3-20.8	Scout Gunnery (Aug 05)
FM 3-20.12	Tank Gunnery Abrams (Aug 05)
FM 3-20.15	Tank Platoon (Nov 01)
FM 3-20.90	Tank and Cavalry HHC and HHT (Aug 04)
FM 3-20.96	Cavalry Squadron (RSTA) (Dec 02)
FM 3-20.98	Reconnaissance Platoon (Feb 02)
FM 3-20.151	Mobile Gun System Platoon (Nov 05)
FM 3-20.971	Reconnaissance Troop (Dec 02)
FM 7-93	Long-Range Surveillance Unit Operations (Oct 95)
PAM 600-3-12	Armor (Aug 87)
IP M1028	Lethality Update for M1028 120mm Canister (Jan 06)
ST 3-20.12	Tank Crew Evaluator Exportable Packet (Mar 02)
ST 3-20.12-4	M908 120mm HE-or-T Char./Capabilities (Sep 04)
ST 3-20.12-7	M1028 120mm Canister Char//Capabilities (Jun 05)
ST 3-20.153	Tank Platoon SOP (Jan 02)
ST 3-20.983	Reconnaissance Handbook (Apr 02)
ST 17-184-1A1	M1A1 Tank Combat Load Plan (May 01)
ST 17-184-1A2	M1A2 Tank Combat Load Plan (Mar 00)

Websites:

Armor Branch	https://www.hrc.army.mil/site/active/oparmor/arnews.htm
Armor School	http://www.knox.army.mil/school/
Armor Univ	http://147.238.144.82/umw/index.htm
Armor Knowledge	https://www.us.army.mil/suite/page/362
Armor Magazine	http://www.knox.army.mil/center/ocoa/armormag/

ARTEP:

17-57-10-MTP	Scout Platoon
17-95F-40-MTP	Cavalry Squadron (RSTA) (Feb 04)
17-97F-10-MTP	Reconnaissance Platoon (Apr 04)
17-97F30-MTP	Reconnaissance Troop (Mar 04)
17-237-10-MTP	Tank Platoon
17-237-11-MTP	Tank Crew (Sep 03)
17-385-MTP	Calvary Squadron
17-487-30-MTP	Regimental Armored Cavalry Troop
34-117-30-MTP	Surveillance Troop of the Initial BCT

Soldier Training Plans (STP):

17-19AII-OFS-1	Armor Officers, 19A (Feb 06)
17-19D1-SM	MOS 19D, Cavalry Scout, SL 1 (Jan 04)
17-19D2-SM	MOS 19D, Cavalry Scout, SL 2 (Oct 04)
17-19D3-SM-TG	MOS 19D, Cavalry Scout, SL 3 (Jun 05)
17-19D4-SM	MOS 19D, Cavalry Scout, SL 4 (Jul 05)
17-19K1-SM	MOS 19K, Abrams Armor Crewman, SL (Jul 04)
17-19K2-SM	MOS 19K, Abrams Armor Crewman, SL 2 (Jan 05)
17-19K3-SM-TG	MOS 19K, Abrams Armor Crewman, SL 3 (Apr 05)
17-19K4-SM	MOS 19K, Abrams Armor Crewman, SL 4 (Feb 05)

17-19Z-SM MOS 19Z, Armor Senior Sergeant, SL 5 (Jun 00)

9.1.3 Aviation

References:

FM 1-100	Army Aviation Operations (Feb 97)
FM 1-112	Attack Helicopter Operations (Apr 97)
FM 1-113	Utility and Cargo Helicopter Operations (Sep 97)
FM 1-114	Air Cavalry Squadron and Troop Operations (Feb 00)
FM 1-120	Army Air Traffic Services Contingency (May 95)
FM 1-506	Aircraft Power Plants (Nov 90)
FM 1-509	Aircraft Pneudraulics (Oct 87)
FM 1-514	Rotor and Power Training Maintenance (Apr 91)
FM 3-04.111	Aviation Brigades (Aug 03)
FM 3-04.140	Helicopter Gunnery (Jul 03)
FM 3-04.300	Flight Operations Procedures (Apr 04)
FM 3-04.301	Aeromedical Training for Flight Personnel (Sep 00)
FM 3-04.303	Air Traffic Services Facility Operations (Dec 03)
FM 3-04.500	Army Aviation Maintenance (Sep 00)
FM 3-04.508	Aviation Life Support System Maintenance (Apr 04)
FM 3-04.513	Battlefield Recovery and Evacuation of Aircraft (Sep 00)
FM 3-06.1	Aviation Urban Operations (Jul 05)
PAM 600-3-15	Aviation (Aug 87)
TC 1-204	Night Flight Techniques and Procedures (Dec 98)
TC 1-210	Guide to Individual/Crew Standardization (Jan 96)
TC 1-210-1	US SPECOPs Aviation (Mar 03)
TC 1-211	Utility Helicopter UH-1 (Dec 92)
TC 1-213	Attack Helicopter AH-1 (Dec 92)
TC 1-215	Observation Helicopter OH-58A/C OH-6 A/AC (Mar 93)
TC 1-216	Aircrew Training Manual Cargo Helicopter, CH-47 (Oct 92)
TC 1-218	Utility Airplane C-12 (Sep 05)
TC 1-219	Guardrail Common Sensor Airplane RC-12 (Jun 02)
TC 1-237	Utility Helicopter H-60 Series (Sep 05)
TC 1-238	Attack Helicopter AH-64A (Sep 05)
TC 1-240	Cargo Helicopter CH-47 (Sep 05)
TC 1-248	OH-58D Kiowa Warrior (Sep 05)
TC 1-251	Attack Helicopter AH-64D (Sep 05)
CALL 05-16	The Modern Aviator's Combat Load: Helicopter Operations

Websites:

Aviation Branch	https://www.hrc.army.mil/site/active/opavn/index.htm
Aviation School	http://www-rucker.army.mil/activities/avprop.html
AV Knowledge Ctr	https://www.us.army.mil/suite/page/607
Kiowa Pilots	http://www.kiowapilots.com/
Scout Attack	https://www.scout-attack.jatdi.mil/

ARTEP:

1-112-MTP	Attack Helicopter Battalion (Apr 02)
1-113-MTP	Utility Helicopter Battalion (Aug 01)
1-114-MTP	Air Cavalry/Reconnaissance Squadron and Troop (Mar 00)

1-245-MTP	Heavy Lift Helicopter Battalion
1-111-MTP	Aviation Brigades (Oct 05)
1-113-MTP	Utility Helicopter Battalion (Dec 02)-
1-425-MTP	Air Traffic Services Battalion (Dec 02)
1-500-MTP	AV Intermediate Maintenance (AVIM) BN and CO (Apr 02)

Soldier Training Plans (STP):

1-15D13-SM-TG	MOS 15D, Aircraft Powertrain Repairer, SL 1/3 (Oct 04)
1-15M13-SM-TG	MOS 15M, UH-1 Helicopter Repairer, SL 1-3 (Oct 04)
1-15T13-SM-TG	MOS 15T, UH-60 Helicopter Repairer, SL 1-3 (Jan 05
1-15U13-SM-TG	MOS 15U, CH-47D Helicopter Repairer, SL 1-3 (Oct 04)
1-93C1-SM-TG	MOS 93C, Air Traffic Control, SL 1(Mar 02)
1-93C24-SM-TG	MOS 93C, Air Traffic Control, SL 2-4 (Mar 02)
1-93P1-SM-TG	MOS 93P, Aviation Operations Specialist, SL 1 (Oct 02)
1-93P24-SM-TG	MOS 93P, Aviation Opns Specialist, SL 2-4 (Oct 02)
9-39B13-SM-TG	MOS 39B, Apache Systems Repairer, SL 1-3 (Jul 00)

9.1.4 Engineers

References:

FM 3-34	Engineer Operations (Jan 04)
FM 3-34.2	Combined Arms Breaching Operations (Aug 00)
FM 3-34.221	Engineer Operations - Stryker BCT (Jan 05)
FM 3-34.230	Topographic Operations (Aug 00)
FM 3-34.280	Engineer Diving Operations (Dec 04)
FM 3-34.331	Topographic Surveying (Jan 01)
FM 3-34.343	Military Nonstandard Fixed Bridging (Feb 02)
FM 3-34.465	Quarry Operations (Apr 05)
FM 3-34.468	Seabee Quarry Blasting Operations (Dec 03)
FM 3-34.471	Plumbing, Pipe Fitting, and Sewerage (Aug 01)
FM 5-7-30	Brigade EN and EN Company Combat Opns (Dec 94)
FM 5-10	Combat Engineer Platoon (Apr 05)
FM 5-33	Terrain Analysis (Sep 92)
FM 5-34	Engineer Field Data (Jul 05)
FM 5-71-2	Armored TF Engineer Combat Operations (Sep 97)
FM 5-71-3	Brigade Engineer Combat Operations (Armored) (Nov 97)
FM 5-71-100	Division Engineer Combat Operations (Apr 93)
FM 5-100-15	Corps Engineer Operations (Jun 95)
FM 5-102	Countermobility (Mar 85)
FM 5-103	Survivability (Jun 85)
FM 5-104	General Engineering (Nov 86)
FM 5-116	Engineer Operations: Echelons Above Corps (Feb 99)
FM 5-125	Rigging Techniques (Feb 00)
FM 5-134	Pile Construction (Apr 85)
FM 5-170	Engineer Reconnaissance (Jul 98)
FM 5-212	Medium Girder Bridge (Feb 89)
FM 5-233	Construction Surveying (Jan 85)
FM 5-250	Explosives and Demolitions (Jun 99)
FM 5-277	Bailey Bridge (Aug 91)
FM 5-410	Military Soils Engineering (Jun 97)
FM 5-412	Project Management (Jun 94)
FM 5-415	Fire-fighting Operations (Feb 99)
FM 5-422	Engineer Prime Power Operations (May 93)
FM 5-424	Theater of Operations Electrical Systems (Jun 97)
FM 5-426	Carpentry (Oct 95)
FM 5-428	Concrete and Masonry (Jun 98)
FM 5-430-00-1	Road Design (Aug 94)
FM 5-430-00-2	Airfield and Heliport Design (Sep 94)
FM 5-434	Earthmoving Operations (Jun 00)
FM 5-436	Paving and Surfacing Operations (Apr 00)
FM 5-472	Materials Testing (Jul 01)
FM 5-480	Port Construction and Repair (Dec 90)
FM 5-482	Military Petroleum Pipeline Systems (Aug 94)
FM 5-484	Procedures for Well-Drilling Operations (Mar 94)
FM 5-499	Hydraulics (Dec 01)
FM 20-11	Military Diving (Apr 00)
FM 20-32	Mine/Countermine Operations (Apr 05)

PAM 600-3-21 Engineer (Aug 87)
TC 5-150 Engineer Qualification Tables (Jun 98)
TC 5-210 Military Float Bridging Equipment (Dec 88)
TC 5-230 Geospatial Guide for Commanders and Planners (Nov 03)
TC 5-340 Air Base Defense Repair (Pavement Repair) (Dec 88)

Websites:

Engineer Branch https://www.hrc.army.mil/site/active/openg/enmainpg.htm
EN Knowledge Ctr https://www.us.army.mil/suite/collaboration/comm_V.do?ci=604&load=true

ARTEP:

5-DRILL	Engineer Drills (Nov 04)
5-025-66-MTP	Engineer Battalion, Airborne Division
5-027-10-MTP	Engineer Platoon, ABN DIV
5-155-66-MTP	Engineer Battalion, Infantry Division (Light)
5-157-10-MTP	Engineer Platoon, Infantry Div (Light)
5-157-35-MTP	Engineer Company, Infantry Div (Light)
5-215-66-MTP	Engineer Battalion, Air Assault Division
5-217-10-MTP	Engineer Platoon, Air Assault Division
5-217-35-MTP	Engineer Company, Air Assault Division
5-337-10-MTP	Engineer Platoon, Heavy Division
5-337-35-MTP	Engineer Company, Heavy Division
5-423-35-MTP	Engineer Company, Combat Support Equipment
5-425-66-MTP	Engineer Battalion (Corps) (Wheeled)
5-427-10-MTP	Engineer Platoon, (Corps) (Wheeled)
5-427-35-MTP	Engineer Company, (Corps) (Wheeled)
5-435-66-MTP	Engineer Combat Battalion, Corps (Mech), Bn Staff
5-437-10-MTP	Engineer Platoon, Corps
5-437-35-MTP	Engineer Company, Corps
5-445-64-MTP	Engineer Battalion, Airborne (Corps)
5-447-11-MTP	Engineer Platoon, Corps (Light)
5-447-35-MTP	Engineer Company, Airborne (Corps)
5-026-11-MTP	Assault and Obstacle Platoon (May 05)
5-026-34-MTP	Headquarters Company, EN Bn (Light) (Jan 05)
5-027-35-MTP	Engineer Company, EN Bn (Light) (Aug 05)
5-053-12-MTP	Engineer Platoon, EN Company, ACR (Jun 01)
5-063-10-MTP	Mobility Platoon, EN Company, BCT (Sep 05)
5-063-11-MTP	Mobility Support Platoon, EN Company, BCT (Oct 05)
5-063-35-MTP	Engineer Company, BCT (Nov 05)
5-113-12-MTP	Engineer Platoon, EN Company, ACR (Aug 02)
5-336-34-MTP	HHC, EN Company, EN Battalion (Heavy) (Sep 03)
5-337-11-MTP	Assault and Obstacle Platoon, (Mech) (May 05)
5-413-35-MTP	Engineer Company, Construction Support (Jul 03)
5-416-14-MTP	Maintenance Platoon, HQ and Support Co (Jul 02)
5-416-34-MTP	Headquarters and Support Company (Jul 02)
5-417-13-MTP	Horizontal Construction Platoon (Nov 05)
5-417-14-MTP	Equipment Support Platoon (Nov 05)
5-417-17-MTP	General Construction Platoon, EN Company (Jul 02)
5-417-35-MTP	Engineer Company, EN Bn (Combat Heavy) (Jul 02)

5-418-17-MTP	Vertical Construction Platoon (Nov 05)
5-424-35-MTP	Engineer Company, Dump Truck (Jul 03)
5-434-35-MTP	Engineer Company, Pipeline Construction (Jul 03)
5-436-34-MTP	HHC, EN Combat Battalion, Corps (Aug 03)
5-438-11-MTP	Assault Platoon (Nov 05)
5-438-12-MTP	Countermobility Platoon (Nov 05)
5-439-11-MTP	Sapper Platoon (Nov 05)
5-443-12-MTP	Engineer Support Platoon, EN Light Equip Co (Oct 02)
5-443-14-MTP	Engineer Equip Platoon, Light Equip Co (Oct 02)
5-443-35-MTP	Engineer Company, Light Equipment (Sep 02)
5-447-10-MTP	Engineer Platoon, Airborne (Oct 00)
5-463-10-MTP	Engineer Plt, Medium Girder Bridge (Jul 02)
5-463-12-MTP	Engineer Platoon, Panel Bridge (Jul 02)
5-463-15-MTP	Engineer Support Platoon, Panel Bridge Co (Jul 02)
5-463-17-MTP	Engineer Support Plt, Medium Girder Bridge (Jul 02)
5-463-35-MTP	Engineer Company, Medium Girder Bridge (Jul 02)
5-463-36-MTP	Engineer Company, Panel Bridge (Jul 02)
5-473-35-MTP	Multi-role Bridge Company (Oct 02)
5-493-38-MTP	Engineer Company, Assault Float Bridge (Nov 02)
5-500-35-MTP	Engineer Companies (Nov 05)
5-500-68-MTP	Engineer Staffs (Sep 05)
5-510-10-MTP	Headquarters, Engineer Fire-Fighting Team (Dec 04)
5-510-12-MTP	Engineer Fire-Fighting Team, Fire Truck (Jun 04)
5-520-10-MTP	Engineer Team, Quarry (Feb 05)
5-520-12-MTP	Headquarters, Well-Drilling Team (Jan 05)
5-520-14-MTP	Engineer Team, Well-Drilling (Nov 04)
5-530-10-MTP	Engineer Heavy Diving Team (Oct 02)
5-530-12-MTP	Engineer Light Diving Team (Oct 02)
5-530-14-MTP	Engineer Team, Real Estate (Nov 04)
5-530-16-MTP	Engineer Team, Utilities (4000) (LH) (Sep 02)
5-540-10-MTP	Topographic Planning/Control Team (Oct 02)
5-540-11-MTP	Terrain Analysis Team (HVY) (Oct 02)
5-540-12-MTP	Command and Control Team (DS) (Heavy) (Oct 02)
5-540-13-MTP	Terrain Analysis Detachment (HVY) (XXI) (Oct 02)
5-601-70-MTP	HHC, Engineer Command (Oct 02)
5-602-68-MTP	HHC, Engineer Brigade (Theater Army) (Oct 02)
5-603-35-MTP	Engineer Post-Opening Company (Jul 03)
5-605-66-MTP	Engineer Battalion, Topographic (TA) (Jul 03)
5-606-34-MTP	HHC, Engineer Battalion, Topographic (TA) (Jul 03)
5-607-35-MTP	Topographic Engineer Company (EAC) (Jul 03)
5-608-35-MTP	Topographic Company (Corps) (Oct 02)
5-615-66-MTP	Engineer Prime Power Battalion Staff (May 04)
5-616-34-MTP	Headquarters Company, Prime Power Battalion (Jul 04)
5-617-10-MTP	Prime Power Line Platoon, Prime Power Bn (Oct 03)
5-617-11-MTP	Prime Power Platoon, Engineer Prime Bn (Jun 04)
5-617-35-MTP	Engineer Company, Engineer Prime Power Bn (Jun 04)

Soldier Training Plans (STP):

5-00B14-SM-TG	MOS 00B, Diver, SL 1-4 (Dec 02)

5-12B24-SM-TG	MOS 12B, Combat Engineer, SK 2-4 (Mar 03)
5-12C14-SM-TG	MOS 12C, Bridge Crewman, SL 1-4 (Mar 03)
5-21G13-SM-TG	MOS 21G, Quarry Specialist, SL 1-3 (Dec 03)
5-21M24-SM-TG	MOS 21M, Firefighter, SL 2-4 (May 05)
5-21V13-SM-TG	MOS 21V, Concrete/Asphalt Equip, SL 1-3 (Oct 03)
5-51B12-SM-TG	MOS 51B, Carpentry/Masonry, SL 1-2 (Sep 02)
5-51H34-SM-TG	MOS 51H, Construction Supervisor, SL 3-4 (Mar 03)
5-51K12-SM-TG	MOS 51K, Plumber, SL 1-2 (Sep 02)
5-51R12-SM-TG	MOS 51R, Interior Electrician, SL 1-2 (Sep 02)
5-51T12-SM-TG	MOS 51T, Technical Engineering, SL 1-2 (Oct 02)
5-51T34-SM-TG	MOS 51T, Technical Engineering, SL 3-4 (Dec 02)
5-62E12-SM-TG	MOS 62E, Heavy Constr Equip, SL 1-2 (Nov 02)
5-62F12-SM-TG	MOS 62F, Crane Operator, SL 1-2 (Oct 02)
5-62J12-SM-TG	MOS 62J12, Gen Construction Equip, SL 1-2 (Oct 02)
5-62N34-SM-TG	MOS 62N, Construction Equip Supe, SL 3-4 (Mar 03)
5-81L14-SM-TG	MOS 81L, Lithographer, SL 1-4 (Oct 02)
5-81T24-SM-TG	MOS 81T, Topographic Analyst, SL 2-4 (Oct 02)
5-82D12-SM-TG	MOS 82D, Topographic Surveyor, SL 1-2 (Aug 01)
5-82D34-SM-TG	MOS 82D, Topographic Surveyor, SL 3-4 (Oct 02)

9.1.5 Field Artillery

References:

FM 6-2	Field Artillery Survey (Oct 96)
FM 6-16	Artillery Meteorology (E) Ballistic Type 3 (Mar 82)
FM 6-16-2	Artillery Meteorology (V) Ballistic Type 3 (Jan 84)
FM 6-16-3	Artillery Meteorology (E/V) Type 2 (Jun 82)
FM 6-20	Fire Support in the Airland Battle (May 88)
FM 6-20-10	Targeting Process (May 96)
FM 6-20-30	Fire Support for Corps and Division (Oct 89)
FM 6-20-40	Fire Support for Brigade Operations (Heavy) (Jan 90)
FM 6-20-50	Fire Support for Brigade Operations (Light) (Jan 90)
FM 6-22.5	Combat Stress (Jun 00)
FM 6-24.8	Tactical Digital Info Link J (TADIL J) (Jun 00)
FM 6-30	Observed Fire (Jul 91)
FM 6-40	Field Artillery Manual Cannon Gunnery (Oct 99)
FM 6-50	Field Artillery Cannon Battery (Dec 96)
FM 6-60	Multiple Launch Rocket System (MLRS) (Apr 96)
PAM 600-3-13	Field Artillery (Aug 87)

Websites:

Field Artillery Branch	https://www.hrc.army.mil/site/active/opfa/fasitrep.htm
FA Knowledge Ctr	https://www.us.army.mil/suite/collaboration/comm_V.do?ci=399&load=true

ARTEP:

6-037-30-MTP	Consolidated.Cannon Battery
6-102-MTP	Corps Artillery, DIV Artillery, and BDE Command/Staff
6-115-MTP	Cannon Bn Cmdd/Staff, HHB, and Service Bty
6-395-MTP	MLRS Battalion Command/Staff Section and HQ Battery
6-397-30-MTP	Multiple Launch Rocket System Battery
6-303-30-MTP	Target Acquisition Battery (Apr 00)

Soldier Training Plans (STP):

9-27M14-SM-TG	MOS 27M, MLRS Repairer, SL 1-4 (Aug 02)

9.1.6 Infantry

References:

FM 3-21.9	SBCT Infantry Rifle Platoon and Squad (Dec 02)
FM 3-21.71	Mech Infantry Platoon and Squad (Bradley) (Aug 02)
FM 3-21.11	SBCT Infantry Rifle Company (Jan 03)
FM 3-21.21	Stryker BCT Infantry Battalion (Jul 03)
FM 3-21.31	Stryker BCT (Mar 03)
FM 3-21.38	Pathfinder Operations (Oct 02)
FM 3-21.91	Tactical Employment of Anti-armor Plt/Co (Nov 02)
FM 3-21.94	Stryker BCT Infantry Bn Reconnaissance PLT (Apr 03)
FM 3-21.220	Static Line Parachuting (Sep 03)
FM 3-22.1	Bradley Gunnery (Nov 03)
FM 3-22.90	Mortars (Jan 03)
FM 3-22.91	Mortar Gunnery (Jan 05)
FM 7-7	Mechanized Infantry Platoon and Squad (APC) (Mar 85)
FM 7-8	Infantry Rifle Platoon and Squad (Mar 01)
FM 7-10	Infantry Rifle Company (Oct 00)
FM 7-20	Infantry Battalion (Dec 00)
FM 7-30	Infantry Brigade (Oct 00)
FM 7-85	Ranger Unit Operations (Jun 87)
FM 7-90	Tactical Employment of Mortars (Oct 92)
FM 7-92	Infantry Recon Plt/Squad (ABN, AA, Light) (Dec 01)
FM 3-97.6	Mountain Operations (Nov 00)
FM 3-97.61	Military Mountaineering (Feb 03)
FM 71-100-2	Infantry Division Operations (Aug 93)
FM 71-100-3	Air Assault Division Operations (Oct 96)
TC 7-9	Infantry Live-Fire Training (Sep 93)
ST SAIB	Small Arms Integration Book (SAIB) (Mar 02)
CALL 05-22	Mortars in the Contemporary Operational Environment

Websites:

Infantry Branch	https://www.hrc.army.mil/site/active/opinf/default.htm
Infantry Assoc	http://www.branchorientation.com/infantry
IN Knowledge Ctr	https://www.us.army.mil/suite/collaboration/comm_V.do?ci=239&load=true

ARTEP:

7-7J-DRILL	Bradley Fighting Vehicle Plt, Section, and Sq (Jun 02)
7-8-DRILL	Infantry Rifle Platoon and Squad (Jun 02)
7-90-DRILL	Infantry Mortar Platoon, Section, and Squad (Jul 02)
7-91-DRILL	Anti-Armor (TOW) Platoon, Section, and Squad (Jul 02)
7-4-MTP	Stryker BCT Infantry Reconnaissance Platoon
7-5-MTP	Stryker BCT Infantry Rifle Platoon and Squad
7-8-MTP	Infantry Rifle Platoon and Squad
7-10-MTP	Infantry Rifle Company
7-12-MTP	Stryker Brigade Combat Team Infantry Rifle Company
7-20-MTP	Infantry Battalion
7-22-MTP	Stryker Brigade Combat Team Infantry Battalion

7-90-MTP	Infantry Mortar Platoon, Section, and Squad
7-91-MTP	Anti-Armor Company/Platoon/Section
7-92-MTP	Infantry Reconnaissance Platoon And Squad
7-93-MTP	Long-Range Surveillance Company/Detachment/Team
71-1-MTP	Tank and Mech Infantry Company
7-32-MTP	Stryker BCT (Oct 03)

Soldier Training Plans (STP):

7-11B1-SM-TG	MOS 11B, Infantry, SL 1 (Aug 04)
7-11B24-SM-TG	MOS 11B, Infantry, SL 2-4 (Aug 04)
7-11C14-SM-TG	MOS 11C, Indirect Fire Infantryman, SL 1-4 (Aug 04)
7-11H14-SM-TG	MOS 11H, Heavy Anti-Armor, SL 1-4 (Mar 00)
7-11M14-SM-TG	MOS 11M, Fighting Vehicle, SL 1-4 (Aug 99)

9.2 Combat Support

Combat support (CS): Fire support and operational assistance provided to combat elements. (Army) Critical combat functions provided by units and soldiers in conjunction with combat arms units and soldiers to secure victory.

- **AVIATION**
  - Air Traffic Services
  - C2 Aircraft
- **CHEMICAL CORPS**
  - Staff Support
  - Decontamination
  - NBC Recon & Surveillance
  - Smoke & Obscuration
- **ENGINEERS**
  - Mobility
  - Countermobility
  - Survivability
  - Topographic Support
- **SIGNAL CORPS**
  - Signal Support
  - Combat Camera
- **MILITARY INTELLIGENCE**
  - Counterintelligence
  - Analysis
  - HUMINT
  - IMINT
  - MASINT
  - SIGINT
  - TECHINT
  - Electronic Warfare
- **MILITARY POLICE CORPS**
  - Criminal Investigation
  - EPW Support
  - Military Police CS
- **SPECIAL OPS FORCES**
  - Civil Affairs
  - Psychological Operations

Figure A-2. Combat Support Capabilities
FM 3-90. Tactics (Jul 01)

9.2.1 Chemical

References:

FM 3-3 Chemical and Biological Contamination Avoidance (Sep 94)
FM 3-3-1 Nuclear Contamination Avoidance (Sep 94)
FM 3-5 Decontamination Operations (Jan 02)
FM 3-50 Smoke Operations (Sep 94)
FM 3-6 Field Behavior of NBC Agents (Nov 86)
FM 3-7 NBC Field Handbook (Sep 94)
FM 3-11 Nuclear, Biological, and Chemical Defense Opns (Mar 03)
FM 3-11.4 Nuclear, Biological, and Chemical Protection (Jun 03)
FM 3-11.9 Chemical/Biological Agents and Compounds (Jan 05)
FM 3-11.11 Flame, Riot Control Agent, and Herbicide Opns (Mar 03)
FM 3-11.14 NBC Vulnerability Assessment (Dec 04)
FM 3-11.19 Nuclear, Biological, and Chemical Reconnaissance (Jul 04)
FM 3-11.21 NBC Aspects of Consequence Management (Dec 01)
FM 3-11.22 Weapons of Mass Destruction Civil Support Team (Jun 03)
FM 3-11.34 NBC Defense of Fixed Sites, Ports, and Airfields (Sep 00)
FM 3-11.86 Biological Surveillance (Oct 04)
FM 3-50 Smoke Operations (Sep 96)
FM 3-101 Chemical Staffs and Units (Nov 93)
FM 3-101-1 Smoke Squad/Platoon Operations (Sep 94)
FM 25-51 Battalion Task Force Nuclear Training (Jun 91)
PAM 600-3-74 Chemical (Jun 87)
TC 3-10 Commander's Tactical NBC Handbook (Sep 94)
TC 3-11-55 Joint Services Lightweight integrated Suit Tech (Jul 01)
TC 3-15 Nuclear Accident & Incident Response/Assistance (Dec 88)

Websites:

Chemical Branch https://www.hrc.army.mil/site/active/opchem/cmbrnew1.htm
Chem Reg Assoc http://www.chemical-corps.org/indexFlash.htm
Chem Knowledge Ctr https://www.us.army.mil/suite/collaboration/comm_V.do?ci=2351&load=true

ARTEP:

3-207-10-DRILL NBC Reconnaissance Platoon (Mar 02)
3-327-10-DRILL CBRN Domestic Support Missions (Dec 04)
3-457-10-DRILL Smoke/Decontamination Platoon (Feb 02)
3-116-MTP Chemical Brigade or Battalion
3-207-10-MTP NBC Reconnaissance Platoon (Sep 03)
3-457-10-MTP Smoke/Decontamination Platoon
3-457-30-MTP Chemical Company Headquarters (Nov 01)
3-477-10-MTP Biological Integrated Detection System (BIDS) Platoon
3-117-40-MTP Nuclear, Biological, and Chemical Center (Sep 03)
3-627-35-MTP Weapons of Mass Destruction (WMD) (Jun 01)
3-635-60-MTP Technical Escort (TE) Battalion (Dec 04)

Soldier Training Plans (STP):
STP 3-54B1-SM MOSR 54B, Chemical Opns Specialist, SL 1 (Nov 02)

9.2.2 Military Intelligence

References:

FM 2-0	Intelligence (May 04)
FM 34-8-2	Intelligence Officer's Handbook (May 98)
FM 5-33	Terrain Analysis (Sep 92)
FM 34-2	Collection Management and Synch Planning (Mar 94)
FM 34-2-1	R/S and Intel Support to Counter-Reconnaissance (Jun 91)
FM 34-3	Intelligence Analysis (Mar 90)
FM 34-10	Division Intelligence and Electronic Warfare (Nov 86)
FM 34-37	Intelligence and Electronic Warfare (EAC) (Jan 91)
FM 34-45	Electronic Attack (Jun 00)
FM 34-52	Intelligence Interrogation (Sep 92)
FM 34-54	Technical Intelligence (Jan 98)
FM 34-60	Counterintelligence (Oct 95)
FM 34-80	Brigade and Bn Intelligence Electronic Warfare (Apr 86)
FM 34-81	Weather Support for Army Tactical Operations (Aug 89)
FM 34-81-1	Battlefield Weather Effects (Dec 92)
FM 34-130	Intelligence Preparation of the Battlefield (Jul 94)
PAM 600-3-35	Military Intelligence (Aug 87)
ST 2-00.102	Objective Force Intelligence Glossary (Oct 03)
ST 2-22.7	Tactical Human Intel and Counter-Intelligence (Apr 02)
ST 2-33.5	Intelligence Reach Operations (Jun 01)
ST 2-50	Intelligence and Electronic Warfare (IEW) Systems (Jun 02)
ST 2-50.4	Combat Commander's Handbook on Intelligence (Sep 01)
ST 2-91.1	Intel Support to Stability Opns and Support Opns (Nov 04)
ST 2-91.2	Intel Support to AntiTerrorism & Force Protection (Feb 04)
ST 2-91.6	Small Unit Support to Intelligence (Mar 04)

CALL	COE Smartcard
CALL	Tactical Questioning

Websites:

Military Intelligence Branch	https://www.hrc.army.mil/site/active/opmi/MI_Home_Page/minews.htm
MI Knowledge Ctr	https://www.us.army.mil/suite/collaboration/comm_V.do?ci=5874&load=true
S2 Company	http://www.s2company.com/

ARTEP:

34-357-10-DRILL	Ground Surveillance Systems (GSS) (Nov 05)
34-387-10-DRILL	Shadow Tactical Unmanned Vehicle (TUAV) (Nov 05)
34-388-10-DRILL	AN/MLQ-40(v)3 Prophet System (Nov 05)
34-143-30-MTP	Military Intelligence Company of the Initial BCT
34-144-30-MTP	Military Intelligence Company, Separate Brigade
34-355-MTP	Military Intelligence Bn of the Joint Contingency Force
34-357-30-MTP	Direct Support MI Company (Light/ABN/AA)
34-358-30-MTP	General Support MI Company (Light/ABN/AA)
34-387-30-MTP	Direct Support MI Company (Digitized)
34-388-30-MTP	General Support MI Company (Digitized)

34-393-30-MTP	MI Company, Separate Brigade (Enhanced)
34-396-30-MTP	HHC of the Military Intelligence Battalion
34-397-30-MTP	Direct Support MI Company (Heavy)
34-398-30-MTP	General Support MI Company (Heavy)
34-399-10-MTP	IREMBASS Platoon of the MI Battalion (Heavy)
34-414-30-MTP	Aerial Reconnaissance Company (Exploitation)(Corps)
34-114-30-MTP	Military Intelligence Company (ACR) (Dec 02)
34-117-30-MTP	Surveillance Troop of the Stryker BCT (Jun 05)
34-143-30-MTP	Military Intelligence Company of the SBCT (Sep 04)

Soldier Training Plans (STP):

34-96B15-SM-TG	MOS 96B, Intelligence Analyst, SL 1-4 (Nov 03)
34-96H14-SM-TG	MOS 96H, Common Ground Station, SL 1-5 (Apr 04)
34-96R15-SM-TG	MOS 96R, Ground Surveillance Sys, SL 1-5 (Nov 03)
34-96U14-SM-TG	MOS 96U, Tactical UAV, SL 1-4 (Mar 04)
34-97B15-SM-TG	MOS 97B, Counterintelligence Agent, SL 1-5 (Feb 04)
34-97E14-SM-TG	MOS 97E, Human Intel Collector, SL 1-4 (Nov 03)
34-98G14-SM-TG	MOS 98G, Cryptologic Linguist, SL 1-4 (Dec 03)
34-98H14-SM-TG	MOS 98H, Comm Interceptor/ Locator, SL 1-4 (Nov 03)
34-98J14-SM-TG	MOS 98J, Elec Intel Intercept/Analyst, SL 1-4 (Dec 03)

9.2.3 Military Police

References:

FM 3-19.1	Military Police Operations (Mar 01)
FM 3-19.4	Military Police Leader's Handbook (Mar 02)
FM 3-19.11	Military Police Special-Reaction Teams (May 05)
FM 3-19.12	Protective Services (Aug 04)
FM 3-19.13	Law Enforcement Investigations (Jan 05)
FM 3-19.15	Civil Disturbance Operations (Apr 05)
FM 3-19.17	Military Working Dogs (Sep 05)
FM 3-19.30	Physical Security (Jan 01)
FM 3-19.40	Internment/Resettlement Operations (Aug 01)
FM 3-22.40	Tactical Employment of Nonlethal Weapons (Jan 03)
FM 19-10	Military Police Law and Order Operations (Sep 87)
FM 19-25	Military Police Traffic Operations (Sep 77)
AR 195-5	Evidence Procedures (Nov 05)
AR 190-45	Law Enforcement Reporting (Feb 06)
AR 190-47	Army Correction System (Dec 05)
PAM 600-3-31	Military Police (Jun 87)
TC 19-138	Civilian Law Enforcement & Security Training (Aug 01)
ST 3-90.15	Tactical Operations Involving Sensitive Sites (Dec 02)
ST 17-16-1	Combatting Terrorism: Mounted Company/PLT (Oct 01)

Websites:

Military Police Branch	https://www.hrc.army.mil/site/active/opmp/default.htm
Military Police School	http://www.wood.army.mil/usamps
Military Police Journal	http://www.wood.army.mil/MPBULLETIN/
MP Knowledge Ctr	https://www.us.army.mil/suite/collaboration/comm_V.do?ci=3963&load=true
Detainee Know Ctr	https://www.us.army.mil/suite/kc/4428067
MilitaryPolice.com	http://www.militarypolice.com/
MP Reg Assoc	http://mpra.freehosting.net/

ARTEP:

19-100-10-DRILL	Military Police Drills (Nov 03)
19-100-SRT-DRILL	Military Police Special-Reaction (SRT) Drills (May 05)
19-313-10-MTP	EAC/Corps/Div MP Platoons (Combat Support)
19-313-30-MTP	EAC/Corps/Div MP Company (Combat Support)
19-333-D-MTP	Digital Division MP Provost Marshal (Heavy) (Oct 05)
19-333-D10-MTP	Digital Military Police Platoon (Heavy) (Oct 02)
19-333-D30-MTP	Digital Military Police Company (Heavy) (Oct 02)
19-472-MTP	MP CS and Internment/Resettlement (Mar 01)
19-476-MTP	EAC and Corps MP Bn and Division PM (CS) (Apr 99)
19-646-MTP	HHC, MP Internment/Resettlement (I/R) Bn (Aug 05)
19-647-30-MTP	Military Police Escort Guard Company (Dec 03)
19-653-30-MTP	Military Police Internment/Resettle (I/R) Co (Jan 05)
19-667-30-MTP	Military Police Guard Company (Dec 03)
19-710-MTP	Military Police Detachment (L&O) (Sep 05)
19-880-MTP	Military Police Detachment (CID) (Jul 04)
19-886-MTP	Military Police Bn (CID) (Mar 01)

Soldier Training Plans (STP):

STP 19-95B24-SM-TG	MOS 95B, Military Police, SL 2-4 (Dec 02)
19-95B24-SM-TG	MOS 95B, Military Police, SL 2/3/4 (Dec 02)
19-95C1-SM	MOS 95C, Corrections Specialist, SL 1 (Oct 03)
STP 19-95C24-SM-TG	MOS 95C, Corrections Spec, SL 2-4 (Dec 03)
STP 19-95D24-SM-TG	MOS 95D, Special Agent, SL 2-4 (Oct 03)

9.2.4 Signal

References:

FM 6-02.40	Visual Information Operations (Jan 02)
FM 6-02.45	Signal Support to Theater Operations (Apr 04)
FM 6-02.72	Tactical Radios in a Joint Environment (Jun 02)
FM 6-02.74	Hi Freq-Automatic Link Establishment Radios (Sep 03)
FM 6-02.76	Improved Data Modem (IDM) Integration (May 03)
FM 6-02.85	Joint Task Force Information Management (Sep 03)
FM 6-02.90	Ultra High Freq Tactical Satellite/Demand Asg Multiple Access Opns (Aug 04)
FM 6-02.771	Have Quick Radios (May 04)
FM 11-24	Signal Tactical Satellite Company (Sep 85)
FM 11-32	Combat Net Radio Operations (Oct 90)
FM 11-41	Signal Support: Echelons Corps and Below (Dec 91)
FM 11-43	Signal Leader's Guide (Jun 95)
FM 11-44	ADA Signal Operations Bn and Co (Sep 88)
FM 11-50	Combat Comms with the Division (Heavy/Light) (Apr 91)
FM 11-55	Mobile Subscriber Equipment (MSE) Operations (Jun 99)
FM 24-7	Tactical Local Area Network (LAN) Management (Oct 99)
FM 24-11	Tactical Satellite Communications (Sep 90)
FM 24-12	Communications in a "Come As You Are" War (Jul 90)
FM 24-17	Tactical Record Traffic System (TRTS) (Sep 91)
FM 24-18	Tactical Single-Channel Radio Communications (Sep 87)
FM 24-19	Radio Operator's Handbook (May 91)
FM 24-22	Communications-Electronic Management Sys (Jun 77)
FM 24-24	Signal Data References: Signal Equipment (Oct 94)
FM 24-27	Tactical Automatic Circuit Switching AN/TCC-39 (Feb 87)
FM 24-33	Electronic Counter-CounterMeasures (Jul 90)
AR 25-2	Information Assurance (Nov 03)
TC 9-60	Alternating Current and Direct Current (Aug 04)
TC 9-62	Soldier State Devices, Power Supplies and Amps (Jun 05)
TC 9-64	Wave Propagation, Transmission,, & Antennas (Jul 04)
TC 9-72	Digital Computers (Sep 05)
TC 24-20	Tactical Wire and Cable Techniques (Oct 88)
TC 24-21	Tactical Multi-Channel Radio Communications (Oct 88)
TC 24-34	COMSEC Logistics and Operational Support (Dec 88)
TC 34-94	Communications Security Monitor Site (Aug 84)

Websites:

Signal Branch	https://www.hrc.army.mil/site/active/opsig/Signal_Branch_Home_Page/1sigcon.htm
SC Knowledge Ctr	https://www.us.army.mil/suite/collaboration/comm_V.do?ci=942&load=true
A&VTR Know Ctr	https://www.us.army.mil/suite/page/206346

ARTEP:

ARTEP 11-067-30-MTP	Co/PLT of Division Signal Bn (MSE) (Nov 90)
ARTEP 11-435-MTP	Corps Area Signal Battalion (MSE)
ARTEP 11-437-30-MTP	Co/PLT of Corps Area Signal Battalion (MSE)
ARTEP 11-445-MTP	Corps Support Signal Battalion (MSE)
ARTEP 11-447-30-MTP	Co/PLT of Corps Support Signal Battalion (MSE)

Soldier Training Plans (STP):

11-250N-SM-TG	MOS 250N, Network Tech (WO1-CW04) (Mar 03)
11-25C13-SM-TG	MOS 25C, Radio Operator-Maintainer, SL 1-3 (Feb 05)
11-25L13-SM-TG	MOS 25L, Cable Systems Installer, SL 1-3 (Mar 05)
11-25M13-SM-TG	MOS 25M, Multimedia Illustrator, SL 1-3 (Feb 99)
11-25R13-SM-TG	MOS 25R, Visual Info Equip, SL 1-3 (Aug 99)
11-25S14-SM-TG	MOS 25S, Satellite Comms Sys, SL 1-4 (May 05)
11-25V13-SM-TG	MOS 25V, Combat Docu/Prod, SL 1-3 (Feb 02)
11-25Z4-SM-TG	MOS 25Z, Visual Information Chief, SL 4(Jan 01)
11-31F13-SM-TG	MOS 31F, Network Switching Sys, SL 1-3 (Jun 01)
11-31U14-SM-TG	MOS 31U, Signal Support Systems, SL 1-4 (Sep 02)
11-31W4-SM-TG	MOS 31W, Telecommunications Opns, SL 4-5 (Apr 04)

9.2.5 Transportation

References:

FM 4-01.45	Convoy Operations (Mar 05)
FM 21-305	Manual for the Wheeled Vehicle Driver (Aug 93)
FM 55-1	Transportation Operations (Oct 95)
FM 55-15	Transportation Reference Data (Oct 97)
FM 55-17	Cargo Specialists' Handbook (Feb 99)
FM 55-21	Railway Operating and Safety Rules (Jul 89)
FM 55-30	Army Motor Transport Unit and Operations (Sep 99)
FM 55-50	Army Water Transport Operations (Sep 93)
FM 55-60	Army Terminal Operations (Apr 96)
FM 55-80	Army Container Operations (Aug 97)
FM 55-450-2	Army Helicopter Internal Load Operations (Jun 92)
FM 55-502	Army Watercraft Safety (Dec 96)
FM 55-511	Operation of Floating Cranes (Dec 85)
AR 58-1	Management, Acquisition, & Use of Vehicles (Aug 04)
AR 385-55	Prevention of Motor Vehicle Accidents (Aug 87)
AR 600-55	Army Driver & Operator Program (Dec 93)
TC 21-305-100	Military Commercial Driver's License Manual (Aug 96)
TC 21-305	Wheeled Vehicle Accident Avoidance (Apr 03)
TC 21-305-1	Hvy Expanded Mobility Tactical Truck (HEMTT) (Oct 95)
TC 21-305-2	Night Vision Goggle Driving Operations (Sep 98)
TC 21-305-3	M939 Series 5-ton Tactical Cargo Truck (Aug 97)
TC 21-305-4	High Mobility Multi-purpose Wheeled Vehicle (May 91)
TC 21-305-5	Equip Transporters (C-HET, MET, and LET) (Dec 91)
TC 21-305-6	Tractor & Semi-trailer (M915, M931, AND M932) (Dec 91)
TC 21-305-7	Light Vehicles (Sep 92)
TC 21-305-8	Medium Vehicles (Sep 92)
TC 21-305-9	Heavy Equipment Transporter System (Jun 97)
TC 21-305-10	Palletized Load System (Sep 94)
TC 21-305-11	Family of Medium Tactical Vehicles Operator (May 99)
TC 21-306	Tracked Combat Vehicle Driver Training (Feb 02)

Websites:

Transportation Branch	https://www.hrc.army.mil/site/active/opfa90/default.htm
TC Knowledge Ctr	https://www.us.army.mil/suite/collaboration/comm_V.do?ci=5873&load=true
LOGNet	https://lognet.bcks.army.mil/lognet/ev_en.php

ARTEP:

42-26-MTP	Bn HQ, Supply and Transport Bn (Light/ABN/AA)
55-62-MTP	Headquarters, Transportation Composite Group
55-158-30-MTP	Transpo Co, Supply/Transport Bn (Light/ABN/AA)
55-288-30-MTP	Transpo Motor Transport Co, DSB (Digitial)
55-406-MTP	Transpo Movement Control Battalion
55-406-30-MTP	Detachment Headquarters, MCB
55-560-30-MTP	Transportation Port Opns Cargo Detachment
55-601-MTP	Headquarters Transportation Command

55-603-MTP	Theater Army Movement Control Agency
55-613-30-MTP	Transpo Floating Craft Maintenance Co
55-716-MTP	Transpo Motor Transport Battalion
55-716-30-MTP	Transpo Agency Headquarters
55-718-30-MTP	Transpo Truck Co (Light/Light-Medium/Medium)
55-739-30-MTP	Transpo Combat Heavy Equipment Transport Co
55-816-MTP	HQ, Transportation Terminal Battalion
55-819-30-MTP	Transpo Cargo Transfer Company
55-828-30-MTP	Transpo Medium/Heavy Watercraft Companies
55-848-30-MTP	Transpo Modular Causeway Company
55-887-30-MTP	Transpo Harbormaster Operations Detachment
55-916-MTP	HQ, Transportation Railway Battalion
55-917-30-MTP	Transpo Railway Operating Company
55-506-10-MTP	Transpo Movement Control Teams (Jun 02)

Soldier Training Plans (STP):

55-88M14-SM-TG MOS 88M, Motor Transport, SL 1-4 (Oct 04)

9.3 Combat Service Support

References:

FM 4-0 Combat Service Support (Aug 03)
TC 63-1 Warfighter Handbook for Combat Service Support Live Fire Exercises (Dec 04)

Combat service support (CSS): The essential capabilities, functions, activities, and tasks necessary to sustain all elements of operating forces in theater at all levels of war. Within the national and theater logistic systems, it includes but is not limited to that support rendered by service forces in ensuring the aspects of supply, maintenance, transportation, health services, and other services required by aviation and ground combat troops to permit those units to accomplish their missions in combat. Combat service support encompasses those activities at all levels of war that produce sustainment to all operating forces on the battlefield.

- **ADJUTANT GENERAL**
  - Personnel Services
  - Postal
  - Replacement
- **AVIATION (GS AVN)**
- **CHAPLAIN**
- **ENGINEERS (GEN ENG)**
- **FINANCE CORPS**
  - Support to local
  - Procurement
  - Pay Services
  - Resource Management
- **JUDGE ADVOCATE**
  - Court-Martial Trial Defense
  - Legal Assistance
  - Contract Advisory Assist
- **MEDICAL**
  - Combat Stress
  - Dental
  - Hospital
  - Evacuation/Support/Surveil
  - Veterinary
- **ORDNANCE CORPS**
  - Ammunition Maintenance
  - Ammunition Supply
  - Electronic Maintenance
  - Explosive Ordnance Disposal
  - Mechanical Maintenance
  - Missile Maintenance
- **QUARTERMASTER CORPS**
  - Supply & Field Services
- **TRANSPORTATION CORPS**
  - Highway/Rail/Water Transpo
  - Movement Control
  - Intermodel (Terminal) Ops

Figure A-3. Combat Service Support Capabilities
FM 3-90. Tactics (Jul 01)

9.3.1 Adjuant General

References:

FM 12-6	Personnel Doctrine (Sep 94)
PAM 600-3-42	Adjutant General (Jun 87)

Websites:

Adjutant General Branch	https://www.hrc.army.mil/site/active/opag/agnews1.htm
US Army Pubs Agency	http://www.usapa.army.mil
Human Resources Cmd	https://www.hrc.army.mil/indexflash.asp
S1.net	https://www.S1.net
AG Knowledge Ctr	https://www.us.army.mil/suite/collaboration/comm_V.do?ci=3931&load=true
S1 Toolkit	http://usassi.army.mil/toolkit/index.htm

ARTEP:

12-402-MTP	Personnel Group (Oct 03)
12-417-30-MTP	Personnel Detachment (Oct 03)
12-426-MTP	Personnel Services Battalion (Oct 03)
12-447-30-MTP	Postal Company HQ, Services, and Opns (Oct 03)
12-602-MTP	Personnel Command (Oct 03)
12-606-MTP	Replacement Battalion/Company (Nov 03)
12-906-MTP	Replacement Battalion/Company (CONUS)

Soldier Training Plans (STP):

12-42A12-SM-TG	MOS 42A, Human Resources Spec, SL 1-2 (Dec 03)
12-42A35-SM-TG	MOS 42A, Human Resources Spec, SL 3-5 (Dec 03)
12-42B-OFS	AOC 42B, Personnel Systems Mgmt Manual (Oct 03)
12-42L12-SM-TG	MOS 42L, Administrative Specialist, SL 1-2 (Oct 03)
12-42L35-SM-TG	MOS 42L Administrative Specialist, SL 3-5 (Oct 03)

9.3.2 Finance

References:

FM 14-100	Financial Management Operations (May 97)
AR 37-104-4	Military Pay and Allowances Policy (Jun 05)
AR 600-15	Indebtedness of Military Personnel (Mar 86)
AR 600-38	Meal Card Management System (Mar 88)
TC 21-7	Personal Financial Readiness and Deployability (Aug 03)

Websites:

Finance Branch	https://www.hrc.army.mil/site/active/opfi/finews.htm
FC Knowledge Ctr	https://www.us.army.mil/suite/collaboration/comm_V.do?ci=3969&load=true

ARTEP:

14-412-MTP	Finance Group (Oct 03)
14-423-30-MTP	Finance Detachment (Oct 03)
14-426-MTP	Finance Battalion (Nov 03)
14-612-MTP	Finance Command (Oct 03)

Soldier Training Plans (STP):

14-44A-OFS	AOC 44A, Finance Corps (Oct 03)
14-44C14-SM-TG	MOS 44C, Financial Management Tech, SL 1-4 (Oct 03)

9.3.3 Medical/Med Service

References:

FM 4-02	Force Health Protection (Feb 03)
FM 4-02.1	Combat Health Logistics (Sep 01)
FM 4-02.4	Medical Platoon Leader's Handbook (Dec 03)
FM 4-02.6	Medical Company (Apr 04)
FM 4-02.7	Health Service Support in a NBC Environment (Oct 02)
FM 4-02.10	Theater Hospitalization (Jan 05)
FM 4-02.12	Health Service Support in Corps and EAC (Feb 04)
FM 4-02.16	Army Medical Information Management (Aug 03)
FM 4-02.17	Preventive Medicine Services (Aug 00)
FM 4-02.18	Veterinary Services (Dec 04)
FM 4-02.19	Dental Service Support (Mar 01)
FM 4-02.21	Division and Brigade Surgeon's Handbook (Nov 00)
FM 4-02.24	Area Support Medical Battalion (Aug 00)
FM 4-02.25	Employment of Forward Surgical Teams (Mar 03)
FM 4-02.56	Medical Field Feeding Operations (Apr 03)
FM 4-02.283	Treatment of Nuclear and Radiological Casualties (Dec 01)
FM 4-25.11	First Aid (Jul 04)
FM 4-25.12	Unit Field Sanitation Team (Jan 02)
FM 8-9	NATO: Medical Aspects of NBC Defense Opns (Feb 96)
FM 8-10-3	Division Medical Operations Center (Nov 96)
FM 8-10-5	Brigade and Division Surgeon's Handbook (Jun 91)
FM 8-10-6	Medical Evacuation in a Theater of Operations (Apr 00)
FM 8-10-9	Combat Health Logistics in a Theater of Operations (Oct 95)
FM 8-10-14	Combat Support Hospital (Dec 94)
FM 8-10-15	Field and General Hospitals (Mar 97)
FM 8-10-26	Medical Company (Air Ambulance) (May 02)
FM 8-34	Food Sanitation for the Supervisor (Dec 83)
FM 8-42	Combat Health Support in SASO (Oct 97)
FM 8-43	Combat Health Support for Army SOF (Jun 00)
FM 8-50	Prevention & Medical Mgmt of Laser Injuries (Aug 90)
FM 8-51	Combat Stress Control (Jan 98)
FM 8-55	Planning for Health Service Support (Sep 94)
FM 8-250	Preventive Medicine Specialist (Sep 86)
FM 8-284	Treatment of Biological Warfare Agent Casualties (Jul 02)
FM 8-285	Treatment of Chemical Agent Casualties (Dec 95)
FM 9-20	Technical Escort Operations (Nov 97)
TC 8-226	Dental Laboratory Specialist (Oct 86)
TC 8-502	Nutrition Care Operations (Aug 02)
TC 8-800	Semi-Annual Combat Medic Skills Validation Test (Jun 02)

Websites:

Medical Corps Branch	https://www.hrc.army.mil/site/active/ophsdmc/medcorps.htm
Medical Service Branch	https://www.hrc.army.mil/site/active/opmsc/1brchief.htm

ARTEP:

8-057-30-MTP	Medical Co, Main Support Bn, Heavy (Sep 94)
8-058-30-MTP	Medical Co, Fwd Support Bn, Heavy (Aug 02)
8-108F-3-MTP	Brigade Support Medical Co, SBCT (Sep 02)
8-158F-30-MTP	Medical Co, Forward Support Bn (Sep 01)
8-257F-30-MTP	Medical Co, Division Support Bn (Sep 01)
8-267-30-MTP	Medical Co, Main Support Bn (Light/ABN/AA) (Sep 01)
8-268-30-MTP	Medical Co, Fwd Support Bn (Light/ABN/AA) (Aug 02)
8-279-30-MTP	Medical Co (Air Ambulance) (Sep 02)
8-403-MTP	Medical Detachment, Veterinary Service (Dec 02)
8-411-MTP	Headquarters, Medical Command (Corps) (Sep 02)
8-411-30-MTP	HQ Company Medical Cmd, Medical Brigade (Apr 02)
8-413-30-MTP	Medical Detachment, Veterinary Service (Apr 04)
8-422-MTP	HQ, Medical Brigade (Corps) (Commz) (Sep 02)
8-422-MTP	HQ Medical Brigade (Corps or EAC) (May 01)
8-422-30-MTP	Headquarters Co, Medical Command (Jun 03)
8-423-30-MTP	Medical Detachment, Veterinary Medicine (Jul 03)
8-429-30-MTP	Medical Detachment, Preventive Medicine (May 01)
8-432-MTP	Headquarters, Medical Group (Feb 03)
8-437-30-MTP	Medical Co, Support Battalion, Infantry/ACR (Jun 02)
8-446-MTP	Medical Evacuation Battalion Headquarters (Jun 02)
8-446-30-MTP	HQ Detachment, Medical Evacuation Bn (Sep 01)
8-453-30-MTP	Medical Co, Ground Ambulance (Sep 03)
8-456-MTP	HQ, Medical Battalion (Area Support) (Apr 00)
8-456-30-MTP	HQ Detachment, Area Support Medical Bn (Mar 00)
8-457-30-MTP	Area Support Medical Company (Oct 03)
8-458-30-MTP	Medical Company, Holding (Sep 03)
8-463-MTP	Medical Detachment, Combat Stress Control (Aug 03)
8-476-30-MTP	Headquarters, Medical Battalion (Dental Service) (Jan 03)
8-478-30-MTP	Medical Co/Detachment (Dental Service) (Sep 03)
8-485-MTP	Headquarters, Medical Bn, Logistics (Fwd/Rear) (Oct 02)
8-487-30-MTP	Logistics Support Co, Distribution Company (Oct 02)
8-488-30-MTP	Medical Logistics Co & Blood Support Detach (Sep 00)
8-496-30-MTP	Headquarters, Medical Logistics Battalion (Jul 03)
8-498-30-MTP	Preventive Medicine (Entomology/Sanitation) (Jun 03)
8-518-10-MTP	Fwd Surgical/Medical Team, Fwd Surgical (ABN) (Sep 03)
8-611-MTP	Headquarters, Medical Command (Theater) (Oct 03)
8-699-MTP	Medical Logistics Management Center (Aug 02)
8-668-30-MTP	Area Medical Laboratory (Dec 02)
8-705-MTP	Combat Support Hospital (Nov 02)
8-715-MTP	Field/General Hospital (Dec 02)
8-753-30-MTP	Area Support Medical Detachment (Sep 99)
8-855-MTP	Combat Support Hospital (Jun 00)
17-236-12-MTP	Task Force, Medical Platoon (Aug 02)

Soldier Training Plans (STP):

8-91A15-SM-TG	MOS 91A, Medical Equipment, SL 1-5 (Apr 03)
8-91D14-SM-TG	Operating Room Specialist (Jul 03)
8-91E15-SM-TG	MOS 91E, Dental Specialist, SL 1-5 (Feb 03)
8-91G15-SM-TG	MOS 91G, Patient Administration, SL 1-4 (Jul 02)
8-91H14-SM-TG	MOS 91H, Optical Laboratory, SL 1-4 (Oct 02)
8-91J15-SM-TG	MOS 91J, Medical Logistics, SL 1-5 (Oct 03)
8-91K15-SM-TG	MOS 91K, Medical Laboratory, SL 1-5 (May 05)
8-91M15-SM-TG	MOS 91M, Nutrition Care, SL 1-5 (Sep 05)
8-91P15-SM-TG	MOS 91P, Radiology Specialist, SL 1-5 (Feb 03)
8-91Q15-SM-TG	MOS 91Q, Pharmacy Specialist, SL 1-5 (Apr 03)
8-91R15-SM-TG	MOS 91R, Veterinary Food Inspection, SL 1-5 (Jul 01)
8-91S15-SM-TG	MOS 91S, Preventive Medicine, SL 1-5 (Jun 03)
8-91T14-SM-TG	MOS 91T, Animal Care Specialist, SL 1-4, (Aug 02)
8-91V24-SM-TG	MOS 91V, Respiratory Specialist, SL 2-4, (Sep 05)
8-91W15-SM-TG	MOS 91W, Health Care Specialist, SL 1-5, (Oct 01)
8-91WN9-SM-TG	MOS 91W, ASI N9, Physical Therapy, SL 1-4 (Jan 06)
8-91X14-SM-TG	MOS 91X, Mental Health Specialist, SL 1-4 (Apr 03)

9.3.4 Ordnance

References:

FM 4-0	Combat Service Support (Aug 03)
FM 4-30.3	Maintenance Operations and Procedures (Jul 04)
FM 4-30.13	Ammunition Handbook (Mar 01)
FM 4-30.1	Munitions Distribution in the Theater of Opns (Dec 03)
FM 4-30.5	Explosive Ordnance Disposal Operations (Apr 05)
FM 4-30.16	Explosive Ordnance Disposal in Joint Environment (Oct 05)
FM 9-207	Ordnance Materiel in Cold Weather (Mar 98)
TC 9-237	Operator's Circular Welding (May 93)
TC 9-524	Fundamentals of Machine Tools (Oct 96)
TC 43-4	Maintenance Management (May 96)

Websites:

Ordnance Branch	https://www.hrc.army.mil/site/active/opfa90/default.htm
LOGSA	https://www.logsa.army.mil
LOGNet	https://lognet.bcks.army.mil/lognet/ev_en.php
Maintenance Univ	https://ommu.army.mil/portal/index.php
PS Magazine	https://www.logsa.army.mil/psmag/psonline.cfm
MotorPool.org	http://www.themotorpool.org/
OD Knowledge Ctr	https://www.us.army.mil/suite/collaboration/comm_V.do?ci=729&load=true

ARTEP:

9-408-30-MTP	Modular Ammunition Ordnance Company (Oct 03)
9-503-10-MTP	Modular Ammunition, Medium/Heavy (Oct 03)
17-236-10-MTP	Task Force, Maintenance Platoon (Sep 01)
43-008-30-MTP	Heavy Ordnance Company, Main Support Bn (Oct 03)
43-009.1-30-MTP	Ordnance Company, Fwd Support Bn (Sep 02)
43-039-30-MTP	Ordnance Company, FSB, Infantry Div (Sep 02)
43-079.1-30-MTP	Ordnance Company, Support Bn, Heavy (Sep 02)
43-107-30-MTP	Forward Maint Company of Interim BCT (Aug 02)
43-167-30-MTP	Light Maintenance Company, Air Assault (Sep 02)
43-168-30-MTP	Heavy Maintenance Company, Air Assault (Sep 02)
43-169-30-MTP	Forward Maintenance Company, Air Assault (Aug 02)
43-187.1-30-MTP	Ordnance Maintenance Troop, ACR (Sep 02)
43-197-30-MTP	Ordnance Maint Company, Separate IN BDE (Sep 02)
43-208-30-MTP	Area Maintenance Company, DS Battalion (Aug 00)
43-209-30-MTP	Ordnance Maint Co (DS), CSG/TAACOM (Aug 03)
43-217-30-MTP	Ordnance Maint Co, Fwd Support Bn, Light (Sep 02)
43-218-30-MTP	Ordnance Maint Battalion, Light (Sep 02)
43-258-30-MTP	Heavy Maint Co, Main Support Bn (ABN) (Dec 02)
43-259-30-MTP	Forward Maint Co, Main Support Bn, (ABN) (Dec 02)
43-388-30-MTP	Ground Maint Company, AV Support (Nov 99)
43-436-MTP	Ordnance (Maintenance) Battalion, CSG/TSC (Sep 03)
43-436-30-MTP	Ordnance Maintenance Battalion, CSG/TSC (Oct 03)
43-439-30-MTP	Service Company & Collection Company (Jun 03)
43-470-30-MTP	Support Maintenance Company, CSB (Apr 05)
43-607-30-MTP	Ordnance Company (DS), Patriot (Sep 03)

43-648-30-MTP	Ordnance Company (Sustainment) (Oct 03)
43-649-30-MTP	Ordnance Company (GS) (Jun 03)
43-888-30-MTP	Ground Maint Company, AV Support, Heavy (Dec 02)

Soldier Training Plans (STP):

9-27E14-SM-TG	MOS 27E, Land Combat Missile Repairer (Dec 02)
9-27M14-SM-TG	MOS 27M, MLRS Repairer (Aug 02)
9-27X14-SM-TG	MOS 27X, Patriot System Repairer, SL 1-4 (Nov 03)
9-35E13-SM-TG	MOS 35E, COMSEC Repairer, SL 1-3 (Dec 03)
9-35F13-SM-TG	MOS 35F, Special Elec Devices, SL 1-3 (Jul 03)
9-35H14-SM-TG	MOS 35H, TMDE Maint Support, SL 1-4 (Dec 02)
9-35J13-SM-TG	MOS 35J, Computer/Automation Sys, SL 1-3 (Jun 01)
9-35L13-SM-TG	MOS 35L, Avionic Communications, SL 1-3 (Jan 05)
9-35M13-SM-TG	MOS 35M, Radar Repairer, SL 1-3 (Dec 02)
9-35N13-SM-TG	MOS 35N, Wire Systems Equip Repairer (Feb 03)
9-35R13-SM-TG	MOS 35R, Avionic Systems Repairer, SL 1-3 (Jun 04)
9-35T14-SM-TG	MOS 35T, Avenger System Repairer, SL 1-4 (Mar 05)
9-35W4-SM-TG	MOS 35W, Electronic Maint Chief, SL 4 (Oct 03)
9-35Y14-SM-TG	MOS 35Y, Integrated Test Equip, SL 1-4 (Mar 03)
9-39B13-SM-TG	MOS 39B, Apache Repairer, SL 1-3 (Jul 00)
9-44B12-SM-TG	MOS 44B, Metalworker, SL 1-2, (Mar 01)
9-44E14-SM-TG	MOS 44E, Machinist, SL 1-4, (Mar 01)
9-45B12-SM-TG	MOS 45B, Sm Arms.Artillery Repair, SL 1-2, (Mar 01)
9-45G12-SM-TG	MOS 45G, Fire Control Sys Repairer, SL 1-2, (Mar 01)
9-45K14-SM-TG	MOS 45K, Tank Turret Repairer, SL 1-4, (Sep 01)
9-52C13-SM-TG	MOS 52C, Utilities Equip Repairer, SL 1-3, (Apr 01)
9-52D13-SM-TG	MOS 52D, Power Generation Repair, SL 1-3, (Apr 01)
9-52X4-SM-TG	MOS 52X, Spec Purpose Equip Repair, SL 4 (Jun 01)
9-55B12-SM-TG	MOS 55B, Ammunition Specialist, SL 1-2 (Dec 03)
9-55B34-SM-TG	MOS 55B, Ammunition Specialist, SL 3-4 (Nov 04)
9-62B14-SM-TG	MOS 62B, Construct Equip Repairer, SL 1-4, (Oct 02)
9-63A14-SM-TG	MOS 63A, Abrams Tank Maintainer, SL 1-4, (Mar 01)
9-63B13-SM-TG	MOS 63B, Wheeled Veh Mechanic, SL 1-3, (Jan 05)
9-63D14-SM-TG	MOS 63D, Artillery Mechanic, SL 1-4 (Aug 04)
9-63H14-SM-TG	MOS 63H, Tracked Vehicle Mechanic, SL 1-4, (Aug 04)
9-63J12-SM-TG	MOS 63J, QM/Chemical Equip, SL 1-2 (Apr 01)
9-63M14-SM-TG	MOS 63M, Bradley Fighting Vehicle, SL 1-4, (Mar 01)
9-63S12-SM-TG	MOS 63S, Heavy Wheel Veh Mech, SL 1-2, (Aug 01)
9-63W12-SM-TG	MOS 63W, Wheel Vehicle Repairer, SL 1-2 (Jun 01)
9-63X40-SM-TG	MOS 63X, Wheeled Vehicle Mechanic, SL 4 (Feb 05)
9-94D12-SM-TG	MOS 94D, Air Traffic Control Repair, SL 1-2 (Feb 06)

9.3.5 Quartermaster

References:

FM 4-0	Combat Service Support (Aug 03)
FM 4-20.41	Aerial Delivery Distribution (Aug 03)
FM 4-20.65	Identification of Deceased Personnel (Jul 05)
FM 4-20.102	Rigging Airdrop Platforms (Aug 01)
FM 4-20.103	Rigging Containers (Sep 05)
FM 4-20.105	Dual Row Airdrop Systems (Jan 05)
FM 4-20.107	Derigging and Recovery Procedures (Oct 04)
FM 4-20.116	Reference for Airdrop Platforms (Oct 04)
FM 4-20.147	Humanitarian Airdrop (Jan 05)
FM 10-1	Quartermaster Principles (Aug 94)
FM 10-15	Basic Doctrine Manual for Supply and Storage (Dec 90)
FM 10-16	General Fabric Repair (May 00)
FM 10-23	Basic Doctrine for Army Field Feeding/Class I (Apr 96)
FM 10-23-2	Garrison Food Preparation and Class I (Sep 93)
FM 10-27	General Supply in Theaters of Operations (Apr 93)
FM 10-27-1	Quartermaster General Support Supply Opns (Apr 93)
FM 10-27-2	Direct Supply and Field Service Opns (Jun 91)
FM 10-27-3	Quartermaster Headquarters Opns (Sep 94)
FM 10-27-4	Organizational Supply for Unit Leaders (Apr 00)
FM 10-52	Water Supply in Theaters of Operations (Jul 90)
FM 10-52-1	Water Supply Point Equipment and Operations (Jun 91)
FM 10-64	Mortuary Affairs Operations (Feb 99)
FM 10-67	Petroleum Supply in Theaters of Operations (Oct 85)
FM 10-67-1	Concepts and Equip of Petroleum Operations (Apr 98)
FM 10-67-2	Petroleum Laboratory Testing Opns (Apr 97)
FM 10-115	Quartermaster Water Units (Feb 89)
FM 10-416	Petroleum Pipeline and Terminal Operations (May 98)
FM 10-426	Petroleum Supply Units (Jul 97)
FM 10-450-3	Helicopter Sling Load: Basic Operations (Apr 97)
FM 10-450-4	Helicopter Sling Load: Single-Point Rigging (Sep 03)
FM 10-450-5	Helicopter Sling Load: Dual-Point Rigging (Sep 03)
FM 10-602	Petroleum and Water Distribution Organization (Sep 96)
FM 100-9	Reconstitution (Jan 92)
FM 100-10-1	Theater Distribution (Oct 99)
FM 100-10-2	Contracting Support on the Battlefield (Aug 99)
PAM 600-3-92	Quartermaster Corps (Aug 87)
TC 10-10	Combined Arms Training Strategy for QM (Sep 92)
ALEDC REF 1-5	Associate Logistics Executive Dev Course (Feb 05)

Websites:

Quartermaster Branch	https://www.hrc.army.mil/site/active/opfa90/default.htm
QM Knowledge Ctr	https://www.us.army.mil/suite/collaboration/comm_V.do?ci=1906&load=true
LOGSA	https://www.logsa.army.mil
LOGNet	https://lognet.bcks.army.mil/lognet/ev_en.php

ARTEP:

10-337-30-MTP	Airdrop Equipment Support Company, ABN
10-414-30-MTP	Field Service Company Modular(DS), CSB
10-416-MTP	Quartermaster Bn (Petroleum Pipeline/Terminal Opns)
10-416-30-MTP	HHC, Petroleum Group, Quartermaster Bn
10-426-MTP	Petroleum Supply Battalion
10-426-30-MTP	HQ & HQ Detachment, Petroleum Supply Bn
10-427-30-MTP	Petroleum Supply Company
10-443-30-MTP	Heavy Airdrop Supply Company
10-449-30-MTP	Airdrop Equipment Repair
10-466-MTP	Quartermaster Battalion (Water Supply)
10-466-30-MTP	HQ Detachment Quartermaster Battalion (Water Supply)
10-468-30-MTP	Quartermaster Company (Water Supply) (DS/GS)
10-469-30-MTP	Water Purification Detachment (GS)
10-498-30-MTP	Collection Company (Mortuary Affairs)
10-602-MTP	HHC, Petroleum Group
10-698-30-MTP	Quartermaster Mortuary Affairs Company (EAC)
11-067-30-MTP	**Companies and Platoons**
17-236-11-MTP	Task Force, Support Platoon
42-26-MTP	Bn HQ, Supply/Transport Bn, Light/ABN/AA
42-077-30-MTP	Supply and Transport Troop, Support Squadron, ACR
42-414-30-MTP	Field Service Company Modular (DS), CSB
42-418-30-MTP	Supply Company (GS), CSB
42-419-30-MTP	Repair Parts Supply Company (GS), CSB
42-424-30-MTP	Force Provider Company
42-427-30-MTP	Heavy Materiel Supply Company (GS)
42-446-MTP	Headquarters, Supply and Service Bn, CSG/ASG
42-446-30-MTP	Headquarters Detachment Supply and Services Bn
43-007-30-MTP	Maint Companies, Fwd and Main Support Bn, Heavy
42-207-30-MTP	Quartermaster Company, Division Support Bn (Jul 00)
42-877-30-MTP	Supply and Transport Company, Support Bn (Sep 03)

Soldier Training Plans (STP):

10-92A10-SM-TG	MOS 92A, Automated Logistical Spec, SL 1, (Sep 05)
10-92G1-SM-TG	MOS 92G, Food Service Specialist, SL 1, (Apr 03)
10-92G25-SM-TG	MOS 92G, Food Service Specialist, SL 2-5 (Apr 04)
10-92L14-SM-TG	MOS 92L, Petroleum Lab Spec, SL 1-4, (May 05)
10-92M15-SM-TG	MOS 92M, Mortuary Affairs Spec, SL 1-5 (Mar 03)
10-92R14-SM-TG	MOS 92R, Parachute Rigger, SL 1-4 (Mar 03)
10-92S14-SM-TG	MOS 92S, Shower/Laundry/Clothing, SL 1-4 (Jun 03)
10-92W14-SM-TG	MOS 92W, Water Treatment Spec, SL 1-4 (Nov 05)
10-92Y12-SM-TG	MOS 92Y, Unit Supply Specialist, SL 1-2, (Mar 03)

10-92Y34-SM-TG MOS 92Y, Unit Supply Specialist, SL 3-4, (Mar 03)

Army Agencies

Part

10 Army Agencies

References:
FM 7-21.13 A Soldier's Guide (Feb 04)

Check you installation website for contact information for the Army Agencies on your post. Make contact with those offices to see what specific services they offer.

Activity	Description
Adjutant General	Provides personnel and administrative services support such as orders, ID cards, retirement assistance, deferments, and in- and out-processing.
American Red Cross	Provides communications support between Soldiers and families and assistance during or after emergency or compassionate situations.
Army Community Service	Assists military families through their information and referral services, budget and indebtedness counseling, household item loan closet, information on other military posts, and welcome packets for new arrivals.
Army Education Center	Provides services for continuing education and individual learning services support.
Army Emergency Relief	Provides financial assistance and personal budget counseling; coordinates student loans through Army Emergency Relief education loan programs.
Army Substance Abuse Program (ASAP)	Provides alcohol and drug abuse prevention and control programs for DA civilians.
Better Opportunities for Single Soldiers (BOSS)	Serves as a liaison between upper levels of command on the installation and single Soldiers.
Career Counselor	Explains reenlistment options and provides current information on prerequisites for reenlistment and selective reenlistment bonuses.
Chaplain	Provides spiritual and humanitarian counseling to Soldiers and DA civilians
Claims Section, SJA	Handles claims for and against the government, most often for the loss and damage of household goods.
Community Counseling Center	Provides alcohol and drug abuse prevention and control programs for Soldiers.

Community Health Nurse	Provides preventive health care services.
Community Mental Health Service	Provides assistance and counseling for mental health problems.
Employee Assistance Program	Provides health nurse, mental health service, and social work services for DA civilians.
Equal Opportunity	Provides assistance for matters involving discrimination in race, color, national origin, gender, and religion. Provides, information on procedures for initiating complaints and resolving complaints informally.
Family Advocacy	Coordinates programs supporting children and families including abuse and neglect investigation, counseling, and educational programs.
Finance and Accounting Office	Handles inquiries for pay, allowances, and allotments.
Housing Referral Office	Provides assistance with housing on and off post.
Inspector General	Renders assistance to Soldiers and DA civilians. Corrects injustices affecting individuals and eliminates conditions determined to be detrimental to the efficiency, economy, morale, and reputation of the Army. Investigates matters involving fraud, waste, and abuse.
Legal Assistance Office	Provides legal information or assistance on matters of contracts, citizenship, adoption, martial problems, taxes, wills, and powers of attorney.
Social Work Office	Provides services dealing with social problems to include crisis intervention, family therapy, martial counseling, and parent or chid management assistance.
Transition Office	Provides assistance and information on separation from the Army.

Table C-3. Support Activities.
FM 22-100. The Soldier's Guide (Feb 04)

10.1 Garrison Resources

IRAC	Internal Review and Audit Compliance
EEO/EO	Equal Employment Opportunity/Equal Opportunity
CPO	Civilian Personnel Office
FAO	Finance and Accounting Office
PMO	Provost Marshal Office
NG/AR	National Guard/ Army Reserve Liaison and Advisors
DPCA	Directorate of Personnel and Community Activities
DPTM	Directorate of Plans, Training, and Mobilization
DRM	Directorate of Resource Management
DOL	Directorate of Logistics
DOIM	Directorate of Information Management
DOC	Directorate of Contracting
DEH	Directorate of Engineering and Housing

10.2 Army Career & Alumni Program (ACAP)

References:

PAM 635-4	Pre-separation Guide (Sep 97)
DD 2648	Pre-separation Counseling Checklist for Active Component Service Members (Jun 05)
DD 2648-1	Pre-separation Counseling Checklist for Reserve Component Service Members Released from Active Duty (Jun 05)

Websites:

Army ACAP	http://www.acap.army.mil/

Timesframes:

Pre-separation briefing	Between 1 year to 90 days prior to ETS Between 2 years to 90 days prior to Retirement

10.3 Army Community Services

References:

AR 608-1 Army Community Service Center (Dec 04)
PAM 608-42 Handbook on Information & Referral Service for Army Community Service Centers (Aug 85)

Websites:

Virtual ACS Site http://www.myarmylifetoo.com/
FRG Website http://frg.army.mil
Virtual FRG http://www.armyfrg.org/

Mission: Improve readiness and increase retention by providing services to assist soldiers and their families in solving problems beyond their ability to solve alone through the provisions of the eight essential services outlined in AR 608-1.

Services:

- Army Basics
- Child and Youth Services
- Home and Family Life
- Lifelong Services
- Moving Assistance
- Managing Deployment
- Money Matters
- Work and Careers

10.4 Army Education Center

References:

AR 621-5 Army Continuing Education System (Feb 04)
AR 621-6 Army Learning Centers (Nov 85)
PAM 621-15 A Soldier's Guide to Education (Feb 84)

Services:

- Functional Academic Skills Testing (FAST): used to improve Soldier's GT score
- High School Completion Program
- English as a Second Language
- Language Training
- MOS Improvement Training
- Read to Lead
- Leader Skill Enhancement Courses
- NCO Lead Education and Development
- Postsecondary Education

10.5 Army Emergency Relief (AER)

References:

AR 930-4 Army Emergency Relief (Aug 94)
DA 1103 Application for Army Emergency Relief (AER) Financial Assistance (Sep 94)

Websites:

AER Homepage http://www.aerhq.org/

AER is the Army's own emergency financial assistance organization and is dedicated to "Helping the Army Take Care of Its Own". AER provides commanders a valuable asset in accomplishing their basic command responsibility for the morale and welfare of soldiers. AER funds are made available to commanders having AER Sections to provide emergency financial assistance to soldiers - active & retired - and their dependents when there is a valid need. AER funds made available to commanders are not limited and are constrained only by the requirement of valid need.

Help with emergency financial needs for:

- Food, rent or utilities
- Emergency transportation and vehicle repair
- Funeral expenses
- Medical/dental expenses
- Personal needs when pay is delayed or stolen
- Give undergraduate-level education scholarships, based primarily on financial need, to children of soldiers

AER Cannot:

- Help pay for nonessentials
- Finance ordinary leave or vacation
- Pay fines or legal expenses
- Help liquidate or consolidate debt
- Assist with house purchase or home improvements
- Help purchase, rent or lease vehicle
- Cover bad checks or pay credit card bills

10.6 Army Family Advocacy Program

References:

AR 608-18 The Army Family Advocacy Program (Sep 04)

Websites:

Virtual ACS Site http://www.myarmylifetoo.com/

Family Advocacy is dedicated to the prevention, education, prompt reporting, investigation, intervention and treatment of spouse and child abuse. The program provides a variety of services to soldiers and families to enhance their relationship skills and improve their quality of life. This mission is accomplished through a variety of groups, seminars, workshops and counseling and intervention services.

Services:
- Command and Troop Education
- Community Awareness
- Conflict Resolution
- Couples Communication Skills
- Stress Management
- Prevention Programs and Services
- New Parent Support Program
- Parent Education
- Domestic Violence Prevention
- Victim Advocate Program
- Relationship Support
- Safety Education
- Respite Care Program
- Emergency Placement Care Program
- Reporting Procedures

from myArmyLifeToo.com

10.7 Army Family Team Building

References:

AR 608-48 Army Family Team Building (AFTB) Program (Mar 05)
AR 600-20 Army Command Policy (Feb 06)

Websites:

Virtual ACS Site http://www.myarmylifetoo.com/

Army Family Team Building (AFTB) is a volunteer-led organization with a central tenet: provide training and knowledge to spouses and family members to support the total Army effort. Strong families are the pillar of support behind strong Soldiers. It is AFTB's mission to educate and train all of the Army in knowledge, skills, and behaviors designed to prepare our Army families to move successfully into the future.

from myArmyLifeToo.com

10.8 Army Substance Abuse Program (ASAP)

References:

AR 600-85 Army Substance Abuse Program (ASAP) (Mar 06)
PAM 600-85 Army Substance Abuse Program Civilian Services (Oct 01)

DA 8003 Army Substance Abuse Program (ASAP) Referral Form (Feb 03)

Other References:

Commander's Guide and Unit Prevention Leader (UPL) Collection Handbook, ACSAP (Nov 01)

Mission: The Army Substance Abuse Program's (ASAP) mission is to enhance readiness and increase combat effectiveness of the United States Army, through awareness and preventive education and training, drug testing, clinical evaluation of individuals identified with substance problems and rehabilitation for those who possess a potential for continued military service.

Identifying Soldiers with Problem:

- Voluntary (self referral)
- Command Referrals
- Biochemical
- Medical
- Investigative or Apprehension

10.9 Chaplains

References:

FM 6-22.5 Combat Stress (Jun 00)
FM 22-51 Leader's Manual for Combat Stress Control (Sep 94)
AR 165-1 Chaplain Activities in the United States Army (Mar 04)
TC 1-05 Religious Support Handbook for the Unit Ministry Team (May 05)

Websites:

Chaplain School http://www.usachcs.army.mil/

Definitions:

Chaplain: A qualified and endorsed clergy person of a DOD recognized religious denomination or faith group. Chaplains are noncombatants and will not bear arms.
Combat stress: The mental, emotional, or physical tension, strain, or distress resulting from exposure to combat-related conditions.

Duties:
- Perform rites, sacraments, and religious services
- Perform weddings and funerals
- Perform invocations and benedictions at ceremonies
- Pastoral counseling

10.10 Command Financial Advisor

References:

AR 600-15	Indebtedness of Military Personnel (Mar 86)
FM 14-100	Financial Management Operations (Aug 97)
TC 21-7	Personal Financial Readiness and Deployability Handbook (Aug 03)

Command Financial Specialist Program (CFSP) is a command program, which helps prepare soldiers and families to deal with financial situations for deployments as well as the financial realities of day-to-day military life. The program is designed to provide commanders a mechanism through which financial education, training, counseling, and referral procedures are established in their units to promote sound financial practices, personal integrity, and financial responsibility. The objective of the program is to enhance and maintain mission readiness and quality of life by providing soldiers and their family members a ready-made program to help achieve personal financial readiness and deployability through the use of sound money management and consumer skills.

10.11 Exceptional Family Member Program (EFMP)

References:

AR 608-75	Exceptional Family Member Program (Feb 06)
AR 614-100	Officer Assignment Policies, Details, and Transfers (Jan 06)
AR 614-200	Enlisted Assignments and Utilization Management (Aug 05)

Forms:

DA 5863	Exceptional Family Member Program Information Sheet (Sep 02)
DA 7246	Exceptional Family Member Program (EFMP) Screening Questionnaire (Sep 02)
DA 7351A	Exceptional Family Member Program (EFMP) Assessment Guide (Sep 02)
DA 7351B	Exceptional Family Member Program (EFMP) Assessment Guide (Sep 02)
DA 7413	Exceptional Family Member Program (EFMP) Assignment Coordination Sheet (Sep 02)
DA 7415	Exceptional Family Member Program (EFMP) Querying Sheet (Sep 02)

The Exceptional Family Member Program (EFMP) is a mandatory enrollment program that works with other military and civilian agencies to provide comprehensive and coordinated community support, housing, and educational, medical, and personnel services to families with special needs.

10.12 Family Readiness Groups

References:

PAM 608-47	Army Family Action Plan (ACAP) Program (Dec 04)
CIR 608-04-1	Better Opportunities for Single Soldiers Program (Sep 04)

Other References:
Commander's Guide to FRG
Spouse's Handbook

Website:

FRG Website	http://frg.army.mil
Virtual FRG	http://www.armyfrg.org/
Army Rear-D	http://reardcommander.army.mil
Virtual ACS Site	http://www.myarmylifetoo.com/
One Source	http://www.militaryonesource.com/

Family Readiness Groups (FRG) are a command-sponsored organization of family members, volunteers, Soldiers, and civilian employees belonging to a unit, that together provide an avenue of mutual support and assistance, and a network of communications among the family members, the chain of command, chain of concern, and community resources. The FRG also provides feedback to the command on the state of the unit "family." The FRG is a unit Commander's program. Unit Commanders at all levels should establish and support FRGs to assist in military and personal deployment preparedness and enhance the family readiness of their Soldiers and families. Normally, FRGs are established at the Company level with Battalion and Brigade levels playing an important advisory role. FRGs assist the unit Commander in providing family members with the tools necessary to educate, enable, and empower them so that they are self-sufficient. The FRG helps boost the morale of Soldiers and family members. FRG goals include: gaining necessary family support during deployments, preparing for deployments and redeployments, helping families adjust to military life and cope with deployments, developing open and honest channels of communication between the command and family members, and promoting confidence, cohesion, commitment, and a sense of well being among the unit's Soldiers.

from Commander's Guide to FRG

10.13 Information Management (DOIM)

References:

AR 25-2 Information Assurance (Nov 03)

Websites:

DOIM Homepage http://www.doim.army.mil/

Email Accounts:

- User accounts
- User Tests

Network Administration

- LAN Accounts
- Service Request Forms
- PKI\CAC
- Firewall Port Access

Information Assurance

- Windows Updates
- Anti-virus Updates
- Network Patches

Telephone Service

- Cell Phones

10.14 Inspector General (IG)

References:

AR 1-201 Army Inspection Policy (Jan 04)
AR 20-1 Inspector General Activities and Procedure (Mar 02)

Assistance Division: conducts, oversees, or assigns the responsibility for investigations and inquiries into misconduct of non-senior Army officials (Army personnel in the grade of COL/GM 15 and below) in response to allegations of impropriety, issues of systems deficiency, complaints, grievances, and matters of concern or requests for assistance received from, or presented by, soldiers, family members, retirees, former soldiers, DA Civilians, or other individuals concerned with the activities of the Army.

Inspections Division: inspect, teach, assess, report, and follow up matters affecting mission performance and the discipline, efficiency, economy, morale, training and readiness throughout the Army.

Investigations Division: conduct investigations concerning allegations made against Active and Reserve Component general officers and SES civilians and other ranks as directed.

Intelligence Oversight Division: conduct inspections and non-criminal investigations of Army sensitive activities which include Special Access Programs and other activities as prescribed in AR 380-381.

Technical Inspections Division: Inspect, teach, assess, report, and follow up matters affecting technical mission performance in the Army's chemical and nuclear material systems.

from OTIG webpage (http://wwwpublic.ignet.army.mil)

10.15 Judge Advocate General (JAG)

References:

AR 27-20 Claims Regulation (Dec 97)
PAM 27-162 Claims Procedures (Apr 98)

DD 1842R Claim for Loss of Damage to Personal Property Incident to Service (May 00)

Websites:

JAG Net http://www.jagcnet.army.mil/

Administrative (Civilian):

- Notarizations
- Change of Name
- Citizenship
- Voting Assistance
- State of Residence
- Consumer Protection (Credit, Debt Collection Problems, Credit Reporting, Contract & "Scam" Problems, Warranty and Defective Products)
- Estate Planning (Wills, SGLI, Casualty Assistance, Advance Medical Directives)
- Economic (Bankruptcy, Debts, Insurance, Veteran's Benefits, Veteran's Reemployment)
- Family Law (Marriage, Nonsupport, Paternity, Divorce/Separation, Adoption)

- Real Property (Landlord-Tenant, Home Sales, Rental Property)
- Taxes (Federal and State)

Administrative (Military):
- Reports of Survey
- OER/NCOER
- Article 15

Claims:
- Loss or Damaged Property

Criminal Law:
- DWI and Substance Abuse

International Law:
- Law of War
- Geneva Conventions
- Passport Assistance

10.16 Logistics (DOL)

Inventory:
- Installation Property Books

Maintenance:
- Work Orders

Supply:
- Contracting

Transportation:
- Installation Unit Movement
- Transportation Motor Pool

10.17 Morale, Welfare, and Recreation

Websites:

Army MWR http://www.armymwr.org/

Services:

- Arts and Crafts Center
- Child and Youth Services
- Community Recreation
- Construction
- Family Programs
- Lodging
- Outdoor Recreation
- Overseas Recreation Centers

10.18 Red Cross

References:

AR 930-5 American National Red Cross Service Program and Army Utilization (Feb 05)

Websites:

Red Cross http://www.redcross.org/

American Red Cross Emergency Services are available to all members of the armed services, and to their families. Both active duty and community-based military can count on the Red Cross to provide emergency communications, emergency financial assistance, counseling, veterans assistance and aid in the field where Red Cross workers are deployed to serve with America's military.

10.19 TASC

References:

AR 25-1 Army Knowledge Management and Information Technology (Jul 05)

The Training and Audiovisual Support Center (TASC) is a great resource for training. You must ensure your company has an account setup on a signature card there before signing out items.

Media Aids:

Slide/overhead projectors

Screens
TV sets
VCRs/DVD platers
Public address/sound amplification systems
Camcorders
LCD projection panels

Training Aids:
see Chapter 8, Training/Operations, Training Aids

10.20 TRICARE

References:
Tricare Fact Sheet

Websites:

TRCARE Website	http://www.mytricare.com
TRICARE for Life	https://www.tricare4u.com/
TRICARE Online	http://www.tricareonline.com/

Services:
- Appointments
- Claims
- Dental
- Pharmacy

10.21 Veteran's Affairs

Websites:

Veteran's Affairs	http://www.va.gov/

Services:
- Burial and Memorials
- Disability
- GI Bill
- Home Loans
- Pensions
- Survivor Benefits

Appendices

Part

11 Appendices

11.1 Post Information

Websites:

SITES Installation Database https://www.dmdc.osd.mil/appj/sites/

11.1.1 CONUS

POST	STATE	WEBSITE	OPERATOR
Aberdeen	MD	http://www.apg.army.mil	410-278-5201
Fort Belvoir	VA	http://www.belvoir.army.mil	703-545-6700
Fort Benning	GA	https://www.benning.army.mil	706-545-5216
Fort Bliss	TX	https://www.bliss.army.mil/	915-568-2121
Fort Bragg	NC	http://www.bragg.army.mil/18abn/default.htm	910-396-1461
Fort Campbell	KY	http://www.campbell.army.mil	270-798-2151
Fort Carson	CO	http://www.carson.army.mil	719-526-5811
Fort Detrick	MD	http://www.detrick.army.mil	301-619-8000
Fort Dix	NJ	http://www.dix.army.mil	609-562-1011
Fort Drum	NY	http://www.drum.army.mil	315-772-5869
Fort Eustis	VA	http://www.eustis.army.mil	757-878-5251
Fort Meade	MD	http://www.ftmeade.army.mil	301-677-6261
Fort Gordon	GA	http://www.gordon.army.mil	706-791-0110
Fort Hood	TX	http://www.hood.army.mil/fthood/	254-287-1110
Fort Huachuca	AZ	http://huachuca-www.army.mil	520-458-7111
Fort Irwin	CA	http://www.irwin.army.mil	760-380-3369
Fort Jackson	SC	http://www.jackson.army.mil/	803-751-7511
Fort Knox	KY	http://www.knox.army.mil/	502-624-1000
Ft Leavenworth	KS	http://www.leavenworth.army.mil/	913-684-2424
Fort Lee	VA	http://www.lee.army.mil	804-734-6855
Fort LeonardWood	MO	http://www.wood.army.mil	573-596-0131
Fort Lewis	WA	http://www.lewis.army.mil	253-967-1110
Fort Monmouth	NJ	http://www.monmouth.army.mil/C4ISR/	732-532-4598
Fort Monroe	V	http://fort.monroe.army.mil/monroe/	757-788-2442
Fort Myer	VA	http://www.fmmc.army.mil/	703-695-0441
Fort Polk	LA	http://WWW.JRTC-POLK.ARMY.MIL	337-531-2911
Fort Riley	KS	http://www.riley.army.mil	785-239-3911
Fort Rucker	AL	http://www.rucker.army.mil/	334-255-3156
Fort SamHouston	TX	http://www.samhouston.army.mil	210-221-1211
Fort Sill	OK	http://sill-www.army.mil	580-442-8111
Fort Stewart	GA	http://www.stewart.army.mil	703-325-3732
Fort McPherson	GA	http://www.mcpherson.army.mil	404-464-4070
Redstone Arsenal	AL	http://www.garrison.redstone.army.mil/	256-876-2151
USMA	NY	http://www.usma.edu/Garrison/sites/local	845-938-4011
Walter Reed	DC	http:www.walterreed.army.mil	202-782-3501

11.1.2 OCONUS

POST	LOCATION	WEBSITE
Baumholder	Germany	http://www.baumholder.army.mil
Camp As Sayliyah	Qatar	http://www-qa.arcent.army.mil
Camp Casey	Korea	http://www-2id.korea.army.mil
Camp Henry-Taegu	Korea	
Camp Hialeah-Busan	Korea	
Camp Humphreys	Korea	https://www-eusa-4.korea.army.mil/usasalll/index.html
Camp Zama	Japan	http://www.usarj.army.mil/
Darmstadt/Babenhausen	Germany	http://www.darmstadt.army.mil/sites/local/
Fort Richardson	Alaksa	http://www.usarak.army.mil
Fort Shafter	Hawaii	http://www.25idl.army.mil/
Fort Wainwright	Alaska	http://www.wainwright.army.mil
Kaiserslautern	Germany	http://www.kaiserslautern.army.mil
Schofield Barracks	Hawaii	http://www.25idl.army.mil/
Schweinfurt	Germany	http://www.schweinfurt.army.mil
Vicenza	Italy	http://www.setaf.army.mil
Yongsan	Korea	http://www.saocsc.org/

11.2 Reading Lists

11.2.1 ArmyToolbag.com

About Face: The Odyssey of an American Warrior / COL David H Hackworth

Company Command: The Bottom Line / John G. Meyer

The Future of the Army Profession / Don M. Snider and Gayle L. Watkins

Learning to Eat Soup with a Knife : Counter-insurgency Lessons from Malaya and Vietnam / John A. Nagl

Men Against Fire: The Problem of Battle Command in Future War / S.L.A. Marshall

Not a Good Day to Die : The Untold Story of Operation Anaconda / by Sean Naylor

On Combat: The Psychology and Physiology of Deadly Conflict in War and in Peace / LTC Dave Grossman and Loren Christensen

On Killing: The Psychological Cost of Learning to Kill in War and Society / LTC Dave Grossman

Once An Eagle / Anton Myer

Platoon Leader / James R. McDonough

Prodigal Soldiers / James Kitfield

Small Unit Leadership: A Commonsense Approach / COL Dandridge M. (Mike) Malone

Soldier and the State / Samuel P. Huntington

Taking the Guidon: Exceptional Leadership at the Company Level / Nate Allen, Tony Burgess

11.2.2 CSA Reading List (Cadets)

For Cadets, Soldiers, and Junior NCOs

The Constitution of the United States

Centuries of Service: The U.S. Army 1775–2004 / David W. Hogan, Jr.
(CMH Pub. 70-71-1)
An easy-to-read and informative pamphlet that describes the many missions the U.S. Army has performed over the course of its history. The booklet covers America's wars as well as the Army's many operations other than war, including occupation, peacekeeping, nation building, exploration, civil administration, scientific research, and disaster relief. This pamphlet is a valuable introduction to American military history for the Soldier and junior leader.

The Face of Battle / John Keegan
One of the classics of modern military history, *The Face of Battle* brings to life three major battles: Agincourt (1415), Waterloo (1815), and the First Battle of the Somme (1916). The author describes the sights, sounds, and smells of battle, providing a compelling look at what it means to be a Soldier.

For the Common Defense: A Military History of the United States of America / Allan R. Millett and Peter Maslowski
This useful, single-volume study covers the American military experience in peace and war from 1607 to 1975. Millett and Maslowski carefully examine the relationship of the military to American society and discuss in detail the military and its changing roles within political, social, and economic frameworks.

Band of Brothers: E Company, 506th Regiment, 101st Airborne from Normandy to Hitler's Eagle's Nest / Stephen E. Ambrose
This excellent account of an airborne rifle company at war is based on journals, letters, and interviews with the participants. The author follows one company from rigorous selection and training through battles in Normandy, Holland, Bastogne, and occupation duty in Germany. A classic small-unit study.

We Were Soldiers Once … and Young: Ia Drang—The Battle That Changed the War in Vietnam / LTG (Ret.) Harold G. Moore and Joseph L. Galloway
A gripping, firsthand account of the November 1965 Battle of the Ia Drang by the commander of 1/7 Cavalry. The Ia Drang was the first major combat test of the airmobile concept and the first battle between U.S. forces and the North Vietnamese Army.

If You Survive: From Normandy to the Battle of the Bulge to the End of World War II, One American Officer's Riveting True Story / George Wilson
George Wilson was a young rifle platoon leader and then an infantry company commander during the costly fighting from Normandy to the German frontier in 1944. He tells his personal story of combat as an ordinary officer during extraordinary times, doing what was required to accomplish the mission and keep his men alive. An inspirational account useful to all junior leaders.

Touched with Fire: The Land War in the South Pacific / Eric M.Bergerud
The land battles of the South Pacific fought between July 1942 and early 1944 on the Solomon Islands and on New Guinea were "a ferocious slugging match between light-infantry armies at extremely close quarters." Written in a clear and engaging style and drawing upon many insightful interviews with veterans, *Touched with Fire* offers a vivid and fascinating look at small-unit combat in the South Pacific that will be of great interest to cadets, enlisted men, and junior officers.

Closing with the Enemy: How GIs Fought the War in Europe, 1944–1945 / Michael D. Doubler
During World War II, the U.S. Army had to overcome many tactical problems, from the thick hedgerows of Normandy to the streets of German cities. Some of these challenges had been anticipated, others had not, but all required the American fighting man to adapt in order to survive.
In this book, Michael Doubler explains how and why the U.S. Army was generally successful in overcoming these many challenges. Soldiers and junior leaders will benefit from his incisive study of the battlefield resourcefulness, flexibility, and determination of the American Soldier.

Patton: A Genius for War / Carlo D'Este
Perhaps the most renowned and controversial American general of the twentieth century, George Patton (1885–1945) remains a subject of intense interest. The author provides new information from family archives and other sources to help us understand why the general is regarded as one of the great modern military leaders. Essential reading for all students of command in war.

In the Company of Heroes / Michael J. Durant
Black Hawk pilot Mike Durant was shot down and taken prisoner during military operations in the failed country of Somalia in 1993. Published in the tenth anniversary year of that conflict, this riveting personal account at last tells the world about Durant's harrowing captivity and the heroic deeds of his comrades.

11.2.3 CSA Reading List (LTs)

For Company-Grade Officers, WO1-CW3, and Company Cadre NCOs

America's First Battles: 1776-1965 / Edited by Charles E. Heller and William A. Stofft
This highly useful book is a collection of essays by eleven prominent American military historians assessing the first battles of nine wars in which the U.S. Army has fought. Each essay is written within a similar framework, examining how the U.S. Army prepares during peacetime, mobilizes for war, fights its first battle, and subsequently adapts to the exigencies of the conflict. *America's First Battles* shows clearly the price of unpreparedness.

Personal Memoirs of U. S. Grant / Ulysses S. Grant
A classic and honest study by one of America's greatest generals. This memoir is one of the finest autobiographies of a military commander ever written. It has valuable insights into leadership and command that apply at all levels.

The Philippine War, 1899–1902 / Brian McAllister Linn
Professor Linn provides a definitive treatment of military operations in the Philippines from the early pitched battles to the final campaigns against the guerrillas. He offers a more thorough understanding of the entire war than did earlier works. Essential reading for all junior officers and NCOs trying to understand the complexities inherent in counterinsurgency operations.

The War To End All Wars: The American Military Experience in World War I / Edward M.Coffman
Professor Coffman has written an excellent synthesis of the totality of the American military experience in World War I. The book's principal attraction is Coffman's use of unpublished diaries, memoirs, and personal interviews to focus on the impact of the conflict on the individual American doughboy as well as on America's military leaders. The lessons from the "Great War" are still applicable today for all the Army's junior and senior leaders.

An Army at Dawn: The War in Africa, 1942–1943, Volume One of the Liberation Trilogy / Rick Atkinson
In this first volume of Rick Atkinson's highly anticipated Liberation Trilogy, he shows why no modern reader can understand the ultimate victory of the Allied powers in May 1945 without a solid understanding of the events that took place in North Africa during 1942 and 1943. Atkinson convincingly demonstrates that the first year of the Allied war effort was a pivotal point in American history, the moment when the United States began to act like a great military power.

Company Commander / Charles B. MacDonald
This is an autobiographical account of a young officer's experiences as an American rifle company commander in France during the Second World War. Fresh from the States, MacDonald led Normandy veterans through the Battle of the Bulge and the invasion of Germany. This absorbing story about the development of leadership in combat is worthwhile reading for all company-grade officers and NCOs who are entrusted with the lives of American Soldiers.

East of Chosin: Entrapment and Breakout in Korea, 1950 / Roy E. Appleman
East of Chosin tells the harrowing story of the Army's 31st Regimental Combat Team of the 7th Division under attack by waves of Chinese just east of the Chosin Reservoir in late 1950. Appleman explains why this unit suffered so badly at the hands of the Chinese and then historians, and he convincingly argues that the sacrifices of the 31st RCT contributed heavily to saving the more famous 1st Marine Division. As a story of men in combat, small-unit actions, and leadership, it has few equals and should be read by all Army leaders.

Leadership: The Warrior's Art / Christopher Kolenda
This wide-ranging anthology brings together noted military minds as they examine the crucial role of leadership in the crucible of combat and relate the lessons learned. They also attempt to apply these principles to the stressful world of business. The book covers both classic and modern concepts of leadership that will serve as an excellent introduction to the study of leadership for junior officers and NCOs.

American Soldiers: Ground Combat in the World Wars, Korea, and Vietnam / Peter S. Kindsvatter
Kindsvatter, a former soldier himself, uses the letters, memoirs, and novels written by other soldiers, along with official reports and studies, to detail the experience of soldiers from entry into military service

through ground combat and its aftermath. Thoughtful discussions of leadership, the physical and emotional stresses of the battlefield, and the various ways soldiers try to cope with these stresses make this a valuable book for all those preparing to lead American soldiers in ground combat.

The Challenge of Command: Reading for Military Excellence, Art of Command Series / Roger Nye
An insightful combat-arms officer, Colonel Nye has produced a one-of-a-kind tool for the professional officer who intends to master his profession. A handbook for mentors as well as junior officers, this work guides the reader through the major aspects of command: developing a professional vision and being a tactician, warrior, moral arbiter, strategist, and mentor. Each topic includes a thought-provoking essay based on interviews and personal reflection, as well as a sizable bibliography.

The New Face of War: How War Will Be Fought in the 21st Century / Bruce Berkowitz
Bruce Berkowitz offers a framework for understanding the new face of combat. As Western forces wage war against terrorists and their supporters, The *New Face of War* explains how we fight and what threats we face. He clearly lays out the four key dynamics to the new warfare: asymmetric threats, information-technology competition, the race of decision cycles, and network organization. *The New Face of War* is an important book for all new leaders.

11.2.4 Insurgency

Reading list from United States Military Academy, Department of History (Nov 04)

Cummings, Bruce. The Origins of the Korean War. 2 vols. Princeton: Princeton University Press, 1981-90.
The Origins of the Korean War (vol. 1, Liberation and the Emergence of Separate Regimes, and vol. 2, The Roaring of the Cataract) details the American occupation experience in post-war Korea. Significantly, US forces arrived in Korea three weeks after the surrender of Japan, which put the Americans on the defensive politically. The Korean people agitated for immediate independence, while the American occupation was distracted with a host of other seemingly equally important issues. The result was a race between the forces of anarchy, dissolution, and never-ending violence; and, an American occupation trying to find its way through a cultural and ideological conundrum. Ultimately, the Americans won, but the result was messy, required a sustained military and economic commitment, and a three year "hot" war.

Herrington, Stuart. Stalking the Vietcong. Novato, CA: Presidio Press, 1997.
Stuart A. Herrington's Stalking the Vietcong provides a first-hand account of an American intelligence officer's personal struggle with Vietcong shadow government. Assigned as an Operation Phoenix advisor to the Hau Nghia province of South Vietnam in 1971, Herrington worked on debriefing and exploiting Vietcong defectors and NVA prisoners in attempts to neutralize the Vietcong infrastructure. His experiences with the both the Vietcong and the South Vietnamese intelligence service officers he came in contact with provide valuable insights into the challenges the United States military faced during the Vietnam War.

Keats, John. They Fought Alone. Philadelphia: Lippincott, 1963.
This is a narrative account of Lt. Col. Wendell Fertig's campaign against the Japanese on Mindanao in the Philippines during WW2. This shows how Fertig puts together an insurgency against the occupation forces, showing important aspects such as recruitment, supply, intelligence, movement of insurgents in denied areas, role of the auxiliary, etc. Critical is the psychological connection between insurgent and populace. For example, at one point, Fertig asks the local women to cut up their curtain rods and slowly sand them down into bullet shapes to provide ammunition for the guerillas. This was not needed from a logistics viewpoint, as bullets made in this fashion

would be less useful than captured Japanese ammunition, but it played a critical psychological role: it provided a direct connection between the population and the insurgents. Each Filipino woman, spending time each day for months working on a bullet, would have an attachment to the insurgency and feel she was doing her part for the cause. It was a seemingly minor task that created a shared sense of resistance. This type of connection is critical, and must be identified and broken or replaced by the counterinsurgency force.

Linn, Brian M. "Intelligence and Low-Intensity Conflict in the Philippine War, 1899-1902." Intelligence and National Security 6 (January 1994): 90-114.
Like Linn's book on the Philippine War, this article emphasizes the paramount importance of local collection and analysis of intelligence in this sort of conflict. Intelligence will (should) flow up more than down, and efforts to homogenize and disseminate intelligences at higher levels of command are often counterproductive.

________. The Philippine War, 1899-1902. Lawrence: University of Kansas Press, 2000.
Linn's book is something of an "instant classic" on counterinsurgency operations. Linn examines the Philippine War as a combination of multiple, smaller regional wars. The U.S. Army achieved success as it recognized the predominance of regional disparities and tailored its efforts to local conditions. The book provides positive examples of decentralized (and therefore effective) operations and intelligence collection, as well as the successful integration of the civil and military components of a pacification campaign.

Race, Jeffrey. War Comes to Long An: Revolutionary Conflict in a Vietnamese Province. Berkley: University of California Press, 1972.
Simply put, this book is a must-read to understand guerrilla warfare or insurgencies as a social phenomenon. Implicitly a scathing critique of conventional military thinking, Race's book equips commanders and their staffs with the conceptual framework necessary on conducting meaningful IPB. This book also questions many of the ways in which we typically measure "progress" (schools built, areas "secured," etc.) in such wars. If you want to know what you're doing wrong, read this book.

Truong, Nhu Tang. Vietcong Memoir. San Diego: Harcourt Brace Jovanovich, 1985.
This is the memoir of a member of the NLF underground in Saigon during the Vietnam War, who then left Vietnam for France after 1975, when the North Vietnamese took over and dismantled the provisional revolutionary government of the south. A good description of the viewpoint of the insurgent, particularly in urban areas. Of particular interest are the strategic thinking of the NLF (e.g. creating the image of a broad-based popular movement, as opposed to purely communist), methods of recruiting, activities of the mole Pham Ngoc Thao (sabotaging the Strategic Hamlet program, "pacifying" a province, thus creating a VC safe haven, coup attempts, etc.) Emphasis is on subversion and propaganda.

11.2.5 Middle East Case Studies

Reading list from United States Military Academy, Department of History (Nov 04)

Battle of Algiers. Directed by Gillo Pontevorco with Brahim Haggiag and Jean Martin. 120 minutes. 1965.
This movie provides a fictional account of the revolutionary movement in Algeria that incorporates documentary-style footage and even incorporates many of the leaders of the actual revolution. It is renowned for its subtle depiction of the internal dynamics of cell-based revolutionary movements.

Islam and Politics / John L. Esposito, 4th edition. Syracuse: Syracuse University Press, 1998.
Islam and Politics provides three critical perspectives to conflict in the Middle East. First is the historical view of Islam as a unifying and expansive force on the Arab peoples. Many of the groups opposed to American influence "yearn" backward for the good old days. Their ideology is focused on how to get there from now. Secondly, Islam has definite and specific political connotations. It has cultivated its own legal systems (the *shariah* [law] and various "schools" of interpretation), social welfare system, and enfranchisement system. Only God is sovereign, and therefore only God may make law. People fall into two categories: those who submit to God's will and are subject to God's law, and those who do not, which by the way includes Muslims who are not aligned with God's will. *Jihad* is therefore required to bring all into submission. Lastly, the proliferation of Islamic groups indicates a dynamic and decentralized movement, with motives, objectives, and tactics that are not necessarily congruent between groups.

The Insurrection in Mesopotamia / Aylmer L. Haldane. Edinburgh and London: W. Blackwood and Sons, 1922.
Personal account by the commanding officer of British forces that suppressed a large-scale insurrection against British occupation in 1920. Methods used were innovative, if brutal, causing short term pacification but long-term resentment of British influence.

The Shi'is of Iraq / Yitzhak Nakash. Princeton: Princeton University Press, 2003.
Most noted Western scholar of Iraqi Shi'ites, Nakash is unique in dealing with the Iraqi Shi'i as a distinct group from greater Iranian/Lebanese influences. An essential read for those serving in the South.

French Revolutionary Warfare from Indochina to Algeria: The Analysis of a Political and Military Doctrine / Peter Paret
Princeton: Princeton University Press, 1964.
The author examines official reports and directives and the large body of writings by French officers who participated in these campaigns. He describes the destructive and the constructive components of counter-revolutionary warfare, stressing the use of psychological tools - re-indoctrination centers, health services, and other techniques - to construct a superior ideological base. After detailing the organization of the French Army's psychological-action units, he analyzes the official case history of an actual operation, Operation Pilote, to demonstrate how the doctrine worked in practice.

11.3 Web Resources

General

Army Knowledge Online	http://www.us.army.mil
Army Homepage	http://www.army.mil
Army National Guard	http://www.arng.army.mil/
Army Reserve Homepage	http://www.army.mil/usar

Administrative

US Army Publications Agency	http://www.usapa.army.mil
Human Resources Command	https://www.hrc.army.mil/indexflash.asp
S1.net	https://www.S1.net
S1 Toolkit	http://usassi.army.mil/toolkit/index.htm
Rear-D	http://reardcommander.army.mil/

Supply/Maintenance

LOGSA	https://www.logsa.army.mil
LOGNet	https://lognet.bcks.army.mil/lognet/ev_en.php
Maintenance University	https://ommu.army.mil/portal/index.php
PS Magazine	https://www.logsa.army.mil/psmag/psonline.cfm
MotorPool.org	http://www.themotorpool.org/

Training

Digital Training Mgmt	https://dtms.army.mil/
Center for Army Lessons Learned	http://call.army.net
Warrior Knowledge Database	https://wkb.bcks.army.mil/
Platoonleader.org	http://platoonleader.army.mil
CompanyCommand.com	http://companycommand.army.mil
NCO-team.org	https://leadernetwork.bcks.army.mil/
Correspondence Program	https://www.aimsrdl.atsc.army.mil/
Army Counseling	http://www.counseling.army.mil
Army Leadership	http://www.leadership.army.mil

Soldier Websites

Army Career and Alumni Prog	http://www.acap.army.mil/
Army Emergency Relief	http://www.aerhq.org
Education	http://www.armyeducation.army.mil
GI Bill	http://www.gibill.va.gov
Morale, Welfare, and Recreation	http://www.armymwr.com
OMPF	https://ompf.hoffman.army.mil/
Officer Preference Statement	https://isdrad16.hoffman.army.mil/AssignmentPreferenceWEB/
Officer Record Brief	https://myerb.ahrs.army.mil/
Tricare	http://www.tricare.osd.mil
Veteran's Affairs	http://www.va.gov/

Current Events

Defense News	http://www.defenselink.mil
Early Bird News	http://www.ebird.dtic.mil

Army Automated Systems

OPSEC	https://opsec.1stiocmd.army.mil
Automated Risk Assessment	https://safety.army.mil/asmis1/default.aspx
Sexual Assault Reporting	http://www.sapr.mil/

11.4 Publication Index

Army and Joint Publications are frequently updated. These publications are the latest as of the publication of this book. Check the accompanying website for updates on what publications have been updated. In some changes the title of the publication was abbreviated to condense space. The date in parenthesis is the publication date. In cases where a change was issued, the date of the last change is listed.

11.4.1 Army Regulation Index

AR 1-201	Army Inspection Policy (Jan 04)
AR 5-13	Training Ammunition Management (Mar 05)
AR 11-27	Army Energy Program (Feb 97)
AR 15-6	Procedures for Investigating Officers (Sep 96)
AR 20-1	Inspector General Activities and Procedures (Mar 02)
AR 25-1	Army Knowledge Mgmt and Info Technology (Jul 05)
AR 25-2	Information Assurance (Nov 03)
AR 25-50	Preparing and Managing Correspondence (Jun 02)
AR 27-10	Military Justice (Nov 05)
AR 27-20	Claims (Jul 03)
AR 30-22	The Army Food Program (May 05)
AR 37-47	Representation Funds of the Army (Mar 04)
AR 37-104-4	Military Pay and Allowances Policy (Jun 05)
AR 40-3	Medical, Dental, and Veterinary Care (Nov 02)
AR 40-5	Preventive Medicine (Jul 05)
AR 40-25	Nutrition Standards and Education (Jun 01)
AR 40-400	Patient Administration (Mar 01)
AR 40-501	Standards of Medical Fitness (Feb 06)
AR 58-1	Management, Acquisition, and Use of Motor Vehicles (Aug 04)
AR 59-3	Movement of Cargo by Scheduled Military Air Transportation (Apr 01)
AR 59-9	Special Assignment Airlift Mission Regulations (Mar 85)
AR 140-111	US Army Reserve Reenlistment Program (Feb 06)
AR 140-158	Enlisted Personnel Classification, Promotion, and Reduction (Nov 05)
AR 165-1	Chaplain Activities in the United States Army (Mar 04)
AR 195-5	Evidence Procedures (Nov 05)
AR 190-8	EPW, Retained Personnel, CI, and Detainees (Oct 97)
AR 190-11	Physical Security of Arms, Ammunition, and Explosives (Feb 98)
AR 190-13	The Army Physical Security Program (Sep 93)
AR 190-16	Physical Security (May 91)
AR 190-40	Serious Incident Report (Feb 06)
AR 190-51	Physical Security of Arms, Ammunition and Explosives (Sep 93)
AR 195-2	Criminal Investigations Activities (Oct 85)
AR 215-1	Non-appropriated Fund Instrumentalities and MWR Activities (Sep 05)
AR 220-1	Unit Status Reporting (Mar 06)
AR 220-15	Journals and Journal Files (Dec 83)
AR 220-20	Army Status of Resources Training Sys (ASORTS)/(BIDE) (Mar 04)
AR 220-45	Duty Rosters (Nov 75)
AR 310-50	Authorized Abbreviations, Brevity Codes, and Acronyms (Nov 85)

AR 340-21 Privacy Act Program (Jul 85)
AR 350-1 Army Training and Education (Jan 06)
AR 350-9 Training Device Policies and Management (Oct 93)
AR 350-17 NCODP (May 91)
AR 350-50 Combat Training Center Program (Jan 03)
AR 360-81 Public Affairs (Jan 87)
AR 380-67 Army Personnel Security Program (Sep 88)
AR 385-10 Army Safety Program (Feb 00)
AR 385-40 Accident Reporting and Records (Nov 94)
AR 385-55 Prevention of Motor Vehicle Accidents (Aug 87)
AR 385-63 Range Safety (May 03)
AR 420-90 Fire and Emergency Services (Sep 97)
AR 525-13 Anti-Terrorism (Jan 02)
AR 530-1 Operations Security (Sep 05)
AR 570-9 Host Nation Support (Mar 06)
AR 600-8-1 Army Casualty Operations/Assistance/Insurance (Oct 94)
AR 600-8-2 Suspension of Favorable Personnel Actions (Flags) (Dec 04)
AR 600-8-3 Postal Operations (Dec 89)
AR 600-8-4 Line of Duty Policy, Procedures, and Investigations (Apr 04)
AR 600-8-10 Leaves and Passes (Feb 06)
AR 600-8-19 Enlisted Promotions and Reductions (Jan 06)
AR 600-8-22 Military Awards (Feb 95)
AR 600-8-24 Office Transfers and Discharges (May 05)
AR 600-8-29 Officer Promotions (Feb 05)
AR 600-8-101 Personnel Processing (Jul 03)
AR 600-8-103 Battalion S1 (Sep 91)
AR 600-9 The Army Weight Control Program (Aug 87)
AR 600-15 Indebtedness of Military Personnel (Mar 86)
AR 600-20 Army Command Policy (Feb 06)
AR 600-29 Fundraising within the Department of the Army
AR 600-55 The Army Driver and Operator Standardization Program (Dec 93)
AR 600-60 Physical Performance Evaluation System (Jun 02)
AR 600-85 Army Substance Abuse Program (ASAP) (Mar 06)
AR 601-280 Army Retention Program (Jan 06)
AR 604-5 Army Personnel Security Program (Feb 84)
AR 604-10 Military Personnel Security (Sep 69)
AR 608-1 Army Community Service Center (Dec 04)
AR 608-18 The Army Family Advocacy Program (Sep 04)
AR 608-20 Army Voting Assistance Program (Oct 04)
AR 608-48 Army Family Team Building (AFTB) Program (Mar 05)
AR 608-75 Exceptional Family Member Program (Feb 06)
AR 614-6 Permanent Change of Station Policy (Oct 85)
AR 614-11 Temporary Duty (TDY) (Oct 79)
AR 614-100 Officer Assignment Policies, Details, and Transfers (Jan 06)
AR 614-200 Enlisted Assignments and Utilization Management (Aug 05)
AR 621-5 Army Continuing Education System (Feb 04)
AR 621-6 Army Learning Centers (Nov 85)
AR 623-105 Officer Evaluation Reporting System (Dec 04)
AR 623-205 Noncommissioned Officer Evaluation Reporting System (May 02)
AR 630-10 Absence Without Leave, Desertion/Personnel in Civilian Court (Jan 06)
AR 635-40 Evaluation for Retention/Retirement/Separation (Feb 06)
AR 635-200 Active Duty Enlisted Administrative Separations (Jun 05)
AR 638-2 Care and Disposition of Remains and Personal Effects (Dec 00)
AR 670-1 Wear and Appearance of Army Uniforms and Insignia (Feb 05)

AR 672-11	Jeremiah P. Holland Award (Mar 93)
AR 680-29	Military Personnel, Organization, and Transaction Codes (Mar 96)
AR 690-12	Equal Opportunity Policy (Mar 88)
AR 710-2	Supply Policy Below the National Level (Jul 05)
AR 735-5	Policies and Procedures for Property Accountability (Feb 05)
AR 735-11-2	Reporting of Supply Discrepancies (Aug 01)
AR 750-1	Army Material Maintenance Policy (Jan 06)
AR 930-4	Army Emergency Relief (Aug 94)
AR 930-5	American National Red Cross Service Program and Army Utilization (Feb 05)

11.4.2 DA Pamphlet Index

PAM 30-22	Operating Procedures for the Food Program (Aug 02)
PAM 40-3	Multilingual Phrase Book (May 71)
PAM 40-11	Preventive Medicine (Jul 05)
PAM 40-13	Training in First Aid and Emergency Medical Treatment (Aug 85)
PAM 55-2	It's Your Move (Jan 94)
PAM 55-16	Civilian Travel and Transpo/ Permanent Change of Station (Aug 91)
PAM 55-20	Uniformed Services Personnel Travel and Transportation (Nov 77)
PAM 55-22	Civilian Travel and Transportation - Temporary Duty Travel (Jan 92)
PAM 190-51	Risk Analysis for Army Property (Sep 93)
PAM 350-9	Index and Description of Army Training Devices (Sep 02)
PAM 350-20	Unit Equal Opportunity Training Guide (Jun 94)
PAM 350-38	Standards in Weapons Training FY03/FY04
PAM 385-1	Small Unit Safety Officer/NCO Guide
PAM 385-40	Army Accident Investigation and Reporting (Nov 94)
PAM 385-63	Range Safety (Apr 03)
PAM 600-2	The Armed Forces Officer (Feb 88)
PAM 600-3-12	Armor (Aug 87)
PAM 600-3-13	Field Artillery (Aug 87)
PAM 600-3-14	Air Defense Artillery (Aug 87)
PAM 600-3-15	Aviation (Aug 87)
PAM 600-3-21	Engineer (Aug 87)
PAM 600-3-31	Military Police (Jun 87)
PAM 600-3-35	Military Intelligence (Aug 87)
PAM 600-3-42	Adjutant General (Jun 87)
PAM 600-3-46	Public Affairs (Aug 87)
PAM 600-3-74	Chemical (Jun 87)
PAM 600-3-92	Quartermaster Corps (Aug 87)
PAM 608-4	Guide for the Survivors of Deceased Army Members (Feb 89)
PAM 608-47	Army Family Action Plan (ACAP) Program (Dec 04)
PAM 600-8-20	SIDPERS - Handbook for Commanders (Apr 86)
PAM 600-15	Extremist Activities (Jun 00)
PAM 600-24	Suicide Prevention & Psychological Autopsy (Sep 88)
PAM 600-67	Effective Writing for Army Leaders (Jun 86)
PAM 600-69	Unit Climate Profile Commander's Handbook (Oct 86)
PAM 600-70	Prevention of Suicide and Self-Destructive Behavior (Nov 85)
PAM 600-85	Army Substance Abuse Program Civilian Services (Oct 01)
PAM 608-42	Handbook for Army Community Service Referral (Aug 85)
PAM 611-21	Enlisted Career Fields and MOS (Mar 99)
PAM 621-15	A Soldier's Guide to Education (Feb 84)
PAM 623-105	Officer Evaluation Reporting System In Brief (Oct 97)
PAM 623-205	Noncommissioned Officer Evaluation Reporting System (Jan 88)
PAM 635-4	Pre-separation Guide (Sep 97)
PAM 638-2	Care and Disposition of Remains and Personal Effects (Dec 00)
PAM 640-1	Officer's Guide to the Officer Record Brief (Apr 87)
PAM 672–6	Armed Forces Awards and Decorations (Jan 92)
PAM 710-2-1	Using Unit Supply System (Manual Procedures) (Dec 97)
PAM 710-2-2	Supply Support Activity Supply System: Manual Procedures (Sep 98)
PAM 735-5	Survey Officer's Guide (Mar 97)

PAM 738-751	Users Manual for TAMMS-A (Mar 91)
PAM 750-1	Leader's Unit Maintenance Handbook (Oct 03)
PAM 750-8	The Army Maintenance Management System (TAMMS) (Aug 05)
PAM 750-35	Guide for Motor Pool Operations (Aug 94)

11.4.3 DA Form Index

DA 2-1a	Personnel Qualification Record (Jan 73)
DA 2-1b	Personnel Qualification Record (Jan 73)
DA 6	Duty Roster (Jul 74)
DA 31	Request and Authority for Leave (Sep 93)
DA 54	Record of Personal Effects (May 99)
DA 67-9	Officer Evaluation Report (Dec 04)
DA 67-9-1	Officer Evaluation Report Support Form (Oct 97)
DA 67-9-1A	Junior Officer Dev Support Form (JODSF) (Dec 04)
DA 71	Oath of Officer - Military Personnel (Jul 99)
DA 78-R	Recommendation for Promotion to 1LT/CW2 (Jul 94)
DA 85-R	Scorecard for M249, M60/M240B Machine Guns (Oct 02)
DA 88-R	Combat Pistol Qualification Course Scorecard (Sep 05)
DA 137-1	Unit Clearance Record (Jun 03)
DA 137-2	Installation Clearance Record (Jun 03)
DA 145	Army Corres. Course Enrollment Application (Oct 00))
DA 200	Transmittal Record (Sep 98)
DA 268	Report to Suspend Favorable Personnel Actions (Flag) (Jun 87)
DA 285A	US Army Accident Report (Jan 92)
DA 285-AB-R	US Army Abbreviated Ground Accident Report (AGAR) (Jul 94)
DA 285-A-R	US Army Accident Report Index A (Jul 94)
DA 285-B-R	US Army Accident Report Index B (Jul 94)
DA 285-O-R	US Army Accident Report Statement of Reviewing Officials (Jul 94)
DA 285-W-R	US Army Accident Summary of Witness Interview (Jul 94)
DA 348-1-R	Equipment Operator's Qualification Record (Except Aircraft) (Feb 86)
DA 581	Request For Issue and Turn-in of Ammunition (Jul 99)
DA 581-1	Request For Issue and Turn-in of Ammunition Continuation (Jul 99)
DA 638	Recommendation For Award (Nov 94)
DA 689	Sick Call Slip (Mar 63)
DA 705	Army Physical Fitness Test Scorecard (Jun 99)
DA 705a	Army Physical Fitness Test Scorecard (Jun 99)
DA 705b	Army Physical Fitness Test Scorecard (Jun 99)
DA 705c	Army Physical Fitness Test Scorecard (Jun 99)
DA 705d	Army Physical Fitness Test Scorecard (Jun 99)
DA 705e	Army Physical Fitness Test Scorecard (Jun 99)
DA 705f	Army Physical Fitness Test Scorecard (Jun 99)
DA 873	Certificate of Clearance And/Or Security Determination (Dec 69)
DA 1059	Service School Academic Evaluation Report (Nov 77)
DA 1103	Application for AER Financial Assistance (Sep 94)
DA 1155	Witness Statement of Individual (Jun 66)
DA 1156	Casualty Feeder Report (Jun 66)
DA 1222	Routing Slip (Nov 00)
DA 1306	Statement of Jump and Loading Manifest (May 63)
DA 1307	Individual Jump Record (Oct 93)
DA 1315	Reenlistment Data (May 98)
DA 1315-1R	Status of Reenlistment Data (Dec 94)
DA 1352	Army Aircraft Inventory, Status, and Flying Time (Apr 93)
DA 1352-1	Daily Aircraft Status Record (Apr 93)
DA 1574	Report of Proceedings by Investigating Officer (Mar 83)
DA 1594	Daily Staff Journal or Duty Officer's Log (Nov 62)
DA 1659	Financial Liability Investigation of Property Loss Register (Oct 04)

DA 1687	Notice of Delegation of Authority - Receipt for Supplies (Jan 82)
DA 1695	Oath of Extension of Enlistment (May 98)
DA 1696	Enlistment/Reenlistment Qualifying Application (Apr 05)
DA 1971-10-R	NBC 4 Radiation Dose Rate Measurements or Chemical/Biological Areas of Contamination (Oct 92)
DA 1971-7-R	NBC 1 Observer's Initial or Follow-Up Report (Oct 92)
DA 2062	Hand Receipt/Annex Number (Jan 82)
DA 2063-R	Prescribed Load List (Jan 82)
DA 2064	Document Register for Supply Actions (Jan 82)
DA 2142	Pay Inquiry (Apr 82)
DA 2166-8	NCO Evaluation Report (Oct 01)
DA 2166-8-1	NCO Counseling Checklist/Record (Oct 01)
DA 2173	Medical Examination and Duty Status (Oct 72)
DA 2204-R	Casualty Assistance Report (May 86)
DA 2366	**Montgomery GI Bill ()**
DA 2386	Agreement for Interment (Jun 82)
DA 2404	Equipment Inspection and Maintenance Worksheet (Apr 79)
DA 2765-1	Request for Issue or Turn-in ()
DA 2806-1-R	Physical Security Inspection Report (Apr 85)
DA 2823	Sworn Statement (Dec 98)
DA 2940-R	Unit Loading Inventory/Checklist (Worksheet) (Dec 75)
DA 2941-R	Unit Vehicle Loading Plan (Worksheet) (Mar 65)
DA 2946-R	40mm Grenade Launcher Scorecard (Nov 02)
DA 3072-R	Waiver of Disqualification for Reenlistment/Promotion (May 88)
DA 3161	Request For Issue or Turn-in (Dec 00)
DA 3254-R	Oil Analysis Recommendation and Feedback (Nov 80)
DA 3265	Explosive Ordnance Incident Report (Aug 04)
DA 3294	Ration Request/Issue/Turn-in Slip (Jul 02)
DA 3517-R	Hand Grenade Qualification Scorecard (Apr 05)
DA 3328-1	Serial/Registration Number Record (Jan 82)
DA 3349	Physical Profile (Feb 04)
DA 3355	Promotion Point Worksheet (May 00)
DA 3355-1-R	US Army Reserve Promotion Point Worksheet (Jan 98)
DA 3356	Board Member Appraisal Worksheet (May 00)
DA 3356-1R	USAR Board Member Appraisal Worksheet (Sep 87)
DA 3357	Board Recommendation (May 00)
DA 3357-1R	USAR Board Recommendation (Sep 87)
DA 3595-R	Record Fire Scorecard (Nov 02)
DA 3601-R	Single Target Field Firing Scorecard (Jun 89)
DA 3645a	Org Clothing and Individual Equipment Record (Oct 91)
DA 3645b	Org Clothing and Individual Equipment Record (Oct 91)
DA 3645-1a	Additional Org Clothing and Ind Equipment Record (Dec 83)
DA 3645-1b	Additional Org Clothing and Ind Equipment Record (Dec 83)
DA 3711	Army Substance Abuse Program (ASAP) Report (RAPR) (Nov 01)
DA 3739	Application for Compassionate Actions (Jan 96)
DA 3749	Equipment Receipt (Jan 82)
DA 3881	Rights Warning Procedure/Waiver Certificate (Nov 89)
DA 3955	**Change of Address and Directory Card**
DA 4126-R	Bar to Reenlistment Certificate (Dec 94)
DA 4137	Evidence/Property Custody Document (Jul 76)
DA 4179	Leave Control Log (Aug 03)
DA 4187	Personnel Action (Jan 00)

DA 4187-1-R Personnel Action Form Addendum (Apr 05)
DA 4237-R Detainee Personnel Record (Aug 85)
DA 4312-R Retention Control Sheet (Oct 74)
DA 4475-R Info from the NOK of a Deceased Service Member (Dec 75)
DA 4817-R Consent/Nonconsent to Disclose Personal Info (Dec 85)
DA 4833 Commander's Report of Disciplinary/Administrative Action (Jun 04)
DA 4836 Oath of Extension of Enlistment/Reenlistment (Sep 04)
DA 4843 Guest/Attendance Sheet (Apr 04)
DA 4856 Developmental Counseling Form (Jun 99)
DA 4881-4 Power of Attorney (Jul 04)
DA 4908 Army Emergency Relief Fund Campaign (Jan 01)
DA 4948-R Freedom of Info Act (FOIA)/OPSEC Desktop Guide (Nov 89)
DA 4949 Administrative Adjustment Report (AAR) (Jan 82)
DA 5006 Authorization for Disclosure of Information (Feb 03)
DA 5011 Training Evaluation Summary (Aug 05)
DA 5109 Request to Exercise Article 15, UCMJ, Jurisdiction (Sep 02)
DA 5110 Article 15-Reconciliation Log (Sep 02)
DA 5111 Summary Court-Martial Rights Notification/Waiver Statement (Sep 02)
DA 5112 Checklist For Pretrial Confinement (Sep 02)
DA 5123 In and Out-Processing Records Checklist (Jun 03)
DA 5123-1 In-Processing Personnel Record (Jun 03)
DA 5164-R Hands-on Evaluation (Sep 85)
DA 5165-R Field Expedient Squad Book (Jul 05)
DA 5234-R OER Control Log (Jul 83)
DA 5247-R Request for Security Determination (Sep 83)
DA 5248-R Report of Unfavorable Information for Security Determination (Sep 83)
DA 5287 **Training Record Transmittal Jacket**
DA 5304-R Family Care Plan Counseling Checklist (Apr 99)
DA 5305-R Family Care Plan (Apr 99)
DA 5381-R Building Fire Risk Management Survey (Dec 96)
DA 5382-R Hazard/Deficiency Survey Record (Sep 92)
DA 5426-R Commander's Evaluation (May 85)
DA 5500-R Body Fat Content Worksheet (Male) (Dec 85)
DA 5501-R Body Fat Content Worksheet (Female) (Dec 85)
DA 5511-R Personal Weight Loss Progress (Feb 86)
DA 5513-R Key Control Register and Inventory (Aug 93)
DA 5517-R Standard Range Card (Feb 86)
DA 5519-R Tool Sign Out Log/Register (Apr 86)
DA 5548-R Unit Climate Profile Questionnaire (Aug 86)
DA 5548-1-R Unit Climate Profile (UCP) (Aug 86)
DA 5627-R Cash, Property, and Reconciliation Record (Feb 88)
DA 5704-R Alternate Pistol Qualification Course Scorecard (Sep 05)
DA 5787-R Military Sketch (Jun 89)
DA 5840-R Certificate of Acceptance as Guardian or Escort (Apr 99)
DA 5841-R Power of Attorney (Apr 99)
DA 5863 EFMP Information Sheet (Sep 02)
DA 5914-R Ration Control Sheet (Jun 90)
DA 5960 Authorization to Start, Stop, or Change BAQ (Sep 90)
DA 5965-R Basic of Issue for Clothing and Individual Equipment (CIE) (Jun 97)
DA 5988-E Equip Inspection/Maintenance Worksheet
DA 5976 Enemy Prisoner of War Capture Tag (Jan 91)
DA 6125-Ra Road Test Score Sheet (Aug 93)
DA 6125-Rb Road Test Score Sheet (Aug 93)

DA 7007-R	Machine Gun Scorecard for M2 (Jan 02)
DA 7246	EFMP Screening Questionnaire (Sep 02)
DA 7279-R	Equal Opportunity Complaint Form (Dec 05)
DA 7279-1-R	Equal Opportunity Complaint Resolution Assessment (Dec 05)
DA 7302	Disposition of Remains Statement (Dec 00)
DA 7304-R	Scorecard for M249 (Feb 94)
DA 7351A	EFMP Assessment Guide (Sep 02)
DA 7351B	EFMP Assessment Guide (Sep 02)
DA 7406	Summary Court Martial Officer Checklist (May 99)
DA 7413	EFMP Assignment Coordination Sheet (Sep 02)
DA 7415	EFMP Querying Sheet (Sep 02)
DA 7425	Readiness and Deployment Checklist (Jan 06)
DA 7425B	Instructions for Deployment Checklist (Jan 06)
DA 7433	Privacy Act Information Release Statement (Apr 01)
DA 7448-R	M2 Caliber .50 Heavy Barrel Machine Gun Firing Table I Day Practice Scorecard (Jan 02)
DA 7449-R	M2 Caliber .50 Heavy Barrel Machine Gun Firing Table II Day Qualification Scorecard (Oct 02)
DA 7450-R	M2 Caliber .50 Heavy Barrel Machine Gun Firing Table III (B) and III (B) Night Practice Scorecards (Oct 02)
DA 7451-R	M2 Caliber .50 Heavy Barrel Machine Gun Firing Table IV(A) and IV(B) Night Qualification Scorecards (Oct 02)
DA 7505	Unit Data Sheet (Apr 03)
DA 7510	EEO Counselor's Report (Feb 04)
DA 7518-R	MK 19, 40mm Grenade Machine Gun, MOD 3 Firing Table I Day Practice and Qualification with Hull Targets Scorecard (Aug 03)
DA 7519-R	MK 19, 40mm Grenade Machine Gun, MOD 3 Firing Table II Night Practice and Qualification with Hull Targets Scorecard (Aug 03)
DA 7520-R	MK 19, 40mm Grenade Machine Gun, MOD 3 Firing Table III Day Practice and Qualification with Pop-up Targets Scorecard (Aug 03)
DA 7521-R	MK 19, 40mm Grenade Machine Gun, MOD 3 Firing Table IV Night Practice and Qualification with Pop-up Targets Scorecard (Aug 03)
DA 7531	Checklist/Tracking for Financial Liability Investigations (Aug 04)
DA 7566	Composite Risk Management Worksheet (Apr 05)
DA 8003	**ASAP Referral Form**
DA 8028-R	US Army Reserve Bar to Reenlistment Certificate (Feb 92)

11.4.4 DD Form Index

DD 4	Enlistment/Reenlistment Document (Jan 01)
DD 13	Statement of Service (Jan 67)
DD 93	Emergency Data, Record of (Aug 98)
DD 137	Application for BAQ for Dependents (Feb 84)
DD 137-1	Authorization to Start or Stop BAQ Credit (May 67)
DD 139	Pay Adjustment Authorization (May 53)
DD 200	Financial Liability Investigation of Property Loss (Oct 99)
DD 214	Certificate of Release/Discharge from Active Duty (Feb 00)
DD 214WS	Certificate of Release/Discharge (Worksheet) (Feb 00)
DD 215	Correction to DD Form 214 (Feb 00)
DD 216	Officer's Certificate of Appointment (Mar 59)
DD 256	Discharge Certificate, Honorable (May 50)
DD 257	Discharge Certificate, General (May 50)
DD 259	Discharge Certificate, Bad Conduct (May 50)
DD 260	Discharge Certificate, Dishonorable (May 50)
DD 261	Investigation, Line of Duty and Misconduct Status (Oct 95)
DD 314	Preventive Maintenance Schedule and Record (Dec 53)
DD 317	Preventive Maintenance Service (Feb 54)
DD 362	Statement of Charges/Cash Collection Voucher (Jul 93)
DD 398	Personnel Security Questionnaire (PSQ) (Mar 90)
DD 399	Casual Payment Receipt (Nov 50)
DD 714	Meal Card (Oct 81)
DD 836	Shippers Declaration of Dangerous Goods (Apr 05)
DD 836C	Shippers Declaration of Dangerous Goods (Cont.) (Mar 05)
DD 1131	Cash Collection Voucher (Apr 57)
DD 1172	Application for Uniformed Services ID Card (Aug 87)
DD 1249	SAAM/JCS Airlift Request
DD 1265	Convoy Clearance, Request for (Sep 98)
DD 1300	Report of Casualty (Mar 04)
DD 1375	Request for Payment of Funeral and/or Internment Expenses (Oct 03)
DD 1384	Transportation Control and Movement Document
DD 1387	Shipment Label, Military (Jul 99)
DD 1387-1	Shipping Tag, Military (Mar 70)
DD 1750	Packing List (Sep 70)
DD 1842R	Claim for Loss of Damage to Personal Property (May 00)
DD 1892	Drug Screening Urinalysis Record (Oct 72)
DD 2026	Oil Analysis Request (Mar 99)
DD 2027	Oil Analysis Record (Aug 76)
DD 2130C	Cargo Manifest Continuation, Aircraft (Sep 98)
DD 2131	Passenger Manifest (Sep 05)
DD 2133	Airlift Inspection Record, Joint (Oct 98)
DD 2280	Fingerprint Card, Armed Forces (Apr 87)
DD 2366	Montgomery GI Bill Act of 1984 (MGIB) (Jun 02)
DD 2390	Data Load Worksheet (Jun 86)
DD 2558	Authorization to Start, Stop, or Change an Allotment (Nov 96)
DD 2594	Separation Pay Worksheet (Dec 91)
DD 2644	Voter Registration Application (Dec 94)
DD 2648	Separation Checklist for Active Component (Jun 05)
DD 2648-1	Separation Checklist for Reserve Component (Jun 05)
DD 2709	Privacy Act Statement (Nov 99)
DD 2775	Pallet Identifier (Sep 98)
DD 2776	Dangerous Cargo Load List (Sep 98)
DD 2781	Container/Vehicle Packing Certificate (Jun 05)

DD 2795	Pre-Deployment Health Assessment Questionnaire (May 99)
DD 2796	Post-Deployment Health Assessment (Apr 03)
OF 41	Routing and Transmittal Slip (Jul 76)
SF 1199A	Direct Deposit Signup Form (Jun 87)
SF 2817-1	Life Insurance Election (Apr 99)
SF 2817-2	Life Insurance Election (Apr 99)

11.4.5 Field Manual Index

FM 1-02	Operational Terms and Graphics (Sep 04) formerly FM 101-5-1
FM 2-0	Intelligence (May 04)
FM 3-0	Operations (Jun 01)
FM 3-5	Decontamination Operations (Jan 02)
FM 3-06	Urban Operations (Jun 03)
FM 3-06.11	Combined Arms Operations in Urban Terrain (Feb 02)
FM 3-07	Stability and Support Operations (Feb 03)
FM 3-07.31	Conducting Peace Operations (Oct 03)
FM 3-35.4	Deployment Fort to Port (Jun 02)
FM 3-7	NBC Field Handbook (Sep 94)
FM 3-13	Information Operations (Nov 02)
FM 3-19.1	Military Police Operations (Mar 01)
FM 3-19.4	Military Police Leader's Handbook (Mar 02)
FM 3.19-13	Military Police Investigations (Jan 05)
FM 3-19.15	Civil Disturbance Operations (Apr 05)
FM 3-19.30	Physical Security (Jan 01)
FM 3-19.40	Military Police Internment/Resettlement Operations (Aug 01)
FM 3-25.150	Combatives (Jan 02)
FM 3-20.8	Scout Gunnery (Aug 05)
FM 3-20.12	Tank Gunnery Abrams (Aug 05)
FM 3-20.15	Tank Platoon (Nov 01)
FM 3-20.98	Reconnaissance Platoon (Feb 02)
FM 3-21.5	Drill and Ceremonies (Jul 03) formerly FM 22-5
FM 3-21.9	The SBCT Infantry Rifle Platoon and Squad (Dec 02)
FM 3-21.71	Mechanized Infantry Platoon and Squad (Bradley) (Aug 02)
FM 3-22.1	Bradley Gunnery (Nov 03)
FM 3-22.9	Rifle Marksmanship M16A1, M16A2/3, M16A4, M4 Carbine (Apr 05)
FM 3-22.27	MK 19, 40-mm Grenade Machine Gun, Mod 3 (Nov 03)
FM 3-22.31	40-MM Grenade Launcher, M203 (Feb 03)
FM 3-22.34	TOW Weapon System (Jan 03)
FM 3-22.37	Javelin Medium Anti-Armor Weapon System (Jan 03)
FM 3-22.40	NLW Tactical Employment of Nonlethal Weapons (Jan 03)
FM 3-22.65	Browning Machine Gun, Caliber .50 HB, M2 (Mar 05)
FM 3-22.68	Crew-served Machine Guns, M249, 5.56mm Machine Gun; M60, 7.62mm Machine Gun; M240B, 7.62mm Machine Gun (Jan 03)
FM 3-22.90	Mortars (Jan 03)
FM 3-22.91	Mortar Gunnery (Jan 05)
FM 3-23.30	Grenades and Pyrotechnic Signals (Jun 05)
FM 3-23.35	Combat Training with Pistols, M9 and M11 (Sep 05)
FM 3-25.26	Map Reading and Land Navigation (Jan 05)
FM 3-34	Engineer Operations (Jan 04)
FM 3-35.4	Deployment Fort to Port (Jun 02)
FM 3-90	Tactics (Jul 01)
FM 3-100.4	Environmental Considers in Military Operations (Jun 00)
FM 3-100.12	Risk Management (Feb 01)
FM 4-0	Combat Service Support (Aug 03)
FM 4-01.011	Unit Movement Operations (Oct 02)
FM 4-01.30	Movement Control (Sep 03)
FM 4-01.45	Convoy Operations (Mar 05)
FM 4-02.4	Medical Platoon Leader's Handbook (Aug 01)
FM 4-25.11	First Aid (Dec 02)
FM 4-30.3	Maintenance Operations and Procedures (Jul 04)

FM 4-30.13	Ammunition Handbook for Munitions Handlers (Mar 01)
FM 5-0	Army Planning and Orders Production (Jan 05)
FM 5-10	Combat Engineer Platoon (Oct 95)
FM 5-33	Terrain Analysis (Jul 90)
FM 5-34	Engineer Field Date (Jul 05)
FM 5-103	Survivability (Jun 85)
FM 6-02.72	Tactical Radios in a Joint Environment (Jun 02)
FM 6-20	Fire Support in the AirLand Battle (May 88)
FM 6-30	TTPs for Observed Fire (Jul 91)
FM 6-20-10	TTPs for Targeting Process (May 96)
FM 6-22.5	Combat Stress (Jun 00)
FM 7-0	Training the Force (Oct 02)
FM 7-1	Battle Focused Training (Sep 03)
FM 7-8	Infantry Rifle Platoon and Squad (Apr 92)
FM 7-21.13	The Soldier's Guide (Feb 04)
FM 7-22.7	The Army Noncommissioned Officer Guide (Dec 02)
FM 7-85	Ranger Unit Operations (Jun 87)
FM 7-98	Operations in a Low-Intensity Conflict (Oct 92)
FM 7-100	Opposing Force Doctrinal Framework and Strategy (May 03)
FM 7-100.1	Opposing Force Operations (Dec 04)
FM 8-55	Planning for Health Service Support (Sep 94)
FM 10-23	Field Feeding and Class 1 Opns (Apr 96)
FM 10-23-2	Food Preparation and Class 1 Opns Mgmt (Sep 93)
FM 10-27-4	Organizational Supply for Unit Leaders (Apr 00)
FM 11-32	Combat Net Radio Operations (Oct 90)
FM 11-43	Signal Leader's Guide (Jun 95)
FM 12-6	Personnel Doctrine (Sep 94)
FM 14-100	Financial Management Operations (Aug 97)
FM 19-25	Law Enforcement Investigations (Nov 85)
FM 21-18	Foot Marches (Jun 90)
FM 21-20	Physical Fitness Training (Sep 92)
FM 21-31	Topographic Symbols (Jun 61)
FM 21-60	Visual Signals (Sep 87)
FM 21-75	Combat Skills of the Soldier (Mar 84)
FM 21-305	Manual for the Wheeled Vehicle Driver (Aug 93)
FM 22-6	Guard Duty (Jan 75)
FM 22-51	Leader's Manual for Combat Stress Control (Sep 94)
FM 22-100	Army Leadership (Aug 99)
FM 23-10	Sniper Training (Aug 94)
FM 24-18	Tactical Single-Channel Radio Communications (Sep 87)
FM 24-19	Radio Operator's Handbook (May 91)
FM 25-4	How To Conduct Training Exercises (Sep 84)
FM 25-5	Training for Mobilization and War (Jan 85)
FM 27-1	Legal Guide for Commanders (Jan 92)
FM 27-10	The Law of Land Warfare (Jul 56)
FM 27-14	Legal Guide for Soldiers (Apr 91)
FM 31-70	Basic Cold Weather Manual (Apr 68)
FM 34-3	Intelligence Analysis (Mar 90)
FM 34-52	Intelligence Interrogation (Sep 92)
FM 34-130	Intelligence Preparation of the Battlefield (Jul 94)
FM 55-1	Transportation Operations (Oct 95)
FM 55-15	Transportation Reference Data (Oct 97)
FM 55-30	Army Motor Transport Units and Operations (Sep 91)
FM 71-123	Combined Arms Heavy Forces (Sep 92)
FM 90-3	Desert Operations (Aug 93)

FM 90-4	Air Assault Operations (Mar 87)
FM 90-5	Jungle Operations (Aug 82)
FM 90-8	Counter-Guerrilla Operations (Aug 86)
FM 90-26	Airborne Operations (Dec 90)
FM 100-14	Risk Management (Apr 98)
FM 100-17	Mobilization, Deployment, Redeployment, Demobilization (Oct 92)
FM 100-23-1	Humanitarian Assistance Operations (Oct 94)
FM 100-60	Armor and Mechanized-Based Opposing Force (Jul 97)
FM 100-63	Infantry-Based Opposing Force Organization Guide (Apr 96)
FM 101-5-2	US Army Report and Message Formats (Jun 99)
FMI 3-07.22	Counterinsurgency Operations (Oct 04)
FMI 3-34.119	Improvised Explosive Device Defeat (Sep 05)
FMI 3-63.6	Command and Control of Detainee Operations (Sep 05)

11.4.6 Graphic Training Aids

GTA 03-04-001A	Depleted Uranium Awareness (Oct 99)
GTA 03-05-015	Chemical Protection and Decon (Dec 95)
GTA 03-06-008	NBC Warning and Reporting System (Aug 96)
GTA 03-08-001	Promotions (Aug 00)
GTA 03-09-001	Grided Template (Aug 95)
GTA 05-02-012	Coordinate Scale and Protector (Jan 81)
GTA 05-02-013	How to Avoid Getting Lost (Oct 01)
GTA 05-02-014	How to Order a Map (Feb 01)
GTA 05-02-029	Conversion Factors and Command Formulas (Apr 05)
GTA 05-02-034	Azimuth-Bearing/Grid-Magnetic Conversion (Apr 05)
GTA 05-08-001	Survivability Positions (Aug 93)
GTA 05-08-002	Environmental-Related Risk Assessment (Oct 99)
GTA 05-08-003	Hazardous-Material-Spill Procedures (Apr 98)
GTA 05-08-004	Soldier's Environmental Ethic Responsibility Card (Jan 02)
GTA 05-08-005	Leader's Field Guide, Assessment, and QA Checklist (Jan 99)
GTA 05-08-012	Individual Safety Card (Dec 05)
GTA 05-08-013	Training the Environment Soldier's Field Card (Jul 05)
GTA 05-08-014	Unit Pre-Deployment and Load Plan (Jan 03)
GTA 05-08-015	Unit Deployment and Sustainment Checklist (Jan 03)
GTA 05-08-016	How to Clear a Base Camp (Jan 03)
GTA 05-08-017	Tactical Risk and Spill Reaction Procedures (Jan 03)
GTA 05-10-031	US Firing Devices, Booby Traps, and Expedient (Oct 89)
GTA 05-10-033	Demolition Card (Jan 94)
GTA 05-10-034	Conventional US Land Mines (Jan 95)
GTA 05-10-036	Mine Card, Part 1 (May 97)
GTA 05-10-037	Mine Card, Part 2 (May 97)
GTA 06-07-003	Observed Fire Fan (Aug 83)
GTA 07-01-005	Target Grid Methods of Fire (Jun 65)
GTA 07-01-30	Range Operations Checklist (Jun 87)
GTA 07-01-032	Observed Fire Reference Card (Jun 87)
GTA 07-01-033	25mm Machine Gun Immediate Action/Troubleshooting (Jun 87)
GTA 07-01-035	Disassembly for MK19 Grenade Machine Gun, 40mm (Jan 94)
GTA 07-01-036	Disassembly for M9 Semiautomatic Pistol, 9mm (Jan 94)
GTA 07-01-038	Infantry Leader's References Card (Jan 95)
GTA 07-01-039	Disassembly Layout Chart, M16A2 (Jan 96)
GTA 07-01-040	M-4 Carbine, Field Stripped (Jul 01)
GTA 07-01-042	M249 Machine Gun Disassembly (Jul 01)
GTA 07-01-043	Basic Rifle Marksmanship Coaches Checklist (May 00)
GTA 07-01-044	M240B Machine Gun Disassembly(May 00)
GTA 07-01-045	Disassembly Layout Chart for the M16A4 Rifle (Jul 05)
GTA 07-02-005	Sight Engagement Trainer, AT-4 (Jan 90)
GTA 07-04-002	Standard Load Plans, M220 (Apr 84)
GTA 07-04-006	Building the Company Team for Defense (May 94)
GTA 07-04-007	Training Meeting (May 00)
GTA 07-04-008	Linkup Operations (Jun 95)
GTA 07-06-001	Fighting Position Construction (Jan 94)
GTA 07-10-001	Machine Gunner's Card (Jun 02)
GTA 07-10-002	Advanced Infantry Marksmanship Strategies (Jun 02)
GTA 07-10-003	Small Unit Leader's Card (IN) (Mar 03)
GTA 08-01-002	Leader's Guide to After Action Debriefing (Aug 96)

GTA 08-01-003	When the Mission Requires Recovering Human Dead (Aug 96)
GTA 08-01-004	MEDEVAC Request Form (Aug 02)
GTA 08-05-051	Preventive Medicine Measures for Companies (Dec 90)
GTA 08-05-058	91B Combat Medic Pocket Guide, Trauma Treatment (Feb 96)
GTA 08-05-059	91B Combat Medic Pocket Guide, Medical Emergencies (Feb 96)
GTA 08-06-012	Adverse Effects of Cold (Aug 85)
GTA 08-07-001	Combat Stress Control (CSC) (Oct 96)
GTA 08-11-011	Artificial Respiration/CPR (May 91)
GTA 08-11-013	Foreign Body Airway Obstruction (Apr 92)
GTA 08-12-005	Med Pak 1 (Jan 88)
GTA 08-12-010	Med Pak 5 (Jan 88)
GTA 08-12-011	Med Pak 11 (Jan 93)
GTA 09-01-181	Truck Wrecker, 5-ton, 6x6, M816 (Sep 76)
GTA 09-01-185	Systematic Inspection Procedure for the 2 1/2 ton Truck (Oct 97)
GTA 09-06-036	M60 Machine Gun, 7.62mm (Jul 69)
GTA 09-06-038	Browning Machine Gun, 50 Caliber, M2 (May 70)
GTA 09-06-044	M16A1 Rifle Malfunction (Jul 76)
GTA 09-10-045	Small Unit Leader's Card (Intermediate Maint) (Oct 88)
GTA 09-10-046	Small Unit Leader's Card (Intermediate Maint Light (Oct 88)
GTA 09-10-047	Command Maintenance Profile Chart Set (Nov 94)
GTA 09-12-001	Unexploded Ordnance (UXO) Procedures (Jan 92)
GTA 09-12-003	.50 Caliber De-armer Aiming Device (Jan 93)
GTA 09-13-001	Ammunition, Missile, Demolitions, and Explosives Safety (Jan 94)
GTA 10-01-003	Kitchen Equipment, Emersion Heater (Dec 75)
GTA 10-01-007	Kitchen Equipment, Layout, Sanitation (Dec 75)
GTA 10-01-011A	Insulated Food Container User Maint (Apr 94)
GTA 10-01-011B	Insulated Food Container Guide (Apr 94)
GTA 10-08-007	.50 Caliber Machine Gun Layout Chart (Jan 83)
GTA 11-01-006	Voice Radio: Communicating Right (Aug 83)
GTA 11-01-007	Send a Radio Message (Jun 87)
GTA 11-03-020	Installation of Antenna Group, OE254 (Jul 83)
GTA 11-04-017	Field Telephone, TA-312/PT, Local Battery (Feb 81)
GTA 11-04-018	Install Telephone Set TA-341/PT (Feb 81)
GTA 17-02-015	Call for Fire (Oct 85)
GTA 19-04-003	Individual Protective Measures (Nov 01)
GTA 19-05-001	Implied Consent Warning (Jan 88)
GTA 19-06-006	How to Inform a Suspect of their Rights (Jun 91)
GTA 19-07-001	Enemy Prisoner of War (EPW) Commands (Feb 89)
GTA 19-08-002	Portable Sign-Making Kit (May 01)
GTA 19-08-004	Nonlethal Munitions (Oct 01)
GTA 21-02-007	Special Orders for Civil Disturbance Opns (Dec 70)
GTA 21-02-008	Soldier's Information Guide (Oct 69)
GTA 21-03-009	Code of Conduct (Aug 89)
GTA 21-06-002	Advanced Land Navigation (Feb 73)
GTA 21-08-001	Risk Management Information Card (Jun 00)
GTA 22-06-001	Ethical Climate Assessment Survey (Oct 97)
GTA 22-06-004	Soldier's Creed Card (Aug 04)
GTA 22-06-005	Warrior Ethos Tag (Aug 04)
GTA 24-01-003	Iraq Culture Smart Card (Nov 04)
GTA 25-06-023	After Action Review Techniques (Jan 97)
GTA 27-01-005	Non-Judicial Punishment for Minor Offense (Art 15) (Apr 95)
GTA 27-01-006	Non-Judicial Punishment within Reserve (Art 15) (Apr 95)
GTA 41-01-001	Civil Affairs Planning Guide (Oct 02)

GTA 44-02-017	Close Air Support (CAS), Fighter-Bomber (Jun 96)
GTA 55-03-030	HMMWV Uparmored Emergency Procedures (May 05)
GTA 55-03-031	Water Egress HMMWV Uparmored (Jul 05)
GTA 55-05-011	Determine Deviation of the Magnetic Compass (Jul 82)
GTA 55-05-012	Taking a Fix using an Azimuth Circle (Jul 82)
GTA 55-07-003	Air Deployment Planning Guide (Feb 96)
GTA 80-01-001	Army Personnel Recovery (Sep 05)
GTA 90-01-001	Improvised Explosive Device (IED/VBIED) Card (May 04)
GTA 90-01-003	Vehicle Search Techniques (Aug 04)
GTA 90-01-004	Logistics Convoy Operations (Sep 04)

11.4.7 Joint Publications

JC 04-01	Distributed Learning/Web Based Training (Jul 04)
JP 1	Joint Warfare of the Armed Forces (Nov 00)
JP 3-0	Doctrine for Joint Operations (Sep 01)
JP 3-07.2	Joint TTPs for Anti-Terrorism (Mar 98)
JP 3-07.3	Joint TTPs for Peace Operations (Feb 99)
JP 3-09.3	Joint Tactics, Techniques, and Procedures for Close Air Support (Dec 95)
JP 3-10	Joint Doctrine for Rear Area Operations (May 96)
JP 3-11	Joint Doctrine for Operations in NBC Environments (Jul 00)
JP 3-13	Joint Doctrine for Information Operations (Oct 98)
JP 3-15	Joint Doctrine for Barriers, Obstacles, and Mine Warfare (Feb 99)
JP 3-26	Homeland Security (Aug 05)
JP 3-50.2	Joint Doctrine for Combat Search and Rescue (Jan 96)
JP 3-55	Joint Doctrine for Recon, Surveillance, and Target Acquisition (Apr 93)
JP 3-63	Joint Doctrine for Detainee Operations (Mar 05)
JP 4-0	Joint Doctrine for Logistic Support (Apr 00)
JP 5-0	Joint Doctrine for Planning Joint Opns (Apr 95)
JP 5-00.2	Joint Task Force (JTF) Planning Guidance and Procedures (Jan 99)

11.4.8 Special Text

ABCS-LRG 6.2	Army Battle Command Sys Leader's Reference (Feb 02)
SH 21-10	Standards of Appearance and Conduct (May 03)
ST 2-22.7	Tactical Human Intelligence and CounterIntel (Apr 02)
ST 2-50.4	Combat Commander's Handbook on Intel (Sep 01)
ST 2-91.1	Intelligence Support to SASO (Nov 04)
ST 2-91.6	Small Unit Support to Intelligence (Mar 04)
ST SAIB	Small Arms Integration Book (SAIB) (Mar 02)
MISC PUB 27-7	Manual for Courts-Martial (MCM) (2005)
TRADOC DCSINT Handbook 1	Military Guide to Terrorism in the Twenty-First Century: Military Guide to Terrorism in the Twenty-First Century (Aug 05)
Handbook 1.01	Supplement 1: Terror Operations: Case Studies (Aug 05)
Handbook 1.02	Supplement 2: Cyber Operations and Cyber Terrorism (Aug 05)
Handbook 1.03	Supplement 3: Suicide Bombings in the COE (Aug 05)
Handbook 1.04	Supplement 4: Defense Support of Civil Authorities (Aug 05)

11.4.9 Training Circulars

TC 1-05	Religious Support Handbook for the Unit Ministry Team (May 05)
TC 3-10	Commander's Tactical NBC Handbook (Sep 94)
TC 3-34.489	The Soldier and the Environment (May 01)
TC 7-9	Infantry Live-Fire Training (Sep 93)
TC 7-98-1	Stability and Support Operations (Jun 97)
TC 9-21-01	IED Awareness Guide Iraq & Afghanistan (May 04)
TC 12-17	Adjutant's Call, The S1 Handbook
TC 19-138	Civilian Law Enforcement and Security Officer Training (Aug 01)
TC 19-210	Access Control Handbook (Oct 04)
TC 20-32-5	Land Mine and Explosive Hazards (Iraq) (Feb 03)
TC 21-3	Soldier's Handbook for Individual Operations and Survival in Cold-Weather Areas (Mar 86)
TC 21-7	Personal Financial Readiness and Deployability Handbook (Aug 03)
TC 21-21	Water Survival Training (Jun 91)
TC 21-24	Rappelling (Sep 97)
TC 21-305	Wheeled Vehicle Accident Avoidance (Apr 03)
TC 21-305-1	Heavy Expanded Mobility Tactical Truck (HEMTT) (Oct 95)
TC 21-305-2	Night Vision Goggle Driving Operations (Sep 98)
TC 21-305-3	M939 Series 5-ton Tactical Cargo Truck (Aug 97)
TC 21-305-4	High Mobility Multi-purpose Wheeled Vehicle (May 91)
TC 21-305-5	Equipment Transporters (C-HET, MET, and LET) (Dec 91)
TC 21-305-6	Tractor and Semi-trailer (M915, M931, AND M932) (Dec 91)
TC 21-305-7	Light Vehicles (Sep 92)
TC 21-305-8	Medium Vehicles (Sep 92)
TC 21-305-9	Heavy Equipment Transporter System (Jun 97)
TC 21-305-10	Palletized Load System (Sep 94)
TC 21-305-11	Family of Medium Tactical Vehicles Operator (May 99)
TC 21-306	Tracked Combat Vehicle Driver Training (Feb 02)
TC 21-305-100	Military Commercial Driver's License Driver's Manual (Aug 96)
TC 21-7	Personal Financial Readiness and Deployability Handbook (Aug 03)
TC 24-21	Tactical Multi-Channel Radio Communications Techniques (Oct 88)
TC 25-10	A Leader's Guide to Lane Training (Aug 96)
TC 25-8	Training Ranges (Apr 04)
TC 25-10	A Leader's Guide to Lane Training (Aug 96)
TC 25-20	A Leader's Guide to After-Action Reviews (Sep 93)
TC 25-30	A Leader's Guide to Company Training Meetings (Apr 94)
TC 26-6	Commander's Equal Opportunity Handbook
TC 38-250	Preparing Hazardous Materials for Military Air Shipment
TC 43-4	Maintenance Management (May 96)
TC 63-1	Combat Service Support Live Fire Exercises (Dec 04)
TC 90-1	Training in Urban Operations (Apr 02)

11.5 Acronym List

AA Assembly Area
AAR After Action Review
AAR Administrative Adjustment Report
AALPS Automated Air Load Planner System
AC Active Component
ACS Army Community Service
ACAP Army Career and Alumni Program
ACCP Army Correspondence Course Program
ACU Army Combat Uniform
ACS Army Community Service
ADSO Active Duty Service Obligation
ADT Active Duty for Training
AER Army Emergency Relief
AIT Advanced Individual Training
AFTB Army Family Team Building
AGR Active Guard Reserve
AKO Army Knowledge Online
AG Adjutant General
AG Army Green
AGR Active Guard and Reserve
APFT Army Physical Fitness Test
ANCOC Advanced Noncommissioned Officers Course
AO Area of Operations
AOI Area of Interest
AOR Area of Responsibility
APOD Aerial Port of Debarkation
APOE Aerial Port of Embarkation
AR Army Regulation
ARCENT Army Forces, Central Command
ARCOM Army Commendation Medal
ARNG Army National Guard
ARTEP Army Training and Evaluation Program
ASAP Army Substance Abuse Program
ASI Additional Skill Identifier
AT Antiterrorism
ATRRS Army Training and Requirements Resource System
AUEL Automated Unit Equipment List
AWCP Army Weight Control Program
AWOL Absent Without leave
BAH Basic Allowance for Housing
BAS Basic Allowance for Subsistence
BASD Basic Active Service Date
BCT Brigade Combat Team
BDU Battle Dress Uniform
BMO Battalion Maintenance Officer
BNCOC Basic Noncommissioned Officers Course
BOSS Better Opportunities for Single Soldiers
CA Combat Arms
CAO Casualty Assistance Officer
CALL Center for Army Lessons Learned
CATS Combined Arms Training System
CDR Commander
CFNCO Command Financial Noncommissioned Officer
CIF Central Issue Facility
CIIC Controlled Inventory Item Code
CIP Commander's Inspection Program
CNO Casualty Notification Officer
CO Commanding Officer
COA Course of Action
COC Chain of Command
CONUS Continental United States
CQ Charge of Quarters
CS Combat Support
CSM Command Sergeant Major
CSDP Command Supply Discipline Program
CSS Combat Service Support
CTA Common Table of Allowances
CTT Common Task Test
DA Department of the Army
DANTES Defense Activity for Non Traditional Education Support
DA PAM Department of the Army Pamphlet
DEERS Defense Enrollment Eligibility Reporting System
DEL Deployment Equipment List
DEP Delayed Entry Program
DFAS Defense Finance and Accounting Service
DG Death Gratuity
DOD Department of Defense
DOIM Directorate of Information Management
DOL Directorate of Logistics
DOR Date of Rank

DPMO	Deployment Process Modernization Office
DRMO	Defense Reutilization and Marketing Office
DTMS	Digital Training Management System
DWI	Driving While intoxicated
EB	Enlistment Bonus
EFMP	Exceptional Family Member Program
EO	Equal Opportunity
ERB	Enlisted Record Brief
ETS	End of Term of Service
FAO	Finance and Accounting Office
FAP	Family Advocacy Program
FAST	Fundamental Academic Skills Test
FCP	Family Care Plan
FEBA	Forward Edge of the Battle Area
FEDLOG	Federal Logistics Catalog
FPCON	Force Protection Condition
FLEP	Funded Legal Education Program
FLOT	Forward Line of Own Troops
FM	Field Manual
FMC	Fully Mission Capable
FORSCOM	Forces Command
FRAGO	Fragmentary Order
FRG	Family Readiness Group
FSA	Family Separation Allowance
FTX	Field Training Exercise
GCM	Good Conduct Medal
GCM	General Court Martial
GPS	Global Positioning System
GT	General Technical
HAZMAT	Hazardous Materials
HHG	Household Goods
HMMWV	High Mobility Medium Wheeled Vehicle
HQDA	Headquarters, Department of the Army
IA	Information Assurance
IAW	In Accordance With
ID	Identification
IET	Initial Entry Training
IG	Inspector General
IPFU	Improved Physical Fitness Uniform
IRR	Individual Ready Reserve
IT	Information Technology
JAG	Judge Advocate General
JODSF	Junior Officer Development Support Form
JOPES	Joint Operations Personnel Execution System
JUMPS	Joint Uniform Military Pay System
KIA	Killed in Action
LAN	Local Area Network
LES	Leave and Earnings Statement
LIN	Line Item Number
LOGSA	Logistics Support Activity
LZ	Landing Zone
MACOM	Major Army Command
MCM	Manual for Courts Martial
MEDEVAC	Medical Evacuation
MEB	Medical Evaluation Board
METL	Mission Essential Task List
METT-TC	Mission, Enemy, Terrain, Troops, Time, and Civilian Considerations
MFR	Memorandum For Record
MGIB	Montgomery GI Bill
MIA	Missing in Action
MILES	Multiple Integrated Laser Engagement System
MILPER	Military Personnel
MKT	Mobile Kitchen Trailer
MMRB	MOS/Medical Retention Board
MOA	Memorandum of Agreement
MOOTW	Military Operations Other Than War
MOS	Military Occupational Specialty
MOU	Memorandum of Understanding
MSO	Mission Support Order
MTF	Medical Treatment Facility
MTOE	Modification Table of Organization and Equipment
MTP	Mission Training Plan
MWR	Moral, Welfare, and Recreation
NATO	North Atlantic Treaty Organization
NBC	Nuclear, Biological, Chemical
NCOER	Noncommissioned Officer Evaluation Report
NCOES	Noncommissioned Officer Education System
NCOIC	Noncommissioned Officer In Charge
NCOPD	Noncommissioned Officer Professional Development

NG	National Guard
NIPRNET	Non-Classified Internet Protocol (IP) Router Network
NMC	Non Mission Capable
NSN	National Stock Number
NTC	National Training Center
NVD	Night Vision Devices
NVG	Night Vision Goggles
OC	Observer Controller
OCOKA	Observation, Concealment, Obstacles, Key terrain, Avenues of approach
OCONUS	Outside the Continental United States
OER	Officer Evaluation Report
OIC	Officer In Charge
OMPF	Official Military Personnel File
OPFOR	Opposing Forces
OPLAN	Operations Plan
OPORD	Operations Order
ORB	Officer Record Brief
(P)	Promotable
PAC	Personnel Administration Center
PAC	Personnel Action Center
PAI	Personnel Asset Inventory
PBO	Property Book Officer
PEB	Physical Evaluation Board
PEBD	Pay Entry Basic Date
PCC	Pre Combat Checks
PCI	Pre Combat Inspections
PCS	Permanent Change of Station
PERSCOM	Personnel Command
PIR	Parachute Infantry Regiment
PLDC	Primary Leadership Development Course
PLT	Platoon
PMCS	Preventive Maintenance Checks and Services
PMO	Provost Marshal Office
PMOS	Primary Military Occupational Specialty
PNOK	Primary Next of Kin
POC	Point of Contact
POV	Privately Owned Vehicle
POW	Prisoner of War
PSB	Personnel Services Battalion
PSG	Platoon Sergeant
PT	Physical Training
QOL	Quality Of Life
RC	Reserve Component
Ret.	Retired
ROE	Rules of Engagement
ROK	Republic of Korea
ROTC	Reserve Officers Training Corps
RSOI	Reception, Staging, Onward movement, and Integration
SALT	Size, Activity, Location, and Time
SALUTE	Size, Activity, Location, Unit, Time, and Equipment
SATS	Standard Army Training System
SBCT	Stryker Brigade Combat Team
SC	Supply Catalog
SCM	Special Court Martial
SDNCO	Staff Duty Noncommissioned Officer
SDO	Staff Duty Officer
SGLI	Servicemembers' Group Life Insurance
SIDPERS	Standard Installation/Division Personnel System
SIPRNET	Secret Internal Protocol Router Network
SITREP	Situation Report
SJA	Staff Judge Advocate
SKOT	Sets, Kits, Outfits, and Tools
SMA	Sergeant Major of the Army
SMCT	Soldier's Manual of Common Tasks
SMTG	Soldier's Manual and Trainer's Guide
SNOK	Secondary Next of Kin
SOP	Standing Operating Procedure
SPCM	Special Court Martial
SPOD	Sealift Port of Debarkation
SPOE	Sealift Port of Embarkation
SRB	Selective Reenlistment Bonus
SDO	Staff Duty Officer
SSN	Social Security Number
STARC	State Area Reserve Command
STP	Soldier Training Publication
STT	Sergeant's Time Training
STX	Situational Training Exercise
T	Trained in the task
TA	Tuition Assistance
TAA	Tactical Assembly Area
TADSS	Training Aids, Devices, Simulators, and Simulations
TC ACCIS	Transpo Coordinator - Automated Command and Control Information System

TC-AIMS II	Transpo Coordinators'-Automated Information for Movement System II
TCN	Transportation Control Number
TDA	Table of Distribution and Allowances
TDY	Temporary Duty
T&EO	Training and Evaluation Outline
TF	Task Force
TIG	Time in Grade
TIS	Time in Service
TOC	Tactical Operations Center
TPFDD	Time Phased Force and Deployment Data
TSP	Thrift Savings Plan
TLP	Troop Leading Procedures
TM	Technical Manual
TMDE	Test, Measurement, and Diagnostic Equipment
TOE	Table of Organization and Equipment
TOW	Tube Launched, Optically Tracked, Wire-Guided Missile
TRADOC	Training and Doctrine Command
TRP	Target Reference Point
TTP	Tactics, Techniques, and Procedures
U	Untrained in the task
UCMJ	Uniform Code of Military Justice
UIC	Unit Identification Code
ULLS-G	Unit Level Logistics System – Ground
ULLS-S4	Unit Level Logistics System – Supply
USAF	United States Air Force
USAR	United States Army Reserve
USC	United States Code
USMC	United States Marine Corps
USN	United States Navy
VA	Veterans' Administration
VIP	Very Important Person
WARNO	Warning Order
WIA	Wounded in Action
WMD	Weapons of Mass Destruction

11.6 Bibliography

All information taken directly from other works is cited in the text. The Field Manuals, Army Regulations, Training Circulars, and Websites listed in the appendix were used in this book. Other works that were consulted during this publication are:

- **A Leader's Guide to Female Soldier Readiness**, U.S. Army Center for Health Promotion and Preventive Medicine (USACHPPM), Mar 2004.
- **Building a Useful Continuity Book,** CPT Leonel Nascimento, (CALL)
- **Commander's Guide to FRG**
- **Commander's Guide and Unit Prevention Leader (UPL) Collection Handbook**, ACSAP (Nov 01)
- **OTIG Webpage** (http://wwwpublic.ignet.army.mil)
- **Reviewer's Checklist to Travel Vouchers,** author unknown
- **US Army Board Study Guide**, version 4.06, from www.ArmyStudyGuide.com, Nov 2005.

Resources from various military websites contributed to this book and were considered open source. If appropriate credit was not given, please go to ArmyToolbag.com, and the issue will resolved in the second edition.

Index

- 1 -

- 3 -

- 8 -

- A -

- B -

- C -

- D -

- E -

- F -

- V -

- W -

Check out:

www.ArmyToolbag.com

for the accompanying website for The Platoon Leader Toolbag. Webpage includes links to all references Army publications, quick charts, and other downloads!

CPSIA information can be obtained at www.ICGtesting.com
Printed in the USA
LVOW131712120912

298543LV00011B/16/P

9 781419 624940